ON SWIFT WINGS

THE TRAVAILS OF CYGNUS

Brett M Wiens

CALGARY, ALBERTA

BW Literature
Calgary, Alberta, Canada

Publisher's Note: This is a work of fiction. Names, characters, places, and incidents are a product of the author's imagination. Locales and public names are sometimes used for atmospheric purposes. Any resemblance to actual people, living or dead, or to businesses, companies, events, institutions, or locales is completely coincidental.

Book Layout by Indie Publishing Group
Book cover design by JD&J
Copy Editing and Proofreading: Bobbi Beatty, Silver Scroll Services

ON SWIFT WINGS/Brett Wiens 1st ed.
ISBN 978-1-9990980-1-8 Hardcover
ISBN 978-1-9990980-0-1 Paperback
ISBN 978-1-9990980-2-5 eBook

Under a Federal Liberal government, Library and Archives Canada no longer provides Cataloguing in Publication (CIP) data for independently published books.

For my son, Des, who inspired me; my daughter, Brooke, to whom I first read it; my wife, Tracy; and everyone else who supported me.

CONTENTS

FOREWORD

A note to my generous, considerate, and supportive readers.

I THANK YOU for taking the time out of your no doubt busy lives to read about a few of my more unusual journeys. These journeys have defined, in both good and ill fortunes, some of the more intriguing aspects of my otherwise torpid existence.

I have always tried to present the facts of my story to interested media. The twisted biases and aggressive challenges to the validity of my reports and the accuracy of my memory have frustrated me. Though I desire only to share my experiences, and some of the lessons I have learned, I have seen my story is always written with a lens of agenda, whether political, social, economic, racial, extravagant, or petty.

Many have focused on trivial matters, about which I think are unimportant, or on insalubrious questions about salacious matters to which I am neither willing nor interested in discussing. I take great issue with the manner in which various outlets have questioned not only my actions but the great deeds of the Blafusechans and the summary dismissal of their politics as either, and often both, fascist or communist.

I find equally reprehensible the uninformed, amaurotic, and frankly deplorable support for the poor Huhuneems. I have long been aware of sects to whom all life is more valuable than that of their cognate species, but to have them suggest that another sentient species, purely because the Huhuneems are not human, are not subject to the decency of humanitarian ideals is beyond the pall. Even amongst their own kind, the Huhuneem espouse unsightly beliefs about natural order and inherent superiority. Defending the villainous, holding the Huhuneem above reproach because they are different, in spite of their cognitive capacities, has vexed me more than I would otherwise care to admit.

As most have heard, though questioned, I have, by virtue of chance or providence, seen and experienced unique peoples, places, and ideas and observed and participated in events that precipitated changes in exotic locales few of our number have had the previous privilege of encountering. It has always been my intention to share the relevant details of my peregrinations with the world in the most honest way possible without unveiling and exposing these singularly isolated and extraordinary, mysterious and antonymous, disparate and peculiar peoples to the corrupting influence of a modern world that has of yet failed to discover them. If lessons are to be learned from these people and their homes, I wish only to faithfully report facts, such that intellects greater and more specifically trained in those areas might apply scientific reason to fairly analyze the benefits and drawbacks that may apply.

To this end, I have concluded my previous efforts at transparency have been in vain. I alone possess the perspective from which to recount the anecdotes, and I sincerely hope I am able to properly convey the narrative while doing justice to both the friends and enemies I've cultivated on my time on the road.

This being my first literary endeavour following several prolonged absences from the English-speaking world, I will try to rouse the atrophy of my tongue to paint a true and vivid picture. Keeping this end in mind, I swear to write only those words that are true and accurate as they were heard, seen, and experienced personally by me.

I know much of the criticism directed towards my person has been born out of the impact my participation in the domestic affairs of each of the islands has had on the development of their societies and the perceived hypocrisy between my actions and my unwillingness to divulge the spatial attributes of the island to limit such interference. I acknowledge and respect this criticism insofar as it has been presented without undue vitriol, or profane invective, which, in today's world, has proven incredibly rare. I defend my actions by saying that one must not allow abuse and mistreatment to go unchallenged in one's presence, and to this end, I was forced, on several occasions to intervene.

Furthermore, I was presented, on occasion, with the dilemma of interfering or allowing myself or those I had grown to care for to come to harm. I chose to draw in those around me and, when possible, protect them. Looking back on my actions, given the information I had available to me at that time, I would repeat the same actions. In response to those zealots who believe I should divulge the location of my discoveries, I maintain that I do not believe the people of your known world will act only in the best interests of the local island populations. I will hold a spirited debate with anyone who believes that history refutes my contention. As long as the location of these races and species are maintained confidentially, it is my belief they will be safer and freer to pursue their own futures.

Though I don't doubt that my oeuvre will result in some actively seeking these places out to fulfill their own interests, and it is inconceivable to hope that none will succeed, I implore those adventure and venture seekers to leave these people to their own ends. I know there will likely be three responses to this book: there will be those who will reject and refute any and every fact presented to them as either falsehood, heresy, or slander, those who will accept as fact the words I write and respect the privacy of these people, and those who will believe, either with skepticism or no, that great fame and fortune awaits anyone who finds the treasures of Brobadingog or the magicks of Glubdubdrib.

I've experienced much of the first group, who accuse and attack me for all I have experienced, and I trust that having no reason to believe, they will leave these exotic locales alone. The second, who trust and respect, like the immortals of Loogenage, would not wish to harm any for their own benefit. It is only the last, those who seek to improve their lot through the plunder of other lands or to rescue and save unbelievers, to whom I aim this request. Please allow these people their peace and tranquility. Left to their own solitudes and devices, they might incubate new inventions and ideas, which may be presented, when they are ready, to the betterment of the known world.

Recognizing the hawkish amongst my readers, I also contend, with strong confidence, that either because of a lack of capacity, interest, or pure ability, that even the most bellicose of the people written herein would not hold any reasonable designs upon the world from which I have returned.

There is no need to fear the Lilliputians, who, though they possess the technology for war, are of little threat to those of our size. Nor is there any reason to fear the giants of Brobadingog or the Huhuneems, who care not a whit about what happens beyond their shores, particularly not about those of us who, being of much smaller stature, they deem insignificant and unworthy. Even the Strulbrugs, Glubdubdribians, and Balnibarbeans pose no real threat to our part of the world as they are technologically limited and numerically vastly inferior. I know of, nor did I experience, any illness during my travels, and I believe these people would likely suffer at our presence more than the reverse.

To the aims defined, I have recorded all pertinent facts in a chronological manner, beginning with some background about who I am and from whence I come. It is true to my mind that beyond any question, we are all products of our environment and upbringing. To understand me, you must know who I am. I will walk you through each of my adventures, including how I arrived at each location without providing specific locational details, and the immediate corresponding events back home that postdated each adventure. I will conclude by elucidating my situation at present, and with more detail about my voyages under your belt, you will better understand how I came to write this book.

I trust a discerning and patient reader, such as one who would read this book, will forgive my failings, find knowledge and entertainment within it, and interpret my experiences to draw what I may only hope to be valuable conclusions to apply to their equally meaningful lives.

Cygnus

PREFACE

The author gives some account of himself and his family, his history and background, and the general circumstances of his travel.

MY FATHER WAS a family physician in Calgary, Alberta, Canada. My mother, to my great fortune, was a stay-at-home mom who took care of me, my younger brother, and two older sisters. Determined to provide for me, but avoid inducing a sluggish work ethic, sloth, or poor attitude common to those of privilege, they enrolled me in public schools, provided me with a small allowance, and supported my academic endeavours through university. I maintained above-average grades and received several scholarships to attend post-secondary institutions. I elected to attend McGill University in Montreal to pursue my interest in global politics, geography, and history. Endowed with a natural linguistic capacity, I also took a few courses in various languages to further the bilingual abilities I had picked up during my grade schooling.

My early employment was a far from atypical mix of retail, selling marked-up goods out of an ordinary, run-of-the-mill shopping centre. It would not be fair to my former employers to share the name of their enterprises, lest judgement befall them for any of my choices or actions. Nor, as I will try to ensure, would it be right to bother the reader with so many details of such trivial importance.

While attending university, in the summer between semesters, I worked for my uncle's rafting adventure company as a guide in the Canadian Rocky Mountains and formed a close bond with nature. This has many times since served me well as the discerning reader may later attest. Through my summer employment, and with the aforementioned support of my generous and supportive family, I was able to graduate without the crushing burden of student loans weighing me down.

To my dismay, the market for broadly educated, polyglottish politicians, historians, and geographers proved not to provide the hotbed of unsolicited job offers and the immediate high-living lifestyle I had anticipated. I did, however, benefit from some charitable work provided by a great professor and supporter of mine from university, who granted me some short-term contracts to work on various academic studies in which he was participating. I was determined to not endebt myself further to my parents, beyond the already unrepayable debt—my rearing—I have since come to realize it was.

As any geographer, and not atypical of my generation in general, I wanted to see the world. I took a job as a flight attendant with an international airline, which I hoped would allow me the opportunity to visit exotic locales and experience the rich diversity of cultures all over the world. For two years, I flew from city to city and experienced primarily the cultural panacea of sterile airport theme parks and their adjoining chain hotels.

I hope my writings are perceived as not too negative. In most every adventure I have had, I have always found positive experiences, and in those two years, I worked with many cheerful, friendly, intelligent—and to be certain—a few quirky characters. I like to think of my story as one of hope and learning. It is a story in which I was incredibly fortunate to have been but an active observer. Obviously, a few turns of the hands of fate have delivered a bounty of immense fortune with respect to my adventures. This has allowed me to overcome some significant hardship, to live a life more akin to that which I had naïvely expected.

At the time, I considered my story to be a frustrating disappointment, and at the beginning of my more unique adventures, I found myself without any significant attachment. I had some pet fishes, overgrown feeder fish, but nothing that truly required regular attention. I rented a small apartment and basically lived out of a rollaboard. I didn't appreciate the detached, nomadic lifestyle I had unintentionally carved out for myself at the time, but I now consider it fortuitous that I had few responsibilities that I could, and most certainly would, have failed in absentia.

I hope this information I have shared offers enough of my history to grant an understanding of my choices, though it gives probably more than anyone would truly care to know about one as common and uninspiring as myself. I share this history only to provide context for my decisions and actions. Whether they are considered wise or foolish, they are the sum of my experiences and nature. One can only be true to oneself. The world may judge as they wish. My mistakes lie bare before you in the subsequent pages of this recantation of events; I hope that you, the astute reader, find some merit and integrity in my actions. As I have said before and will surely repeat, for good or ill, this is how my story unfolded.

PART ONE

THE ISLAND OF THE HUHUNEEM AND YAHOO

CHAPTER 1.1

The author describes the beginnings of his first adventure and the near catastrophe that nearly ended it.

WHEN CHOOSING WHERE to start this adventure, I could have chosen to recount stories of my youth. Or I could have chosen to reveal how I got my job at the airline or some of the memorable experiences I did have when not confined to a tin can with wings or the termini from and to whence they fly. These experiences, while meaningful to me, add little pertinent background for what was to come. The best place to begin is the day Flight 1726 departed from Toronto.

The day began not unlike most others in my ordinary life. I've always maintained a schedule of when I need to be at the airport, the time we leave, and to where we fly on each flight. I could be in Toronto in the morning, Los Angeles in the afternoon, and on my way to Tokyo that night. Sometimes I wasn't even sure where I was going, only that I next had to be somewhere at 6:00 am.

My job wasn't as glamorous as some might think. I woke up in a hotel almost every day and then crisscrossed the planet, barely seeing so much as a spot of it. On this day, though, I woke up in my king-sized memory-foam-topped bed in my apartment close to Toronto Pearson International Airport. Every night I spent in my own bed was the best night. Compared with hotels that clean the sheets daily and maintain strict controls, there was just something about home and sleeping in my own rarely laundered sheets that was more comfortable.

As I looked around the room upon waking, I noted, warmly, the lack of decoration on my walls and the suitcase, always packed and ready the night before, sitting on the floor next to the bedroom door. The air smelled stale as I had been out of my apartment for six days, and the apartment had grown accustomed to my absence. I kept little food in my fridge and rarely had time to cook, so little greeted me that morning, as usual.

But something was unusual that day. Not that it would presage the events to come, but for some reason, I awoke fifteen minutes before my alarm was scheduled to hammer the morning into my ears and remind me that I had places to not be. I mention this only because when sleeping at home after and before a long trip, it was especially rare that I didn't wake to the despised alarm just slightly out of arm's reach on the left side of my bed. Waking up before the alarm, however, is somehow equally disappointing. It is, after all, a missed, once-in-a-lifetime opportunity to sleep for an additional fifteen minutes. Instead, I was awake and ready to take on the world with safety presentations, in-flight sales, and complimentary food service. I turned off the alarm, to avoid mindless morning-show banter, and just lay in bed thinking about how great it would be to sleep for fifteen minutes, perhaps twenty minutes, before realizing that, in effect, I had now overslept.

I broached the cabinet, raided some cereal, and emptied the last drops of milk into a bowl just seconds before it was to expire, according to the label. Rushing, I had a quick shower, brushed my teeth, threw on my uniform, and grabbed my luggage as I locked myself out of my house—I had left my keys on the night table in my haste. No time to waste; that was a problem I'd have to deal with another time. It's one thing to be late for your flight when you're a paying guest, but airport public announcements rarely ask if the plane's steward is in the building. The threat of having one's bags offloaded means something entirely different to a steward.

No, it really wasn't as dramatic as that unless I was more than an hour late. An hour before the flight, the whole crew met to discuss and plan everything including the route, weather, duration, any possible turbulence, and the safety equipment of the jet. I inspected a few of the safety features before the passengers began to trudge aboard the plane, and everything appeared to be in certifiable working order. I adjusted my uniform, tightened the laces on my shoes, straightened my lanyard, and took out a torpedo level to straighten my tie bar. My crewmates would often give me a hard time about my proper appearance and attire. We were all required to maintain a professional appearance to keep the passengers at ease and knowing everything down to the complimentary beverage service was being handled to the highest standards, so I always felt my appearance reflected my commitment to the clients and my coworkers. I trusted that my guests and comment cards supported that decision.

I took up position midcabin to assist the passengers. As an aside, the first passenger on a plane is almost never one who needs the most assistance, despite the preboarding protocols and announcements. Usually, the first passengers are able-bodied, thirty-five-year-old couples eager to get to their destination faster than anybody else on the plane. It may seem obvious to most people, but the plane arrives at the same time for everyone regardless of when you board. Waiting in the airport lounge is actually more spacious and comfortable than the airplane itself, and the loading routine is designed to get people on the plane in the most efficient manner possible. Those requiring assistance and those with small children need the most time to settle, and while they settle, the more self-sufficient can settle quickly and easily. In fact, the faster a plane can turn around, the more profitable a carrier can be. All airline employees are incentivized to get the plane out of the terminal and off the ground as quickly as can be.

This trip began no differently. Sure enough, a well-dressed couple jumped up at the first announcement for preboarding and made a beeline onto the plane. I have always been of the opinion that during an emergency, these are exactly the kind of people one would want manning the emergency doors rather than sitting elsewhere on the plane. Their hurry would be an asset if they were in a position to be the first off but a liability to everyone around them if they were expected to wait. Anyway, they positioned themselves almost perfectly halfway between the mid and rear cabin exits, stuffed their oversized carry-on luggage into the compartment, and reclined their chairs.

Most of the remainder of the boarding went about usual. As 1726 was a long-haul flight to Sydney directly from Toronto—a brutal twenty-two-hour trip—most passengers carried as much on board as they could manage: books, electronics, headphones, pens, papers, clothes, snacks, pillows, blankets, even toiletries. As anyone who has been on a long flight like this can imagine, this meant the overheads and under-seat storage spaces were filled to bursting. A giant game of Tetris ensued to try to make sure everyone's things were stored safely and securely.

My colleague, Justin, lays claim to the international high score. On this flight, once again, he proved it by deftly stacking soft- and hard-shelled luggage, leaving a cyclopean Samsonite wall that couldn't fit a toothpick more.

Once the plane was loaded with fuel, service, crew, passengers, and luggage, we taxied to Runway 5 and got away clean from the metropolis of Toronto. As an early morning flight, the window passengers were sent off by the lights of the CN Tower and the downtown skyline. The long flight went by in a typical manner. There were a few teeth-chattering bouts with minor turbulence, but nothing worthy of reporting. We knew we were heading in the general direction of a large storm, but reports from aircraft in the area and satellite showed it was well within the tolerances for which the aircraft was designed and capable of handling.

I hesitate to admit it, but somewhere after the first meal service of the flight, I put my head down, in the allocated space for such activities, and fell into a deep slumber, the kind from which one awakes pondering whether he is still asleep and dreaming or if he is actually awake. The air was gravy thick, and the passengers tittered as they looked out the windows into the dark clouds surrounding the plane. It had started to shudder and drop as the storm outside the cabin created bubbles of pressure. The plane shook and the passengers became alarmed. Most travellers will tell you turbulence is a likely hazard for most any flight, and the current turbulence didn't exceed my own comfort.

I marched down the aisles in an effort to soothe the children on board and to exude the necessary confidence that all was well with the state of things. This was a normal event, one well within the normal range of flight experiences. Little did I worry while meandering to the back of the plane. The plane jolted, the screens flickered, and the captain announced that it looked like we were in for some stronger turbulence ahead and to please stay seated and fasten seatbelts.

Then a bright light filled the cabin, and a loud boom alerted everyone that we had been struck by lightning. I looked at the passengers nearby, their spines suddenly bolt straight and eyes open as wide as possible. They were desperate for reassurance that the plane was going to be all right.

The plane suddenly dropped. I lost my footing and lay sprawled in the aisle near the back of the plane. The sight of a fallen attendant is troubling to passengers. One reached down to help me up. Several others were now filling the air with a chorus of piercing screams. As I scrabbled to my feet, I could see that a number of passengers had suffered minor injuries from the drop and several were bleeding, compounding the panic. One woman nearby had fainted, slumping over the arm of the chair, her head sagging in the aisle. The turbulence had caused a number of weaker stomachs to fail, and the atmosphere was thick, warm, humid, and somewhat foul. The public announcement system, like the screens, was now not even emitting static. A warm trickle of blood poured from my own forehead, meandering its way to my mouth and chin.

A number of people had gotten out of their seats, whether from discomfort or to help a loved one or neighbour I could not really say. Suddenly the craft crabbed and jolted upwards. All those near me, myself included, who were not restrained were sent flying into the seats on the left. The plane started to list. The pilot was trying to regain altitude, but a right-side engine had failed. The plane continued to bump and thrash. The oxygen masks fell from the ceiling and all calm was lost.

The plane must have been in pretty bad shape; maybe the engine had fully detached in the storm, or maybe the storm had damaged another engine. All souls on board Flight 1726 felt their stomachs rise, literally, towards their throats as we felt the plane descend from the dark sky into a darker, still unknown, space below. Time passed both in the blink of an eye and as a glacier in slow motion. I can't honestly say whether we fell for a fraction of a second or for full minutes. It seemed without a doubt now that we were going to go down somewhere in the South Pacific Ocean in the middle of the night in a storm. I was sure the pilot was doing everything he could to make that touch as gentle as possible, but I abandoned my efforts to help discombobulated passengers. I tucked myself into the best impromptu bracing position I could manage, stuffed on the floor of the seating area with several people close by.

CHAPTER 1.2

The author affects his escape and hopes for rescue from the wreckage.

I KNOW THE reader will forgive the gap in my narrative for when the plane struck the water; the deceleration caused a second knock to my head and a temporary period of unconsciousness.

I regained consciousness in an eerily quiet scene of destruction. Once there had been panic and pain. Now all was still, at least as far as the inside of the fuselage. Outside the tube, the storm raged on. As any vessel on an unfriendly sea, the cabin lurched and dropped, rose and twisted with each wave and windy gale. I'm not much for the action of the waves at the best of times. The smarting, flourishing knock on my temple wasn't helping me to establish my sea legs.

On board, nothing and nobody moved. The crash had made a great shamble of Justin's Tetrisian achievement. I will not endeavour to account the further description of what I encountered. In honesty, I didn't, at the time, enumerate or evaluate in detail. The fair reader may choose to skip over the subsequent description of the wreckage if they be of weak constitution. In such a case, I recommend that they avoid only the next paragraph.

The first thing one notices when looking about the cabin of a crashed plane are not the bodies or the baggage, but the oxygen masks dangling limply from the ceiling of the overhead compartments. Each and every mask hung down from above the seats in the eerie darkness permeated only by some poor emergency lights. The shadows of the cords and masks give the feeling of a dark jungle, with vines dangling from thick foliage. Of course, there were many bodies in various states of burial amongst the piles of luggage strewn about randomly. I shouldn't like to discuss too much the individual bodies I saw; it is the most difficult memory I possess to think of my helplessness to help them. I checked a few of those nearest to me and found their vital signs were not detectable. I could hear no signs that would suggest to me that any other survivors were hidden amongst the chaos. The smell of the cabin was as chaotic as the dimly lit scene. Food, drink, blood, perfume, and all manner of broken and burned glass and plastic permeated my nasal passageways. This is a scene I sincerely hope nobody ever has to witness for themselves.

Here I found myself, stranded somewhere in an unknown ocean, in a violently rocking aircraft, and becoming no more combobulated. I had to find a way to safety. The survivors of the crash, whatever their number, had already removed the evacuation slides from the doors to use as a life raft as they fled the cabin. I made no effort to adjudicate their actions.

The first escapees may have waited for several minutes after the crash, or conversely, the first one out the door might have seized his opportunity and shoved off immediately, stranding others to share more crowded rafts. My period of blankness would forever keep that knowledge from me. It was not possible to determine whether they had checked on the welfare of others aboard. Perhaps they had, and I was either too buried to spot, or they believed me dead, but I was not amongst those who escaped in the first wave; thus, I was without the best possible conveyance.

Whatever had occurred, I found myself with no ready route of escape and armed with the knowledge that an aeroplane will not float indefinitely on the ocean. And with a storm pummelling her, it will indeed not last very long in a buoyant state. Water was lapping at the doors of the cabin and time was running short.

I began tearing apart the seats nearest the emergency exit. Aircraft seats may be used as floatation devices, but they are not the same as life jackets. The seats, at least aboard this flight, were equipped with a couple arm loops on each side of the cushion and floated like a pillow on the water. If I lost consciousness again—a distinct possibility—my head would not be held above the waves. I knew neither where the flight had landed nor when or if a rescue was coming. Nor did I know how long it would take to arrive. So, I gathered a dozen of the seats and tied four together in a square using some rope that had fallen from the overheads. I then tied eight together end to end as firmly as I could and quickly secured them to my square. Grabbing a couple water bottles, little caring that they were both open, I shoved my raft out the door into the choppy water and jumped onto the middle of the square of four cushions, sinking to my waist but free floating safely, with a long tail of eight seat cushions trailing behind me in a line.

I wish I could have investigated the plane as I cast off, but my first priority was to make my seat-cushion raft as seaworthy as possible. The storm was still blustering and dark. I had no idea what dangers lurked in the water.

The four-cushion square acted as the floor of my boat while I feverishly tied the eight remaining cushions around the outside of the square as a one-cushion tall wall. I intended this to be my little walled raft, floating like an open-topped box in the waves. I cursed the clouds, the rain, the wind, the waves, and the unyielding pains in my body, particularly my head. The rain lashed at my skin and clothes and numbed my hands while I endeavoured to finish my boat. Every gust and wave blew bitter saltwater into my eyes and mouth.

I lashed the seats together as best I could, but found my teacup, which in my mind was supposed to appear like a square-bottomed, open-top box, instead was more of a twelve-panelled wet sock. I found that trying to sit or lie on one or several of the seats just resulted in either falling into the water or into a crevice between two lines of seats. After much effort, I surrendered, lying prostrate on one side of the craft, which was folded in half like a pita pocket. My arms splayed out to the sides in another gap, wrapped amongst the ropes. The remaining six seats more or less sat on top of me, providing little more than a wet, dripping, porous umbrella against the rain. As secure as I felt I was going to get, I strained to look back at the plane that so nearly had become my resting place.

It had not been a conscious thought, but I became dimly aware that the plane was no longer above the waves. Without a means of propulsion, the hulking mass of aluminum behind me had silently tucked in beneath the waves not to be seen by my eyes again. The realization that it was gone left me with a desperation and loneliness only someone who has experienced a similar shock and trauma could understand. There I lay on a pile of seat cushions, completely alone, with no idea where I was, other than in the vast Pacific Ocean, floating in a hurricane. I was rapidly losing hope, realizing that even if a rescue plane was on the way, even if the wreckage could be found, my little makeshift raft wouldn't look like much more than debris. The depressing reality of my predicament was clear. I had two half-drunk bottles of water to sustain me. If I survived the night in the blowing hurricane, I would still have to survive days floating in the direct, burning, unrelenting sun, somewhere in the tropics, and my fair skin was liable to singe. If my adventure wasn't to be ended by the water, it would surely be by exposure, heat stroke, or dehydration.

I began to consider more radical alternatives to my situation but succumbed to rest. I kept as hydrated as I could and hoped and prayed against Herculean odds that somehow I would, in some way, be delivered to safety. In no way was I a religious person, and I did not know how to pray to a god, whichever god that would be. I blindly hoped that some power, human or divine, would pluck me from the waves, though I knew the odds were against me. As the water sapped the energy from me and the pain of my injuries began to overtake the adrenaline that had thus far sustained me, I submitted at last and rested my head to the side on a salty seat cushion and slept.

CHAPTER 1.3

The author awakens in the care of a strange woman on a strange island.

THE MEASURE OF time can be a fickle thing. Compared to the ghastly excitements on board the carefully engineered vessel that was my previous conveyance, the gentle oscillations of the egregiously named, "Pacific Ocean," seemed an apprehensive tedium. I bobbed about the waves in a state of alert sleep, as though sleepwalking but while not fully asleep. With little upon which to focus but an endless azure field and surrounded by a wet cocoon of jetsam, I drifted in and out of consciousness. Vaguely, I was aware of my own consciousness, but dragons and krakens, in my current state of mind, would have been no more or less surreal than the sight of a ship or land. The fight had long since left my wearied limbs.

I floated in these conditions for hours or days. With honesty, I cannot truly say whether it was the former or the latter. I was sustained only by the small ration of water in the bottles and the meagre shelter provided by the raft.

My first clear memory—and I pray you believe me when I say it took some time for me to accept that this was indeed a memory and not just a ridiculous dream—was of sensing my leather-upholstered swaddle no longer surrounding me. Heavy, dark air and a solid, slanted deck had replaced the bright, wet environment. Activity around me informed me I was not alone.

Dimly, it became clear I was in a small cave and was being attended to by a small but strong woman. My lips were burnt and parched from the sun and dehydration. I knew I had been given water. A point to note, however: if you happen upon an unconscious person in your travels, you should not give them food or water. They are most likely to aspirate rather than revive. In my circumstance, somehow, I had been resuscitated.

The woman in the cave was clearly attending to many disparate emergencies, of which I was apparently secondary concern. As she flitted about and fiddled here and there, I adjusted to the light that entered the cave through numerous fissures in the rock. I took an estimation of the woman as I could not yet ascertain if she was my saviour, captor, or companion of circumstance. She was short, but with defined musculature like that of an athlete, and was thin and unkempt, with long, messy hair. I hesitate to print this, but in the interest of full disclosure, she was also completely naked. Her back was marked by numerous scars, with cuts and bruises, which suggested to me we were imprisoned together in our subterranean dungeon. She stood stooped and crooked and possessed long, jagged, untrimmed fingernails more resembling an animal's than a well-groomed human's.

Sensing there was nobody else around and I was not in any immediate danger, I endeavoured to prop myself up with the ultimate intent to quietly rise to my feet. At almost the first movement, before I thought I had even made the slightest whisper, she whipped her head around and glared at me like a deer in the forest upon the slightest snap of a twig. She and I shared a long, breathless stare as we both took the measure of the other. I could see the bruises on her back continued to her front, on her face, arms, and legs. Her entire body was covered with hairy, almost fur-like matting. One might draw the impression from this description that she bore the appearance of a Neanderthal. I can't claim to have ever before seen one in person, but she seemed to me more a feral human, with delicate features like a small nose and a flat, near vertical forehead camouflaged behind a tough façade.

I had barely managed to lift my body centimetres off the slab and had found the exertion of staying here was proving too great for my current physical condition. My arms gave out on me suddenly, and with a light, but solid, bump, I fell back onto the rock upon which I had recently laid. My cavewoman companion was at my side almost immediately, raising and funnelling a liquid towards my mouth with a large leaf. She spoke in a sort of whisper saying, "way-o, way-o, way-o," showing me I should drink from it. Unable to put up a struggle, I reluctantly complied and drank the water. It was dirty and thick with what I still hope was just silt from the stream. The water fell into the cave, not far from my bed, through an algae-plugged hole in the ceiling. Despite the taste and texture, I could not help but drink deeply and greedily from the proffered cupped leaf. As I finished the beverage, which I spilt embarrassingly onto my once again soaking wet clothes, she offered me another and another, repeating "way-o, way-o, way-o" each time.

Finally, I pushed the leaf away, and as gracefully as I could, thanked her but refused any more. Though I thought it unlikely she would speak English or any other language to which I could stake any claim, I could not foresee her reaction to my voice. Her eyes and mouth burst open, and she jumped back, without making a sound, into the stream on the floor. The sudden violence of her action startled me as well, and I jerked away from her. We returned to the stare we had shared before. This time she was noticeably shaken and apparently as afraid of me as I was of her. She silently exclaimed a single word, "Huhuneem." I'm certain the look on my face was one of pure confusion. My brow furrowed and I repeated back, "Huhuneem?" Her eyes stretched wider as she turned and fled deep into the cave, ducking under stalactites and veering around stalagmites as she ran out of sight, leaving me alone once again in a strange cave, lying on an inclined rock.

I tried to lift myself up to explore the cave but found I could not muster the energy and lay back down to rest. The wild cavewoman didn't return, and I fell back to sleep on my rock on the floor of the cave.

CHAPTER 1.4

Stranded in a cave, the author meets more natives of this place, but not all of them are like the feral runaway.

GRADUALLY, STRENGTHENED BY the subterranean water, I pulled myself back together in the dimly lit grotto. Though it was sparsely, to put with a mild sense of humour the exaggeration, decorated, it was evident this cave had been lived in for some time. While nothing existed to cause one to believe a civilized person called it home, the twigs, moss, and leaves were arranged in such a way that suggested some areas were used for rest. A pit against a wall, near where I first saw the wild woman, led upwards to a fissure in the ceiling. A low rock wall surrounding the pit showed this was used for fire. My indulgent stone bed was posited against the wall opposite the fire pit. Nearby, the aforementioned stream trickled from the ceiling—which was thick with falling stalactites—roughly twelve feet above the ground, falling to the middle of the floor and out in a sinuous stream to my left towards a brightly illuminated part of the cave. I took this to indicate the mouth of the cave. This entrance was opposite the direction the woman had fled.

The air was thicker than before now, and I noticed that at the entrance, where the stream trickled out, a pool of water lapped gently. I shambled over to the water—after surveying the path the woman had taken into the depths of the cave—and carefully tested it. It was warmer than the stream water, and the seaweed and salty aroma suggested to me that beyond the entrance lay the expansive ocean. I smelled my fingertip to confirm my suspicion. Judging by the layout of the room, and the proximity to the gathered accoutrements, this was likely to be high tide. The water appeared shallow around the bend of the cavern entrance, which had shrunk from its height inside to just slightly taller than my measure. From the light that shone brightly on the dark rock of the right wall, an opening to the outside existed ahead and to the left.

I found myself faced with three options. Ahead of me lay an opening to the sea and whatever hazards awaited me out there. It was clear from her direction that my companion did not believe this to be an attractive option. Behind me, a room devoid of all but a stone-age culture—and water—awaited the possible return of either the woman or our captors. Beyond that beckoned an unknown cave system and perils I could only imagine.

No choice shone forth as obvious, but I decided to go towards the light. At the very least, I would be able to try to ascertain my position. Though stable and safe, the unknown cave to which the woman fled repelled me, as did a fear of dark, unknown passageways. My sore feet and ruined shoes contributed to negating that option. I carefully plodded forwards towards the entrance. I inspected the water with the tips of my toes and bent over, checking for any sharp objects or sudden depressions into which I could fall. I could see, but still I proceeded as though blind, feeling every nook and cranny of the portal, alert to every flicker of light from ahead or slosh of a wave behind. With each step, the reverberating waves grew in volume and the sun's rays grew brighter. The thick, musty smell of the cave gave way to a light sea breeze as I reached the mouth of the cave.

I squinted at the bright sun that reflected both agonizingly and with a resplendence I can scarcely describe. As I acclimatized to the bright daylight, it finally occurred to me that I was alive. A discombobulating mess of emotion struck me at that moment. Once more I realized I had lost track of time. Its relative passing was a forgotten memory as I stood and digested some of the fates that had befallen me. I suppose in my dumbfounded stupefaction at my good fortune, I was vulnerable to the same people from whom I had just escaped in the cave. I had a moment of clarity as I thought about what my survival meant and wondered what my survival meant to the others from the plane. I knew some, or maybe all of them, would never be seen again, and I paused, unable to wrap my head around the magnitude of my thoughts.

I surveyed the scene, and I found myself on the right side (looking to the sea) of a horseshoe-shaped cove. The near side of the cove presented a rocky cliff a few metres tall, craggy and jagged. Somewhere around the horn to my right, invisible to me, I heard a small cascade of water fall into the sea. Apart from my rocky perch, the cove was surrounded by a thick deciduous forest. A sandy strand ten metres wide separated the water from the trees. The opening of the bay was about half a kilometre wide. The water was the colour of a robin's egg, and a slight breeze created only the smallest waves that licked at my feet and the sand all around the beach. In the distance, two-thirds of the way around the harbour, at the edge of the forest and the sand, was a dark pile of rectangular cubes and rope. The only apparent anthropogenic disturbance in sight was this eyesore of debris, this jumble of wreckage. It was amongst the most beautiful sights I had ever seen, my salvation from the sea.

Several metres beyond my seat-raft, out of the thick forest, something astonishing appeared. A red-brown horse stepped from the brush onto the beach and slowly performed his own reconnaissance. He swept his gaze gradually from left to right, and as his gaze passed about halfway around the cove, his attention was drawn to the detritus. He did not spot the human interloper on the far side of the beach but cautiously moved towards the heap of aeroplane seat cushions.

I apologize to the reader. My knowledge of equines is not extensive. To my eyes, the horse's behaviour seemed unusual for an animal of its constitution. He moved around the pile calmly and deliberately, warily keeping an eye on the forest, as if expecting something to disturb the discovery. The horse settled to the ground with his hind feet positioned forward, as a child sits to play with a new toy. He reached forwards and grasped one cushion with a hoof. He held the pillow between the hard part of the hoof and the softer top, which I have since been informed is called the pastern. He looked at all sides and was clearly confused and awed by its composition. I marvelled at this great creature and gasped at the display of dexterity by the beast and the careful, studious nature it was demonstrating.

An eagle called out from the skies above me, and the horse glanced over in my direction. It seemed to me he was acknowledging the bird's presence rather than showing alarm. The horse noted me and rose confidently to its feet. The sorrel walked with no great urgency across the beach. I felt it unlikely he would be able to manage the steep cliff around me. I decided to work my way towards the animal.

It might not have been the wisest decision in my current state to try to scale an unfamiliar cliff face on an island somewhere in the Pacific Ocean with not a soul around save a curious horse and a strangely behaving wild native woman who had fled into a dark cave. I hope the reader will excuse the folly of my action at this time. It would have been wiser to wait until the tide was low and instead explore the relative safety of the cave from which I had come. My curiosity overcame reason, and I set out towards the beach. The water directly beneath the bluff was shallow. Like the cliff above the tide, the rocks were sharp and slippery, covered with barnacles, seaweed, mussels, and a variety of other marine life to which I remain ignorant to this day. My brine-soaked hands blistered quickly and were cut upon the rock. My feet suffered no better fate as each hand and foothold proved treacherous.

I would love to report I handled the cliff like a seasoned climber and scampered to the beach without incident. I'm afraid that wasn't to be. After about ten metres of scaling, hands and feet aching and bleeding, an important foothold suddenly gave way. Flailing with both arms, I failed to grasp anything more solid than a gnarled tree root that tore from the escarpment easily and caused me to crash with great impact on the acuminous shelf a metre below. A peaked stone scythed through my pants and thigh. Several smaller gashes covered my arms, leg, and back. The shallow water of the ridge, not more than a foot deep, changed hue gradually to a crimson red. I tore the left sleeve off my already haggard white uniform shirt and tied it over the cut on my thigh as a bandage to stem the bleeding.

From this vantage, I could see that the cliff dove deep into the water at this point along the rock wall. I decided rather than continuing the punishing crossing, I would dive into the water and swim for the beach. It was roughly two hundred metres to the nearest sand. In spite of the throbbing of my hands, feet, and mostly my thigh, I swam as hard as I could towards the sand. I picked up speed when a large fish brushed in front of my leg and I realized I was a glowing beacon for sharks if the water was deep enough. In a rare turn of good luck, there were none around. Still, I swam for shore as a man being chased by an armada of great whites. I suppose fear and the associated rush of adrenaline helped to push aside the pain and got me to shore faster than my swimming skills would otherwise have allowed. The beach shallowed for the last fifty metres, and I was able to touch the ground and keep my shoulders above the water.

Ahead on the beach, the horse had made much faster time than I and was watching me intently from the shore. I could hear it neighing, but each sound had a distinct tone and rhythm, not like a normal neigh and whinny, but something entirely more complicated and intelligent. As I emerged from the water and incrementally celebrated my burgeoning security, both she, for I could at this point see my mistake in believing the horse was a male, and I were measuring each other thoroughly. I found myself focusing on the noises she was making and the poised, assertive position she took on the shore. She seemed to focus on my clothing and hair. As I drew my waist and leg above the water, she seemed to whinny a word that most closely resembled "Yahoo." Had I not thought I knew better, I would have said she was voicing the word with astonishment.

As I approached the animal, I adopted a cautious pace. I had ridden horses before, but only a handful of times. I was certainly not an expert in dealing with wild mares. I grew ever more conscious of my size and capabilities as compared to the powerful beast before me. By my estimate, I had the advantage of mind and dexterity, while my counterpart possessed size, strength, and speed. I approached the horse with humility and caution and spoke in soft tones I intended to be soothing. I did not succeed in soothing the sorrel nag. As I whispered, she reared back and repeated the same word, "Yahoo," with an even greater tone of awe and incredulity. I put my hands up to simultaneously show I wasn't a threat and to defend myself in case she was to strike. She settled her front legs back on the ground and stood a few feet outside of my reach. I suppose I expected a wild animal, this close up, to smell something between a zoo and a wet dog. The horse possessed no ill pungency but rather an almost faint flowery fragrance.

We stood apart for a moment or two more before I took a step forwards and staggered to the ground, stung by the pain in my leg. She swiftly closed the gap and stood over me. I reached up, intending to use her leg to stabilize myself and stand again. She batted my hand away and neighed to me in a manner that convinced me she was telling me something; again, I made out the same word as before, but with a note of contempt. I cowered in fear, completely at her mercy. She stood over me, a tower of flesh and muscle.

Still she continued to neigh with various inflections and tones. It seemed crazy to me even in the moment. I felt like the noises she was making were a form of language unlike I had experienced before. Repeatedly, I picked out the familiar word. As she pawed at my shirt with curiosity and confusion, I endeavoured to replicate the word. I translate the word into a Latin script as "Yahoo," but the sound involves the passing of much more air through the mouth and a sort of assonant stutter around the soft consonants. I mimicked the sound as best I could, but in a typically Indo-European manner, I added a raised inflection at the end to indicate a question. This spooked the horse more than I anticipated. She pulled back a few feet from me entirely. She and I stared at each other again, and she repeated the word almost perfectly as I had, inflection and all, while bobbing her head. Suddenly, thrusting her head forward, she repeated it in the tone she had used before while pointing her front left leg towards me. I interpreted this to mean she wanted me to echo her. Still at her mercy, but more amazed than afraid, I obliged as best I could, with the upwards inflection. This to me indicated an uncertainty. As I later discovered, it had an entirely different meaning to her. We practiced this several times. Each time, she bobbed her head and thrusted it forwards with the correct resonances. Gaining confidence, I dropped the intonation and spoke it most compatibly with the way she had.

I had risen to my feet by this point, though it caused great pain to do so. It occurred to me that she was identifying me. I was to discover later that my entire species were Yahoos. At the time, I took it to indicate her identification of my person. I pointed to myself, recognizing that her front leg was likely pointing not to me to take a turn, but to indicate she was referring to me. Once more I repeated the word to her, and she stomped her foot twice on the ground and expelled air through her nostrils noisily, as if exasperatedly saying, "Finally!"

Amused by this exchange, and utterly incapable of walking away both literally and figuratively, I pushed the issue a little further. I pointed my right hand towards her and said, "horse." She looked at me with derision but immediately sensed what I was doing and bent her leg in such a way that I had never before seen a horse do and pointed towards herself and said "Huhuneem." If it pleases the reader, I will skip the intricacies of the pronunciation. It is difficult to translate to a written script such as this. It will have to suffice to say it took a great deal more practice before I achieved the foot stamp of approval.

I had formally been introduced to Huhuneem, or Hue, as I came to think of her. Not your average name for a female horse, I believed, but much easier to wrap my tongue around. The question arose, what to do next? I was in too great a pain to stand up straight, much less walk, and here I found myself face-to-face with a magnificent and obviously intelligent horse on an unknown island somewhere in the South Pacific—I would suppose—Ocean.

Not more than a moment later, a sort of horn sounded. Hue's ears, which had been lying flat back on her head, perked up and rotated towards the forest, from whence the sound had come. She was in a hurry as she lifted a hoof towards me and importuned me to follow her. Out of instinct due in part, I credit, to my injury, I reached towards her back, either to try to ride her or to use her as a crutch. I can't specifically recall my intent, but this drew a sharp rebuke, and she struck my hand forcefully. The blow caused me to cry out in pain, and having lost my support and being unable to catch my weight on my damaged appendage, I once again fell to the ground. Hue looked back with a mixture of tenderness and abhorrence, as though somewhat sorry for causing injury but unimpressed at my exasperatingly frail condition.

The horse apparently decided I wasn't the greatest priority. She left me crumpled on the ground like my cushion raft. It seemed likely, through all I had been through, that I would see this animal again. After all, how many people could be in this place near enough I could hear the horn blast that called her.

I rested on the beach as the wind picked up and the waves grew into small breakers. The tide receded some, revealing the entirety of the sharp shelf upon which I had been gored. My poor beached body, having washed ashore, been laid upon a slab, and shredded and pulverized by the cliffs, deserved a rest. I dragged it towards a large chunk of driftwood, lay back, and drifted into a pleasant afternoon nap on the sandy beach.

CHAPTER 1.5

The author meets more locals who bring him back to their home.

I WOKE WITH a start as the light on my closed eyelids fluctuated several times. Three completely naked and unkempt souls circled, gawking and prodding at my person. They intermittently blocked the sun and consequently woke me. As the woman I had met in the cave, they were diminutive in stature. I would notice this later, as this was hardly evident looking up at them from the ground. They possessed a wiry musculature, which I supposed they owed to a primal existence. I found myself most concerned, apart from my own welfare of course, with the distinct and regular bruises and scars, particularly across their backs. Their bodies were covered in hair. Two males and one female cautiously scanned me as if I was the threatening party. All three possessed long, black, lank hair on their heads. The men had thick hair on their faces, arms, legs, backs, and chests, while the woman was covered in the stubble that would more naturally occur amongst the women of my home, if not for frequent interference. I shall avoid the salacious details.

Their bodies, by means of violence, not birth, possessed numerous deformities. Both men showed telltale signs of broken noses and cauliflowering of the ears such as would be seen typically on a professional boxer. One had a scar across his left eye as if he had been struck with a bat. None of the scars were particularly clean, as would suggest a blade or the puncture of a bullet. It was also clear none of the scars had been treated with stitching as the wounds were particularly wide. They didn't speak but seemed to whinny and neigh in a manner reminiscent of Hue.

It is certain my evaluation of these people fell far short of what they had ascertained about their interloper as I have denoted the features that would be of remark to one such as me. I could only believe they were most interested in the same details—but in reverse—in me. I had short brown hair, blue eyes, stubble on my face that on takeoff had been freshly shaven but was nonetheless much closer shorn than theirs. My body was virtually untouched by scars. I believed they were mostly intent on focusing on my clothes and skin, which, being of a fair complexion, must have seemed quite the rarity in this land. I have tried many times since, but I can only imagine what I would think if somebody similar to me in core body, but possessing materials of which I could scarcely conceive, was covered in a skin of a tone unprecedented in human history or memory. It would cause quite a stir to see an unaltered person with glowing green skin. Perhaps this is not a fair comparison, but I digress.

The observant reader will remember that I fell asleep in the afternoon, somewhere in the Pacific Ocean, on a bright, sunny day. I received some criticism about this action, failing to protect myself against the damage of the sun. I believe this criticism misplaced, even humorous, considering my physical condition and recent events. My skin, at least those parts visible, was saturated with a scorching scarlet sear. The evaluation of the natives of this island must have been one of curiosity and disgust. Every part of my body was in great pain from one or another injury.

I certainly felt myself at their mercy and physically intimidated, both by their relative health and statures. My defensive instincts at what would occur next clearly were misplaced. I tried to introduce myself, but the words escaped as barely more than a hoarse exhalation. These people were afraid, constantly turning their attentions to the bush and the beach at every sound, small or large. Like skittish deer, they reared their heads back and scanned their surroundings cautiously and with such a degree of care as to cause me to assume these were perhaps equal prisoners to the first woman I had encountered in the cave. A thought occurred that I might have washed ashore in some sort of penal colony, though I was unaware of such a place existing in the modern world. These people were in an awful hurry and terrified of something. Fear is as contagious as the flu, so I began to listen carefully for sounds from the bush.

It was only thus for a couple minutes before they, recognizing the wound to my leg and my obvious inability to stand, offered me a metaphorical olive branch. It is here that I made my error. I saw a group of possibly dangerous, certainly fearful people, and assumed the stick they thrust towards my prone and terrified body was an act of hostility. I batted the stick aside sharply yelling, "No!" and shielded myself lest they repeat the attack. To this they responded with an incredible diversity of emotional responses. They seemed angry, distressed, concerned, and confused and recoiled from me a couple feet.

The smaller male recomposed the quickest. He picked up the stick, which in honesty, was a thickly foliated branch from a nearby tree. He said, "Way-o" as he gestured to me to grab onto the branch. I remained suspicious of these people, but I knew I was very much at their mercy. I heeded his gesticulation and propped myself back on my feet. This revealed the back of my arms and legs, which had not been exposed to the sun and were lily white in comparison to the sunburnt bits. My hosts seemed resigned to my unusual colours and physique and must have interpreted this as within the acceptably preposterous normal of the present situation. The branch they extended was not usable as a cane or crutch. I was in no condition to make a long walk, or really any sort of perambulation, with these inhabitants. The larger man and the woman caught me on the first stagger. As with an athlete being helped off the playing field, the two of them took my weight on their strong, broad shoulders and helped me hobble off the beach into the brush.

Quickly, they all but carried me along the dense forest floor, just out of sight of the beach but always within earshot. They walked on stones, twigs, roots, and fallen trees, though their feet were completely barren of footwear. They moved with a rugged gracefulness. In spite of the burden presented by their arm candy, as I began to think of myself, they swiftly jogged between the trees. At times, they even used low branches to swing over particularly rough ground. We were moving far faster than I thought possible through such terrain. I would not say their motion was graceful; it seemed appropriate and natural: perfect for this environment. Suddenly, we were next to the sharp rock cliff. If not for the beach, I would have lost my bearings entirely during the run, but the vertical wall of rock in front of me was immediately recognizable in its geology.

In front of us was a thin crack in the rock, scarcely large enough to edge through sideways. The crack did not extend very high; it was perhaps as tall as my nose, two metres or so from ground to top. The smaller man disappeared quickly into the crack, like a mouse into a woodpile. My attendants wayo-ed that I was to follow, and quickly. Their panic was as obvious as their distress at my slothfulness. They prodded me into the crack as a cow into a pen. They watched their backs, covered our tracks, and jammed me through. I crouched and twisted with great pain, scrabbling, with the walls close on both sides for several metres, into a new, uncomfortable darkness.

CHAPTER 1.6

The author describes the abode and is introduced to the local culture.

I'VE BEEN TOLD that some had expected a description of some marvellous, mystical, underground karst cave system illuminated by some eerie but wonderful glow. Therein would lie a hall that was a refined, artisanal crafted cavern that would make my sufferings so far seem of little consequence. It only would have been fair considering what had befallen me to this point. Sadly, I would be disappointed. It would be much more pleasant to describe and imagine such a place. However, it did not exist in this realm.

I struggled assiduously through the uncomfortable crack in the wall, pursued closely by the two remaining inhabitants of this land. I was affronted by the putrid smell of acrid, untreated faeces and a thick, mouldy must in the air. It only got stronger as I pushed further, or more candidly, as I was pushed further. We could no longer see the beach side of the rock wall, but they pushed as though we could be caught at any moment. Their irritated grunts, punctuated by my awkward position, limited the energy I could devote to preparing for the future. The passage was not so long, altogether, but it snaked and curved over a course of roughly five metres. Each jog in the track required strange new contortions, and never was the ceiling tall enough for me to stretch out. Gradually, we escaped into a larger cavern.

I emerged from the tight crack, and my welcome to the subterranean room proved similarly distressing. I wiggled my head and upper body out first and found myself surrounded by a semicircle of cautious natives. There were about ten of them within a few strides of the entrance, within which I was still half entombed. Behind me, my friends from the beach were still impatient with my progress. They shoved the rest of my body with their typical great strength out of the doorway and onto the slippery, wet rock of the main room, where I fell to the ground. In the semicircle I recognized two figures. The first was the smaller man who had preceded me into the cave. No doubt, he had forewarned that some sort of strange visitor was approaching. The second was the wild woman I first encountered when I awoke in the same cave system. My view of the room was obscured by the strapping but unclad people around me.

I think it wise to describe my condition once more. After crashing into the ocean, a thorough soaking at sea, a bit of spelunking through a dimly lit unfamiliar cave system—twice—some ill-fated rock-wall scaling and interactions with both natives and wildlife in this place, I looked hardly the prim and proper flight attendant in a well-pressed uniform. Based on the growth of facial hair, I could only have been absent a few days now. However, from the looks of me, one might have estimated I had been marooned for months. In addition to the cuts on my arms, legs, and torso, the significant gash in my leg from the climbing accident had soaked the shirt I had tied over it, my skin glowed from sunburn, and I had a cracking headache. My clothes were scarcely better than tatters, stretched and tumbled by the harsh salt water. They hung off me and were torn in dozens of places as I was bundled back into the cave. My lips were parched and bleeding, and I smelled, well, compared to my current surroundings, I suppose I didn't smell so awful.

Here was I, battered and broken, scarcely able to stand on my own feet, surrounded by a dozen strangers who had thus far indicated no ability to speak in any language to which I was familiar. I was the helpless ward of strange beings in a foreign place. Little of the environment was visible behind the strong, tortured legs of my company. The smell, were it not for the adrenaline coursing through me, would likely have overwhelmed me. I had even failed to notice that my original wild woman had deserted. She returned with a leaf full of water and indicated with a "Way-o" that I should drink. I'm not of the type who accepts food and drink from strangers, but I could tell I was starved of alternatives. I heartily drank the water as though it were Juan Ponce de Leon's fountain of youth. The large leaf held a surprising amount, and though I was likely seriously dehydrated, I felt sufficiently quenched to hoarsely gulp out without thinking, "Thank you."

These two words, barely uttered, drew a similar but muted reaction to that which the woman first showed when I spoke. The woman puffed up a bit, and a knowing smile crossed her lips. Her companions repeated the same word I had heard most often, "Huhuneem." They did not demonstrate a great vocabulary. I might have expected them to draw into council, or discuss what to do with me, but they didn't seem to possess such linguistic capabilities. I shifted into a more natural and marginally more comfortable position on the moist floor while I attempted a more dignified pose. I felt a little proud to be as upright as I was, considering what I had been through. They seemed less impressed with my comportment. I suppose that with the number of scars they each displayed, my wounds were only par for the course. They did seem to care for my well being, though. Perhaps my injuries were the entry fee to join this band of blemished brothers (and sisters).

Trying to introduce myself, I pointed to my chest and spoke my name as clearly as I could. I skipped the pleasantries and just used my first name. Those around me were surprised again by my verbal perspicacity but seemed at a loss as to what to do. The first woman, closest to me and the calmest in my presence, tried to respond. She said something like, "Huweehunum." I had no intelligent answer. I thought it universal that the first thing one would do is try to introduce oneself, so I said my name. She responded again, this time making a sound more like "Weehnum," but she pointed to her chest, as I had done when introducing myself. Every sound she made was a heavy, breathy whisper. It reminded me of Hue on the beach. I pointed to her and said the same, mimicking the sound as best

I could, "Weehnum." She pointed back at me, just the same, and repeated the word I had said virtually identically, but puffed out some more. Confused, I pointed back to myself and said, "Cygnus," and she smiled and pointed to me with a childlike delight, "Weehnum." The rest of the group, taking their cue from the first, mimicked my pointing gesture and said the same thing.

It was then I realized, to their ears and in their language, I was "Weehnum." I had not the first clue what, if anything, she or her people were called. I pointed at her and asked, "Who?" The entire group, as though playing a game of Simon Says, pointed at her and responded, "Whoo." I knew I really didn't have her name, but, I hadn't a good idea how to go about getting it. It seemed I had ingratiated myself to the natives, who were now repeating "Weehnum" and "Whoo" with a goofy sort of pleasure. I resolved, until better informed, to refer to the first woman as Whoo.

Whoo possessed a childlike innocence, despite her mature, muscular physique. I relished looking into her dark brown eyes awash with the puzzle of language and an unusual person. She was glowing with satisfaction, pleased with herself for having been the first to interact with me in the cave as with a child who finds a treasure and presents it to all their friends only to learn that it is even better than they had first estimated. Those who had the least interaction with me bounced away with similar childish abandon until I remained in the company of only Whoo. She sat next to me on the rock in a great grotto. Whoo looked me over again and again, occasionally daring to touch my clothing, but only lightly, and then pulling back once again. I, with characteristic awkwardness, tried to look away and not gawk at the woman before me. I focused on her eyes intently, as if to pointedly demonstrate I was not intruding.

The excitement abated around me, and I developed an increased awareness of the area. I was seated in the flat section of the wall of a fairly large D-shaped chamber. Like the first room, the ceiling was punctuated by a number of cascading stalactites. Between the stalactites was mixed a number of small fissures. These fissures provided the lion's share of light from the ceiling. A hole in the cave directly opposite me, ten feet off the ground, diffused a further dull light.

There were no furniture, tools, or decoration to note. A small stream trickled through the room, enlarged by a few tiny waterfalls in the ceiling, from which the company drew their water. The source of the foul perfume became evident. I noticed one of them openly defecating into the stream close to one of at least a dozen tunnel exits from this place. It was to my relief that I realized that while this cave was used as a lavatory and water source simultaneously, they did have the good sense to befoul the downstream and drink from a separate font. Close to the dripping fresh water lay a pile of large leaves, the only sign of environmental manipulation by these people.

Not a word was spoken between my companions save for the occasional squeal of "Weehnum" and the associated chortles and giggles that would follow. Whoo sat beside me and continued to marvel at my tattered clothes. She said not a word. Awkward of manner, I tried to maintain eye contact with her, but she was focused on the many things that made me completely out of place in the cave. Everything from my feet to my head, clothes, and what lay underneath were visibly different and unique. Initially, I hadn't been sure if this woman was a captive with me or a captor. Now I knew little better, but it seemed to me I was not being held by these people. A curiosity, I was treated more like a guest and long-lost friend than any sort of adversary. The cave reeked, and the rock was uncomfortable, but I was safe. I tried to explain to Whoo about my clothes, but every word was returned with an awestruck, wide-eyed look. Occasionally she replied with a breathy "Huhuneem." I wondered if these people knew Hue, the incredible horse from the beach. Perhaps she belonged to them and somewhere near the cave was a stable. I tried to ask, but my whispered "Huhuneem" only left her more confused.

We sat quietly for some time. The light that filtered through the cracks in the ceiling gradually faded away, and the cave drew just too dark to see more than a few inches. Down one of the exits, a light appeared suddenly. Unmistakeably, a fire was being struck. The light grew and smoke replaced some of the less desirable aromas. Whoo tugged at my arm, and with the same easy grace and strength, helped me to my feet and assisted me, shuffling, towards the fire. In the dark, the pain from the sunburn was diminished, aided by the moist air of the ocean and cavern.

Gently, she guided me towards another room, where all the natives I had first encountered, and a number more, were squatting around a small, crude fire surrounded by large rocks. On top of several rocks were various animals, some familiar and others foreign to me. A couple fish, a rabbit, and what I assume was once a rat were being gradually cooked in proximity to the fire. The dining hall bore none of the smell of the large cave; thankfully, it seemed they kept some activities separate from their kitchen. The room was thick with smoke. A passage out of the room opposite the side I entered was clearly the main escape for the exhaust from the fire.

Our entrance was not unexpected. They were still obviously inquisitive about my singularity. I felt a bit as a captive animal at a zoo, with the public gawking at my every feature. The new faces seemed as surprised as those who had first met me. Apparently, the newcomers had been uninformed of the details of my presence. I had begun to suspect that language was as foreign to these people as I was. The hoots of "Weehnum" probably didn't clarify much to anybody.

One, bearing the most scars of the entire bunch and most clearly hobbled through great injury of his own, stood and spoke as clearly as Hue, "Huhuneem." I should note there was no inquisitive tone to this statement. His furrowed brow solicited a response. I didn't realize I was being asked an important question. I pointed towards where I had come from and repeated his question. In my mind, I was confirming I had seen their horse, Hue, and that she was in that direction. I would have happily shown them the direction in which she fled, but he was not asking me about the horse. He was not assuaged by my response. He pointed at me and repeated with greater emphasis. I responded with my name, "Cygnus." He and those who had not heard me previously were deeply perplexed and turned to Whoo, who nodded, pointed to me, and repeated, "Weehnum." In this place, with these people, I was Weehnum, the stranger. Whoo took up a role as a sort of lingual interpreter and defender. She took up a position in front of me, to defend me from the others if necessary. She stood as tall as she was able and protected me from harm. It was ultimately an unnecessary gesture on her part, as the others were far more curious about me than they were legitimately concerned, but it began to develop a feeling of trust in my friend.

Whoo gathered a few bits of food and offered them to me, taking a role as provider and guide. I tried to eat all she presented, save for the rodent.

I couldn't bring myself to eat rat, even in my present state. I'm proud to say I was mostly able to stomach the cooking. The fish was the easiest to manage, and the meat was, put generously, rare. The meal was hardly five stars but enough to push back at least one of the pains of which I was suffering. We sat by the fire, and normally I would have watched the flames, transfixed by their flicker. I couldn't help but look instead upon my friends, for they were all looking at me in the light of the fire. The same man who approached me at the fire picked up a stick from the blaze and carried it down a passageway. The others took their cue from him and followed.

Whoo urged me to follow as well, and we entered the third room. It was clear this was the dormitory. The ground of this cave was covered with fine sand. As with every other cave so far, there were no signs of furniture, no pillows or blankets, no sleeping bags, no sheets, no mattress, nor any sort of bed. Whoo ushered me to a vacant spot close to the door, lay me down, and took a spot across from me.

The dormitory cave was laid out in a line, and each of the dwellers slept with their heads towards the middle and their feet to the wall. There was no separation between us, but that didn't seem to bother anybody else.

I can report I did not sleep well that night, but eventually, despite the extremely Spartan accommodation, I did fall into a strange, dream-filled slumber, in a cave, on an unknown island, surrounded by strangers. I would become increasingly accustomed to this accommodation in my time here.

CHAPTER 1.7

The author is initiated into the activities of the natives.

I BELIEVE NONE will be surprised that I awoke in the morning feeling somewhat worse for wear in these conditions and marginally better from the wounds I had suffered. Evidently, I had slept a fairly deep sleep, if not necessarily a restful one. I awoke alone in the bunkhouse cave. Alert, I roused and rose from the sandy floor and carefully felt my way back towards the dining space, hoping to find some foo, and perhaps a suitable place to relieve other common morning distresses. Recalling the memory of the path from the evening past, I wound my way back towards the firepit.

Though the fire was long since extinguished, there were some scattered remains of carrots and apples strewn about the vacant space. I ate as much as I could handle, uncertain of when my next repast would occur. I retraced my steps back to the main chamber, and, remembering the activities of the night before, micturated as near as I could remember to where the fellow had himself thus composed before.

Light streamed through the cracks in the ceiling brighte than the evening preceding. I guessed the hole in the ceiling must point more eastward than not. Unknowing for certain whether it was morning or afternoon, I could not confirm. The caves, with the exception of the quite dim bedchamber, were quite brightly illuminated. They were easily bright enough for me to move confidently despite my lacerations. Both kitchen and hall had similar gaps in the ceiling, and while my evening companions were not to be found, I decided this place seemed sufficiently safe, if not plush and comfortable. I decided to do some intrepid spelunking to better acquaint myself with this home. Alone in the caves, I found myself thinking of Whoo, my defender, guide, provider, and perhaps friend. I wondered to where she had disappeared but didn't fear I wouldn't see her again. I trusted she and the others would return to me in due course.

There were no shortage of passages, tunnels, and open spaces, though few of the size of the three rooms to which I had been introduced. I saw no marks of tools on any walls, and I concluded the caves must be wholly natural, or so subtly modified as to appear so. I chose not to venture down the downstream channel, for reasons that must be clear to the reader. Instead, I tried to pass through the larger, uphill, upstream corridors of the cave. Most did not travel far before reducing in girth to a point that neither I nor surely any of the group would be able to squeeze through. Several of the walls were drawn upon, nothing so detailed as Lascaux, but virtually all of them depicted horses. A suspicion of mine was confirmed upon discovering a number of drawings that portrayed several men, on their hands and knees, guiding horses through some obstacle. It was my belief these people were masters of horse and somewhere nearby were the stables.

From the kitchen, I followed the tunnel down which the smoke had escaped the previous night. I found this tunnel wound upwards for several metres before opening to a bright, sunny rockface not altogether unlike the one I had scaled in my movement towards the beach the day before. From this vantage, I could see only ocean. The rock bent back on either side as I stood at the edge of this place. I believe it understandable that I wasn't in a hurry to test new rock surfaces. I turned back into the cave system to explore other passageways.

The hallway from which the greatest stream trickled proved to be the most fruitful. The path, though wet and slick, and covered with some sort of algae, wound upwards for quite a distance. Never straight for very long, and occasionally thinning, it remained just wide enough to pass through. I slipped numerous times. The walls were of scant assistance, themselves mostly dampened and moist. As I gradually worked my way upwards, I began to see a brighter light ahead than that of the fissure-illuminated space. At the end of the passage, I came into a most enchanting space. A room was perched at the top of the corridor, and occupying most of it was a small lake, roughly the size and shape of a large hot tub. The room was shaped like a dome, though not very tall. It was about one to two metres at the highest point, and that in the middle of the chamber. The pond appeared to be of roughly the same dimension in the ground, like the Ink Pots of Johnston Creek. The pond dipped under the wall of the cave, and the room was illuminated by the reflection of the bright sunlight off the pool. The room glowed with beguiling swirls of the reflections of the water, creating beautiful, moving artwork across the low ceiling. I took a seat against the wall and found the thick, humid air most comforting.

I cannot say how long I sat there enjoying my rest, but I imagine it must have been an hour or so. I was in no hurry to either head back through the entrance from which I had come or to explore too far downstream. The calm and tranquility of this place soothed my aching body. The room smelled faintly of sulphur, and I knew the stream was fed partly by a natural spring. As I rested, I was startled when a sudden splash came from the centre of the pond. One of the inhabitants from the previous night emerged. He swished his long, unruly hair from side to side a couple times, spraying the room and me with the stowaway water. With a final nod upwards to get the bulk of hair behind his back, he became aware of my presence. For a pleasant change, he didn't seem surprised to see me there; in fact, he seemed to hardly care at all about me. He stepped out of the water, and in his left hand, he clutched the neck of a recently dead chicken. Gradually, in succession, each of the others came into the grotto in the same manner. Each of them carried some sort of food: some carried carcasses, while others brought wraps of a selection of fruits. As they entered, one after another, each one was startled, but unconcerned, by my presence. Then without a word, they moved down the corridor from which I had come. Eventually, Whoo came in through the aqueous portal.

I read from her face that she was pleased to have found me in this place and apparently in reasonable health. With a gentle wave and gesture, she indicated I should follow her. I acquiesced to her desire, having no pressing appointments, and we went back towards the main hall.

In the main hall, the fruits were arranged near the fresh water spout like appetizers at a dinner party. My hosts partook of the food, and I joined in. As the light dimmed, several of the gathering headed back out towards the waterlogged entry. The rest sat about the room, until one of them, one of the youngest men, said my name, the first word I had heard all day, "Weehnum." I was startled. After hours with barely a word, this one young man was trying to speak to me. As the first time, I pointed to myself and repeated my name properly, and the group animatedly tried to replicate it clumsily. When I pointed at them, beseeching an introduction, the answers were uniformly my name. I tried a different tack and pointed to the water and said, "water." The group looked confused, and pointed in random directions and said, "way-um." Thus began my first language lessons with these people without a language of their own.

My following days and evenings were primarily spent in a consistent fashion to this: waking up alone and exploring the caves until settling beside the luminous lagoon until the residents returned from their foraging. A midday meal would be consumed, a party would set back out, and a few would stick around with me and try their hand at some linguistic gymnastics.

I've not before or since heard of a people with no language of their own. Teaching them all but the most basic names of common things proved to be beyond my capabilities. I was able to impart upon them words for water and several varieties of food including chicken, crab, apple, berry, and leaf, but even slightly abstract concepts like food were beyond them. Even those they did learn could only be pronounced with the limited alphabet they possessed on my arrival. Their phonetic alphabet is transcribed thusly:

A (ə): as in Canada
A (æ): as in mat
A (ej): as in mate
E (i): as in meat

U (u): as in shoot
U (^): as in cut
O (ow): as in coat
H (h): as in hat (but with a particularly breathy exhalation)
M (m): as in bottom
N (n): as in note
W (w): as in witch
Y (j): as in yes

In an effort to mimic my tongue, they fabricated a couple other sounds: a tongue-slapping click they used in place of "K" sounds and a glottal stop, such as one might use in place of the letter "T" in button when speaking quickly. As I'm certain the reader might ascertain, trying to speak English with eleven letters and two constructed stops renders the agility of the language substantially accented.

In their own sort of Pidgin English, I had named each of my companions for my own sanity and tried to base their name on something about them. Each one was pleased as punch with their handles and owned them proudly, even jealously. First amongst these was Hu (formerly Whoo), to whom I had given a name in my mind long ago. The three who had found me on the beach were named Amma (the female), Nom (the shorter male—I apologize to the reader, but he was a short man, and yes, it is pronounced "gnome." I thought it a cute name at the time.), and Ya (the taller male), for he took to nodding his head frequently in accord.

Some of the cavers possessed a greater aptitude than others, though none reached solid fluency in the week or so I repeated this pattern. On the seventh day, Hu woke me up as the band prepared their morning expedition. My leg had scabbed over, and I had since removed the torn-sleeve-bandage. The smaller cuts had mostly healed, and though I was absolutely at the mercy of infection, I seemed free for now of such worries. The crimson sunburn was fading to an amber tan, which brought me closer to the dark skin of these aphotic people. The crew brought me to the cave pool, and one after another, waded into the water towards the lighted entrance, took a deep breath, submerged, and departed the cave. After Nom went through, it was only Hu and me remaining in the room. Hu looked at me with confidence and the care most characteristic of an elementary school teacher, and with a "Way-o," urged me to proceed. This felt a milestone for me; she was trusting me beyond the water room. I was being entrusted with their most important secret, and at no little risk to themselves. Comfortable in my place, I accepted her goading, took a deep breath, and swam towards the light.

It was not a particularly long swim to reach the other side. I groped along the smooth ceiling with my hand, and carefully felt my way forward. The passage could only have been a few feet long and was only the same depth. The water, warm and calm but for my efforts, was almost crystal clear. The floor of the passage was littered with what felt like broken shells on my feet but reflected the light like millions of tiny pieces of glass. When my hand reached no more ceiling, I knew I had reached the other side, and I broke the surface with a gasp. On my head a warm shower of water splashed from a small cascade from the cliff. On this, the other side of the glowing pool, the water thinned quickly at a slope of roughly forty-five degrees, only a small half-moon shaped pool. Had I not just swum through it, I wouldn't have even thought to try.

I emerged into a small clearing, alone again. It was apparent those who had preceded me had already left. The natural clearing was encircled by old-growth, moss-coated jungle. The sun shone brightly through the trees, and the cliff down from which the tiny torrent descended was brightly illuminated. The face was also thick with green moss. The wall was but a few feet high and gradually gave way to rocky plateau just slightly higher than I could see from the ground. The air was thick with the pungent, characteristic, sulphurous odour I smelled in the caverns. Only a step away from the pond was a dense wall of thick, broad-leafed fern, the same as the cave people used to cup their water. Throughout the busy canopy was a cacophony of birds and other wildlife, a tiny oasis of pure beauty on this island.

As I marvelled at the beauty, Hu succeeded me. Actually, she bumped headfirst into the back of my knees, causing me to buckle. I laughed as I fell into the pool, playing like a young boy. Almost immediately, I recognized I was blocking the way, so I stepped out of the water, and as she joined me, I apologized, not that she understood me. She grabbed me by the arm with the kind of urgency I sensed when I was first introduced to the caves. She pulled me through the fern wall and ran nimbly through the forest. Apparently, she knew exactly where she was going. I tried to follow as closely as possible, but stumbled and tripped on the twigs, roots, and various understory. Hu alternately stopped to wait and pulled me along. My poor, coddled feet hurt, but my guide showed no ill effects. On my own, I stood no chance of finding my way home. She held her head high and alert, looking deep into the trees instead of watching her steps closely. I would have spent the day just enjoying my surroundings, but my focus was firmly locked on the ground between our feet, searching for the next thing upon which I would trip, cut, bruise, or stub myself with. We ran for several minutes, and the thick vegetation seemed indistinguishable from one minute to the next. The smell of sulphur faded and was replaced by the crisp, sweet smell of the woods. The reader would also perceive a hint of seaweed that grew stronger as we ran.

Hu ran through another wall of fern but with the same muscular grace and confidence of foot she exhibited with persistence. I crashed through the same, tearing several leaves, stepping onto the loose sand on the other side, and splashed face first into a patch of dry sand. I looked up, expecting to see my companion enjoying the spectacle, or worse, running further away, but she was focused on her task at hand.

We had apparently reached our destination, for Hu already had picked a leaf and was quickly picking berries from a large bush. Her practiced hands brushed away the thorns and thistles of a blackberry-like bush with rolled leaves and easily removed the fruits from the branch. I brushed the sand off my sweat-drenched face, arms, and legs, and plucked a handful of the berries (and ate a few as well). In the time I managed to pick a handful, Hu had almost filled her entire leaf-horn. She had carefully rolled the leaf in such a way that she could hold it with one hand, use it to brush the branches aside, and then use the same device as a container to store the berries. I was no match for her skill, speed, or dexterity. I tried to roll a leaf in the same manner but could barely manage to keep the leaf from snapping.

Hu finished filling the horn and folded the leaf over, closing the opening. She was able to hold the entire thing securely with one hand. I took my shirt like a bib and filled as much of it as I could. Hu looked at me and seemed impressed at my collection aid. As she had back in the caves, she marveled at my shirt and its heretofore unknown benefits. By this time, she was more comfortable around me and actually took a firm grip of the shirt in her hand and pulled on it. She did not understand the way the shirt was attached to me, or the inelastic qualities it possessed. I was surprised by the strength and firmness with which she tugged it, and I was yanked off my feet, crashing into her and back into the sand, dropping my collection. She maintained hers, in an incredible display of balance and agility, while she fell under me. Her eyes showed how startled she was by this, but no anger. She seemed more concerned with my well being than her own. Embarrassed, I abashedly went about recovering the food, and taking a cue from my actions, she followed suit, adding the fallen fruit to my improvised shirt-pouch.

Our job complete, she urged me back through the ferns in the direction we had come. In the sand, my crashed sand-angel provided evidence of our presence, but Hu didn't concern herself with that as we raced through the forest again. I couldn't say for sure whether we were heading to a new place or back to the caves. The jungle floor was as dark as the caves in the middle of the night, and I couldn't locate the sun. It would not have been much help, as I could identify neither my latitude nor the time of day beyond a rough approximation. I felt it was likely almost noon, but I couldn't have been sure.

We ran, and I did my best to avoid losing my load. More comfortable with the ground, I made marginally better time on this second leg. Hu continued to outpace me effortlessly. I panted and sweated; she ran with heavy steps yet light tread. She slowed a little as we approached another clearing. Had I been less exhausted, I would have smelled and heard the waterfall and known we were home. I came to a stop before the ferns, gingerly pushed through, and saw the familiar waterfall. Hu goaded me back into the water, and mindful of the pattern from previous days, I understood how I was to return to the cave.

I carefully stepped into the water, tightened my grip on my shirt, ducked under, and swam back into the grotto. On the other side, Hu reappeared quickly after, and together we returned to the dining hall. As I had observed numerous times before, we deposited our findings and partook in the shares of the other parties. I had contributed a little to this place, and anticipated, correctly, that I would be expected to continue to do so.

I would follow Hu out most days on these gatherings. Sometimes we collected berries, and other times fruits, particularly apples. We were becoming a foraging team, and I learned from her faster ways how to collect, how to make less of an impression on the ground as I walked and ran, and even how to track a little bit, all without any but the most limited of vocabulary. Daily, we would go out together into the forest looking for the supplies necessary to help the larger group survive. The trust and respect shared between us would only grow during this period of time.

I learned a little of the geography of the island and could find my way back home on my own from short distances away. Never while on our hunts did we ever encounter another forager, not from the caves, not from anywhere. I began to understand these people were operating methodically and that we were, if not alone on this island, at least operating in a space exclusive to other humans.

CHAPTER 1.8

The author learns about other sources of food on the island and makes a startling discovery about the natives.

AS I AWOKE on my last day with the cave dwellers of the island, I would have no indication that today would be the final time I would take my rest on the soft sand of the dormitory chamber. Nothing unusual would happen until the scavenging party departed through the pond. Through my efforts over the preceding weeks, the people of the cave had developed a crude vocabulary. We had created words for a few common things like water, "wa^em," and berry, "newwy." I shall spare the reader greater detail into the linguistic achievements of these people. Though they possessed an infantile excitement at self-expression, it needs to be noted they were not altogether receptive to my labours. Conversely, I had deduced a trio of words of their nascent language:

"Way-o" meant simultaneously, "here," "look at this," "take this," and "give me that."

"Yahoo" and "Huhuneem" were said with some frequency, though I could not at the time identify their true meaning.

On this day, as we left the security of the cave, Hu and I were joined by two others, Nom and Ya. We took a different path through the woods. My tracking skills had dramatically improved in my time with these people, and I trusted I could retrace my steps to the cave in an emergency. It was apparent my companions were more diligent than usual to not disturb the underbrush or leave a distinguishing footprint. They moved slower, though still faster than I could easily manage, and Hu, following me, was cleaning my still clumsy trail. I had become better at leaving fewer tracks but evidently not enough for today's activities. There was no time for her to teach me more today; the hunt was long. We crossed a distance several times longer than previous foraging missions. Today we travelled to the edge of the forest.

As the darkness of the canopy thinned and the busy sounds dimmed, I could imagine the forest would soon give way to a novel biome. The party slowed to a halt and swiftly swung from the ground into the trees with the nimble agility that until now I had seen only as they ran along the ground. Ya reached down and swung me up onto a branch. The reader would be kind to forgive my boastfulness, but in fact, I have climbed many trees in my life. Yet never have I seen a person climb so quickly and easily from branch to branch up a tree. They nearly brachiated while I struggled to do a single chin-up. They were already at their desired vantage point, surveying the area, when after several minutes of intense effort, I reached the large branch upon which they were squatting. The ample bough was easily strong enough to hold all our weight at least ten metres off the floor. The tree was most thickly leafed at this height, and I imagined it would have been fairly difficult to spot us from the ground. Furthermore, it provided a sweeping panoramic view of the enormous verdant savannah.

Our ascendant view offered me the first glimpse of what must have been indicative of the majority of the island. The landscape was dominated by thick grasses, roughly a metre tall, and an undulating landscape of hills and valleys. Several streams and rivers flowed forth from the forest from which we'd come out across the grasslands. There were rows of trees growing across the plain, not regularly spaced so as to indicate practiced intervention, but almost so. The trees on the plain grew almost dead straight, defying the otherwise flat aspect from which they rose. In the distance, I could see the first sign of civilization. I could see what appeared to be a thatched longhouse with a number of livestock milling about. In the distance, only a few horses and cattle were visible. Smaller creatures could be seen by virtue of their movements.

While I admired the scenery and took note of the beauty of the place, the others' with their more practiced eyes, were clearly looking for something else. Their movements were as guards surveying the scene for threats. I knew this need be the reason for our care in travel and our pause in the arbour. After about ten minutes, they each dropped from the branch to the tree floor, grabbing and swinging quickly but safely to the ground. I scraped along the trunk of the tree slowly and eventually met my less-patient-than-usual friends. We set out along a row of trees in the general direction of the farmhouse.

Along the way, I noted that amongst the grasses were a variety of cereals. Though no farmer, I was familiar with what I saw to be wheat, barley, and the occasional cornstalk, but the most common was oat. The grasses were not organized like a typical farm, with machine-groomed rows, but it still seemed to my untrained eye that they had been sown intentionally. Those with me cared little for the grains, which, processed appropriately, could have been an important food staple. The objective lay ahead further still.

They moved in a crouch, staying close to the trees, but keeping their heads below the grasses. I struggled more, due to my advanced height, as well as my lack of experience moving this way. Anytime my head bobbed too high, Hu quickly reached out to silently put it back down. It was at least a kilometre between the forest and the house, and it was clear this was where we were headed. We moved like a tiny raiding party, which I fashioned we probably were considering the parcels I had become accustomed to in the caves. I hoped that ahead I would find a civilized people who would be able to help me return to my world.

Once more, as we approached, the advance slowed. My companions grew uneasy, particularly with regards to my tendency to rise above the vegetation. Short, darting glances were all my crew would afford, and even then, only very close to the trees. I knew not what hazard it was for which they were scouting. I didn't think I was to be equally afraid. As we got closer, we could hear the animals of the farm, the cattle and chickens raising a typical commotion. A number of fine horses neighed and whinnied calmly. I could hear no voices amongst the group but felt certain there must be somebody nearby from whom my companions were avoiding detection.

The first animal we came across was a cow. I made the mistake of using the cow as a shield. As I looked from behind the cow, I could see a couple horses close by. Hu reached up to pull me down with urgency and a look of abject terror seared into my mind even today. It was too late. Both horses suddenly charged towards us. The cave people turned and fled. They ducked and weaved through the trees as they attempted to escape. I stayed close to the cow. I hoped to avoid the stampede. One horse, the dappled grey, broke away to chase my companions. The white charged straight at me. He struck me at a gallop, and I was knocked under the cow.

As I gathered myself, I thought of Hu and the others. I didn't realize the great danger in which I had put them. I felt, while laying dazed and badly hurt, that I was sufficiently safe despite what had just occurred. I couldn't really imagine a sustained attack by a horse, but I could hear the gallop and crashing in the near distance, and I worried for Hu, who had been the closest to me, and sincerely hoped she had been able to evade the vicious horses. I could scarcely imagine a situation where my comrades were able to evade their pursuer. Despite their strength, agility, and speed, I can't help but think they would be caught by the angry beast. With limited experience with horses, I was nonetheless bewildered by the ferocity and suddenness of the attack. I lay broken on the ground. The white horse, contented with my incapacity, raced off to join the pursuit.

I never did discover what it was we were hunting, perhaps chicken for protein. As I lay on the ground with what I assumed to be a number of broken ribs and possibly a broken ankle, it didn't seem important. I was lying under a cow. This shielded me from one danger, but I was afraid of what my impromptu shelter might do to me if she decided to take umbrage. A third horse came, a black horse. This one nudged the cow away and investigated my clothing. Taking my arm in her hoof, in a manner that I would have believed impossible for a horse, it stroked my hand curiously. Loudly, she neighed over her shoulder. Several malformed people, worse off than those of the cave by a wide margin, came to me and plucked me from the ground harshly. Stunned and completely winded, I didn't even test resistance. I tried to ask, "English?" but none answered me. The black horse swung her head back towards me and neighed, as clear as Hue on the beach, "Yahoo." As the beastly kidnappers hauled me away, I drew upon my memory and responded quietly, "Huhuneem."

CHAPTER 1.9

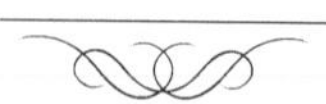

The author makes the acquaintance of the equine masters of the island.

I WAS UNCEREMONIOUSLY, and with no little discomfort, dropped into the dirt outside the long wood and thatch house I had spotted from the forest edge. The air was forced painfully from my lungs by my assumed broken ribs. My distempered captors smelled of a foul faecal odour that seemed sunken into their skin and hair, which grew wildly from their heads and bodies. The four brutes snorted in derision, spat, and receded around the side of the house. The abysmal stench lightened but lingered with their departure, and the great black horse returned and stood at a distance and investigated me more closely. She softly paced around me. I watched from the ground as I had the first time I encountered Hue on the island. As she investigated me, a distinct look of confusion and curiosity was plastered firmly to her face. I heard her regularly repeat, "Yahoo." I struggled to raise an arm in her direction and asked, "Huhuneem?" She reared back as if I had just uttered some magic and perilous phrase.

A second black horse, male, rushed forwards and they exchanged a series of neighs and whinnies, of snorts and exclamatory exhalations. The pattern and cadence were foreign but perceptibly linguistic. At frequent intervals, I heard the two familiar words, "Yahoo" and "Huhuneem." Often, one or the other would point to me and bob their head or shake it vigorously. In turns, they reached towards me and tapped my right forearm. The two horses engaged in this discussion, which to my ears and eyes could not but be mistaken for conversation, and they pulled away a few feet to confer together in privacy.

I marvelled at the incredible sight before my eyes. Before me stood two of the most majestic looking horses upon which my eyes had ever before beheld, speaking and exchanging their thoughts. I lay on this unknown island thinking never would I have imagined witnessing such a thing as this. I wondered what sort of people it was that possessed both the foul humanoids and these rational, intelligent horses at their service. I was certain that if I could just make the acquaintance of their owners, not only would they be able to heal the wounds I had sustained, but they would surely be able to put me in touch with some authority to facilitate the necessary operations that would lead to my ultimate recovery and rehabilitation to my beloved homeland. To such an end I strove, the sole way I could at that time imagine, to request of the horses to take me to their master. In a voice as calm, confident, and with so great a poise as I could muster from the hard dirt ground, I asked, "If I may interrupt, I am a survivor of Flight 1726. My plane crashed into the ocean, and I was washed ashore on this island. If it is possible that you may direct me to your master, I would appreciate that greatly."

As the reader will no doubt consider consigning me to the nearest mental health facility, I do admit and proclaim in sincerity that I didn't truly believe the horses in front of me would understand my words. That being said, in the desperate circumstance in which I presently found myself, I was willing to try the ludicrous, for when no other course of action is available, the ridiculous must surely be worth the effort.

Alas, my request did not achieve the desired, if unlikely, result. It did serve to recapture the immediate attentions of the two black horses. They opened towards me and returned once again. The mare advanced a little closer than the stallion. She pointed to me and said again, "Yahoo."

I pointed to the horse and answered, "Huhuneem" in the most practiced, careful pronunciation I had endeavoured since encountering Hue on the beach several weeks previous. It was then that I understood a folly of all my previous efforts, both with this group and with the natives of the caves. Huhuneem was not the name of a particular horse that I had met on the beach. She had not named me Yahoo. The horses referred to themselves as Huhuneem, and humans, including me, were Yahoos. With this seemingly obvious and elemental understanding under my cap, I pointed first to myself confidently and repeated, "Yahoo," and then back to the horses and pointed my hand in an arc from the mare to the stallion, "Huhuneem." I propped myself off the ground, and instinctually reached out my arm as if to shake theirs. To my amazement, the stallion stepped forward, reached out his front right hoof, and tapped me on the forearm. They both were similarly incredulous to what they had witnessed as I was. It seemed they were most impressed at what I had achieved.

The two horses turned to each other and spoke briefly before tapping hooves again, at which point the mare turned and headed in the direction my former colleagues had fled. The stallion urged me forward, in the direction the vile Yahoos had left. I cradled my ribs with my left arm, and we walked around the longhouse, past the chickens and cattle to the opposite side, where the Yahoos were fighting unreservedly amongst each other. They took little notice of my person while the stallion urged me into the long log house.

CHAPTER 1.10

The author is afforded a tour of the village of the horses and learns to make a home in these circumstances.

THE DOOR OF the house, the walls, ceiling, and roof were framed with long, straight log timber. At a crossing diagonal, these same wooden logs, for to call them beams might suggest they had been squared, were lashed together by a natural sisal-like rope. Every remaining space bore a woven thatch of straw and reed, the quality of which was justly incomparable to any place or thing I've seen. As I was pressed through the wide but low entrance, I had to duck under the threshold. It ought to be noted that the low clearance would cause me ample distress in my subsequent time in this place. The door rose just under two metres from the ground, and on the ground was laid a timber, like all the others, over which I was forced to step.

The room I entered was long and straight, a single hall about two metres across and a ceiling not more than two and a half metres from the hard clay floor. Across one entire length of the room sat a series of rack and mangers right up to the ceiling, full of straw, oats, and hay. A gap of about a foot divided the ceiling from the wall at the top of each manger, providing a place for the grains to pour into the manger, like a milk chute. This gap also created the primary point of luminescence into this room without electricity, or even lanterns, though one small fireplace sat opposite the door at the long end of the hall. Next to it, as a trough, a small stream funnelled through the room along the wall through some hollowed logs. I still expected some sort of druidic master to emerge from one of the many doors along the other side of the log house at any moment.

On the side of the room with the doors, the horses were seated. Mind that I mean seated on their buttocks, as any human might do while sitting on the ground. And they were seated upon carefully and intricately woven carpets. Lacking in colour, they were nonetheless clearly the proud work of an excellent artisan. The horses here behaved as though the masters of the house. The air did not possess any of the thick musk one might expect in a building full of horses. The ground was neither covered in hay nor other natural decoration typical of livestock. In fact, it appeared to have been recently swept clean. If I could describe the smell, it would be more like potpourri, causing my mind to race back once again to my encounter on the beach with Hue. Scarcely furnished, apart from the mats under the equines, the room was clean, orderly, and altogether pleasant. The horses conversed calmly amongst themselves, primarily concerned about my appearance, it was clear. Outside in the courtyard, the rough and tumble natives, who I did not believe could be responsible for these horses, continued to roar and howl as their scrap continued. I was accompanied by one of the larger horses, and deference was paid to him by the lot of the others.

I was directed to the side of the room. The horses rose and rearranged the mangers to the centre of the room in a circle as a table. A perpetual source of surprise, these horses worked together and moved the racks quickly and effectively, and it was clear the mangers were designed with this purpose in mind. Eight even pieces locked together to form an octagon and the horses calmly stepped forward, two to each side, paired off as males and females of the same colour.

One lateral at a time they approached the central table full of both hay and oats, and without any further ceremony, began to eat their fill. The first to the table was the black stallion and a similar mare beside. While the others ate, these two communicated. Through gestures and unfamiliar words, he indicated I was to join them. I acquiesced to his command but had no interest in the raw grains. As the assembly ate, they spoke frequently. I judged, based on the repeated word, and through gestures, that this was mostly about the Yahoo.

I recognized that the open end of the table might be acceptably occupied by me. Recognizing an opportunity, no matter how slight, I guardedly took a handful of oats. Finding a large bowl of clay affixed to the manger, normally used to carry grains to and from the room, I used a rock as a pestle and ground the husks off the oats as well as I could while trying to keep the grain intact. Finding a second bowl, I filled it with water from the trough and placed it by the fireplace to heat. The oats husked, I carefully placed them in the tepid water to soak. After a few minutes, I ground out the oats with the rock as best I could then went over and set the bowl over the fire to dry them. It took more time than I would have liked, so I stirred the oats around in the bowl in an attempt to hasten the process. Eventually, I winnowed them by tossing them in the air at a bit of an angle, allowing the chaff to blow away. My progress was hampered throughout as I had to protect my broken body at every stage.

My actions had drawn the attention of the horses in the room, who noted my every move and action with curiosity. I thought about Hu and the first night with her people. I missed my friend, but my current predicament required a more immediate concern. Through a series of charades, I managed to ask the master horse to milk a cow, and with a few quick whinnies, another horse hurried to a door and revealed a store of bowls. She presented one to me full of the white gold. I thanked them as best I could with words and gestures. I'm sure I looked quite the fool as I bowed with my hands together, thanking them in every language of which I could think as if, somehow, they would understand. I prepared what could only be described as the worst oatmeal I've ever tasted, but it was enough to keep me nourished and warm. The horses were impressed, though their emotion was tempered.

As the dinner wore on, the horses urged me to repeat the words they had heard me say, repeating "Yahoo" and "Huhuneem" until I responded. It was clear I was being tested. The horses seemed to revel in my repetition of the words and were in the best of humour, as one would be if watching a pet suddenly start to speak in understandable, if broken, English. Over the course of the dinner, they taught me the pronunciation of several words for hay, oats, milk, and water. I walked to the fire and pointed, and they taught me the word for fire as well. I was reminded of my time learning my second language in immersion in childhood. In tiny strides, I developed my tongue and was able, by the end of the dinner, to recite a half dozen words, all nouns of course.

The horses were a clever and most intelligent species, and related to me, by pointing to themselves one at a time, that they were each "Huhuneem." I understood. The black pointed at me and spoke that word, "Yahoo." I understood that "human" was pronounced as "Yahoo" by these gifted steeds. I hoped he would not see me the same as those in the courtyard. Though I shared a great deal of genetic material with them, my behaviour, I hoped, would set me apart. To emphasize the point, he pointed out towards the yard where the Yahoos did battle. I affirmed to him that they were Yahoos. It seemed that despite my assumptions, they weren't quite sure whether or not I was actually a Yahoo or something different.

At the end of dinner, I was guided with an "Huhun, huhun," which I took to mean, "Hurry, hurry" across towards one of the doors. I was taken from the first room across to a second laid out just the same, but mirrored to the first, along the axis of the wall with the doors. Here, too, sat a number of horses on their mats, as well as a couple of foals resting close on the large mat with their mares. These would evidently have eaten separately from the group with which I had most recently shared a meal.

In this second room, a great black stallion arose and approached my guide. They reached out and tapped their right forelegs, just above the hooves, and there between them quick and urgent exchanges followed. The two apparently reached a decision and took up positions on either side of me, urging me towards the exit. We passed through the courtyard, where the combatants had still evidently not settled their dispute or perhaps had discovered a new one. As we neared, they pulled away, and the horses cut a direct path straight through the area moments ago occupied. The Yahoos avoided eye contact with the horses but cast squinted glares at me and hissed in my direction. My escorts paid no heed to those they had displaced and walked with their heads tall, masters of the space.

Across the courtyard was another squat building. This, too, was composed entirely of wood, constructed as a palisade. The wooden spikes sharpened at the tops, and the crossbeams that reached out through the wall were equally sharp, giving an imposing, fortified impression. The exterior was not nearly as well maintained as the first longhouse, with mosses and vines growing up the walls. From the door spilt out a mess of hay, and with each step forward, the smell elevated and permeated my nostrils.

The smaller horse reached forwards and opened the door, and a foul blast caused me to wretch. The smell was incomparable. Like an old outhouse in the summer, the house exuded an odour multiplied by the heated air. A number of Yahoos turned and howled a horrible wail. The noise from the dozen or so inside was deafening, and I sheltered my ears, but the horses prodded my disinclined body through the door. Inside, a single long log was suspended a few feet off the ground. Tied every couple metres was the source of the loathsome racket. Fourteen naked, scarred, and deformed—by cause of violence—humans were secured by their necks by a length of rope to the trestle. Only a racist and pretentious fool would not see they were as human as I, and, but for their grooming, history, and colour, of the same ilk as me. Their hair, as everyone I had met on this island, was long and scraggly. Their posture was stooped, with sharp nails and a strong, muscular physique conditioned by heavy labour. At their feet were slivers of raw flesh. Some held handfuls of it, and several had blood, both dried and wet, on their face. It was clear these brutes had been interrupted mid-meal and that the Huhuneem cared not, or knew not, to cook the flesh. Perhaps that may have explained these Yahoos' feral nature compared to my cave-dwelling friends. They focused their screams in my direction and threw several scraps of carrion at me. They were not particularly gifted with their throws and missed me narrowly despite the confined space.

The horses, clearly feared by the prisoners in this jail, suffered no such ill treatment. They joined the single horse already in the room, a white mare. It seemed she was the keeper and guard. She was not so large and impressive as the two black stallions. Nevertheless, she was an imposing figure of authority in this edifice. She kept an eye on the inmates, and a similar gaze upon my person, as the two greeted her and communicated their intention. It was only a moment before she stomped her feet and the barbarous folk settled obediently, cowering behind the bar. My two chaperones stepped forwards and untied the largest of the convicts and drew him out to the courtyard. They shoved me out along with him, causing bursts of blinding pain from my still untended injuries to spark to life. In the bright light, they lined him up with me. They poked and prodded me and the other, comparing our countenances, body posture, tone, musculature, skin, nails, arms, legs.

My counterpart stood three feet from me, and through clenched teeth, spittle dripped from his bloodied face. His skin was as dark as the others of the island, and he never took his eyes off me. My own appraisal of him was simple. He was a poor man who had suffered a terrible twist of fate. Thick hair covered his entire body, and long hair covered his head and chin. Despite that thick cover, a number of scars, from both cuts and bruises—many of which were caused by human hands by the looks of them—were apparent. This unfortunate person had led a difficult life. Despite the intense hatred that burned from his eyes, I felt pity for him. At intervals, he took swipes at me with his sharp nails and caught me across the left cheek, drawing blood.

The horses intervened on my behalf. Apparently satisfied, the two stallions indicated to the white mare to return the prisoner. The two seemed most interested in my clothes, which were the most obvious differentiator between me and the other. They guided me back towards the longhouse of the Huhuneem, to my unending relief. Their deliberations would no doubt continue, but I was led to the fields, to a pile of hay near the cattle. I was granted a bed of straw, separated from the Yahoos who were being herded back into their own structure. Drawing roughly half the straw about me, I constructed, as I began to know it, my Yahoo nest. I was sleeping rough amongst the cattle of a nonhuman sapient species. I was unsure, but the weight of evidence now suggested that in this place, these empyreal Huhuneem were, in fact, the masters, the civilized, the supreme. The lamentable humans, these Yahoos, were slaves, servants, exiles, and undesirables.

CHAPTER 1.11

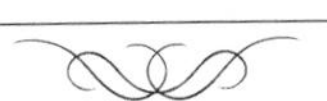

The author receives horse language lessons.

I WAS RETAINED in this land as something between a prisoner and a guest of the Huhuneem. In their country, the horses want for nothing, for they have fewer desires than we. Food, though not particularly satisfying, was nonetheless plentiful. The Huhuneem took care of many animals, even those they did not use directly for farming. I would happen to come across many animals, both familiar and not. Amongst those for which they cared, I recognized of course the cows and chickens, but also donkeys, geese, and pigs. The nearby plains also teemed with exotic rabbits and rats and birds of various sorts. I was treated evenly and fairly by my hosts, but I was not free to leave or to travel without a close escort. Usually this, and the pain of my still-healing ribs, meant I was confined to a close proximity from the longhouse.

In these circumstances, I applied myself to learning the Huhuneem language. In this endeavour, my masters were unexpectedly satisfied to oblige. They taught me a foundation based on the objects at hand. I learned the words for animals and plants and those words they used for their homes, the island, and the ocean. They were most interested in me and from whence I had come. Some of the horses showed a greater interest in me than others. Big Black, as the leader of the harras, was of course often one of the regulars, but a few others were as well. One in particular, a white nag, stood apart from the rest. She was a small, somewhat broken-down horse, but she seemed more interested in me than many of the others and took more time with me to teach and learn. I would come to appreciate her greatly.

I made use of a stubby pencil I carried in my shirt pocket to label everything they taught me. I had to invent a system by which the language could be translated. To this end, I employed a number of accents and diacritics, particularly to emphasize when a syllable was to be expressed with a strong exhalation. I was judicious with the use of the pencil, recognizing that when it ran out, I would no longer be able to write. As I lacked paper, I wrote upon the wood directly. Sometimes I had to use a stone to knock the bark off rougher segments or to create stakes.

The Huhuneem understood only slightly what I was doing but didn't object to the graffiti on their property. They didn't seem to mind the damage I was causing as long as it didn't compromise the structure itself. The horses possessed little understanding of literacy, though they weren't unfamiliar with the concept. It just seemed they found no desire to adopt the technology for their purposes. As such, their knowledge was passed orally. With limited desires, few events were of such note that they felt the need to store them in their collective consciousness.

I would learn much about their society, which I will relate in time. In my early learnings, I was able to question only the most common words, and I was able to teach only a few words in my language to them. I learned that Huhuneem was used simultaneously to express the horse people as well as the paramount of evolution. Conversely, Yahoo was used to denote not just the suffering humans of the island, but everything bad, nasty, and unfortunate.

As I became familiar with the local words, occasionally I would be granted carefully monitored peregrinations through the fields and nearby forests. On these, I would frequently point to various things as a child learning his first words. I would ask about the trees, branches, leaves, rain, sun, roots, berries, and all the various animals and birds. I would not memorize these words as easily, for my little cheat sheets posted around the farm were not available to me out in nature. I was supervised at all times, sometimes by the Big Black, who was the principal, sometimes by the others, but most commonly by the white nag. I named her Honey. She was often around, and the most communicative, but also quite impatient, urging me to hurry with a "Huhuun, huhuun."

On my field trips with Honey, I would get the best sense of the island. To some eyes it would seem quite plain, to others, perhaps idyllic. There were few outstanding geographic features such as mountains, lakes, or even particularly deep valleys or steep hills. The island was characterized by a relatively flat, rolling hill terrain with mostly uniform vegetation and wildlife. The land was divided roughly equally between deciduous forests and the grasslands upon which the Huhuneem settlements were all located. Honey and I would walk side-by-side to all corners of the island. Rarely would we stop at any settlement, and even though word of my presence on the island was spreading rapidly. I was seen with some suspicion whenever we met another of her kind. There were a number of rivers and streams, and I would be sometimes allowed to bathe there while Honey looked on. She played the role simultaneously of guide, protector, friend, and teacher, and I nurtured a fondness for this particular Huhuneem.

I was never able to identify names of the other Huhuneem, and they weren't willing to share such with me. I didn't really develop close relationships with any other than Honey and Big Black. Unlike my learnings of other languages in the past, learning to speak to and by another species proved a significant hurdle and one I think nobody could properly understand. In my former life in my beloved Canada, I learned from teachers who shared a similar development and physiology. I shall relate several examples that typified this trial.

When a human teacher provides lessons to a student, at least in any context that I have encountered, the student demonstrates a lack of comprehension by furrowing their brow, hoisting their shoulders, or exposing their hands. In the society of the Huhuneem, the horses possess none of those physical indications of confusion. This resulted frequently in poorly understood lessons and delayed me numerous times, when, out of embarrassment or misunderstanding, I failed to ask for a greater explanation. Even when I would attempt to ask a question, particularly early in my stay, I would repeat a word, or a phrase with the elevated intonation, that to me was the natural way of asking a question. Amongst my teachers, this caused great confusion, for their alphabet, being limited by physiology, made greater use of tone, duration, and volume to modify meaning. Asking a question more slowly, or louder, or with a different emphasis thereby meant something entirely different. Were it not for my situation being as dependent on, and my grasp of this language being so critical to, my survival, in retrospect, I am assured my mistranslations might well have been of great humour to me. Pointing to a tree and asking its name, but by mistake declaring a desire to eat that same thing, which to my ear sounded altogether identical in material structure, was hardly a way to convey intelligence.

Often, I would be visited by distant travellers, of an equine nature of course. In this place, all were treated as friends and family. In fact, I could identify no distinction but for the familiarity and regularity with which I was acquainted with those I lived with. The infirm would come to visit, carried on sledges hauled by a team of four to six Yahoos, bound by the waist and equally tied by the neck. The Yahoos bound to this service snapped, snarled, and swiped at each other, but not at their masters. I was taught all Huhuneem, regardless of ability, was provided with the same quality of life. Each family kept a pair of Yahoos at their disposal. If one Yahoo was rendered lame by injury or old age, they would be granted the service of a pair more from their village. In this place, because of the absence of greed and desire, I imagined such an equitable distribution was acceptable, for each individual Huhuneem was asked to share the same duties taking care of the settlement.

Despite a facility and aptitude for language, I found it took me several weeks to comprehend even the most basic questions. After around six months, I could not only understand but rudimentarily answer and ask a measure as well. To expand upon my understanding of the language of these people would be an endeavour far beyond the scope and scale of this book. I believe from what I have relayed, the reader might have a sufficient understanding of the challenges and unique nature of such a language. I have no doubt that doctors of linguistics would take great joy in pursuing my learnings further and would embrace an opportunity to experience some of these tribulations firsthand.

On occasion, I have been asked about how I relieved myself in this place. I can assure the reader that I did not adopt the Yahoo's way of defecating as I pleased and the thoroughly disgusting practice where they would frequently throw their faeces at each other. I would beg leave to go behind a tree, but remain otherwise visible, to visit the lavatory, and while my chaperones could not understand why I would conceal such a natural function, never could I disabuse myself of the practice. Honey would often urge me along impatiently at a distance, frustrated at the duration of my evacuations. They accepted the compromise that while I desired my privacy, a concept for which they had no comprehension, they would remain nearby and always able to see at least some part of my body to ensure I was not fleeing.

In this act, many months after capture, I was come upon by an unsuspecting Huhuneem. My escort, Honey, remained a suitable distance away for my comfort when a second emerged from around a corner and caught me with my pants at my ankles. As a course of habit, I quickly hove my trousers up to my waist. The horse, in distress, hurried back to the house. I concluded my business, having been startled, and rejoined my guard. She knew little of what had transpired, beyond having seen her compatriot, and demonstrated the typical impatience with the amount of time it took me to void my bladder.

We began to resume the lesson when the Big Black stallion rushed back with the bay that had come upon me minutes ago. The bay was assigned to keep watch over me while the stallion took aside the white nag to communicate some new command. The bay who kept watch over me did so with great unease, reminding me of Hue's behaviour upon the beach. With her ears peaked, and highly alert with respect to her surroundings, she kept a steady eye on me. I began to wonder if my actions had offended her. This was only the tip of the iceberg. While she had not in fact been offended by my action, I would soon be informed that it was my person, and more specifically, the aspect of my clothes, that had caused distress.

The Big Black returned, having sent the nag away to the farm, and excused the two of us from the charge of the discomfited bay. He made to ask about the nature of my clothes. Amongst the horses, and the other natives of this place, they had no parallel for such items, nor any words. He reached out and asked the meaning of what the bay had told him. He asked me why I was one thing in private, and another in person. I understood that in his way, he was asking about my clothes and how I could look one way with my clothes on, and another with them off. I tried to explain to him that amongst my people, we had developed an art of creating accoutrements and accessories to our person that provided us numerous advantages. Through these things, we could be protected from nature, whether wind, heat, cold, rain, or snow; we could be provided protection from injury; or we could be protected from the malicious intents of other people, insects, or animals.

He commanded that I show him my true nature. Being at his mercy, I was compelled to comply. Even though most of my clothes were already in tatters, they still concealed and protected much of my body. I removed the shirt and my pants. I kept my underwear on me, as I clung to old traditions of propriety. Not knowing any differently, as the informant had not shared every detail, he was unaware to even ask.

He posited that from the less than civil behaviour of the Yahoos, it was understandable we would avoid exposing ourselves to others of our kind. He made clear through this conversation, having seen me in my nonartificial state, that he was now certain I was indeed a Yahoo. Despite a great many similarities between those he had encountered, I was of a type he had not before come across. I could not, nor would I try to, persuade him any differently, for though I differed in behaviour, I could not necessarily attribute those differences to nature. Perhaps, given the same upbringing, I might behave as the Yahoos of this land. I wouldn't reveal that stream of thought to him, but I conveyed I desired to be kept separate from the Yahoos, in the presence of whom I felt quite insecure. He remarked that my body seemed inferior to the other Yahoos. He could understand, having numerous times observed their ill intents towards me, that I would not be eager to be placed in a confined space with them. I urged him to preserve the truth of my being from the others.

With this shared understanding, but perhaps more because he was now convinced I was an extraordinary Yahoo, he redoubled his efforts to teach me. Further still, he desired to learn about my origins and how I came to possess the faculty for rational thought, whereby my brethren in this place were sorely deficient.

As the Huhuneem became increasingly convinced I was just an unusual Yahoo, they sought to experiment on the other Yahoos to determine how much of an aberration I truly was. They would put me in the yard with the Yahoos under close scrutiny and watch. I learned quickly I had to impose a dominant position early lest they think me submissive and attack me as the first had done in the yard that first day here.

The she-Yahoos were particularly aggressive, in a manner most unbecoming, but by virtue of my stature and wary of the Huhuneem masters so close by, they mostly made gestures, snarled, screamed, and occasionally proffered their faeces at me forcefully. The males were similarly perturbed by my presence, but more frequently I found their aggressions slightly more civil.

Above all the others, the one Yahoo who had drawn my blood on the first day seemed the least intimidated. Of course, he would remember me; I was a strange Yahoo in this place, but he was not in the least afraid of me for my height and didn't care a whit about the Huhuneem watching him. Like a prisoner who knew he had nothing to lose, he loathed me, and the pure hatred burned in his eyes for only moments before he charged at me full speed to attack whenever given the chance. Twice he caught me off guard, the first day in the yard, and the first time he and I had been placed together for experimentation. On this first time, he came at me with such fury. Before the horses were able to intervene, he'd managed to cut away a piece of my ear and caused several painful scratches on my arms. The horses pulled him away, and I was left alone, blood flowing easily from my wounded ear most of all.

I retreated to my nest after this encounter and swore to never be taken so ill-prepared by this Yahoo again. The white nag, Honey, would come by later with some paste she tenderly applied to my ear and arms. It cooled the burning feeling of the cuts and slowed the bleeding. I hoped I would not face infection.

CHAPTER 1.12

The author's grasp of the Huhuneem language improves, whereupon the author sets about to detail his story and the place from whence he came.

AS MY VOCABULARY, articulation, and accent ameliorated and I became able to resolve and elucidate upon the inquisitions of my master, my lessons, already expedited and prioritized, shifted focus from the plain language arts to matters of practical importance and relevance.

The first line of inquest focused predictably on how it was I had come to this place. Why had I been caught in the presence of wild Yahoos trying to steal livestock? To answer these questions directly proved to be an impractical impossibility. I began with a response accepted as plausible. I had come from a faraway place. This certainly came as no surprise to the Big Black horse. It was patently obvious I was not from a nearby place. I bore so little in common with the natives with whom the horses were familiar. Neither the wild nor captive Yahoos shared many obvious features with me. He could fathom neither the capacity for rational thought nor the propensity and penchant for learning amongst the local aborigines.

I could not say with precision the distance from which I had come. Little did it matter, for amongst the Huhuneem, distance was only measured as a function of how long it would take to travel, and all travel was by hoof. Even the measure of time was only broken into days and years. Their culture found little need to break up time into any sort of arbitrary construct as ours has with seconds, minutes, hours, weeks, or months. I explained I had come from a distance, which by foot, if it were possible to travel over the sea at the same speed as a horse on land must probably exceed a hundred or more days.

Suggesting so great a distance, far beyond the known limits of the land, led to another sequential question, and I told the black stallion I would reveal wonders he had never before known. He predictably asked how it was I had travelled so great a distance across the sea. It was known Yahoos could swim a short way before having to return to land and the Huhuneem tended to distrust and avoid the water, so the idea of travelling by water so great a distance from a land unseen was incomprehensible. I've never been one to arc from authenticity and felt no compunction against revealing the truth even though I suspected he would think me daft. Any who lacked the sufficient technology must surely believe me a liar.

I informed him I had arrived by air, in a sort of enclosed sledge, shaped like an enormous bird, itself powered by a sort of fire that kept it aloft for great distances and travelling at incredible speeds. I think he would have had a difficult time imagining I could have come by boat, if he knew what such a thing was. So, to explain aerodynamics, engineering, and aviation theory was obviously going to stretch not just my understanding of his language, but the boundaries thereof and the capacity of any mind to imagine such a thing. It is said that any sufficiently advanced technology is indistinguishable from magic. If somebody describes something that must be magic, the only protection of the mind is to reject such folly.

Predictably, when I spoke the words, my host struggled to understand my meaning. To his mind, the description of a craft shaped like a plane, or the concept of flight, of course, seemed impossible. For me to speak of such a thing that could not be sent his mind racing in directions it had never explored before. Amongst these horses, there is no word for deceit, lies, falsehood, slander, or distortion of the truth. The nearest concept around which he could wrap his head was the unknown. With certainty, he could state that there were things that were unknown. In his tribe, one could never say what one did not know. Dishonesty was a concept only barely known, and this too was only the product of interaction with Yahoos. I will not go into too great detail, but he granted that I said a thing he did not know. Big Black reacted as if allergic to the concept of lies, but eagerly pressed to push on to other details.

Accepting the idea of an aeroplane, he sought to know more about the Huhuneem that would commission such a craft and enquired what had happened to his kind in my crash. I informed him that horses had no role at all in the production. The craft was conceived, designed, manufactured, and operated by humans. It caused him such consternation he was obliged to recess from that day's lessons.

The Huhuneem live a completely agrarian lifestyle, without science or art. To develop technology such as flight was beyond comprehension. A number of days were spent mostly in the objective of explaining the complicated subject of deceit. My record of the things about which we spoke only contains a few of the highlights. Over the course of some three years, and engaging, for most waking hours, in conversation, one can imagine many subjects were covered. I discovered that without elaborating and establishing the indispensable foundation on this subject matter, no amount of language would be of any use. I would ask the reader to think about all of the things we have created because of our own duplicity. Law, war, stories and fiction, mythology and religion, exaggeration, tactics, trust, and inspiration are all begotten from the ability to lie. It was upon frequent meditation, which I utilized to formulate the appropriate words such as would fit into their language, that I discovered the good we receive through the evil of deception.

In the mind of the horses, they had achieved their perfection. They were content to live the same lives in the same way they had always lived and sought neither to better themselves nor their surroundings. They possessed a lack of ambition and innovation that, to me, is fundamental to my being. It is not the same to suggest they had given up: upon achieving the pinnacle of what there is, there is no point in striving for anything else.

I explained to him the idea of stories, ideas created out of the mind alone, not based upon, or at least not entirely, relating to pure facts. Through a series of detours, I tried to explain that humans try to elucidate that which we did not or could not know. Using the forest as an illustration, I asked whether there was an animal hiding behind a tree. The lord answered that he did not know. When I told him, with childlike innocence, a hurt Huhuneem was behind the tree and unable to communicate, he immediately broke into a run to provide assistance. When he arrived and found there was none, he was at a loss to explain where it had gone. I told him I did not actually know what was behind the tree but had imagined a scenario he would find plausible. Through a series of like examples, I was able to explain to him the basic tenet of lying.

It was a most uncomfortable thing around which for him to wrap his head. Communication was the conveying of information and fact. This way of speaking, of saying things one could not know, made communication less than neutral. I explained that while there were indeed drawbacks to mendacities, there were also benefits. A story that invents new ideas, alternate approaches, and imagines new technologies—another word that took more than a fair amount of time to illuminate—might create inspiration for someone to solve the problems therein presented. Otherwise, one might try to achieve what was otherwise not even thought of. These works of art and literature focused the energies of wise and clever people towards the betterment of others.

In much the same way my fiction about the horse behind the tree was intended to help him understand an otherwise complicated subject, stories could also be used where actual examples were limited to teach important morals and behaviours without having to experience everything firsthand. We, humans, use stories and mythology to explain those things that make us uncomfortable because we cannot know them. I brought forth the obvious example of death. We cannot know what happens when we vacate this existence, leaving our loved ones to mourn our loss. This was met with a look I learned to equate with confusion. When a horse died, it was explained to me, they did not mourn his passing but took the body far away and buried it. There was no reason to try to know that which they could not, and as such, no thought, time, or effort was devoted to it.

I explained that for Yahoos, the need to understand the world was a driving force. Through art and science, whereby we would methodically study the causes and effects of all manner of things, we strove to understand the intricate workings of nature. Those things we could not study, therefore could not adequately explain, became the fodder for fiction and theory. Many people had created explanations of what might happen at the end of our time. As I had convinced him about the horse behind the tree, they had convinced others of the truth of their fictions. So great was the power of their convictions that wars were fought, and people were killed over who was correct.

Even in situations where things are known and can be proven to be true, blind belief in a contrary fiction leads people to reject fact in favour of sometimes dangerous ideas. The horse assumed I referred to mental deficiency, for familiar he was with those, both equine and Yahoo, who had lost their capacity for reason due to injury. I corrected that, in fact, a large number of otherwise intelligent and capable Yahoos had developed a mistrust of any authority, caused either by bad experiences or by a conflict between their established fictions and the studied facts and they chose to reject fact—or confuse fact with belief. No amount of argument is likely to change the mind of one who cannot distinguish between fiction and fact. This, of course, was a discussion that took many days and was of a depth too great for the horse to really understand.

I tried to explain that a belief is an idea that can't be proven or disproven. A fact is something that can be tested and repeated, or at least not disproven. A lie can be disproven if studied carefully and fairly. In the words of the Huhuneem, a belief is something that cannot be known. A fact is something that is. A lie is something that is not, as was the case when I suggested a wounded Huhuneem was behind a tree. I will speak more on this later.

As the Huhuneem had no place for incorrectness, the need for a word to mean its contrary was equally unconceived. The stallion would even ask me about the concept of war. Fighting, particularly amongst the Yahoos, was common, the concept of war was novel. This I will convey in due course.

As we talked about words such as correct and true, another word derived from falsehood became apparent to me: the knowledge of trust.

In the absence of all lies, trust, one would assume, is implied. This was not my experience. It is only in the absence of something that one has had before that one can truly understand its importance. The Huhuneem formed no great bonds between themselves, but equally, neither did they create enemies. To the horses, this lukewarm way was simply the only way. I have learned that though we can mostly agree that lying is an undesirable behaviour, it is only through this knowledge that we can develop stronger bonds with those we trust.

Big Black was only able to comprehend this after many days of frustratingly unproductive effort. I believe he had to draw upon a Yahoo behaviour that had been frequently witnessed but never understood. When one Yahoo possessed something he believed another would covet, he would often hide it away where neither of them would be able to benefit from it, but at least only he would know of its location. The deceit shown by the less civilized on this island provided the only context by which he could fathom that which we call duplicity. In their language, no word existed to handle such an incongruous thought, so we created one. It had already become clear this subject would undoubtedly come up repeatedly. As the horse said, anything made by the minds and hands of Yahoos must certainly be the product of this behaviour. It was clear they would work backwards and opposite from what is good and normal. The word we came up with was "Huhuhoo," a mash-up of their words "Huhuneem" and "Yahoo," which basically meant good-evil or that which does not mean what it means. Even as we explored this, I never would sense that he could really understand. For the sake of furthering our conversations, he accepted that we must possess a common lexicon.

As for the aeroplane, whereupon this adventure began, my host was still desirous of greater detail. If a horse had not commissioned the aeroplane and had had no role in its production, then how was it possible that Yahoos had created such a thing he thought could not be built? Why would the horses of our world even allow the brute Yahoos to try such madness?

I told him that in our world, Yahoos were the masters and horses the servants. At this, he was certain I had spoken a huhuhoo. There was no possible way a Huhuneem would suffer a Yahoo to lead him anywhere. So weak and fragile were the constitution of the Yahoo that even the weakest of horse could easily crush the mightiest of human. I told him that in the world from which I came, horses were not sentient, and no more capable of rational thought than the cow in his paddock. Yahoos were not just the dominant species but were calm and rational. Through such rational thought, we had overcome the limitations of our frame to bring to heel all other species. My master could accept that a race, gifted with reason, as from where I claimed to have come, through rational thought, would be able to take advantage of less intelligent beings like cattle or chickens. But for that race to be detestable Yahoos, and for them to have overcome the Huhuneem, was huhuhooing.

I must admit he learned quickly. Applying logic and reason, he tried to catch me in a lie when he asked about the status, numbers, and occupations of the Yahoos and Huhuneem of my world. I told him that in the known world from whence I came, there were several billion humans. On its own, this took a substantial amount of explanation, for their numerical system was limited in scope. He was shocked at the incredible size of our population and that the corresponding horse population was in the tens of millions. I drew some figures on the ground to provide some scale so he could more easily grasp that there were two entire orders of magnitude between humans and horses. He could not but marvel at the necessary size of an island to support so great a population. He could not say exactly how many Yahoos and Huhuneem there existed on this island, but from his description, I hazarded to guess not more than a thousand of each. On the occupation of horses, I admitted I was no expert, for I neither possessed nor regularly rode horses.

If the reader will excuse me for the deviation once again, this left my host aghast. Despite the thought of humans running things, he never imagined a Huhuneem would allow a human to ride upon his back. Any horse could easily unseat and roll over the human with little risk to himself, killing the rider easily. I was forced to explain we had created ways to take the fight out of difficult horses, and that through tools, we could ensure they behaved with docility and civility towards us, their masters. I explained that in some instances, they were used as draft animals. One or more would be tied together, similarly to the Yahoos who pulled the infirm on sledges and dragged carts and carriages around with either goods or persons. I begged his forgiveness, but mostly this was used nowadays as a ceremonial function because the horses weren't really necessary. Alternative forms of transportation were more efficient, but the symbolism and the historical romanticism kept these things in vogue. I contended that in spite of our usage of his kin, they were nonetheless held in high regard and high demand. They were treated well, with the exception of the indignities I've already presented, and a small number of humans kept as their only occupation the responsibility of ensuring they were managed to the highest possible standard. Often these horses were treated even better than some of the least well-off humans, the plight of whom I would have to explain to the black stallion and will reveal in time. It pleased him that they were well treated, but my master was unable to believe I was speaking the full truth.

CHAPTER 1.13

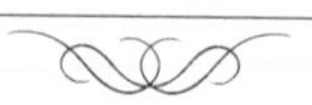

The author describes the food and drink of his homeland.

MY KEEPERS WERE most enthusiastic to hear about how a world ruled by Yahoos could function. Preconceived as they were by the notion that Yahoos were incapable of reason, I, if they assumed I was a Yahoo, must be merely a unique aberration. As Honey pointed out, in spite of my capacity for rational thought and ambition to learn, I had shown no facility for convincing the others of this place to abandon their ways and to follow a comparable path to reason. On numerous occasions, Big Black continued to facilitate a sort of exchange program, now with the intention that I was to teach a bound and snarling Yahoo any one thing of meaning. I asked on one occasion for the Yahoo, not the vicious one of course, to be unbound. I felt this would calm the brute and provide a more suitable environment for learning. Upon being released, and the Huhuneem stepping away, the Yahoo immediately assaulted me, and I suffered several sharp fingernail scratches while fighting off his attempts to bite. I evidently lacked the wherewithal for such an endeavour, which, I'm disappointed to admit, tainted the impression of our world.

In many conversations, I was presented to various visitors: big and small, male and female, all shades of hide and hair. Word had spread throughout the island of the Huhuneem of the presence of a strange and exotic Yahoo who could speak and looked different from the others. I was usually accompanied by and led in the conversation by Big Black. Occasionally others would ask for elaboration, particularly those who had missed out on large chunks of previous conversations. This would frequently cause delays. I was forced to go over the same subject numerous times with different adjudicators. Big Black would either participate in these conversations to try to help speed things along, or he would leave us to avoid lecture reruns.

I spoke of my native land, and he asked on our shelter and food. I could see his line of inquiry was likely to follow Maslow's hierarchy. I told him we built houses of stone, wood, and a great many other materials. Some houses were built to suit just one family. Others were manufactured with distinct enclaves for numerous. I used sticks and earth to illustrate to Big Black the size and scale of our edifices. I spoke of great buildings of steel and glass and summarized the creation and composition of such materials, which in itself took quite a while to explain.

These towers, I told him, could house hundreds or thousands of people far above the ground. He sought to understand from what distance we would carry these materials, and I told him our homes are created from materials gathered all over the world. Various stones and wood were needed for a diverse range of utilities. Stone might be quarried from nearby mountains, where the stone possessed the appropriate qualities of strength, texture, and aesthetics. Others might be retrieved from huge mines half a world away. The stone would be worked on by specialists in a number of professions who would mine and refine the stone then entrust it to others. These others would specialize in the shipment of it over the seas, either by boat or by plane. It would then be passed along to craftsmen near to us who would produce the final product and install it. In all, our houses often require materials from every corner of the Earth, transported by every type of conveyance conceivable.

The reader must understand that for each of these concepts, apart from that which can be readily seen in nature, most required great elaboration. I knew the seed of doubt I had only so recently planted was by now growing and flowering in my master's mind. It was feasible to explain specialization, for some Huhuneem were more predisposed to some forms of labour than others, and he informed me that some Huhuneem were naturally born with a greater proficiency for thought and strength. The black were born with the highest natural abilities, followed by the dapple grey, the bay, iron-grey, sorrel, and finally, the least capable were the white. It was the way of nature for these lesser beings to achieve less. The superior sorts of horses were therefore treated preferentially, and with deference, by the lesser castes.

He sought confirmation that amongst humans, the same distinction had been made, and that it was this I meant when I spoke of specialization. I responded that the same form of discrimination had once been viewed as the norm. Truthfully, it had been practiced based, too, on just the colour of a person's skin. I further elaborated that in the majority of the world today, at least in those places I had visited and experienced myself, this was no longer the accepted view of those most learned. In most places, and particularly amongst the most rational people, it had been studied and determined that while no person is born to be exactly the equal of another in all abilities, the pigmentation in their skin was no more useful an identifier of a person's mental or physical capabilities than the length of the hair on their head.

On this point, it was made abundantly clear to me that what I was saying was certainly a huhuhoo, for it wasn't necessary to study anything to see that the lesser Huhuneem were inferior to the others, particularly the black. It could only be so amongst other species. Perhaps we were unable, through our inherent limitations, to accept such facts. I recognized I was stirring up a sort of anger I hadn't previously witnessed amongst the horses to this point.

I tried to step down from the topic when Honey asked how it was that we had studied this thing. I said the place from which I had come had decided it did not matter where one came from, or what they looked like, but they should be treated the same way and given the same level of respect as any other. The horses, who live a mostly egalitarian lifestyle, concurred with this assessment. I had never previously witnessed any ill treatment pass between any two of their kind. However, as I had long ago witnessed, the higher castes were granted a number of small privileges such as the right to eat first and a usual deference to their leadership. I hadn't attached significance to the skin tone of the horses, assuming the leadership was a function of capability. In this dialogue, I began to understand this was not necessarily correct. I should reiterate again that I was no expert in horses or Huhuneem. Amongst their kind, I could not say with any certainty that colour was not an accurate indicator. I only spoke of my own kind, and amongst humans, the same visual traits were not indicative of what lay beneath. I had known people of all colours to be bright and dull, weak and strong, friendly and hostile, altruistic and malevolent, agile and awkward. A product of my environment and my raising, it is my firm, unshakable belief all colours are created equal and together form the one true race of mankind.

Honey was most interested in this conversation. Long after the others, excepting Big Black, had left to attend to whatever matters they needed, she remained and pressed on.

Tiring of the subject, my master asked of our food and whether it was quite the same as with our houses. I responded that it was even more so. A meal, particularly for a well-off person, might require ingredients taken from every corner of the world. Grains and cereals were produced close to my home, and certain animals were raised for meat and dairy nearby as well. Spices, fruits, vegetables, and other exotic animals were raised by specialists in far off places. The wealth of the planet could be seen on many plates around the world, particularly on those in greatest contact with the rest. In some countries, only a single product was produced by most people, and it was shipped rapidly around the world in exchange for things that could not be grown due to climate or soil. Rice was produced primarily in Southeast Asian countries, while barley, oats, and wheat were often produced by northern, colder-climate countries. Various fruits were grown around the world in quantity but were available everywhere. Drinks, such as tea, coffee, or wine had to be imported to create a complete meal.

The horses judged this was unimaginably complicated and inefficient. It must be a poor country that cannot provide its people with all the necessities of life. I could not agree with this assessment. I said that my country produced enough food and drink to satisfy several times our population, but then our diet would be restricted to a small variety. I tried to explain that in almost all things, humans traded around the world. Both in services and products, various locations specialized in different things.

Though not universally accepted, I went on to explain, amongst the most educated, those with the greatest predisposition to learning and rational thought, globalization was generally viewed as a force for good and development. I tried to explain it thusly: One man could produce five apples and five litres of milk in a single day, or that same man could produce twelve litres of milk but no apples if he focused on milking cows because he was better at this particular skill. His neighbour could produce five apples and five litres of milk, or he could produce twelve apples but no milk if he focused on picking apples because he was better at picking apples. If both men produced both apples and milk, together they would produce ten apples and ten litres of milk in a day. If the first man only produced milk, and the second man only produced apples, together they would produce twelve apples and twelve litres of milk. This example was only a local scale, but forces of globalization validated it at a global scale. While it may seem a complicated and impossible system to manage, it actually works without much oversight to the betterment of most people in the world.

There are undoubtedly some flaws in the system. Through economies of scale, if one person particularly good at making milk lives in a place otherwise specialized in producing oranges, that man may find he can't compete evenly with people and places that specialize in his field of expertise. The Huhuneem present seemed particularly engaged with this case and asked if that man would not be more efficient with the others of his kind, why would he not move to join them?

This question brought up a small conversation of mobility and international politics. I tried to explain that a person from one country cannot easily move from one place to another, even if it was his desire to do so. The governments of all places restrict the free flow of people for a variety of reasons. Many prevent others from coming purely out of fear, either for personal safety or economic concerns. Other countries prevent people on more racist or religious grounds, desiring to maintain a purity of people or to keep their lands for people like themselves in body or spirit. In almost all cases, this leads to the impoverishment of all.

CHAPTER 1.14

The author describes politics and war and peace amongst Yahoos.

EVENTUALLY, THE HUHUNEEM I had named Hue came to visit the strange Yahoo. It was no surprise, of course, to her when she confirmed her suspicion that the unique Yahoo was the same one she had encountered months ago on the beach. A number of conferences brought her up to speed with relative quickness, and she was eager to pursue the subject of colour and capability. With regards to specialization, if there was not a natural hierarchy of status in Yahoo society, how were difficult decisions made? I came to understand that by this, she was really asking about the governance of our people. Amongst the Huhuneem, the highest status (dominant black) horses would meet in a sort of conclave to determine necessary courses of action. The decisions were made exclusively by these horses for the entire group and were passed down without any question and without any concern or dissent. It is my supposition this form of basic government sufficed amongst the Huhuneem, who faced few conflicts, no external threats, and few desires.

I explained the world is divided into a number of political units, which might best be compared to settlements. While the Huhuneem live in groups of a couple dozen only, humans formed towns and cities that varied from a few hundred people up to great megacities with tens of millions of inhabitants. These cities thrive on the various skills, desires, cultures, arts, sciences, ideas, and efforts of the different people therein. Each word required many circumlocutions to explain. Perhaps I had best elaborate to my readers that the Huhuneem visit with little formality for long stretches of time and are welcome to stay for weeks as equals amongst their compatriots. I feel the need clarify this, for my confabulations with Hue took several weeks, and we only rarely spoke privately. I told her these cities of men are amongst the greatest achievements of our people. A vocal few view the mixing of people and cultures as weakness, while the best see the great strength of diversity. These cities are grouped into like-minded provinces and states, which are formal collections that share a common leadership. A number of provinces or states are grouped to form countries. How these countries are governed is left to the people to decide.

In some countries, such as my own and most of our closest neighbours, all adults are granted the right to pick their government through a democratic process. The government is selected by the people, to serve the people, to make decisions on behalf of the people, and to represent the people of their country. There is freedom, power, and responsibility in this system for each person to stay informed, to understand the issues and candidates, and to exercise their vote to ensure that leaders best represent their concerns. Honey, as usual, seemed most intrigued with this concept while Hue and the other Huhuneem present thought this most complicated, and could little relate, with no general distinction made between skill and preference. I confirmed it was not a simple solution and there were a number of flaws, particularly when subjected to dishonesty and corruption.

These concepts are most difficult to explain to a thoroughly honest and uncorrupt race, to whom lying was only recently explained. I was able to take the example of the Yahoos in the yard fighting over the flesh of dead animals: even when there were ample supplies, the foulest Yahoo would commandeer the lion's share of the food and horde it from the others. Amongst humans, a leader has some authority to distribute all the food (amongst other things) and may decide to keep more for themselves, due to their position, while claiming to be taking only their fair share. These politicians may say one thing, but mean another, or say a huhuhoo but be so convincing, or have supporters so fervent in their belief, that the people will ignore all logic and reason to vote for a person many other Yahoos can see is presenting themselves falsely.

The Huhuneem were unconvinced of the value of democracy. If these politicians I spoke of would lie and cheat, then why would the millions of people of their country allow them to lead? With such great numbers as I had claimed, it would be simple to remove that person from power or to ignore their authority. I agreed this was indeed a possibility and one that happens from time to time in many countries. We have, however, developed systems of laws and policing that protect the government from such discord. One disgruntled person, a small group, or even a large group, cannot easily overrule the will of the state. Furthermore, the government is also responsible for the military, which includes those Yahoos with the best fighting skills and who have the best tools for the job.

On this too, the Huhuneem were unimpressed. Having witnessed frequent fighting by the Yahoo—for it was nearly incessant in the yard—it seemed clear we were ill-equipped for such fighting. Even though the Yahoo could be seen fighting regularly, our small frames, relative lack of muscles or the weapons found on other animals like sharp teeth, horns, hard feet, pure mass, or even claws sharper than our fragile nails, made it clear we were not made for fighting. The most vicious Yahoo wanted to cause me damage over any other objective, and yet given multiple opportunities, he only effected some minor abrasions and a small portion of my left ear. If my people all possessed my capacity for rational thought, why would the masses fear a small number?

I could easily see this question coming. The Huhuneem made use of only a limited number of tools, and the only sort of fighting I had witnessed was when I was captured. That could hardly compare to the human invention of war. I begged Hue to forgive me as I pressed forwards with my description of battles and cautioned her that that which I was to convey was unlikely to create a good opinion. Hue impatiently pushed me on, and I reluctantly explained about the history of war as best I could. I spoke of simple weapons, such as pointed sticks, like the Huhuneem used in their houses, though smaller, such that they could be carried by one person. I talked of refinements and the ability to throw and demonstrated the use of atlatls and bows. Then, too, the invention of bronze and iron and steel and sharp weapons of such were capable of killing easier and faster.

I detailed the creation of great machines, small and large, that could heave boulders at people or towns or hurtle numerous smaller rocks at groups. I told Hue about the discovery of gunpowder and its rapid deployment and dissemination around the world, with its ability to kill at a distance with ease. In an earlier discussion, I had already taught about planes and boats, but I described the invention of closed bowls full of fire that can destroy entire cities and the development of fast planes and boats that could deliver them.

Then I broached the subject of cars and carts that can move armaments to the battle with unprecedented speed and the further invention of great boats that can move on land carrying huge guns that can make war on others. Beyond the development of weapons, I was asked about scale, for each weapon was more powerful than those that preceded it, and I talked of wars between small groups of people, gangs, and tribes. Wars were once fought between towns but had grown in size to encompass cities and states in the recent past. Not in my lifetime, thankfully, but entire countries had once even waged war on each other over resources, land, space, religion, or pigmentation.

The Huhuneem were unfamiliar with hatred except what they witnessed amongst the Yahoos. I will speak more of their social structure in time, but while they were not particularly fond of the Yahoos, and especially their behaviour, they no more hated them for their nature than they hated a snake for its. Discomfited but unconvinced by the thought of Yahoos with such great weapons, and eager to turn the subject to something less disturbing, Hue asked, if such people held such power, why would they choose to relinquish it? Why would a government willingly hand over power to another? More to the point, why would the armed forces, who actually possess the real power, not simply confiscate it for themselves, as the largest Yahoo in the yard was prone to do?

I confirmed this was a normal occurrence in countries other than my own. A particularly strong Yahoo or one who possessed the loyalty of those with great strength could decide to seize power for themselves, taking charge of all the resources and deciding exclusively who would receive what and which laws would be passed, usually to their own benefit. Even in many countries where a legal government had come to power by the will of the people, so entranced did those elected people become with the luxuries granted that many created laws that served to preserve their authority. Sometimes they strove to maintain power through disenfranchizing efforts that prevented specific people from voting, including, sometimes, the threat of violence, the inhibiting of an opposition group from being allowed to vote, or the prohibiting of candidates altogether. In other cases, at the reins of power, some Yahoos would just abolish elections altogether and govern on an elapsed mandate, silencing dissent.

I recognize this may not sound a very pleasant or optimistic view of governance. Certainly, the Huhuneem were not particularly sympathetic to the plight of humans, especially as man was the creator of such systems, therefore responsible for its own complications. As I have said, the Huhuneem are a strongly rational race, and though they doubted my veracity, they agreed that if a Yahoo, such as the ones with which they were familiar, were to achieve through some magic a level of enlightened understanding, then our same base qualities—a deficit of reason and the weakness of our bodies and spirit—would only be amplified in the presence of intelligence, and our systems of governance and law, owing to our rancid birth from the unbalanced mind of Yahoos, could only be a reflection of that source. That Yahoos would seek out more food than needed was no surprise to the Huhuneem. The avaricious ways with which the Yahoo pursue all the things they value, though not previously understood, certainly seemed affirmed by my descriptions of our society.

CHAPTER 1.15

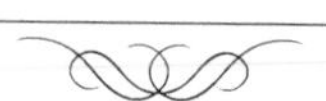

The author compares and contrasts family and social structure.

HUE SEEMED NOT to be particularly surprised by the enormous population of which I spoke. They had observed that Yahoos were a particularly promiscuous people, who, if supplied with sufficient food, would gorge themselves upon virtually anything that could be eaten, from roots to berries to cereals and flesh. So long as food was available, the males would mount almost any female, though some more than others. The females were found, if not prevented by their masters, to be carrying children most of the time. In spite of the children of Yahoos being the least viable of offspring, for they could not even walk for upwards of a year and lacked the strength or coordination to feed themselves for several years after that, Yahoos nonetheless were prone to rapid multiplication. Hue found it easy to believe that over the thousands of years that I described in our history, an unchecked human population might well grow wildly out of control until it stripped the land of all useful resources, and in so doing, precipitate a calamitous crash in its own population. Unlike all other animals, Yahoos, it seemed, didn't form a balance with nature, growing with reckless abandon and then declining rapidly when forced.

Hue asked how, with so many people, such a reckless tendency for growth, and our anarchic method of procreation, we were able to form any sort of society. I explained that though many of the tendencies she had witnessed remained within human societies, the same rules of law she derided and upon which she liberally poured her scorn also helped to protect people from harm. Most humans form small family groups, where a male and female come together, agree to create a partnership, and decide how many children they would like to produce. I told her men and women shared the feeling of love that bound them to one another and provided a shelter and stable upbringing for their children. She asked who selected the mates; in a place of millions of people, it must be difficult to select the appropriate match so as to ensure the correct offspring are generated. I told her that again, in most parts of the world, the matches were created by individuals themselves, who seek and find another with whom they are desirous of building a life together. In some places, the parents create matches, often based on economic criteria, but most have moved beyond this practice.

To the Huhuneem gathered, this seemed an appalling system. To assist the reader, I shall make the best effort I can to describe the Huhuneem family structure. The Huhuneem were not a kind to practice the permanent marrying of two individuals. Leaders of settlements gather to select appropriate couples, based principally on their colour and secondarily on their strength, speed, and hardiness. A male and a female would be matched with the intent that their offspring be the most appropriate for their station. The strongest males would be combined with the most attractive females, all within the same colour group, to avoid the creation of undesirable mixtures.

The Huhuneem were educated, both male and female, to be orderly, polite, and to treat all others as equals. They were subject to strict exercise to identify and refine their physical attributes and spend a great amount of time at play or grazing in the fields. I must also note that when I say they treated all others as equals, this is not strictly, or really even liberally true. A stranger of a superior class of Huhuneem was treated with the same dignity and respect as a local and afforded all the same privileges and honour.

Those of an inferior class, particularly the white and sorrel, were actually treated quite differently.

As I've previously mentioned, the white were understood to be the lesser in both physical and mental arenas. They were therefore afforded less time amongst the grass, by a matter of almost half, and were made to serve the others. They did not complain about their lot, for it was understood without question that this was the way the world was and should be. It was immediately apparent they were the servants of their masters. Male and female were, however, treated with utmost apparent equality. They were educated the same way and treated to the same luxury afforded by their stations, except for when it came to leadership. The highest office was always held by a principal male.

The reader might pardon my slight deviation here from the description, but I will also acknowledge that while they believed they offered each gender of Huhuneem an apparent equality, minus the leadership that they out-of-handedly discounted, they did so in a manner that was actually discriminatory. The "best" males are matched with the most attractive females. This created an inherent discrepancy between the genders for one is evaluated for their strength, skill, and abilities, while the other is valued purely on appearance. This is no equality at all, but a façade, behind which I sensed there could be some frustration. I sensed this frustration foremost in Honey, whose face, I was learning to read, belied her emotions on the subject.

The Yahoo, on the other hand, were treated at a level far below, as disgusting and despised slaves. The women Yahoo were viewed as good at nothing but creating children and being less strong but even more vicious, both towards each other and the males. Their promiscuity was used as a weapon to entice the males, whom they lorded over one another and the other males, all while fighting amongst themselves. Though the Huhuneem were constantly occupied surveilling and keeping order amongst the Yahoo, a role not unlike a referee but closer to a guard, at most times the Yahoo females were kept away in pens and only infrequently allowed to mingle, under close supervision, with the others. It is of little value to spend much time presenting more of the social structure of the Yahoo. Their society, if it could even be called such, was entirely managed and maintained by the Huhuneem. Their lives consisted of caged subservience to their masters.

Returning to the Huhuneem, their couples, matched by the elders, were formed for the simple and direct purpose of perpetuating the species and their stable numbers. Each of the highest stratigraphic castes produced precisely two offspring, and it was the desire that these be comprised of one male and one female. In the event that a pairing produces two of the same gender, the second was exchanged with another couple who had likewise produced two of the complementary gender.

As strange a thing as it is to us, this didn't create any apparent malice or jealousy. I had learned from Honey that this had happened to her quite some time ago; in fact, she'd had two fillies, one of which was exchanged with a settlement on the far side of the island, and who she never again saw. I expected her to demonstrate some displeasure, but as this was the way of their people, she actually seemed calm about the idea. The Huhuneem felt no more for their own children than they did for all others'. Maternal and paternal instincts were defined by the care of those fillies and colts in their charge, not by those to whom they had conceived and delivered. As all members of the village raised each foal, this was decided to be the optimal family unit. It was apparently unimportant to know from whence a Huhuneem had descended, for this history was considered irrelevant. There were no illnesses amongst the Huhuneem, and few amongst the Yahoo. With no need for inheritance, and a common, shared history passed through oral tradition, they had little need, nor any particular desire, to seek out their dames and sires.

Amongst the lesser horses, subservient to their superiors, they were occasionally exempted to conceive of a third foal. This was to ensure a sufficient working class. These horses were expected to tend to the fields and do the largest share of the work, but they were treated otherwise to similar standing.

In the event an individual should come to an untimely passing before they'd had their two children, due almost exclusively to accident, the parents of the deceased Huhuneem were expected to replace them with another. In the event this was not possible, another couple would be made to produce a child for the pair unable to. In all other ways, however, all couples ceased such activities and drifted apart, free of any compulsion to remain together, either through feeling or obligation. As theirs was a purely rational society, they found no need for supplementary consortation. I could recognize a few of the benefits, but to my mind, this form of pure, uncaring, nonspecial life was most cold and mechanic.

Even in death, as previously noted, there was little energy devoted to the deceased, who were taken far away from the town and buried in some place unknown to the others and quickly forgotten. There was no service, wake, celebration, or any feelings of joy or grief at the passing of a Huhuneem, for it was but a regular part of life and of little importance in the grand scheme of things. No one horse mattered more or less than any other to any other. Therefore, apart from the unceremonious burial, there were no other observances.

The choices they made, if indeed there ever was any decision to be made by the Huhuneem, were based on pure, simple, basic reason at the expense of any emotion. This is not to say they possessed no emotion at all, for they were obviously curious and inquisitive, as evidenced by their continued conversations with me, they were caring of one another, in a strictly impersonal way, and they showed disgust, with respect to the Yahoos exclusively. In our world, we have explored through many of our arts the idea of cold, rational beings. In my mind, it is just not imaginable for a normal, healthy human to be more or less than the sum of their emotions.

A boundless amount of time did I spend trying to elucidate the idea of emotions. I would, with great pleasure, enlarge upon the subjects of love, friendship, trust, pleasure, inspiration. So, too, did I explain the contrasting grief, and those of pain, suffering, loss, defeat, misery, and sadness. Hue and Big Black would listen aloofly and dismiss such absurdities as the wasted efforts of a distasteful species. They noted that all of the good I described had a corresponding ill; therefore, it made little sense to seek one when the other would certainly follow in equal measure. To take joy in the birth of a child, only to grieve the loss of a parent, only served to be an irrelevant distraction, and too frequently, an undesirable one.

No amount of conversation would move the Huhuneem from this position. I was forced to abandon the effort. I must make the reader aware that though my efforts could frequently be seen as endeavours to convince the horses of the merits of mankind, most often, I was trying less to mollify and modify their position than I was cementing my own position, as we are all wont to do from time to time. Faced with a race of intelligent, but uncaring, aliens, I was presented with an opportunity to question, explore, experiment, refute, and validate my thoughts regarding humanity. I have concluded that though our lives are full of the slings and arrows of outrageous fortune, it is through our struggle and frequent victory over these that makes us happier, healthier, and better than ones who do not experience such emotions.

CHAPTER 1.16

The author finds himself the subject of unwanted attention and suffers a traumatic event at the hands of a Yahoo.

THOUGH I SPOKE to many a Huhuneem about diverse topics during my time with them, I never revealed anything or asked anything about the Yahoos with whom I had been discovered. They held those Yahoos in the highest of contempt as criminals, pirates, and raiders. I was wise to avoid reminding them of my association. On my escorted field trips, I discreetly sought to discover what had become of my original hosts. The forest was a fair distance from the village. If they were watching, or present at all, I could not discern. In truth, I knew not whether they had survived the event in which I was captured, but I felt it wiser to downplay that particular interaction. Nevertheless, I did think of Hu regularly, and often my mind would wonder back to the wild woman in the caves who first took care of me.

I knew, from personal experience, the speed and dexterity of my masters. Many might question whether a horse is capable of true dexterity. On this subject, I've had to complete some research to explain that in the place of hands, of course, the horse has hooves. The Huhuneem used their hoof, which was jointed more flexibly from that of a typical horse, to form a pincer grip against the long pastern bone. The action best resembled the action of holding a pencil between the tips of all fingers in a glove against the wrist. Their dexterity in this effort was defter than one would assume. On one occasion, I was able to convince one visitor to hold my now blunted writing instrument. She was able to hold the dull pencil and trace the motions of written words.

Now as for speed, I had witnessed the horses move with great speed through the forest much faster than I could manage and well above even the velocity I witnessed amongst the spelunkers. If I were to run from them, I would not be able to get far unless I were to climb high into the trees. I felt certain that even then there was not much chance I would be able to escape, even if I had a place to which I could return. After a couple years amongst the Huhuneem, I had heard nothing of my former friends. Even were I able to stray beyond the grasp of my escorts, I could only stay in a tree for so long. I would be forced to either reveal the location of the cave or find forage on the ground and certainly be captured. Such a prospect, recapture, was enough to keep me in line. I feared my misbehaviour might result in my expulsion from my nest, to live in confinement alongside the antagonistic Yahoo.

I had, of course, over the years spent some time and effort improving upon my dwelling. With permission, I first sought some branches and created a kind of teepee made of sticks. Unable to manoeuvre the logs of the trees, and without tools or assistance and aching ribs, I instead found the longest, straightest branches I could in the forest and carried them in small loads back to my nest. Gradually, I built and expanded upon the structure. I learned through observation and inspection of the long log house how to use grasses to thatch and enclose the building. With practice, and an intense workout regime to first bring my body back to health and then to keep it mobile, I was able to construct a livable structure and camp near the cattle. Big Black provided me with a mat, which I placed on top of the straw for a more cushioned bed. I collected discarded feathers from the fowl to improve it further. It was a modest but manageable home, and the Huhuneem ensured no Yahoo was allowed in proximity. It was no match for the log house in terms of size, sophistication, or stability, but it was nevertheless a small wonder amongst the Huhuneem. Like a great monument, it always demanded the attention of whoever came to visit.

In time, I came to view this place as my home, albeit one surrounded by savage and revolting Yahoos and cold, uncaring, and potentially hostile equine captors. I scrounged my existence from the grains I could process and collected berries, nuts, and roots, and even trapped the occasional squirrel, rabbit, or rat for a rare bit of meat. My clothes gradually dissolved through wear, so I patched them with that which was available. I was scarcely able to maintain all but the most basic covering. It was of little concern to my hosts, but my increasing exposure began to draw some additional unwanted attention from the female Yahoos.

On one occasion, I was out in the open, preparing to excurse to the woods with Honey. I made eye contact with a red-haired she-Yahoo, who was standing next to the vicious male. I expected the male to be the threat as the two of them split apart keeping their eyes locked firmly on me. As they spread to a point where I could no longer watch both of them simultaneously, I kept my eyes on the male. The she-Yahoo took advantage of a moment of distraction amongst the Huhuneem, who were engaged in their own activities, and broke into a run directly towards my person. She covered the distance quickly, despite her low, squatted run and a hobble. I was barely able to gulp out a short "Whoa!" before she was upon me. I would have been better served to run, but she leapt upon me and I braced for the impact. She hit me high and struck me to the ground with her momentum. She encompassed my body in her arms on the ground, in a flattering, if immoderate manner. I howled in terror. She howled too. In short order, Honey arrived, and she released me to retreat back to her point of origin. The male stood some distance away with a wry smile curling his lips.

This proved, too, to be a matter of some humour to the Huhuneem and a traumatic experience for me. This aged Yahoo, for I estimated her age to have been between twenty and twenty-five, which amongst the Yahoo was virtually ancient, made it clear to all that I was certainly a Yahoo. Only one of their own kind would elicit such a rash and reckless action. These same two Yahoos afterwards stood at a distance, howling at me, and were joined in the chorus by several more. I realized they were mocking me and my yell. They hooted and hollered loudly until corralled back into their dormitory.

I took to carrying a weapon after that day, a shillelagh I fashioned from a stick with a particularly large knot. In actual fact, to say I fashioned this deterrent is an exaggeration. The truth is, I found a reasonable one and tucked it into my waistband to fend off future attacks. In so doing, I provided evidence of the industry of man in the art of war and would be further prodded on the need and innovation of such devices.

CHAPTER 1.17

The author discusses technology and development.

I THINK SOME censure has been directed over the openness with which I criticized the people of my world. As I relate the tale of this adventure, my narrative is perhaps tinted by the lens through which the Huhuneem viewed my thoughts. On one subject, though, I felt there could be little dispute on the value of human innovation, and it all came about because of a stick.

When I took up arms, I was asked to explain the utility of the short knobby rod I carried. I explained I would use it for self-defence and demonstrated with the assistance of some sticks the additional power the torque of the stick would provide me. In my previous encounters with aggressive Yahoos, I had been ridiculed for my inability to fend off either the man or the woman. I confirmed I could not break a stick of sufficient diameter with just my arms and hands, but with the aid of the shillelagh, I could do much more. Big Black concurred that while the Huhuneem, being the most powerful and wise, needed no such technology, we, the

Yahoo, would have need of such tools, particularly as all species possessed a hatred of Yahoos above all other.

Apart from the weaponry, of which we had already spoken, Big Black desired to know all the other tools that had been created by man. I told him I should never be able to explain all the tools man had constructed. Nevertheless, he implored me to try.

Starting with some basic agriculture, I described the plough. Explaining the need to soften the ground, I described the heavy metal blades we had created that could till the soil when drawn by a beast of burden, such as an ox. I spoke of axes and knives and the extensive list of occupations towards which they are applied. I described the use of fire for preparing metal, for melting and sealing, and of course, for its use in the generation of electricity through the burning of fossil fuels such as coal, gas, and oil. Expanding on that subject, I explained that lightning was a concentrated form of electricity, and we had learned to harness the same power through practice and experimentation using a scientific method. I talked of communications and the invention of machines that allowed us to speak and even see others on the other side of the world from our own homes.

To better explain human innovation, I said that for every difficulty we face, we search for, and generally find, a technological solution. Our lives are enriched by the work of countless generations of innovation and improvement. Anything that made our lives difficult in the past is mitigated through the incessant progress of society. We found minerals in the ground that contain huge amounts of stored energy, and when burned, release it. We harness that potential to great industry. In a world full of billions of humans, there is an enormous need for such things. Those places that lack them live uncharmed lives of poverty and sadness. Humans work every day to make the world a better place through scientific advancement.

I could have prattled on endlessly about technology, but my audience cared little for this huhuhooing. They noted that things must have been most horrible in our history to necessitate so much invention. I replied about the ingenuity of people throughout our history. Of course, I know little of times prehistoric. However, great works still remain that prove the authenticity of many stories from our history. At length, I described the empire of Rome and the network of roads they constructed to make movement across prodigious distances fast and consistent. Further, I spoke about their aqueducts: huge stone troughs held high above the ground and reservoirs, enormous bowls to store months worth of water, that provided a stable, secure supply, even in times of drought. Then came my stories of the Incans who carefully crafted terraces into steep mountainsides, turning inhospitable and unproductive land into high, productive oases and the Chinese who invested enormous time and effort to tame great rivers to stabilize and normalize the flow of these hydraulic lifelines.

I spoke of the many uses we had contrived for those places where a course of water proved to be stable and predictable, where we used wheels powered by water flow to turn turbines that powered machines, generated power, or directly milled grains into flour. We harnessed the water's buoyancy to transport logs from upstream to down where they would be processed into materials suitable for construction. We cut canals to link waterways, and I explained the utility of two of the most famous, the Suez and Panama Canals, that shorten the maritime distance between oceans.

The Huhuneem took particular interest in my description of a mill. They had no need for such intense processing of their grains and were happy to eat it raw, but they had seen the work I had to perform to produce my hard tack. If they had been cursed with weakness of body and lack of strength, it was agreeable we would have need of such aids.

I would format my lectures on technology and advancement with a simple template. First, I would speak of the need and explain how our inferior bodies necessitated such an innovation. Next, I would speak of the innovation and how it worked, most often building on previous devices and ideas, which often would require me to circle back to explain one or another fundamental concept. Then, often, I would have to admit the several new, smaller challenges that subsequently followed.

I had even spoken of and demonstrated written language. I presented to them the need thusly: due to our complicated society and the increasing number of inventions and technology, no single person possessed sufficient knowledge, and they could not be expected to remember everything and how it worked to be able to pass on that information to their progeny. A system of permanent record had been created over generations to store that information. I told them about the numerous languages and alphabets that had been created and tried to explain the benefits of a written account over oral tradition.

I even tried to play the telephone game, but the Huhuneem, with strong hearing and a stubborn resolve to not pass along uncertain truths, were always successful in translating the message. I had to explain that human ears were not so efficient, and that a competitive spirit implored us to pass along our best guesses instead of confirming for certainty.

Creating a written record required inventing new devices to copy, write, store, and transfer that information. Early writing had been done on clay tablets and stone before papyrus and paper were invented to make transportation easier. With the invention of paper, tools were needed to pulp trees. This led to a demand for more lumber and tools to better harvest it. Each invention, every idea, created more less significant needs, and each subsequent invention solved a less critical issue.

I spent a great deal of time discussing mathematics and philosophy. Basic arithmetic was a concept within the grasp of the Huhuneem, though they had not formalized it. To build and maintain their simple villages, basic addition and subtraction were obviously understood. More complicated concepts such as multiplication and division were less well formed. Advanced subjects like algebra, calculus, computation, probability, and formalized logic proved to be too great a challenge to convey. Some might criticize my methods, but as I was not trained in education, I only drew from what I could. The reader will remember, too, that the language of instruction contained none of these words and little width for satisfactory and supplementary elaboration.

In my life, I had spent most of eighteen years in the full-time pursuit of knowledge and education. During the prevalent share of this, all of my other needs—housing, clothing, food, entertainment, companionship, and love—were provided to me by my family and friends, allowing my pure focus on my pursuits. The Huhuneem engaged with me on a part-time basis, and all the while, I learned about their history, culture, language, and society.

Furthermore, I was subjected to the flowering concept of doubt. If a teenager struggles in school, they might ask why they would ever need to understand how to solve a quadratic equation. The reader, I hope, will understand that this sort of questioning, when posed by a horse on an isolated island somewhere in the Pacific Ocean, with no desire higher than to eat, sleep, grow, and perpetuate their society, is particularly difficult to answer. Even the Huhaneem's curiosity was limited by a lack of desire to improve. Gradually, the interests of my master students diminished. Despite a reduction in conversations, I continued to seek out more about their traditions.

CHAPTER 1.18

The author ruminates on the subject of the history of Yahoos and Huhuneems.

AS THE INTEREST of the Huhuneems declined, I asked as much as I could of Honey about their island and history and what had been passed down through their oral history. The other Huhuneem were becoming less willing with time, perhaps because my novelty was fading. I feared for the consequences of this. My uniqueness, and the interest I elicited from my masters was an important staple of my continued existence here. Honey, on the other hand, seemed to still be most interested in my world and willing to share about hers, but only away from the settlements while we explored the countryside.

As the events of the past are not seen to be of particular importance, a lifestyle whereby little of great events or unexpected news occurs and where supposition, philosophy, and theory have no place, the history of the island was relatively pure and simple. In this chapter, I will relay the history of the Yahoos, the history of the Huhuneem, and the three major events in the interaction of the two races worthy of any mention and remembrance.

On the subject of the Huhuneem, it was understood that they were the peak of perfection. All other things paled in comparison, and little else mattered. The Huhuneem had lived on this island forever, or for as long as anybody cared to remember. I poked and prodded at this, trying to pry out some semblance of theology, but the door was firmly barred. What was here before the Huhuneem, or how the Huhuneem came to exist in the first place, was inconsequential, unknown, and not worth understanding.

Amongst our kind, there are those who desire to live a simple life, free of the contrivances of modern living, of byzantine complications, fully understood or understandable by none. It can feel like life and society are balanced upon the head of a pin, and by virtue of the offices and artifacts thereupon balanced, the imminent collapse of its entirety is virtually assured. Amongst the Huhuneem, there was beauty on the simplistic surface, but underneath boiled a cauldron of unaddressed affliction. Of this I'm fairly certain.

The Huhuneem had always been the supreme species, and it was as simple as that. I suppose this history is a little light on detail, but without conjecture or archaeological evidence, I can provide little more.

It was known that Huhuneems had settled in one of the other villages first, and gradually, very gradually, they had spread to cover the island in equally spaced settlements of identical size and importance. The village in which I found myself had been founded at least one hundred generations ago. This would equate to something in the environs of four to six hundred years. The impetus to create a new village occurs only when an existing village is destroyed by some natural disaster. In such an event, the village might split into two to settle a new area. If a single new settlement is successful, the other can be reincorporated. If both gain a foothold, both settlements will grow to the ideal, original size, creating two sister colonies from one former source. Other communities, of course, welcome and support the refugees while they stake out, but in short order, they create their own homes in the new locales.

The Huhuneem kept no track of exceptional people or leaders, for all were considered the same. No wars, no innovation, philosophy, or art had rendered any need to remember great people moot. My recognition of Big Black and Honey might be the only two recorded members of their civilization, a fact that even today gives me pause at the enormity of such a statement.

On the subject of Yahoos, the Huhuneem tracked only three events. The Yahoos were not of this place originally. How they arrived is unknown, but the original Yahoos, a breeding pair evidently, were first seen on a mountain. The contemporary Huhuneem had been unimpressed with these beings and had devoted little attention to them. In a short time, the Yahoos had spread and multiplied to encompass the entirety of the island. This caused a strain on the resources, even of the Huhuneem. The Yahoo were a plague that was seen to have infested the island.

The Huhuneem had made quarry of the Yahoos, and through the slaughter of the elders, the infestation had been brought to heel. Then each Huhuneem took a number of them to use as draft animals as I had myself witnessed. It was thought that all of the Yahoos had been captured and pressed into the service of the Huhuneem, but some few remained and continued to flourish on the margins.

Many generations ago, a semirational Yahoo, similar to me, named Lemuel, appeared on the island. I learned it was this experience that informed their treatment of me. This man, who I believe must have come by ship around three hundred years ago, also taught the Huhuneem about the places from whence he had come and about the world of man. He had apparently taken quite a shine to the Huhuneem, who he came to view as his family, and sought to distance himself in every way from the filthy Yahoos. He spoke of the corruption and gross defect of man, and the Huhuneem judged, that based on his description, there was not a single merit in the existence of his people or the developments of the Yahoo.

I had asked why, with this history, they had chosen to accept me into their midst. Honey informed me it was because Big Black was uncertain I was truly a Yahoo. By the time they were all completely sure, they had found themselves willing to carry my slight burden.

The last major event had precipitated by the subsequent departure of this one man. The Huhuneem, finding the presence of the Yahoo noisome, filthy, malicious, and deplorable, had long debated a concerted effort to eradicate the pestilence from the land. Through the learnings presented by my predecessor, the decision had been made to eliminate all those but the tamest and most docile of Yahoos already in service. Long ago, then, this final resolution had been made, agreed to, and committed. The wretched Yahoos had been systematically destroyed as would be cattle that had contracted some communicable disease. Those Yahoos that remained in the service of the Huhuneem thus were the descendants of a pliable minority, and though they continued to be known for their abhorrent and atrocious behaviour, I was assured that these were of substance better than their forebears.

I admit to feeling shock and disappointment at hearing of the treatment of these people. Even though they had a tendency to treat me with loathsome habit, in my mind, they were still people. I could not imagine a more horrendous punishment than to serve a master who had pursued and decimated my ancestry on a decision resolved upon the teachings of a single person and the natural acts they betook. I thought to the behaviours of caged, mistreated animals and found I could identify with the Yahoos, even the vicious male, confined though they were to their cages and taught to be hostile to every living thing. I hoped my interaction with the Huhuneem would produce a dissimilar service to those unfortunate souls than as befell them the last time a visitor had dropped in.

I inquired as to the whereabouts of the man, Lemuel, and to where he had fled. I was told he fashioned a boat and stitched together the carcass skins of several Yahoos as a sail and fled the island to another smaller island visible off the shore. He was not heard from after. It seemed to me there could be no way I would have a similar impact on this place. What sort of an abhorrent aberration was this man who had so misrepresented his people? I became determined, more than before, to present my conversation in a positive, though always truthful, light.

CHAPTER 1.19

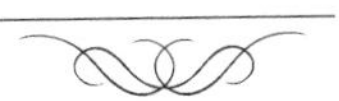

The author experiences the quadrennial.

THE PRIMES OF each hamlet met every four years on the summer solstice to reconnect, take inventory, and discuss important affairs, of which there rarely were any. I had been told that at these quadrennials, historically, they used to debate the extermination of the Yahoos, up until the year following Lemuel's departure. It was at this meeting they had decided to proceed. The affair was highly regimented and ritualized, and each village took their position according to the order in which they had been founded. One representative was present, no more, no less, to bring forward matters, and in the same order, they prepared their brief oration.

And so, after three and a half years living amongst the Huhuneem, the first quadrennial coincided. It is a matter of course that I was not present for the meeting, nor was I anywhere nearby. I was informed of the structure and format by Big Black only upon his return. Those who were not privileged to be part of the highest position in each township were not informed of anything that went on in this place and never asked. I, being a curious observer to their activities, did not observe the same respect for blind tradition and grilled my host at the conclusion of the quadrennial.

It no doubt comes as little surprise to my readers the principal topic of discussion at this summit. As far as I'm aware, the subject, "What about the unique Yahoo?" was probably the only matter discussed. The representation of every village on the island knew of me. In truth, most had come to see the exceptional and incredible Yahoo. I was told by my host that this meeting lasted longer than any he had before attended, and the discussion evidently focused on what should be done with me. Though not inclined to lie when posed with a question, my master had learned to avoid answering, whether through a change of subject or by simply going quiet. In this way, it was no demanding thing to circumvent his limited capabilities. I deduced through direct questions that my presence was not particularly desired by most. I, as with the previous visitor, was seen to be a source of trouble. Honey, my usual source of information, also became quiet on the subject.

Quietly, I began to make my preparations to flee the island. I gathered supplies of food and collected leaves from the forest as I had been taught years ago. I stocked up twine and prepared ropes. At every chance I got, I practiced my swimming and worked hard to get into peak physical condition.

After a few stiflingly quiet days, I received word from my friend; the decision had been made to push me into a low tide from the same beach from whence the previous visitor had made his escape. They were not to provide any warning, as she was to me providing right now. I was to have but one chance to swim to safety on the far island. It was to be adjudicated that my fate would be determined by my ability to swim. Honey took me to where I had been beached, and the seat cushions of the aeroplane had been discovered, and she permitted me to scout out my point of exile.

We jogged to the beaches, a trip that took a few hours, and burst through a thin veil of forest to the very spot I had first encountered Hue. It was, coincidentally, near to where I was to be set to sea. My fortune proved great. My original vessel had only washed a little higher up on the beach, and I hoped it would still maintain buoyancy. The beach had the same salty smell I remembered in detail, and I imagined I could feel my burning skin scorched from the sun. By way of distance, this beach was much closer to Hue's settlement. In fact, my white escort brought me close enough to see this village.

She permitted me to return several times over the next few weeks while we awaited the date of my expulsion. The conversations with my host, Big Black, became fewer and fewer. Apart from a few brief tête-à-têtes with a few red and white Huhuneem, it was clear my time was coming to an end. I asked Big Black direct questions about whether my fate would be determined in the next week, and he said no. I pressed further and asked if in the next fortnight, and that answer he diverted. It was clear I had only a week of safety to prepare for my next odyssey. Each day, I was taken by Honey to the beach, and from there I moved the cushions to the launch point. We continued our conversations, but they grew more focused on my plans. It didn't occur to me that I ought not to have trusted Honey, as many have since suggested. I suppose it might be seen as a weakness that I see individuals not as part of their encompassing group, but as individuals and measure them on their own merits. I see now that trusting her could have led to my downfall. On the other hand, by virtue of my transparency and trust placed in her, she developed a sense of trust in me that would probably have otherwise been impossible. Especially considering the dominant view of Yahoos in this place, and the only one she had ever known, I found her leap of faith to be far more laudable than my own.

As I scouted the beach at my point of exile, in the distance, I could make out the dark silhouette of an island. I could not say how large, only that there was some solid ground towards which I could aim. I felt that despite my efforts, I was not going to be able to swim there, and certainly not while carrying supplies. I beseeched my companion to allow me to work on some provisions, and thankfully, she complied. She even helped by providing some articles from the settlement. The waves on this beach were fiercer than those of the beach upon which I landed. Instead of sand, this was a rocky and unprotected shore.

I carefully hid my craft within the brush, lest it be discovered prematurely, and moved my supplies to this beach. Each day, we ran for several hours to and from the strand, and each day, my preparations better manifested. I had lashed together three large logs, bored a couple holes in them with the help of my equine friend, and stuck two smaller logs through. At the ends of these, I strapped the floatable aeroplane seats and thatched a sort of triangular mesh from the centre hull to both of the outriggers. I had no sail and could certainly not bring myself to replicate the reported Yahoo-skin sail of my predecessor. Instead, I found a wide and thin chunk of wood to serve as a paddle. I fortified the middle with a pair of straight, round, smoothed sticks from the village. These I also tied together down the entire length with my rope.

Then one day, my companion could see I was nearing completion and had been made aware that we were to host an unusual number of guests in the coming night. She cryptically told me she had found informative many of our discussions and appreciated those things I had shared. I knew beyond any doubt this would be my final night on the island, and I thanked her sincerely for her service. We returned to the village, and I retired to my nest for the night.

The next day, visitors, all great, black males of the stature of Big Black, began to arrive early in the day. I was met, not with the usual formality and dialogue with which I had become accustomed, but with more of the disdain I had first encountered. This was no surprise. These visitors were arriving to observe and validate my execution by sea. Big Black took only a moment to inform me that we would all be going on a long walk the next day, the sort of half-truth I had grown to expect. He would not take any questions and hurriedly returned to the care of his guests. My senses peaked as I mentally prepared myself for my escape.

As night fell, the Huhuneem receded into the long log house with their guests, leaving me alone in my nest. I gathered up my final supplies and went to deliver one last gift for this island. Instead of heading directly to my escape, I went to the kennels. As quietly as I had learned, with the grace and strength I had developed, I eked through the portal. To my delight, the Yahoos therein were already asleep. The Huhuneem had fed them extra to make them more pliable and less ornery around the distinguished guests, and with such a great gathering, even the usual guards were pressed into service in the main house. I loosened and cut the ties to each Yahoo I safely could without waking any. Several were asleep too close to the bindings, and I was unable to approach, but I was able to release twenty-one males and eighteen females. Carefully and quietly I propped open the door and took my leave. I hoped the Yahoos would awake before the Huhuneem returned. It was a long shot at best to think the Yahoos would flee to safety without alerting their masters, but it was the only option I could provide.

Under the cloak of darkness, I ran towards the beach where my craft lay in wait. No time was there for me to find the white horse, nor could I risk it. As I carefully skirted Hue's village, now in the middle of the night, a risky thought came to me. Deciding my fate was already tenuous at best, I headed through the tree rows towards the settlement. Here I found, laid out almost identically to my former home, a similar, but larger log house, and a correspondingly sized kennel for their Yahoos. As I had in my village, I ducked into the prison and carefully cut the bonds of my fellow men and women. Aware of every swish of straw under my bare feet, and alert to the smallest groan from the prisoners, I was able to free the entire lot and ensure the door was unable to close.

Finally, I made my final trip to my escape craft. The low tide coincided with a full moon, and I understood the Huhuneem had selected a neap tide to give me the fairest chance at survival. I quietly thanked them for their foresight. The same moon that provided me with illumination would, I hoped, grant me the outgoing tide to propel me towards my destination.

CHAPTER 1.20

The author affects his escape from the island of the Huhuneem towards an uncertain future.

BY THE LIGHT of the new moon, I hauled my trimaran from the bush towards the shore. Somewhere to the northeast lay my destination. Even in the full light of day, I could scarcely make it out. A cool breeze blew in from the sea. As I dragged my craft across the smooth rocks in a tense haste, I lost my footing on more than a few occasions. Shins and knees would turn black and blue later, but for now, my survival depended on this one shot. I was a marked Yahoo, sentenced to exile. Even if it were not for my final acts, never again would I be allowed on this land.

The waves rippled on the rock high on the seashore. Reading the seaweed, I believed this to be the highest tide. Providentially, I had chosen what must be deemed the perfect time.

I took a break from pulling the boat and collected several long, straight-as-I-could find logs. With these, I formed a ladder from the bush to the sea to use as rollers as I had not previously considered the combined weight of the craft and supplies I had to carry. I was grinding the ship too slowly and was apprehensive of every second it took. I gambled that a few minutes of preparation might save me an hour or more of brute force and ignorance. It took several excruciating minutes to transport the heavy raft, made heavier by my exertion and push to reach the beach in a minimum of time, to the water.

When it was halfway engaged, I withdrew my supplies and tied them to the triangular cargo meshes. I had not gathered a great many, but these added mass to the enterprise. To me, they felt like anchors. With all my strength, I heaved the boat off the final roller, and to my eternal relief, it mostly floated. The water eventually picked up its share of the weight, and it became easier. As I watched the tree line, certain I had or would hear some noise, I broke free of the land and waded into the sea.

I walked the boat as far as I was able, conscious my arms would likely be taxed again by the next part of the dubious voyage. I hoisted myself up onto the centre hull. There, I swung my leg over the central hump and straddled the trio of logs just ahead of the crossbeams. I picked up the paddle, held it to my right and paddled with everything I had to escape the bay.

I thought back one last time with mixed emotions to the island of the Huhuneem and Yahoos. I thought of Hu, who I hoped was well; I thought of Honey; and I even spared a brief thought for the Yahoos and the fate to which I had exposed them.

In spite of the low chance of success that lay before me of reaching an island of unknown size, whereupon I was determined to land and create for myself a permanent home, there arose in me a feeling of relief and even exaltation. Even if the odds were against me, they were still better than any alternative. The fear of what lay behind diminished quickly with each inefficient stroke. I knew the Huhuneem had no interest in swimming in the ocean, nor would they be so disposed to vengeance or punishment to overcome their reticence. As long as I never stepped foot on the island again, I would be permanently free of this peril. The adrenaline drove me forward, and bit by bit, I was able to pull the boat out into the bay.

The receding tide aided my escape, but the wind, combined with the ocean current, drove me further north in the darkness than I had intended to go. I relaxed my stroke as the excitement wore off and settled into a more consistent, regimented pace. I continued to pull in the direction towards which I believed the island lay, but with the only landmark behind me, I was at some disadvantage. For several hours, I pulled at my one oar until the new day dawned.

I must have crossed a distance of several kilometres during the night. When I looked back, I saw an unfamiliar part of the coast, and the island I was fleeing to, in the direction I was now facing, was no longer visible on the horizon. The only option was to continue away from the island of the Huhuneem and Yahoos.

Quite different from when I arrived on the island, my skin was now a much darker hue, able to withstand greater exposure to the rays of the sun. I had prepared for a long day-or-two ferry followed by a period of settling. To this end, I had food enough for a week or so but only enough water enclosed in leaves to last for a couple days. I carefully rationed my food, sheltered under a couple leaves, and converted my paddle into a mast, hanging a few more leaves as a weak sail.

The boat then sailed east at a decent clip, considering the relative seaworthiness of the craft. I have no measure of the distance I travelled, but on the third day, just after noon, a land mass emerged from the sea directly in my channel. As the land got closer, trees became visible, and several other islands materialized. I had sailed towards a Pacific Ocean archipelago.

Amongst the islands were even a number of boats. Tired and exhausted, I made an effort to flag them down as I approached. A Melanesian fisherman from Vanuatu came over to investigate my crude craft. Over the years, as my clothes had disintegrated, I had lost a modicum of modesty. I wore only my belt, my club, and a few tattered rags. The gentleman greeted me in French, a language I had once known but had not heard or practiced during my time with the Huhuneem. The gears of my mind ground out the word "Allo!"

Then he asked me, "Où allez-vous? D'ou venez-vous?" I answered him clumsily, "Je suis Canadien! Où sommes?"

CHAPTER 1.21

The author describes his adventure and is returned home.

NOT LONG AFTER our brief exchange, my first with another, contemporary human in much time, the fine man threw out a rope and provided a pair of shorts. He commented on my strange, breathy, accent and fed and clothed me.

I should note to the reader something of the way it feels to be back amongst one's own kind after such a long time in the presence of an entirely different sentient race. I had grown accustomed to being viewed as the inferior body, the inferior race, and it had actually sunk into me a little bit that I was not worth as much as the Huhuneem around me. With the fisherman, I was treated as an equal, and even as an honoured guest. I didn't scrounge for food that I made poorly myself; he provided me with a simple meal, by most standards, but a luxury that was to my elation.

There is an amazing feeling of liberation when one is granted a right of equality, true equality. It was as though a weight were taken off my back, restraints removed from my wrists, and a gag removed from my mouth. I had spent much of my time with the Huhuneem in conversation, trying to explain to them how my world worked, and it was freeing to speak with the fisherman without feeling judged and disrespected.

This may seem contrary to that which I have just reported, but of course the first thing I told him certainly aroused some suspicions. I told him I had been marooned on an island where the horses were civilized and the humans were feral. You can imagine that he did question my sanity, particularly considering he met me floating on a raft with no clothes. Whether he truly believed me or not, I don't know, but he listened quietly and patiently. I suppose he might have been lonely, and like me, eager to share in the company of another human. He made for Honiara, the capital of the Solomon Islands.

We made our way to the British High Commissioner in the Solomon Islands. I related my story to the high commissioner, who certainly questioned my sanity, but passed the word along to my government.

It took some discussion with Canadian authorities to prove that I was who I said I was, being that I had been dead some time according to the record. A complicated process took place where they validated my records, reviewed photographic identification, and challenged my memory to recall details of my past life. Finally, they arranged for my safe return home.

The reader will understand my trepidation at boarding a trans-Pacific flight, or really any aircraft. After suffering the crash and subsequent events, I could have easily consigned myself to a quiet life secluded on an island inhabited by only sentient species, and at that, only one of them. Such a fate was not due unto me. I prepared for another trek back, across the great ocean, home.

My case developed a sort of celebrity. As far as the world had known, I had been deceased these last four years, killed on the infamous Flight 1726. I spoke with my recently unbereaved parents by video chat courtesy of the BBC and assured them I was, by all measures, fine. My hosts at the British High Commissioner had me thoroughly evaluated by the best doctors available on the island, both physically and mentally. Apart from my experiences on the island of the Yahoo and Huhuneem, I was determined to be in excellent health. The doctor's report read that I was physically strong and healthy, and emotionally and psychologically reactive and responsive. Tests of my identity, including the conversation with my parents, had confirmed I was indeed who I claimed to be. Thus, was I to be repatriated to Canada at the first opportunity.

My former employer—or perhaps they were still technically my employer as I had never resigned, been fired, retired, laid off, or otherwise had my employment formally terminated by either party, though I believed my death certificate had perhaps formalized my cessation of employment—was eager and willing to participate in my recovery and restoration to my home. A small commercial jetliner was sent to the island for my recovery. The costs for this were shared between the governments of my homeland, my employer, without acknowledging fault or responsibility, and a small detachment of reporters who hitched a ride to interview and catalogue my story.

I boarded the plane in the morning, and contrary to expectations, the distraction of the press corps assisted me in forgetting my previous incident. Aboard the plane were half a dozen print reporters representing magazines and news conglomerates, two crews of camera reporters, and a number of representatives of the Canadian government dispatched to help me reintegrate while minimizing the culture shock inherent in someone who has been absent for several years. I had dissuaded my family from joining the circus, hoping to see them instead on the ground at home.

I boarded the plane and took a seat near the back. I had been near the back of the plane in my previous flight when we had fallen, and in this position, I felt more comfortable than I think one might imagine. Conflicting emotions arose in me for sure. On the one hand I had significant experience on aeroplanes, most without any sort of incident. Of course, my most recent flight had provided more than enough of a counter-example to merit some slight anxiety. I told myself one bad experience ought not to weigh as heavily on me as the many positives. I even told myself that the likelihood of suffering two accidents was so minuscule as to be laughable. Evidently this worked, and I sat with unexpected calm and comfort.

The reporters asked me about every detail of my harrowing experience and noted every word in their laptops, recorders, cameras, and notepads. They asked about the flight, and I told them all the details I could remember. They, in turn, filled me in on some of the publicly known details. The plane had flown directly into Typhoon Horai, against advisement. It had maintained elevation without radio contact for some time before disappearing from radar. A search and rescue operation had been hampered by the weather, but to my great amazement, three other passengers had survived and been recovered in an emergency life raft. The remains of the plane itself had not been found, nor had the black box. After an exhaustive search, it was determined there could be no other survivors. Using some surface current models and the rescue location several days after the accident, the crash site was only confined to a small four million square kilometre area somewhere off Vanuatu.

The decision was made to minimize the time over the ocean, at my behest. We flew first towards Japan, skirting over Papua New Guinea, Indonesia, the Philippines, and Taiwan. I wished never again to find myself in the open sea, whereabouts unknown and without emergency equipment and was determined to avoid ever testing fate again. At my insistence, I was eventually allowed to carry a pocket knife, compass, pencils and a sealable notepad, and a sardine can full of waterproof matches. In ordinary circumstances, I'm aware these provisions, several of them at least, would not be permitted, but exceptions were made for me at every turn. I thoroughly inspected the plane myself. Not that I possessed any knowledge of advanced aerospatial engineering or mechanics, but I looked anyway to make sure everything looked clean and properly maintained. The pilot was sent specifically for his experience as a test pilot with the air force. No expense was spared to make my flight as comfortable as possible.

The bird took off gracefully, after scooting down the runway, and as my white knuckles grasped the arms of the chair for the dearest of life, the cacophonic sounds of the runway and roaring echo of the engine faded to a familiar quiet liftoff into the forbidding blue sky. Never before had I feared takeoff so, and a nearby reporter, sensing my panic and terror, tried to soothe me with assurances, reminding me of the precautions that had been taken. As anybody with a phobic mind may explain, this did not give me any solace. As telling a depressed person to just be happy, telling an air disaster survivor it is perfectly safe is of little value. As we reached cruising altitude, I avoided looking out the window. I can't recall the smells, or even the first-class food that was provided. Those memories are void in my mind.

Every detail of my visit to the island, whether delusional or a fiction of my imagination, had been noted and recorded, packaged and prepared, to be shared with the world upon arrival, or likely even the moment we touched down in some location connected to the rest of the planet. I freely shared every detail that came to mind, as with this correspondence to you, my readers. I even shared specifics of location, having not considered the possible ramifications. I was possessed by a mind finally at peace amongst like-minded (and bodied) mortals, headed back to the place from whence I had come, and to those who loved and missed me greatly.

PART TWO

LOOGENAGE: IMMORTALITY

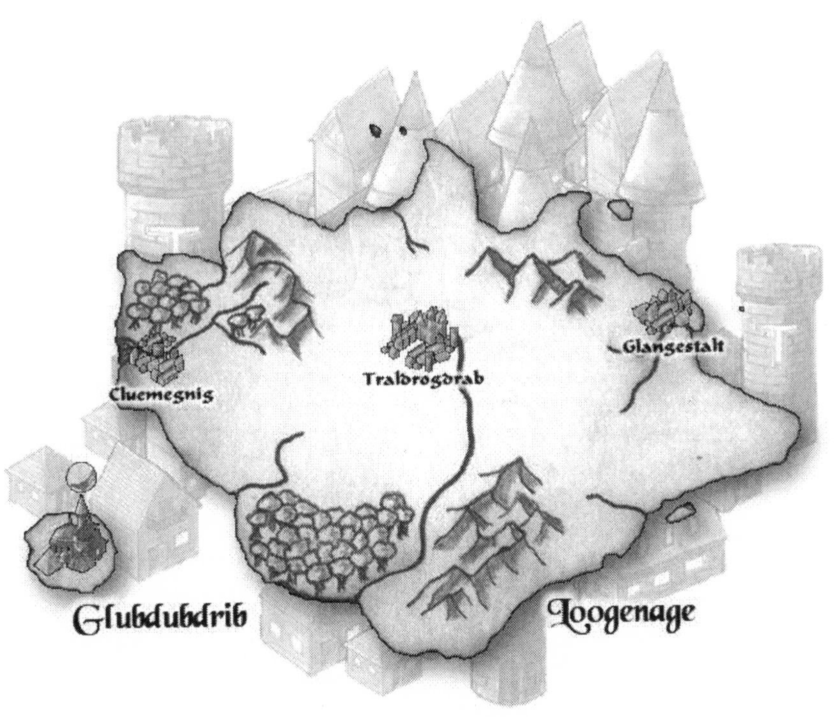

CHAPTER 2.1

A second incident befalls the author, who, though better prepared, relates his harrowing tale of survival once again.

THE WELL INFORMED and au currant amongst my readers are undoubtedly aware that my homecoming and restitution were not meant to be. After several hours of intense media scrutiny on board the flight, we ran into a sort of cascading mechanical and electronic failure I had never before encountered. Flying along the Pacific Rim, also known as the Ring of Fire, comes with certain slight, but real, threats.

A volcano in the Kagoshima Prefecture had briefly erupted as we were taking flight, spewing an exudate of tiny ash particles into the sky. I would only learn about this much later. The particulate matter had silently wafted several hundred kilometres directly into the path of my plane. As we approached the cloud, it appeared no more menacing than any normal atmospheric disturbance. I continued to avoid looking out the window until the lights flickered. When the main cabin illumination failed, the emergency lights took over. Considering the cargo on board, by which I, of course, refer to myself, there was more than the usual trepidation.

My company consulted their windows as they would a most trusted source. By this time, we were long removed from the small cloud. Unbeknownst to us, the fate of our flight was already foreordained. The experienced pilots were doing their utmost in the cockpit to secure control. With each effort, they lost more of the battle. A small but significant amount of tiny glass, metal, and stone particles had already coated the engines. One at a time, they were slowly shutting down, and the captain had begun to descend as gracefully as possible as the multiple hearts of the bird failed.

From our high cruising altitude, it was not clear to the unsuspecting passengers that the plane was dropping with such great precipitancy. As we approached the waters below, those around me began to panic in an altogether familiar manner. Those nearest my seat looked to me for guidance. It is a strange feeling to be the grizzled veteran of an air disaster, being looked to for leadership when truly, nothing but luck had preserved me in my previous experience. I gathered about me what soft objects were at hand and prepared to brace for impact. A funny thing about head trauma, for I'm certain this is what I suffered, is that my true memory ends here, long before we would strike the water. I'm almost certain I did no such thing, but the last thing I remember was standing up, wishing everybody the best of fortunes, and waving wider than the standard cabin width would have allowed.

I would awake some time later, floating in a personal life raft. I had ensured that redundant floatation and survival supplies had been stocked before departure. Beside me were several bottles of water and some fruit and cans of food. Once more, yours truly found himself floating somewhere in either the Pacific Ocean or the South China Sea, hoping for somebody, anybody, or rather, any human, to provide rescue.

I'm sure the reader will easily understand that I was less than excited at the prospect of landing on yet another unknown island. My desire for empiricism was easily outweighed by my desire for calm and security. Little was my disquietude directed towards the possible return to the island of the Huhuneem, but more towards a place of hostility, inhospitability, or maybe worse, uninhabitation.

I drifted lazily on the waves for several days, thankfully sufficiently outfitted with supplies and shelter to survive a week or more. I took note of my injuries, which, despite the duress of the trauma that must certainly have occurred, were only demonstrable through a single, penny-sized nip that must have been the foremost point of impact of my head, just over my eye.

Much of my time was spent trying to recall my last moments, but even to this day, I find I can no more remember those last minutes than I can grow a third arm at will. Often, I wondered to whom I was indebted for their service in stowing me aboard the craft and what had become of them. I tried to stay mentally strong, focusing on simple math problems and logic puzzles knowing I was suffering from a cruel concussion. Solving simple questions took longer than I felt they should, and whenever night fell, I felt my ability to see any distance diminished more quickly than the luminescence would otherwise command. In my head swam the language of the Huhuneem, along with the English and French I had recently had occasion to practice.

Late one night while I slept, the gentle undulation of the waves transitioned into rough surf. Waves broke around me and I realized I must be close to land, very close. Vision blurred by the diminished concussive nocturnal state, I struggled to make out the shore. I could see the waves and knew that with no great wind, they must be crashing towards the coast. I swung my arm into the water and paddled with the waves. In short order, I made landfall on a quiet beach of soft, fine granules of sand. I pulled the raft behind me beyond the sand and lay back in the raft and slept until morning.

CHAPTER 2.2

On this, a third island, the author meets a native and settles in for another stay in an alien land.

AFTER FOUR YEARS living amongst the Huhuneem and the Yahoo, one might imagine I would be well prepared for any adventure. Equally, it has to me been suggested that the prospect of another stranding on unknown shores would be beyond comprehension or even survival. Faced with the ludicrous reality, it is perhaps but sober pragmatism that best described my perspective.

As I awoke, still suffering from the obscuring curtain over my eyes, my first action was to survey my surroundings. It was a beach, not altogether unlike any other. A thick smell of brine hung in the air, and seagulls picked away at driftwood and stones, striking for food in the rocks amongst the barnacles and seaweed. I had pulled my raft above the high-water line indicated by the seaweed by a good two vertical metres, nearly a three metre distance from the gradually sloping sandy beach. I found myself at the foot of a steep sand escarpment with huge, erratic boulders jetting from the cliff as though fired into place by monumental ordnance.

Some fifty metres from where I had landed, when looking out to sea to the left, was a prodigious stone of about six metres in each dimension. I'm certain it must have weighed near to six hundred tonnes and was roughly the size of a two-car garage. It was towards this rock I made my first expedition. With my raft in tow behind, I hauled it farther up the shore, and finding a shallow slope, raised the craft on top. I applied a weighted ballast to preserve it against the tide.

It was tempting to try and scale the sandy precipice. Thinking better of it, I decided to round the beach beyond the point. Doing so meant walking beneath several large, exposed, but, I trusted, firmly ingrained monoliths, the kind that could easily crush your author should this be his time. I rounded the point and found a convenient dip in the slope where a slide had occurred and left in its wake a trail of smaller crushed boulders. A craggy path, it afforded me a passage to the superior vantage of the sand walls' peak. Unencumbered by my vessel, I scrambled up to discover the details of this new place. Sincerely, I hoped to find friendly and familiar civilization at the top of the cliff. I was not to find that which I sought.

As I crested the peak, before my eyes sprawled a display of profound beauty. I looked down upon a vast, undulating valley draped beautifully in a verdant sheet, represented by all tones and hues of green. It was composed of unconquerably great terraces, meticulously hewn and built of stone containing paddies of rice. Upon each stone wall dividing the terrace paddies were planted a row of cherry blossom trees, which, being of the late spring, were in magnificent pink bloom. Scarcely can I illustrate the scene, for I stood upon a high perch, looking towards a valley with all the beauty of Machu Picchu combined with Hiroshi Park.

Amongst the terraces were a connected series of pathways lined with compact almond trees, themselves blossoming with white flowers, highlighting and identifying the paths with a most beautiful ivory focus. Amongst the setting, I would have been justified to anticipate a dense populace, but as far as I could see, to the tall hills that enclosed the valley, scarcely a body could be found. Such was the beauty before me that hardly did I spare a thought for the striking panoramic view of the ocean at my back.

An entrancing concoction of the sea breeze and an unseen citrus grove filled my nose and raised my spirits. I felt such hope and wonder that I lost track of time. I failed to notice a young man emerge from a nearby paddy and step tentatively but deliberately to my perch on the dune.

I guessed the boy to be about sixteen years old. He stood tall to his height of about 170 cm, with posture fine, and he wore a magnificent royal blue silk kimono with a navy blue haori and hakama. Each piece seemed to me to be of the utmost quality. On his feet, he wore the simplest wooden sandals, as though in intentional contrast to the rest of his garb. By countenance, his face belied a Japanese heritage, his head nearly fully shaven excepting for a small cluster tied up in a knot on the top of his head. On his face was one distinguishing feature: a bright red, as the colour of ruby under a bright light, birthmark two centimetres superior to his left eyebrow.

The young gentleman bowed deeply, folding at his waist to a degree of an almost perfect ninety. Then he spoke swiftly with a well-practiced tongue in a sort of smooth pidgin that seemed to blur the sounds and structures of numerous languages, chiefly Japanese and Dutch. Obviously at a loss, for though I consider myself to be an able linguist, I could understand not a single word he spoke. I searched for gestures or clues to his speech but could find none. As near as I could ascertain, he was either introducing himself, asking who I was and from where I came, or welcoming me to the country. I also admit I do not speak any language of an oriental nature and could not discern from his speech where I had landed.

I returned his genuflection clumsily and feared I might have demonstrated a lack of respect in waiting so long. He had spoken so quickly upon meeting me that I felt to interject myself while he spoke could be equally disrespectful. Showing no insight into his language, I tried to say the only thing that came into my mind. I told him I had recently survived an air mishap, and I had come to this place by portentous fortune. I desired to return to my home in Canada. As an added aside, I pointed to myself and informed him of my name. His expression contorted into a confused yet determined look.

I was stunned when, moments later, he was able to duplicate my entire introduction with similar inflection and emphasis. It was clear he was parroting my every syllable. Such an impressive feat I had never before witnessed. When he reached the part where I had pointed to myself and indicated my moniker, he paused before pointing not to himself, but back to me, and repeated it. In so doing, he demonstrated he understood that this word was characteristic of my person. Subsequently, he repeated the final sentence, pointed at himself, and indicated that his name was Ryuudrikje. He then gestured to the lands behind him and named it Loogenage. By virtue of some clever kinesics, he made clear he wished me to follow him.

He repeated each word I had spoken with only the slightest of accents. It was a walk of a couple hours, but in that little time, I was able to teach Ryuudrikje basic body parts and actions such as walking, throwing, smiling, and running. He absorbed these words as a sponge would a small spill. In moments, he was able to understand numbers and could count and perform elementary mathematics in English as though he had been born to it. I told him every word I could think of, and with each one, became further flabbergasted at his ability to not just comprehend, but his faculty to store and repeat every single unit of my mother tongue.

I shall admit that upon the conclusion of our first walk, I had been thoroughly disavowed of my linguistic prowess. He was speaking English after two hours at the level of a child and picking up subtleties as fast as I could think to teach them. Me, I found it only possible to retain a few dozen vital words of his language, and these only after he carefully repeated them several times. I struggled to ensure their passable pronunciation. It even seemed to me that my mistakes became easily understood, and his diction morphed towards my erroneous patterns.

I would eventually learn that the people of Loogenage are all capable linguists, and the language of these people changes so quickly and easily that it can be difficult for the more aged to follow a conversation, due principally to their less agile and flexible capacity.

It was fascinating to think of a people so capable of communication that even I, with a novel tongue, could only stump a teenager for a couple hours. It is no small understatement that I announce I found my first impressions of this place and people to be inconceivable and unfathomable. It was with sincerity that I expressed to Ryuudrikje my excitement to learn more about these people and this place and to see what other wonders they had in store for me.

CHAPTER 2.3

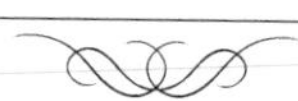

The author is introduced to a city in Loogenage and learns about the incredible nature of the natives of the country.

EXPECTATIONS SUFFICIENTLY ELEVATED, they would be swiftly dashed as we entered the city of Glangestalt, which I learned to be the largest city in the country, though not the capital. I was also to learn Glangestalt had once been a bustling trade city, serviced by ships from the great empire of Japan and occasionally visited by those intrepid explorers from places farther afield. In an overreaching response to the influx of new ideas and materials beginning to flood his country and which threatened his world view the king had ordered the complete isolation of trade and travel to and from their partners. Systems were implemented to ensure word of the outside world was filtered through official channels, and social engineering punished anybody who was not measured to be a quality citizen.

This city was described by Ryuudrikje as once the jewel of the world, a gleaming, shining example of civilization. Today, it seemed a backwards cesspool. Sewage drained openly in custom-cut channels along the edges of otherwise beautifully crafted cobblestone roads. Inquiring directly, I was assured this indeed led to frequent outbreaks of cholera and all manner of illness. Those same notions and designs from which the king sought to shelter his kingdom and subjects had brought the remainder of the planet forwards in great strides. In their absence, they had left the country of Loogenage dreadfully behind the times. The small river that lazily coursed through the heart of the city was fetid and ruined. Starved of resources, including fossil fuels like oil and natural gas, the air was thick from the burning of dried animal faeces for heat as the residents had long since consumed all coal supplies. The city possessed not even a single solitary tree, the last having been burned for fuel many years ago. Built on a rolling terrain, and without any root structure to retain the earth, frequent mudslides sharply eroded the hills of the city. Every typhoon wreaked havoc with the residents, and much of the populace lived in shanties constructed of rough stone and fabric.

It was evident the absurd protectionist policies had brought little but devastation to the people. In contrast to the beauty of the surrounding countryside, where I learned it was strictly forbidden under penalty of death to disturb a placed stone or royal tree, the stark harshness of the city was all the more appalling. Despite these failings, Ryuudrikje described his home in nothing but the most beholden terms, and even the king, who it was said could trace his descendancy directly from the gods. As Ryuudrikje spoke, in terms such as that I would ascribe only to one brainwashed, it was clear an additional effect of the isolation was that not a single person on this island was aware of the true state of the rest of the world. Though the country had once been an active member of the international community, today, never should one who sets foot on Loogenage touch down on any other land mass. This bode ill for my hopes. Amongst the king's royal subjects, there could be none who had reason to leave their idyllic lives for the awfulness of the outside world. Even to speak quietly otherwise in the wrong company could lead to one's re-education.

I was told the country consisted of three such cities. To the west side was another port city of Cluemegnig, and in the centre of the island, midway between Cluemegnig and Glangestalt, was the noble capital city, Traldrogdrab. Ryuudrikje assured me he had visited both cities during his life. He spoke most highly of Traldrogdrab, blessed as it was by his magnificent highness.

It was only later, upon personal contemplation and rumination, that I was to reconcile this apparent dichotomy. Through isolation, separation, and detachment from the greater sphere, the kingdom of Loogenage could not see beyond their own walls any alternative. We accept the reality of our situation. For those presented with no substitute, we need only to secure ourselves in the rationalization of what we know. It is only through the most inclusive and expansive world view that we can better understand the benefits and drawbacks available. Through open experimentation, and the wisdom acquired thus, we cultivate our civilization to its greatest degree. In this kingdom, however, a single, solitary reality had to them been prepared, through which and within the bounds of which, they had to live their entire lives.

I could speak of the great developments that had been forwarded in the past three centuries, when last the kingdom had not been a recluse. Little could Ryuudrikje harmonize his love of home with the possibility of something better. I must note to the reader that these exchanges took place over a period of less than a week. So great was their perspicacity into the workings of language that he and I could speak at length and depth on near any subject in virtually irreproachable English.

It was on the fifth day that he asked me why I had said nothing about our, and by which he referred to his and my, people. I demonstrated my confusion as we had long and frequently spoken about the inclusive family of humanity. He believed me to be intentionally obtuse but humoured me nonetheless and asked about Strulbrugs. I answered that to this I had no reference point. He pressed with greater elaboration. What names have you for those of us, again indicating a shared experience and camaraderie, who never die?

The reader must surely understand my confusion. All men die. If there is a single thing of which I am confident and doubtless, it is that all humans, man or woman, irrespective of circumstances, must eventually reach the conclusion of their lives and do whatever follows. As muddled as I was by his question, my answer befuddled him to equal measure. Ryuudrikje asked about the mark on my forehead, above my left eyebrow, and what it meant amongst my people to hold such a feature. I touched the spot and realized the young man was referring to the injury I received during the crash. It was then I saw that this birthmark meant a great deal more to him and the people of Loogenage than I could have ever anticipated. My mark, I confirmed, was merely the result of an abrasion suffered in transit and held no further meaning.

Aghast, the realization dawned upon my friend that I was not as he and I did not know of the plight of the Strulbrugs. This was to be the most illuminating exchange of my time here. I would learn about a subject of fantasy and fiction, but here, a reality. He told me a small, randomly born, minority of this kingdom were brought into the world with a small but obvious birthmark above their left eye. This was understood to mean the child was a Strulbrug. More than that, they would never die. I felt my years of knowledge and certainty melt away as I considered the great possibilities that such a gift would offer. The glory at the prospect of never fearing death overcame my thoughts and a torrent burst forth from my mouth of the incredible joy at such a revelation. I nearly forgot he had himself unto me just revealed he was immortal. He could never die from the passing of time. My first question was answered that he could still pass away from accident or injury.

It was obvious to me that to him, this was but the usual way of things. I wondered how he could be so blasé about so incredible an opportunity afforded him. I asked, though with such a tone as to really tell, what it was he and those like him did with such an endowment? I suggested, without waiting for his response, that I would take the opportunity to build the greatest empire of knowledge ever known to man. Upon myself, I would take to visiting every place on the planet, to know the minds of as many people as possible, and to absorb the greatest of all the best minds in any subject. I would be an oracle of knowledge, consulted on all matters of great import. I would refine my body and be the greatest athlete and seek to build the greatest artworks of all variety. Unbound by the shackles of time, I could and would devote myself to the pursuit of all things glorious and great and build the world into a paragon of virtue.

And yet, as I described the things I would do, I saw in his eyes a sort of disappointment, a melancholy of such depth as I could scarcely comprehend. You see, I spoke of possibility and of the potential that could be achieved through living in a perpetual state of youth. It was at this point it dawned on me to ask how old he actually was. If he was, as he claimed, a Strulbrug immortal, perhaps my young friend was simply not young.

He was, for I had grasped an assumption in my ignorance: to be a Strulbrug immortal meant eternal youth and vigour. In fact, this state of being was considered more a curse than a blessing. The Strulbrugs age at the same rate as all the rest of us. As we reach infirmity and our bodies inescapably falter, they continue to function in an ever-diminishing efficiency. Ryuudrikje was only fourteen years old, but even at this young age, he knew he was doomed to a perpetual existence whereby his body would fail, his mind would slow, and all those he cared about would move on. He would descend into a silent prison, trapped behind his own eyes, a burden on those around him and unable to contribute anything meaningful to the world.

CHAPTER 2.4

The author explores the curse of the Strulbrug and the treatment afforded to the poor souls.

THIS WAS THE way the life of a Strulbrug was presented to me. At birth, the bright red birthmark appears over the eye immediately and without fail. At this very moment, even before their cords are cut, the basic blueprint for their life is sealed and confirmed. Their name and vital statistics—date and time of birth, family, parents, and location—are all carefully noted and recorded in a central register. Strulbrugs are regularly checked upon. As though their defining birthmark were insufficient, an official with royal authority is assigned to ensure all Strulbrug are present and accounted for. On the day of their birth, at the break of dawn, the inspector comes, and when the mark is present, gathers all details mentioned earlier plus height, weight, colour of skin, hair, and eyes, and of course the identifying birthmark, which is carefully determined according to a detailed chart, and any other identifiable feature, beyond the facial identifier.

As the Strulbrug grows, they are treated not as productive members of society but as perpetual burdens on the state. In school, they are bullied, receive a lesser education, and are ostracized with abandon. A variety of proclamations serve to protect the Strulbrug to some degree. The abandonment of one by their parents is prohibited. Despite this, many are nevertheless deprived of proper care, and their growth is stunted by this same act. They are subject to the worst forms of discrimination, and they are rarely able to excel in any venue. They are locked geographically to the area in which they were born and outside this, are prohibited from entering schools or hospitals or receiving any sort of public service.

The mark above their eye changes over the course of time. My friend, Ryuudrikje, expected that at any moment, his would turn to green, a colour that usually appears two years earlier. In early adulthood, it would darken into a navy blue. By the midlife, when for a normal person that would signify some fifty years, it blackens entirely into an onyx as large as a quarter.

The attitudes of Strulbrugs themselves are equally scripted. I interpreted it as being more a matter of consequence than of necessity. The young Strulbrugs generally see a hopeful future, in spite of their surroundings, but they are gradually sanded and polished by continuous spite and failure until, by the age of thirty, or forty at the latest, they succumb to a sort of deep and unrecoverable depression. It is their inability to achieve anything, and the certainty to come of a painful and unending, unendurable future, that drives them to this state. They are promised cared for perpetuity, but the reality is they will suffer a most bleak existence from age 80 onwards. It is at this time the most egregious of laws that ever has before been passed takes effect. The Strulbrug are declared to be legally dead. All obligations of the family are declared void. All the Strulbrugs' possessions are taken away and replaced by the least generous of stipends upon which they will survive for the rest of their being.

Such is the lack of incentive to achieve and to create value for society. Given the net sum of life achievements is nullified at age 80, surely no fair judge reading this would begrudge the Strulbrugs their depression. These laws are passed so the immortal population, perpetually increasing but always decrepifying, need not ever overburden the tiny kingdom. In my judgement, however, these laws serve to ensure no Strulbrug is motivated to succeed. Even knowing the future before me is guaranteed to be one of great suffering, I should think, and perhaps this is what keeps the younger Strulbrugs engaged, I would try to achieve as much as possible that I might create a more comfortable nest in which to decline in my exceedingly advanced years.

And yet the Strulbrugs have no reason to achieve. Everything they earn is taken away in their old age, so why would one bother? It is not even possible to strive for anything else. The regular and carefully monitored visits by the general inspectors guarantee no Strulbrug goes off the grid. Even if a Strulbrug were to escape detection, and evade inspection, the mark would immediately give them away for what they are. The punishment meted to a Strulbrug who attempts to escape their duty, or to any mortal who provides shelter, assistance, material, or advice, or who is considered to have done so, is imprisonment in a stone castle—which sounded akin to the Château d'If—on a small island at the mouth of the largest river that flows through Cluemegnig into the ocean. There, without any support from the country, those imprisoned have to survive on their own, with no hope of escape to the mainland. All currents flow strongly out to sea. The sanction for helping a prisoner to escape is immediate death upon return to the shore, and few would dare to undertake such a venture to save either a single Strulbrug or any who would side therewith.

Thusly, the greatest secret of this forgotten country was to me recounted. The incredible horror of living indefinitely, that which I had considered a great bestowal, now, a torture unfit for any living creature. I admit that Ryuudrikje having explained this to me sent me into a state of desperate dejection and despondency from which I myself could ill find a reasonable or possible escape. Ryuudrikje tried to comfort and support, ironically, as it was for him, and his kind, that I felt such distress.

CHAPTER 2.5

In an effort to calm and rejuvenate the author, Ryuudrikje introduces him to a secret society and an alternative.

IT WAS MY uncomfortably profound response to the predicament he faced that prompted Ryuudrikje to reveal to me a secret. It seemed to me an awful tragedy to live one's mortal life assured that in the postscript of the most productive times, quality of life would be reduced to the barest of minimums. These considerations had not been exclusive to me. Ryuudrikje told me that a small, informal support group had been cobbled together in the past half century. A minuscule number of mortals, and the few Strulbrugs around whom they coalesced, had formed this secretive society to the protection of their members.

The group had been founded by the wife of a "young" sixty-year-old Strulbrug by the name of Furoud. Having shared their lives over a quadragennial years and the raising of four children, his devoted wife, Tsuvra, decided she wished not to see her husband spend his days wandering alone and uncared for as was the expectation of a Strulbrug. At fourscore, all marriages wherein a Strulbrug has been a party are formally and officially dissolved by the Crown. As is so often the case, the best of intentions has turned into the foulest of results, and the family, wife, and children are pushed away from the Strulbrug by a nanny state that seeks to provide the minimum requirements of life from this point forward.

To mitigate this bleak future, Tsuvra had gathered as many Strulbrug together as she could find, their rarity a blessing for the stability of the state as they were only born at a frequency of one every hundred thousand live births. Amongst the population of the kingdom of Loogenage, this generally meant one was born roughly every other year. Tsuvra had congregated two dozen and promised to care for them personally with the scarce funds she possessed. With the utmost of care and secrecy, she had also gathered a small group of like-minded mortals who had pooled their resources together to support their neighbours, friends, and family. Upon her passing, these last thirty years, her children continued her work. Her husband, Furoud, still lived. He had long since misplaced his grasp of the world. An unsanctioned, and if discovered, illegal, association remained, operated by the children of Furoud and Tsuvra, who took care of this dozen, and recently another five more, including Ryuudrikje.

My kindhearted reader might assume that with the glowing of such a bright and compassionate light, all of Loogenage would surely see the tenderness and humanity of such work and that many might follow their lead. Alas, by virtue of the commands and proclamation of the king and his sycophantic cabal, who sought to control civil society and keep his subjects firmly within his grasp, such operations could only operate beyond the law.

I truly believe the king meant to create such a system with the purest of intentions. His aim perhaps was to protect his great principality from the ever-increasing burden of those afflicted with this condition and to protect families in particular from an eternity of carrying the weight of an unfortunate ancestry. It was a generosity offered in perpetual care, in full spite of their dwindling capacities, at the expense and the infinite largesse of the reigning monarch. The alternative that had been summarily rejected was a promise to euthanize all those upon the tenure of eighty years being reached. The word of the king, coming directly from the gods but more as the representative of the people, in no uneven manner decided it to be incompatible to end a life for all but a criminal sanction. Those who exceeded certain age strictures were precluded from the commission of criminal acts by the simple fact of their infirmity.

A great achievement of the nongovernmental organization was the discovery of the value of hope. Those Strulbrugs who had yet to fall into the depression of the deep blue phase found the assurance of care extended their spirits far deeper. Even those who had succumbed to the malaise of their age were to a degree improved. One of the originals had studied medicine, and it is a pleasure to report he had made some great strides in two distinct but related fields.

He had spent much of his time studying the brain and cognitive preservation. It could be seen from his work that a number of the black-phase Strulbrug were extending their capacity far longer than was usually the case. It was said a Strulbrug could not remember his descendants beyond his grandchildren, and yet a pair were quite familiar and enamoured with their great progeny.

Secondarily, this original had searched for a way to harmlessly remove the mark from the visages of his peers. Even if by accident the mark was cut deeply from the face, it would return within a matter of days. So many Strulbrug had tried such a thing and had been marked with both the spot and a deep scar underneath. This was a clear sign of foul play and was often sufficient to be banished to the castle in the river. This young doctor had taken a different approach. Instead of stealing the dot from the face, he would stretch the skin near the mark with a number of herbs and fluids. When loose enough, he would fold the skin from one side over the other and carefully sew it together, concealing the mark tightly underneath. Early efforts resulted in some significant scarring, but lacking the blemish, officials would assume only that a mortal had suffered some accident.

It was found this surgery could only occur after the age of thirty when the skin begins to loosen naturally, and so my friend was not yet able to be cleansed of his dollop. So great were those medical achievements that the aspirations for betterment were tangible. Optimism abounded now at what could be achieved with these sciences further explored.

CHAPTER 2.6

The author is approached on the street by an official inquiring about his papers.

SUCH IS THE way of the world that when things seem at their worst and hopeless, or at their best and most buoyant, fate has a way of levelling things out again. I had been free to travel about the city at my leisure. I'd lacked the necessary language skills to make any meaningful enquiries but could find my way home in a pinch. Such as it was, the dilapidated and crowded state of the city worked to my advantage. Daily, I would travel about in clothes borrowed from my hosts. On only two occasions did somebody deign to speak to me.

The first to approach me came up with a sort of unearned hostility. He walked straight up to me and pushed me a few times brusquely while uttering something about Strulbrugs, the only word I could make out in his entire rambling. I humbly shrugged him off as a supplicant as I could not communicate with him without possibly revealing too much of myself. After a minute or two, the bitter man kicked some road waste (from the edge of the road) towards me and stormed off.

I was a little shaken by the encounter and begged Ryuudrikje to teach me a few key phrases. He imparted enough to let somebody know I'm not a Strulbrug, and I'm sorry, but I have to be going. Ryuudrikje was surprised and frustrated with how difficult I found it to learn his language. Over the course of a couple weeks, he had achieved basic fluency in my language and could probably walk through the middle of any big city talking to every person without raising an eyebrow. I, on the other hand, was barely able to string a basic sentence together to acquire food, water, or find a bathroom. Confident now that I could handle an interaction with an ill-tempered ruffian, I continued my explorations of this city.

My second approach by a stranger went much more poorly than the first. I had taken a different path every day, and my early perambulations took me uphill first as I sought to find the highest path possible to see as much of the city as I was able. I also did it to ensure that the path home was always downhill. By the third week of my stay, I had exhausted all the uphill routes and had begun walking in the lower parts of the city, closer to the water, docks, and former trading and administrative areas. Most people were busy with their own activities and took little attention of a stranger walking down the street, even a visible minority such as me.

One man, an official of the royal inspection corps of the city of Gluegenstat spotted me, and in particular, the large black scab on my forehead. He came up to me and with a tone full of terseness shouted an order and thrust his hand forward. I tried to tell him I was in a hurry, a suggestion to which he responded even more angrily. He stuck his finger straight into my face at my nose, and in a sudden move, struck his other fist directly into my gut, forcing me to double over on the street. On the ground, he kicked me while yelling commands I could not understand and clamped a heavy pair of crude handcuffs over my wrists. A huge crowd had gathered at the scene, and to my dismay, most, if not all, of the spectators were clearly and firmly on the side of the grand inspector.

The inspector hauled me through the streets with impressive strength as the gathered crowds threw produce and pebbles at me. A second officer came over to provide assistance when he was struck by a stray rock intended for me. I was dropped at once, and they nabbed the stunned perpetrator as the crowd fell silent. The pair slapped a set of cuffs on the unfortunate pitcher and hauled the two of us several blocks down the street. I suppose I found it a bit amusing. The silent mob that had attacked me now still followed but without a peep towards my captors. When we reached the largest building by the quayside, a formidable stone fortress, we were hustled up the stairs and through the great wood and iron doors.

The edifice within which I then found myself was immediately apparent to be a gendarmerie. Inside were officers of the army, with swords at their hips and pistols as one might imagine being carried in a brace by a pirate. The soldiers spared not a glance at us in spite of the commotion we were causing. We were taken forcefully down the stairs into the dungeons. I was placed in a tiny cell, and the ill-aimed flinger of stones was thrown into the one adjacent. The iron bars of my cell faced outward, and between us stood a wall of stone. The doors were slammed and locked firmly, and the jailors marched up the rocky stairs. When they slammed the door, the jail was completely dark.

In the cell adjacent, I heard the grumblings and mutterings of the other prisoner but felt little desire to speak with this person. It is usually better to know the mind of the people around you, but I decided this man's mind might be better off unknown. In my own, I tried to play back the words, the place, the people, but there seemed little information of value stored in my mental vault. I explored the jail with my hands, but in the complete darkness, I could find no furnishings much less a weakness I might exploit. Even the stones of the jail seemed consistently cemented in place. I was at the mercy of my situation and the jailors who held me.

CHAPTER 2.7

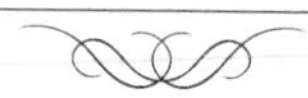

The author is transferred through the countryside to the capital.

IT WAS A dark, cold night in the lockup. The floor was moist, and it smelled of previous occupants. At my side, my neighbour fell asleep after grumbling for a period of only several minutes, a fact made abundantly clear by the unmuffled snores that ricocheted around the enclosure and seemed to amplify, not dull, the nasal sound waves. It was perhaps a blessing. The irritating sound of his slumber provided unto me a focal point for my frustrations, distracting my mind from the more pressing issues concerning my future, and my present, predicament. Enclosed in the cave, those sounds marked the only clear passing of time. They were so regular and routine I could not say if I ever fell asleep though I'd propped myself up in a corner as far from the bars as I could manage.

After an indeterminable period of time, the door at the top of the staircase creaked open, and a man of extravagant corpulence squeezed through the portal. He first went to the other cell and unlocked the occupant, who obediently stepped forth, received a sharp cuff to the back of his head like some disobedient child, and was then freed of his bondage.

Following his example, I attempted to mimic his actions exactly when my turn soon followed. There were other activities in store for me. It seemed that whatever my crime, it was unquestionably greater than striking an officer with a stone. I bowed as low as I could and reached my handcuffed appendages towards him that he might free me. Like my roommate, he struck me firmly behind the head, while announcing something in his, to me, still foreign tongue. He seized the irons about my hands and hoisted me easily onto his broad shoulders. He carried me up the stairs, past the officers, who snorted derisively in my direction, through the great door, and into the street where a jail cart awaited, drawn by a troika of horses. The cart door was slammed firmly behind me, and like a criminal in an old paddy wagon, I held the bars and looked at the street behind me, wondering where I would next be found.

The cart clattered down the king's highway, a magnificently laid cobblestone trail cut with deep wagon tracks. The wooden wheels, drawn from a time before rubber softened the way, bounced and shook violently. The driver enjoyed a marginally smoother journey, his carriage buffered by rusty springs that screeched in protest at every bump. My cage, conversely, was equipped with none. I supposed the comfort of a detainee, such as was I, was hardly a concern for the designer or operator of this transport. The voyage was a contrast of antitheses. My immediate surrounding was a rough, cacophonic, callous cage, driven by a quite unsociable chauffeur. On quite the other hand, the beauty of the countryside was striking and remarkable.

The wagon wound its way through a number of farms and orchards. Impoverished in the technology and materials advanced in the past three hundred years, this country did not lack for food, or silk, for a number of fields were clearly devoted to the cultivation of the worm. It could be little doubted that this country possessed a wealth of natural resources, which, if connected to the rest of the world, would surely enrich the citizens therein. The edges of this two-lane country road were lined with perfectly tended flower beds of tulips, violets, chrysanthemums, and a number of others I could not name. Behind these were hedges of berries, and every hundred yards or so, an arch of stone wide enough for a cart to pass under, if one could imagine it leaving the deep grooves. I was certain a method existed for this as the fields and flora were so perfectly tended. I was led to assume an army of master gardeners was employed in the maintenance of this beautiful place.

The horses, though I could not observe them from my current position, besides, having seen my fair share of their kind recently, I was not altogether interested, trotted along at a fairly decent clip. I took note that we were travelling along the only artery I could see. Not once did we cross another similar road, and the thought of our destination gradually cemented itself in my mind. If all roads led to Rome, then certainly, I was heading to the capital, to the city of Traldrogdrab. In my current state, I did not conjecture that the king was inclined to meet me. It seemed more likely, being the seat of power, and as in most places, the ruling city often housed other agencies of government, the most pertinent being the offices of judicial inquiry, tribunal, and sanction. It seemed likely to me that I was heading to court, still unsure of my offence, increasingly confident that it had to do with the mark over my eye.

The wagon trundled over hills and through valleys. After a few hours, at about noon, the driver dismounted to speak with some officials on the road. They kept repeating the immortal noun. Evidently satisfied, the driver climbed back onto the throne, and with a lurch, we rounded a cliff face to head down into another valley. This path was defined by a number of hairpin turns. The driver was forced to proceed slowly. On a few occasions, I caught sight of a magnificent palace of pure white limestone in the valley surrounded by a large city that consisted of mostly tattered and broken shanties as at Glangestalt. It was a beautiful scene of majesty and poverty all in one place.

Down the middle of the city, leading directly to the castle, was a golden path. It was lined with the same cherry trees from the fields, all blooming in white and pink. The buildings on either side were kept to the highest standards, themselves immaculate architecture of gabled roofs. Brick and stone walls, with tiny windows underneath intricately carved façades, lined the street all the way to the palace. This single road, punctuated by the falling cherry blossoms, need be added as a true wonder of the world, the most beautifully built entrance to a city that would make the Champs-Elysees in Paris look downright dowdy in comparison.

I took all this in through the less impressive bars of the jail car. It was a surprise that this vehicle was allowed on the carefully manicured street. Gradually, we approached the palace, and as we did, the great portcullis opened.

CHAPTER 2.8

In the king's dungeon, the author meets some new people who clarify his situation and provide assistance.

THE CARRIAGE CAME to a halt just inside the gates in a grand courtyard cleared of all but three large trees. The main keep, a tall, square, stone building, sat at the far right of the fortress, at least a hundred metres from the main gate. Several smaller buildings huddled close to the main keep, likely residences or barracks of important people of the state. Then the carriage was pulled to the left of the gate, and I was removed by several guards, each armed with a halberd. Whilst I was escorted to a large building on the left of the castle, I took careful note of the layout of this place.

This building was attached to the main outer walls of the palace. I entered upon the gentle suggestion of the armed guard and came into a room arranged as a church, with pews on either side facing the anterior of the chamber. At the front of the room was a large painting of a man in the finest kimono I could imagine. Without hesitation, I knew this to be none other than the king. Two guards followed me into the room and took positions on either side, standing straight and erect but saying nothing.

In a moment, the door at the front of the room opened, and a portly man wearing flowing red robes muddled his way to the front of the room. He wore glasses on his entirely bald head and poked through some book as he walked clumsily towards the middle aisle. Taking a brief look towards me, he proceeded in my direction, muttering something under his breath. I could not tell if he was reading or speaking his mind. Sensing an opportunity, I tried to tell him I was no Strulbrug, but the guard to my right must have noted my inhalation and struck the back of my knees, forcing me to kneel before the magistrate. The judge stopped, took one look at me, in particular the scab on my eyebrow, and gestured that I be taken through another portal on the left. I tried to protest but was stifled before the words even formed in my mouth by the strong arm of the guards striking my back firmly, expelling the air from my lungs and the voice from my tongue.

The magistrate turned and made his retreat. The guards escorted me through the door and up a long, winding flight of stairs into the castle dungeon.

Unlike the dungeon in Glangestalt, this prison was quite large and illuminated by thickly barred windows. A hundred or more cells lined the hallway that curved with the wall of the fortress. One side of the prison faced the exterior of the castle to the west, and the other, the courtyard on the right. The prison was about twenty feet in width, the same as the wall wherein it was located. Through this prison, one could look all the way from the outside of the castle into the courtyard beyond. I was guided past many prisoners who made a general clamour at my presence. Some scoffed at me as the guards threw me into a large cell at the end of the curved hall, this one with windows on both sides and space enough for several inmates by my reckoning.

The more senior guard announced something sounding official I could not understand in the least. I felt it a fool's errand to try to reason with the guards, who seemed unwilling to speak. So, silently, I took up residence in the west wall of the castle of Traldrogdrab. Between my cell and my nearest neighbours were walls of iron bar set in a diagonal grid. I took a seat on the floor.

The nearest of residents here waited barely a minute before whispering, "Strulbrug." I looked to see a short, skinny young man of about twenty years. I tried to answer him with the best accent I could muster to tell him I was not a Strulbrug. Eyes full of doubt, he pointed to my scab and beckoned me forward. Cautiously, I approached the bars, and as I got closer, he laughed. In much the same manner as my first interaction with Ryuudrikje, I found in him somebody more than capable of linguistic acrobatics. He learned to speak English at the usual local prodigious rate. Other eager ears did likewise as they eavesdropped on our conversation.

I was most interested to understand why I was here and for how long I could expect to be retained. In not more than a few hours, he was able to inform me I had been arrested for failure to report. He laughed as he explained that the man who had arrested me mistook me for a Strulbrug in the black phase because of the scab. My inability to speak had been likely mistaken for an early onset of Strulbrug dementia. A series of unfortunate events had prevented the second officer from verifying the charge.

And apparently, the bumbling royal magistrate, a figure with whom every prisoner in the room was adequately acquainted, had failed to exercise his authority properly. The grunts and nods from the other prisoners suggested to me the same was felt universally. This man was in good favour with the king. It was to this fact, and not his own merits, that he owed his lofty position. With nary a second glance, I had been arrested, detained, charged, and found guilty. The prescribed punishment had not been announced, but surely, I was to be exiled to the island of Michijokima, in the river of Cluemegnig. Alternatively, it was possible I would be sentenced to execution by boiling, burning, or the separation of my body at one or more joints.

I protested that I was not a Strulbrug, as accused. I could therefore not be guilty of not reporting and producing my papers. My neighbour just laughed. Any fool could see this, he said. The lord magistrate, having rendered his verdict, would not suffer to have it reversed. Short of an intervention by the king himself, by whom I could be certain not to be received, I possessed no chance. In this land, the word of the king are all but worshipped. He had published tomes of self-promotion that highlighted his most important ramblings, and these were viewed by the people with near sacred reverence. With such an established cult of personality around him, my friendly felons had taken to abundant and uncontrolled fits of laughter at my suggestion of being seen. I was ever so glad my predicament was so humorous to these convicted criminals in the wall. I had rather hoped for some better news.

I asked my fellow prisoner why there was no chance I could speak to the king. The loud guffaw from the others strengthened his position as he explained to me that the king expressly prohibited the visitation of foreigners. After composing himself, he explained that in any situation where one had been granted an audience, that man had been executed in a ritual most unpleasant. All visitors of the king must kneel and lick the ground at his feet, or more precisely, at a distance of several metres. At the king's orders, the ground may be made to be more or less dusty, depending on his will, and in the most undignified cases, a poison was spread that would result in the ultimate and untreatable punishment several hours later. Such was always the case these last three hundred years when any audience had been granted to a foreign traveller. He said I was quite fortunate to have been found guilty of failure to report and not to have been granted an audience with the king.

It was apparently my turn to share as the men gathered in the prison were amongst the most curious types. I told them much about the world and about the judicial system in the land in which I had grown up. Of lawyers and trials I spoke, all designed to maximize the chances of a fair judgement, and above all, to minimize the risk of conviction of an innocent person. I elaborated on the subject of juries and judges, whose role it was to determine guilt through careful examination of the facts. I told them of our jails and compared and contrasted them with the lot I had witnessed here. They were intrigued but underwhelmed. There was a sort of acceptance and resignation amongst the people of Loogenage. Theirs may not be perfect, but it was the best it would ever be. It was with a disquieted mind that I took my rest that evening.

I was to learn the next day the story of each of the men in the jail. Most of them claimed innocence, having been accused of serious crimes such as murder, theft, or rape. A number admitted guilt but to charges of treason or simply not being good enough citizens. On more than one occasion, I was forced to stifle my own laughter at the ridiculous charges that brought them here. One man was arrested for high treason when he was caught urinating too close to a royal tree, which, having just recently been planted, had not yet sprouted above the ground. The tree had been planted by the youngest daughter of the king and was considered to be part of the princess by extension. Therefore, this man had been found guilty of urinating directly upon the princess. Another, in an effort to put out a fire burning on a patch of farmland, had tripped over a placed stone, knocking it out of place in the sight of a soldier. The soldier had promptly arrested him for the desecration of the king's royal road and garden. The stone had separated the road from the garden. He was found guilty of two distinct offences in one accidental action.

Amongst those who claimed innocence, most recanted stories of being in the wrong place at the wrong time or of stumbling upon a situation and quickly having been accused by the perpetrator, who, being of nobility, or of higher rank, had made guarantee of their guilt. There was one man who admitted to the most heinous of crimes, so loathsome that I wish never to repeat them. The hearing of his actions and the tone he used, almost playful and friendly, still chills my bones to this day.

I formed a collegial bond with all but that one man. That afternoon, a large mountain of a man in the cell on the inside, courtyard-facing wall of the prison, whispered for me to come closer. He told me I was locked in the Strulbrug cell. Unlike the other cells in this place, this one was less secure. For a favour, he would show me the way out. I told him I would do what he asked if I was able. He asked if I would pass a message along to his family on his behalf indicating his location in the castle. He told me that off the king's road at exactly half the distance between the capital and the city of Glangestalt was a gate to a field with a mark on the capstone. The mark, an "X" resting on an isosceles triangle, was to be unmistakable. If I walked directly perpendicular to the road at this portal for a distance of four hundred metres, I would come over a hill and into a shallow valley. Here I would find a flat rock with the same mark. I was to follow the mark, as the tip of the triangle pointing to the "X" would guide my way. I would have to follow several more of these until I reached a door buried and hidden in the hill. Though I was sure to be watched, as long as I showed no sign of authority or threat, I would be allowed to continue. At my destination, I should knock thrice upon the door, not more, not less, and it would be opened, whereupon I was to repeat a simple message and the precise location.

I swore myself to this pact, and he told me how to escape my prison. The king and his men knew this cell was less secure than the others but also that it would only be occupied by Strulbrugs of the black phase. The melancholy of this stage ensured they would lack any ambition to escape. There was no purpose in such an endeavour if the only reward was their predestined fate.

The latrine in the cell, by which I mean a hole in the floor with a metal grate covering, led to the eavestrough along the side of the wall, which would eventually empty into a river. At the time of construction, this cell had been intended for the highest security, thus its position at the end of the hall. The first prisoners, amongst the fiercest and strongest of their kind, had clawed and struggled in an effort to reach the outside, to little avail. Over time, weakened by the acidity of its natural contents, the cement had weakened. Later prisoners had, bit by bit, worked the stones around the evacuation hole until they could almost taste and smell freedom. To the misfortune of the prisoners who had attempted to affect their escape through this tunnel, a stone had dislodged at the face of the wall and had fallen, striking a sergeant-at-arms on the shoulder. Alerted, the alarm was raised and the prison gang summarily executed. My opportunity lay in the way the facility had been rebuilt: instead of closing the prison, cementing the hole, and reinforcing the cement, the cell had been redesignated for the black-phase Strulbrug and a metal grate laid in place over the hole. The informant revealed that if I was to remove the grate, only a few stones would sit between my cell and freedom.

I was faced with the prospect of my imminent demise, and not for the first time as the reader must surely remember. I decided to seize the opportunity. That night, I would attempt my escape. Shortly after the guards left the food at my cell door and retreated to their posts outside, I pulled out my pocket knife, thus having not been searched in this country where such fashion receptacles were unknown. I found that, true to his word, the cement that held the stones of the castle in place was quite soft. It was almost like putty, and I could easily pry off the grate and peel away the rocks. Though a disagreeable occupation, it was made easier by the pungent smell to which I had grown accustomed back in Glangestalt. I found the former inmates had been quite industrious and had enlarged the hole to a width of about a metre, easily large enough through which I could squeeze. The tunnel had been bored to a distance of about four metres, at an angle I estimated at near 45 degrees downwards. I shimmied and slithered down the chute until I reached the outside portal. I was to discover then a vital element had been omitted from the escape plan.

The cells were located at least thirty feet off the ground. If I were to fall, or the old rotten troughs to break, I would surely meet my conclusion prematurely on the grounds of the courtyard. If the fall did not do me in, I certainly would be in no position to run away. Finally, sticking my head out the small hole, tearing the scab painfully from my forehead, I realized I would have to scale at least the same ten metre distance along the trough. From previous experience, this as well probably would have exceeded my abilities.

I carved my way up into the rock wall above the tunnel. For my new plan to succeed, I only needed to clear about one cubic metre of stone, and it didn't matter one single iota where that detritus ended. I dug around some of the larger rocks that filled the loose cement of the wall, prying these and putting them aside as I worked. I laboured all night at this occupation and hollowed a cubbie just large enough in which to tuck myself. As day broke, checking first that nobody was in the area at the base of the hole, I kicked out the last stones from the wall, making a portal large enough to escape through. The rocks dropped to the ground and hit the grass with a thud and crash. This drew the attention of the guards on the top of the wall high above the prison.

The alarm was raised. Horns and trumpets blasted around the castle. Soldiers streamed out of the barracks and into the courtyard. Half ran to the keep to protect, I assume, the royal family. Others took up positions along the walls. A small detachment sprinted up the stairs of the prison and slammed open the cell from which I had been emancipated. The officers ran down the hall checking each prisoner and discovered my room empty but for a pile of rock and the metal grate in the corner. The most junior soldier removed his overcoat and was made to crawl into the escape tunnel. When he resurfaced, he detailed a one metre hole all the way to the exit and the waste trough at its mouth. At the base of the wall, directly beneath the hole were the stones; he concluded confidently that from this portal I had affected my escape.

Meanwhile, the repugnant and nefarious inmate whose crimes were so loathsome squealed with glee as he informed the guards I had outsmarted them and announced triumphantly every detail of my escape. Furthermore, he fingered my source. The lousy snitch revelled in his malignant enmity, and a guard opened my mentor's cage, fixed cuffs to his hands, and swore they would return to deal with him upon my recapture. The guards left and began to trace the eaves towards the outer walls of the palace, tracking my movements.

The bustle of the guards, soldiers, officials, and stewards of the palace was impressive in its chaos. None took notice of the man wearing a junior officer's overcoat—minus the key ring—carelessly abandoned hurriedly in an empty jail cell, striding purposefully and confidently across the courtyard and straight out the main gate.

CHAPTER 2.9

The author was free of the palace but still remained in danger in the capital city of Traldrogdrab as he made his preparations to return to Ryuudrikje in Glangestalt.

OUTSIDE THE CASTLE, things were also pandemonious. Dozens of deputies and the king's watch investigated walls carefully, searching for signs of penetration or weakness. I departed the king's highway as quickly as I could manage without drawing suspicion and cast away the officer's overcoat. Even the peasantry of the capital was in a state of confusion and excitement. Rumours raced about the prisoner who had escaped and that it was a black-phase Strulbrug who had failed to report.

I walked amongst them openly today, my scab having been pulled off. I had only a small lesion on my forehead now. No longer would even the most inattentive guard consider me to be immortal. My skin may have set me apart from the majority, but there were others, descendants of the time when this land traded openly. We accept the reality which to us is presented. A far simpler explanation for my ethnicity than being foreign-born was simply that I belonged here, a visible minority.

So busy and carefully observant for the dangerous convict, the people took notice of nothing else. I walked through a city full of energy and skittish clamour. I remember thinking I could probably have stood in the middle of the street and bellowed, "I am Cygnus, a foreigner in your lands who has just escaped your castle," in plain English, and not a single soul would have noticed. If I was not a Strulbrug, today, I didn't matter.

I paid close attention to the buildings around me, making sure not to stall or dwell, but equally cognizant of any which might house the king's officials. Briskly I walked, but I didn't break into a run. I needn't have been worried. I was not hassled by a single person as I left the city. I walked out past the city walls into the hills to the east.

My fortune was great. Only a half dozen people had bothered to look closely at me when I was brought to this city, and I believed they had really only seen the mark above my eye, nothing else. I avoided the guards at the entrance of the city by walking through a ravine by the river. Skulking about in the river valley seemed like a dangerous thing to do, for I could only think that a guilty person would bother with such an endeavour. As soon as I figured I had gone far enough to avoid being seen, I climbed out of the ravine towards the king's highway. I would have liked to have found a different way back to Glangestalt, but I knew of no other trail, and I felt time was of the essence.

I had also made a promise: I had told the inmate I would deliver his message to the door halfway down the highway. To find that place, I needed to find the crossed-triangle marker to point the way. I had no need of ceremony the first time I took this track and felt I had to discover the customs before I could move forward. I took a position on a rocky hill overlooking the road and waited and watched as the travellers passed each other on their way. I ascertained several key behaviours described herein:

- Upon meeting, each passing traveller, whether on foot or in a carriage, would pause, bow ninety degrees, and salute their opposite.
- The traveller heading towards the capital would usually bow first and most deeply.

- The salute was achieved by raising an arm, extending a single finger, which was not always the same finger, though I wouldn't learn the reason until much later. Most pointed their pinky finger.

I watched the trekkers for over an hour. There was no shortage of travellers along this main kingdom artery. When I felt confident I could replicate the formalities, and a gap in traffic permitted my vigilant merging thereupon, I set forth, checking, but surreptitiously, my compass to ensure I was headed to the right place. Each voyager I passed, I made sure to greet silently in the way I had observed, pointing my pinky finger. I furtively checked each gate along the road for the crossed-triangle marker. The further I went, the fewer the interruptions. I walked for a few hours until I found the foretold opening. The symbol looked exactly as described: a deeply incised triangle, which at its peak was crossed by a wide "X." I could not but mistake the shape for a windmill.

I walked off the main road, repeating to myself the message I had promised to deliver. Following the directions that had been provided, I found the first way marker easily. All told, I followed a trail that included almost twenty of these. At times, they led me to cross a path I had already taken. I spent the better part of the afternoon hunting windmills in the hills until finally I came to the promised door in the wild. It had the look of a hobbit hole, with a round door well camouflaged in the hill.

With trepidation, I approached the door, and true to the prisoner's word, I felt as though a number of eyes were upon me. I reached out my hand to knock, but even before I struck the wood, the door swung quickly open. There standing before me was the prisoner from the adjacent cell who had revealed to me the way out of the prison. We smiled widely and laughed. I asked how he had beaten me here. He said that after I had walked out of the prison and thrown the guard's ring of keys back to the other inmates, they had taken their turns unlocking their cells. Waiting for an opportunity in the chaos, they had made a break for it. Some chose to run towards the gate, while he had instead run towards the barracks. A hundred inmates running through the courtyard had provided ample time for him to find clothing for a disguise. Just as I had, he strode out through the fracas and into the town. Inside, the battle between many of the other inmates and the guards drew attention away from him. He had marched out almost as easily as I. The rumour of a full jailbreak took longer to spread with the Strulbrug event already moving like wildfire.

While I had tarried and struggled in the riverbed and watched behaviours, he had hurried along back routes directly to the house in the hill. He didn't have to follow the markers and had easily beaten me by several hours.

I asked my prison friend about the finger pointing on the king's highway and was informed it indicated the direction of the capital and the location, therefore, of the king. The finger raised indicated rank. The vast majority raised their little finger to indicate the rank of commoner. Officers in transit raised their ring finger, while lesser nobles, of which I saw none, would raise their middle finger, and the royal family, barring the king, would point their first finger. The king himself would not raise his arm and finger to point. He would instead have raised his thumb. Obviously, this was not something I witnessed, but something related to me by my associate.

He asked me what had happened at the prison, and I revealed the entire story. I didn't think I could make the climb, so I had instead carved a hiding place above the tunnel. Believing the guard would likely not look closely in the poop chute and that he would probably crawl on his belly, I hid above him as he looked below. As soon as he had left, I crawled back into the jail, put on the coat, and walked out the door. Again, he laughed and asked where I was headed with my freedom. I told him I had friends in Glangestalt who I hoped would be able to help me further. I was offered a place to stay, a bath and clothes I sorely needed, and a warm meal with his group, and he promised to point me in a safe direction in the morning.

CHAPTER 2.10

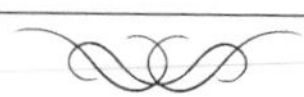

Dinner is spent with the hill folk. The author becomes acquainted with the Tegens and their particular worldview.

I HAVE FOUND I am not well versed in the etiquette of name reminiscence. As a product of this failing, I often forget to even ask someone's name. When they do introduce themselves, I find myself too little focused on the one crucial element of their locution. Such was the case with my recently liberated jailbird friend. To all the assembled deities, I would swear I knew not his name from the jail or that he ever offered it. As he introduced to me his family, I could attain familiarity with their names in this more relaxed atmosphere, though I still could not title the man who had started me on the path to freedom.

The Family, as he called them, though unrelated by birth, were known as the Tegens: a closely knit extra-judicial sect, convened by a common ideology. Drawn from every part of society, these folk were united by a common mistrust in authority of all forms. It was not to say they were well educated or informed on any matter as would be described by science or logic but by means of the perception of a consistent conniving and the presumptive perfidy of the most educated, prosperous, polished, and powerful. All authority was suspected, even assumed, and through such assumptions, verified of its unscrupulous malfeasance.

I, a near stranger to their lands but one who had already been falsely convicted for failing to prove I was not that which I in actual fact was not, whereby any person of innocence would by equal measure find it impossible to so prove, felt it not advisable to test an alternative hypothesis.

What had begun as an invitation for the night turned into a class that lasted a couple days. It was conveyed to me the falseness of the sciences of the land and how the example of a single collapsed building settled beyond any doubt that all construction was founded upon faulty logic and reason. The guilds of masons and carpenters, amongst the most highly trained in the land, were the epitome of greed and corruption. It was believed they possessed the skill and knowledge with which buildings could have been made of a permanence that could never fail; instead, they manipulated fact and reason to support the otherwise failing lumber industry. They fabricated inferior structures with materials and designs that artificially inflated the demand for their industry and occupations through additional services in their repair and replacement. Furthermore, The Family charged, the guilds, their avarice being so well verified, sought to create buildings that necessarily and intentionally would fail by building fragile structures above the ground, prone to damage from wind, fire, and quake. This conspiracy was only further proven by the dismissal by the ruling class as the nonsensical ramblings of uneducated fools.

The evidence of the misdeeds of the masonic cabal was plain and evident because the established powers therein produced endless false evidence to promote their conspiracy. It had been so proven from the work of a celebrated builder who constructed buildings below ground. In the unanimous agreement of all gathered, these were the most magnificent dwellings ever conceived. It was declared they were safe from all forms of disaster. This builder, the greatest ever to have lived, concurred the Tegens unilaterally, had shown to The Family such incontrovertible evidence in the form of his personal testimony against the strictures of aboveground development that no reasonable person could presume to question the soundness of his logic.

By consequence, the Tegen family had sworn off construction of aboveground shelter and moved below. It was proclaimed that building above ground was too dangerous. The collaborators to the conspiracy, the trained masons and carpenters of the realm, must never be allowed to pollute the purity of a Tegen home, which would certainly lead to sabotage. Of course, I could see from the particularly poor craftsmanship in the house and the design flaws, such as the nonreinforced walls, the noninclusion of chimneys, and poorly finished floors, that a number of hazards were present in this place. It seemed a fool's errand to ask about cave ins, which I knew must be common. Instead, I inquired of unseen gases. Unsurprisingly, there was no concept or understanding of such things, so I asked about visible indicators such as a reddening of the skin at death. They acknowledged that a number of them had succumbed to the red death, as it was known, but, and the tone of my hosts darkened as they began to sense I might not share their core ideological opinions, they spat back that even in those (aboveground) houses, sometimes people die of the red death, so it had nothing at all to do with the way the building was created. Besides, as they pressed on, the freedom from the tyranny of the masons, and the savings from their gouging, more than made up for any possible risk.

Sensing I was playing upon a nerve and needing the assistance of these people to reach another phase of my journey, I decided to change the subject from the secret-guild conspiracy. I thought it most ludicrous to believe these people of the guilds, who spent long years in the study and practice of their trade, would do so for the malevolent aim of harming the public. I have always held to the belief that nobody, at least few people, aims to misbehave. Those who spend their time following a noble profession, particularly one that requires skill and practice, usually do so for the benefit of mankind. For their tools and troubles, they are often well remunerated in return. It is not, in my opinion, the usual case that they practice solely for the purpose of fiduciary gain. That is seldom sufficient motivation amongst the greedy and lethargic.

I found this subject, and others, to be a matter of faith amongst The Family. For the Tegens, you either believed in innumerable conspiracies, or you accepted those with power and fortune were out for exclusively their own gains and only through the thorough and complete rejection of all their edicts, designs, trappings, and manipulations could one live a true, free, and happy life.

Most unnerving was the belief that all those who had achieved success in this kingdom, and by extension, surely all others, were colluding in a secret league to preserve their station while exploiting all others. It may be difficult for me to explain their convoluted logic, but it held that the masonic order, aligned with the carpenters, were close conspirators of the royalty who created the upper system. Upon those foundations, the officials and the officers of the army, being privileged to the machinations of the state conspiracy, protected through force that which it sought to construct and maintain. Through schools that pushed their agenda, they kept the lower classes from achieving their potential. Systematically, they disadvantaged those of lower caste and denied all but a tiny minority the opportunity to succeed. Thereafter, they sought to trick the poorest into believing that opportunity was available to those who worked for it while holding up a tiny few as examples, all the while ensuring the failure of all others secretly behind the puppet show curtain.

In this house of cards, The Family's beliefs were held together by an intricate network of fear. For each weakness, another layer of the grand plot was woven, further reinforcing their beliefs. Their fear would only grow. To the Tegen family, the entire world had been set against them by great forces. Only their tiny group had stumbled upon the secret, and only by separating and living apart could they truly live. They had quit a world of grand delusion to survive in a simple and free, but much more challenging, alternative.

The reader may understand that for the purpose of brevity, I should only convey a small amount of the conversation. Many of the details I have decided are too eccentric or fantastic to explain. My time spent with the Tegens proved to strengthen my respect for the firm basing in science appreciated by my own land, where evidence and proof trump fear and suspicion. As a traveller to this land, one must be aware of the Tegens and their strange views. If my writing should ever come to their family, though I doubt they would choose to read it if it did, I'm certain the esteem earned through the freeing of my fellow prisoner would be eroded entirely. An architect of the conspiracy I would be labelled.

I am to believe the people of the family of the Tegen, who knew me to be a foreigner captured by the authorities they so despised, therefore an enemy of their enemy and friend for freeing one of their own, thought highly of me. Even my inability to speak the common tongue of this place lent me a certain anti-authoritarian credit.

After two evenings and a day, I was determined to set out for Glangestalt and the supportive friends I had developed there. Disappointed but understanding of my loyalty, my colleague showed me back to the road in the morning and provided me insight into the unwritten rules of travelling the king's road. My return to Glangestalt was thereafter uneventful. Free of the cage that brought me there at first, I was liberated to take in the unparalleled beauty of the immensely spectacular environment.

CHAPTER 2.11

The author, returning from the capital to Glangestalt, arrives to find a ghastly change amongst the Strulbrug community.

OUT OF, I assumed, an abundance of caution, I tarried in the fields outside Glangestalt until dusk began to fall. My concern was that I would be recognized by some official or by a "good citizen" alerted to the completed escape from Traldrogdrab. I wore the change of clothes that to me had been given by the Tegens. It was a plain and shabby kimono. Amongst the people of Glangestalt, who wore such fine garments prepared from the bountiful silk forests, it surely would attract attention.

Cloaked in night's sombre shadow, I skulked into the outlying slums of the town. I pulled a wool mantle up over my neck to hide my identity while I retraced my previous perambulations. The edges of the town, as is typical in many parts of the world, were also the poorest. The wealth was focused closer to the centre and main trading areas. The edges also possessed the highest altitude in the town, making it easier to locate landmarks. Even in the darkness I could see them silhouetted against night's curtain.

I cut swiftly back towards the house of Ryuudrikje. Literally and figuratively, I was running downhill towards my friend's home and sanctuary, intent on allaying my fears about my well being. I sought to find a way to escape from this situation. On the cobbled streets, I stumbled several times in the dark. It was a moment of providence when, as I rounded the final corner before my intended street where Ryuudrikje and the other Strulbrug supporters inhabited and operated, I rolled my ankle and had to lean against a street post to check for a sprain. I crouched down to inspect myself, and before I brought myself back to my feet, I noticed an unusual number of people on this particular street, just standing around. They weren't speaking to one another. There did not seem to be any reason to be standing observing this place in the twilight. I felt a pang of suspicion shoot down my spine, and an icy wave of fear spread through my body. I stood and calmly walked across the road. Instead of turning into the street as I'd meant to, I continued past it while stealing glances back at the sentinels.

I discarded my plans to visit Ryuudrikje that night and instead sought the home of the immortal doctor. Jittery and shivering, I crept through the streets, first inspecting every road to decide if it was one down which I wanted to travel. Down some I concluded I would not go. The thought of leaving town occurred to me as well.

As a direct result of the watchers I'd encountered, I set about limiting the number of people I would pass. Any street with more than two people standing still was stricken from my travel plans. I checked carefully that I could see no tail and chose several back ways. I added many blocks to the trip but eventually found my way to the good doctor's back door. I poked about, making sure to not be seen by any observer, before I addressed the door with a reticent knock.

All senses heightened, I listened closely and heard somebody moving about the house quietly. They came to the window, and I saw them draw the corner of the blinds ever so slightly so as to pilfer a quick look. In the dark, I could not make out the lookout, nor, as I assumed of them, me. In a flash, the door opened a crack, and I spoke to him my name. The door opened only wide enough for them to yank me through the portal and into the house.

Inside, dimly lit only from a covered lantern outside, the room was dense with nervous energy. As my eyes attuned to the darkness, I began to make out the shapes of a dozen people. I realized these were Ryuudrikje's people, keeping watch over this place. The doctor pulled me into a side room, and in the faintest of hushed tones imaginable, asked where I had been. Dressed in fear, every sound still felt like cannon fire. I told him my story, about my capture, imprisonment, transport, conviction, and escape, and finally my return and my suspicions relating to the home of Ryuudrikje. The doctor confirmed what I feared.

Through intense investigation, the constables that had arrested me in the streets several days before had discovered I had been sheltered in the home of another Strulbrug. He, Ryuudrikje, had been found and arrested for harbouring an illegal immortal. It was some little irony that he had been arrested for harbouring me, a mortal human, when he had originally intended to do just as I was charged, as his group did of principal. The punishment for harbouring an immoral illegal immortal, for which no judge was required, was exile to the island in the river. Ryuudrikje had since disappeared. There was no doubt he had been taken where no person would dare follow, to the last home he should ever know.

I felt my heart drop into my plain sandals at this revelation and prayed and hoped the doctor had better news to share. Alas, he continued that as I had witnessed, upon the news of my escape, the net had been cast about the house of Ryuudrikje. It was expected I might consider a return. Had I walked to his door, I would have surely been captured and executed in the street. The Strulbrug now felt great fear that their miniature society might soon be discovered by the zealous officers or citizens and exposed. The great work and progress that had been made in secret would wither under the intense scrutiny and certain sanction by the Crown. All those implicated would be exiled or executed, and the fates of the Strulbrugs would undoubtedly be secured.

It was unclear how much was already known to the police. I could be sure of only one thing: My presence, despite the incredible courage and hospitality of this group, could only be considered a supreme peril and liability. None of these kind and miraculous souls would speak it, but I knew each masked a desire, borne purely out of mortal fear, to shove me out into the streets to protect themselves. Even from a purely selfish standpoint, I could see there was no gain to be made by staying in this place any longer. Sheltering beneath a rock, they could no more help me to escape as I could they. Even had I the courage to turn myself into the police, I couldn't be certain whether they wouldn't torture more names out of me or cease their investigations. The best thing I could think of to do was to flee this city, probably to never return.

The doctor prepared for me a small, cold meal, and I thanked him, and he me. He understood my reasons for leaving without me having to speak them. I took leave of the Strulbrug brotherhood of Glangestalt and stole away into the dark night.

CHAPTER 2.12

On the road in the night, the author develops an audacious plan and enlists help to refine and execute it.

SO, I FOUND myself out in a cold, dark night, with only a first-quarter moon in the sky above to light my way. In this kingdom, little travel is conducted outside of the waking hours. In fact, a paucity of activity of any sort prevails but for when the sun illuminates. I decided it unwise to stand out in so public an arena, and resolved, after a short period of brisk jogging beyond Glangestalt, to find a shelter for the night.

A swift notion had briefly flitted through my mind to return to the beach where my life raft surely rested still atop the rock. The distance, if I could even have remembered the way through the terraces, trees, and fields in the darkness, would have meant I could not have found it in less than a few hours, by which time it would have been closer to dawn than to dusk, and I would have wasted much sleep. I could have attempted another escape by sea on my raft but had been better persuaded by two thoughts. Firstly, my concern was that even if I were to find the raft in good working order, and not deflated in these last few weeks, it would not prove seaworthy enough to haul out. Secondly, I could not but think that the currents of this island, which had drawn me in in the first place, would surely fight my escape. I was only prepared for an evening on the road, with one cold meal, and no water. Unless I was, miraculously, to be rescued immediately, I would almost certainly succumb to termination by dehydration.

Then, too, the better part of me felt a responsibility to Ryuudrikje. He had been taken to the castle on the river where he faced his own peril, all because he had tried to protect me, a stranger to his land. I felt compelled to do something to help my friend, even if I had no solution at hand.

I ran until I could see a forested area near enough to the road. I veered into the shadows, darting amongst the trees and concealing my tracks as an outlaw Yahoo would have. When I had deemed I had travelled a sufficient distance so as to not be visible from the road, or by any ranger that might inspect the roadside for interruption, I tore some low branches off some nearby trees and dedicated myself to digging a burrow at the base of a tree. I covered the hole with the branches to conceal where I would lay and rest.

Of the poor places and spaces wherein I had recently slept, this was only exceeded in discomfort by the stoney prison. Beneath my austere Tegen cloak, I was not just uncomfortable but feared being found, unknown insects, other wildlife, and any manner of unknown forest hazards. My fears were overblown. It took some time to grasp a slumber, but the fatigue, exhaustion of days on the road, and heavy labour assisted me into the depths of torpor. In this quiet forest, for far enough had I wandered to be far away from the king's road and wherein few animals did frolic, under a thick canopy, I awoke. The sun's fingers rapped gently on my leafy blanket, and I arose to face the day.

In my efforts, vain though it be to seek that which may only find you, a puzzle had resolved itself in my mind. Epiphanically, I had pieced together a possible solution to all things ailing me. The island whereupon my friend was forsaken and marooned was guarded by a wide and powerful river, the crossing of which would be prevented by Cluemegnig city officials. Its principal defence was the ocean and one's inability, once swept to sea and disgraced by conviction, to return to Loogenage. As with other infamous prisons, its natural defences against escape were the greatest obstacle for the ill-prepared. The unwillingness of anyone to provide the support to prepare such an escape, due to the punitive response on the mainland surrounding, provided the necessary bulwark to punctuate the discussion.

However, my situation was opposite the one for which the prison had been designed. I sought not to return to Loogenage, but to flee to the sea, to return to the outside world. I did not fear the current of the river. Instead, I welcomed it as an assistant to my flight from the island. If I could, at some gentle inlet upstream of the city, put together a seaworthy vessel, I might be able to float, or even sail, directly to the island, pick up my friend, and current abetting, rush off to sea before any sort of concerted response could be enabled.

To this end, I needed great assistance. I had not the tools, the material, or even the necessary knowledge to build such a ship. While I had become something of an authority in raft making, I intended to do more than just float away. I was going to escape with command and control. This was not, I intended, to be a skin-of-my-teeth, pray-for-rescue, and barely-survive-if-all-fortunes-smiled-upon me getaway, but a confident, well-provisioned ocean expedition.

I knew just where I was going to find my help: the Tegens. Instinct told me they would be more than eager to stick one to the authorities they loved to defy. I would ask them to lend me their hands and their minds to defeat the fortifications of the castle, and by so doing, thumb their noses to the royal conspiracy. I, in turn, would share with them the generic ship-building knowledge I possessed from the general experience of modern, outside life. We would gather food, water, and tools to craft a boat with minimal draft and a hull that could sustain light shelling from land and survive the ocean waves. My other hope was they could provide some direction that would lead me to the island of Japan, their most recent trading partner—300 years ago—which I assumed to be their nearest neighbour.

Buoyed, I ate the meal provided to me by the doctor and started back towards the road. I thought better of it when faced with the realization of how close to discovery I was on the road. Instead, I would walk through the fields, orchards, terraces, and forests. I would keep contact with the road to maintain my direction, and with my compass, make certain I was going west. It meant a longer trip, but I knew moving towards the capital directly, and all of the assembled forces amassed against me there, would serve me poorly. Decision made and path determined, I set off on my journey. Along the way, I stopped and picked fruits from trees and berries from patches. I kept from breaking into a run, for no peasant would be running about rather than working the fields in the middle of the day.

As I approached the Tegens' underground dugouts, I looked about for the silent and stealthy sentinels. I knew them to be there, but their veils were too effective. I stumbled upon the crossed-triangle marker that would eventually lead me to the door. Upon the door, I knocked twice and grew uneasy at the lack of response. I thought about the most probable location of the nearest sentry. The near peak of a hill, I figured, would give the greatest line of sight, and I considered striking out in that direction when I recalled the words of the prisoner and knocked upon the door a third time. The door opened with caution, and a pair of wary eyes peered out. Once those eyes identified me, the door swung open, and in front of me stood a teenage boy. His face lit in recognition, and he hurriedly turned back down the hall and rang a sort of gong that gave the all clear.

My host emerged from a small depression near the door I had not seen previously. Several others cast off their camouflage and approached me with relief. My friend told me they had almost shot at me, thinking me a trespasser. They had not expected anyone, and as their watch had observed my progress, they had prepared for a fight. My fortune was greater than I could know. Their bows had been drawn and only moments separated me from an ignominious end. I noted my thanks at their not having welcomed me so as he embraced me with a hand around my shoulders. He said I must be possessed of the greatest fortune.

Our welcome concluded, my host inquired as to the reason for my return. I told him of Ryuudrikje, of the trap I had evaded, and of my idea to spring Ryuudrikje from prison, though I withheld a few details of the Strulbrug community to protect the immortals from harm. He sat in deep thought as he decided what to do with my unusual request.

CHAPTER 2.13

A plan is refined and agreed upon, and preparations begin for an audacious and adventurous escape.

TO NO GREAT surprise on my part, convincing my associate to marry his aims with my own was only the smallest of hurdles. He held concentration for mere moments before a smirk creased his lips. The suspense in the air dispersed with a jovial laugh from he, I, and the Tegens gathered. The Family was thrilled by the prospect, but a few riders were attached to my plot. I found their demands sufficient and tolerable, and we bowed deeply together, affirming and closing the deal.

I had hoped to get moving as quickly as possible, not knowing in what state my friend Ryuudrikje to be. The leader of the Tegens justifiably and wisely restrained my craving to prepare our supplies. It would take a couple days of hard riding to reach Cluemegnig, and if we were to complete our enterprise of fashioning a river-and-ocean faring vessel in a short time-frame, the threat of discovery aside, the more provisions we could prepare in advance, the less time we would be exposed to curious eyes.

We gathered axes and saws, hammers and nails, buckets, and

silk—which is common in this land—sheets. I helped my hosts with what heavy lifting they would permit, but I was disallowed to see their stores and warehouses out of an abundance of caution on their part. So instead, I drew up plans for the vessel, and along with the chief, who possessed geographic knowledge of the prison-castle, focused my efforts towards scripting the details of the escape. The Tegens knew of a place outside the city, by a distance of a few kilometres, where a kill fed into the Keimokaw River. The river flowed quickly through a wide floodplain, where therein it became a large volume of water, and numerous large rocks, always shifting downstream, would provide a few extra hazards and currents. Armed with that knowledge, I modified the plan to strengthen the bow of the ship with thicker beams and a fortified prow to skip off any obstacles I was unable to avoid.

The city of Cluemegnig straddles the Keimokaw River, which flows principally from the east to the west. In the middle of the fast-flowing river and near the geographic centre of the town is a rocky island whereupon the castle-prison is located. The river splits evenly at this island and unifies shortly thereafter.

Encircling the near entirety of the island were the outer walls of the castle. Only one connection to the island from the mainland existed: a single cable, suspended above the water, whereupon the prisoners were sent to the island down the line from a single, strong, solitary sentinel tower on the mainland. Access to the sentinel tower was protected by the city keep and defended by scores of soldiers; it would not be breached by our tiny contingent. The cable ran from the southern end of the city towards the island. To the north, the slums of the city sprawled across a wide alluvial delta. This land was rich in all kinds of farmland vegetation and beautiful but for the destitute squatters occupying its breadth. It was on this northern side we could expect both hostiles and friendlies, but the leader put into action a plan to attend to the unfriendly through a combination of distraction and subversion, the details of which I was not made privilege.

Two long, strenuous, taxing, disquieting days were spent solely in the art of packing and preparing. We attended to every detail including the shipment of both me and our leader in a covered and sealed compartment. To avoid suspicion, we set out to look like regular traders on the road between Glangestalt and Cluemegnig. A façade of fruits, vegetables, and grains was erected about the cart to disguise the true content. These supplies formed a critical part of the plan themselves: They would sustain us during the building and escape portions.

So, on the third day, the leader and I were closed into our coffin-shaped boxes and slid into the cart, completing the Tetris puzzle. The cart was driven by three of the most skilled Tegens. The cart lurched forwards on the road to our launch point. It took two full days of pandemonious rattle as we dared not stop but when absolutely necessary. Neither did we speak, lest outside our sarcophagi things went ill. We spent the entire time in sonorous silence. Batts of silk made the boxes all the more like a funerary box but gave us a measure of comfort on the rough lumber.

The first night, we stopped at a roadhouse operated by Tegens and tucked into the back. We disembarked for the night and for our only meal since the early morning when we had departed. I packed a little more silk into my crate, and early in the morning, we set off again down the turbulent road.

Upon reaching our destination, we, the deceased, sprung, or perhaps more accurately, oozed, out of the coffins when the covers were removed and we were freed. There, we stepped into a rainforest paradise. The stream that fed the great river trickled into a pool of calm water at the edge of a raging whitewater, rapid-filled waterway. The dense forest was beautiful and noisy, full of life, and not like the lands around Glangestalt. It was unkempt and anarchic as one would expect of nature.

We arrived late in the evening, unpacked several boxes, and erected tents just beyond the sight of the Keimokaw. I was recalled to my youth in the Rocky Mountains camping with my family. Here, in the solitude of the forest, we celebrated the true beginning of our venture. In the morning, the final preparations would begin in earnest.

CHAPTER 2.14

The schooner is assembled, final preparations are completed, and the boat is launched amid a flurry of arrangements.

FOR THE SAKE of brevity, I shall spare my patient reader the details of the ship's construction. We spent the entirety of one full week in the manufacture of the sailboat and tested each component as best we could in the calm waters at the conflux of the Keimokaw and the kill. We felled and milled several trees, a crime in itself. In the end, we produced a small, seaworthy craft with the strength and buoyancy to test the rapids and carry a couple passengers and the water and food needed to keep us alive. We erected a single mast to the ship and prepared sails.

The barge was a single hull, shaped as a punt. Over the hull, except in a small space for the occupants, was a great silken tarpaulin, arched in the middle to force any water to drain off the edges. The passenger compartment directly beneath the sail was isolated from the cargo areas by wooden crossbeams. Style was secondary to function, and so the wood on the outside was not sanded or shaved. The logs, where possible, were left raw, bark exposed. She was not the most luxurious craft, but she would float, could handle a few challenges, and would, with luck, provide enough power to sail Ryuudrikje and me to safety.

The leader of the Tegens left early on the morning of the launch day with two of his lieutenants. With me he left a single man to assist with the trip to the island. The plan hatched earlier had included carrying a single passenger and one chest, uninspected, to be dropped off at the island fortress. The boat was floating in the still waters and needed only to be punted from shore by long, strong oars, which could be secured to holes to serve as paddles or pulled to length to use as punting poles.

Without life jackets or flotation devices, we had decided to set out as near to noon as we could to maximize our visibility as we sought to navigate the unknown rapids. We heaved off against the eddy of the big river and immediately faced peril as the boat was jammed firmly against the rocks at the mouth of the confluence. Immediately the boat began to tilt, and my first mate and I leaned hard on the opposite side and pushed for all we were worth against the rocks with our poles. The boat creaked and bent under the strain of the current, but finally we swung the bow of the boat past the rock. Then with a lurch, the boat swung into the river, the high side dropping and nearly submerging us as both my shipmate and I tumbled overboard and into the river.

My neighbour reached out with one hand and seized a corner of the loosened tarp. He held strong. Each of us held our oars with one hand, and with my spare, I held onto his oar. The boat swiftly barreled down the river, dragging us two rats behind it. We were pummelled by the waves and the raging water. Without a pilot, the boat chose the natural path, which seemed to include every protruding boulder.

We were flung about as I tried to haul back towards the relative safety of the hull. I made slow progress. I threw my paddle aboard and grabbed at an oar hole with my one free hand. Just as I began to pull myself aboard, the ship struck a boulder, flipping me head over heels into the boat. Momentarily safe, I looked back out to see the Tegen had been jolted free. He was struggling mightily just to avoid drowning. I tried to reach him with my oar, but fully engaged with survival, he couldn't see the assist offered. I reached past his arm, leaning far over the wall of the boat, and tapped his chin with the paddle. Out of reflex, he grabbed the oar with both hands, and he released his own. The instant I felt resistance, like a fish on the line, I pulled with all the muscle I could muster. Flush with adrenaline, I landed him on board the boat. Exhausted and waterlogged, he coughed and vomited on the deck. I took up a position near to the back of the craft manning the tiller and bemoaned the loss of the oar.

The rudder proved of little value. The bulk of it had been shorn off in the original push off the kill. I dipped my oar behind the boat at long reach to act as a makeshift rudder. I managed to steer the boat into a calmer current while my mate regained his composure. With the speed of the river, and the panic of our steering, it was a short time before we reached the city. Already we had passed farms and cabins, uncaring livestock, and many astonished onlookers little predisposed, or capable for that matter, of providing assistance. The river widened and slowed some as we approached the huddled shanties of Cluemegnig. The river continued to meander around walls of great boulders deposited over centuries by the wild river until it opened widely. Ahead, in the centre of the still swiftly progressing watercourse, we could finally see our objective, the castle-prison: an island that jutted straight out of the river as a column of stone with three terraces, each at least ten metres tall, gradually decreasing in height. True to the description of the leader of the Tegens, a single cable descended from a high tower on a greater fortification on the shore of the mainland south of the island to the lowest terrace on the island.

Across from the castle, on the southern shore that hosted the source of the zipline, horns blared, and we could make out guards and soldiers running to their stations. On the northern shore of the mainland, a few people beckoned, while in the distance, an inferno raged. Great black billows of smoke poured out towards the ocean from flames that licked high into the air. The Tegen shipmate told me to steer to the north side of the island where we would be protected from the guards in the south. With all the strength remaining in my cramping muscles, I obliged. A small number of prisoners observed our approach, and unsurprisingly, they possessed few tools to assist. We crashed against the rocks, but the boat held firm under the stress. We pulled into a shallow cove, by which I mean a slight inlet created by the shelter of a particularly large boulder. I steadied the ship, hands locked and fingers closed tightly about the oar, and my partner pitched a rope up the wall. To our relief, it was collected by a resident of the island, who secured it in place.

I was urged to go up the rope first. Drawing on what little energy still resided in my arms and legs, I climbed up towards the prison. When I looked back down, I saw my shipmate had secured the chest to his back, and with fortitude and determination, he was climbing behind me with the heavy load strapped to his back.

At the top of the rope, I was greeted by a group of five. I tried to inquire on the well being of Ryuudrikje but ended up having to wait for my partner to arrive to interpret. When he got to the top, winded by the effort, I bade him to ask on my behalf, and he pointed to his brow. The group pointed to a building, which I was told was where the immortals lived. Here, too, they lived separated from the other prisoners. I took a second to check on my shipmate's well being, but he assured me he was in good hands and beckoned me to find my friend.

I found Ryuudrikje in a small dormitory with several other, much older Strulbrugs. I told him I had prepared a boat and we could probably take a couple others if necessary. None showed the slightest inclination to join us. Thankfully though, Ryuudrikje assented to the escape and ran back with me towards the boat. This life-threatening trek would have been difficult to justify to the Tegens had he not. The Tegen and the other prisoners had been crafting something out of the contents of the box as I'd run off to find Ryuudrikje, and when I got back, I found they had assembled a ballista that they were busy aiming, not towards the assembled troops on the southern shore, but at the impoverished shanties on the northern shore.

To the south, horns, bells, and whistles rang out, calling all men to barracks. Battalions mustered on the riverbank, but at a great distance. They were impotent to but watch our progress. In the north, fifty or so organized peasants were erecting a wooden wall out of a pile of rough logs. In the distance beyond, the fire still raged. Some white steam now mixed with the black fumes, suggesting a bucket brigade had joined that fight. Out of the shadows, for the rickety shelters to the north could barely be said to possess organized thoroughfares, the leader of the Tegens swaggered. At the sight of him, a cheer arose from the ballista crew on the island. My former shipmate approached and told me what was to follow was not for my eyes. He requested that I take my leave below. The tone he presented left little room for argument. Ryuudrikje and I climbed down the rope into the boat.

I pushed it towards the current. Having learned from the previous near-catastrophic casting off, I held a higher line and pushed hard to enter the current more directly. On the fortifications above, activity continued briskly. As Ryuudrikje and I navigated the tricky waters towards the ocean, I spared a moment to look back as an enormous bolt, tethered to a long, thin cord, was shot across the water from the island towards the northern shore. I saw it strike the wooden wall directly, where it stuck firm. At a signal from the leader of the Tegens, the prisoners began to cross the river along the rope, hanging upside down over the perilous waters, their legs crossed above the rope as hand over hand they pulled themselves to safety.

From the southern shore, archers had taken up positions and were occasionally firing towards the fortified island. None that I could see were finding a mark, their prey being protected by the prison walls. With the power of the current, Ryuudrikje and I were blown out past what must have once been a bustling harbour in the south. Today, the docks, quays, wharfs, and all the assorted buildings and infrastructure that once offered a lifeblood of import and export to and from the island kingdom now sat in decrepit disrepair, their utility no longer required in this hermit kingdom.

Gradually, the rushing water of the river was replaced by the gentle undulation of ocean waves. I realized soon thereafter that Ryuudrikje had never before travelled upon waters of any kind. He became very seasick, very quickly. There was understandable panic in his face and voice as he soiled the waters repeatedly with the contents of his stomach. He struggled to grow sea legs while I set about unfurling the sail and unpacking a few of our provisions. I was concerned he might suffer from dehydration or perhaps a lack of nutrition from his time spent in the prison. I urged him to try to drink and eat, against the flow from his body.

Slowly, a tired and empty immortal peeled his depleted body off the bulwark and slouched apologetically in the hold of the boat. I felt a deep sorrow for the poor man, who must certainly be questioning his decision to come aboard. In the most comforting voice I could muster, I tried to convince him this feeling would pass. Doubt and hope shared equal measure in his eyes. What man, faced with the illness I have described, not understanding its cause, does not feel they must surely be dying? Upon my friend, I kept pushing fluids to replace those he had lost, and after some time on the water, he began to hold some down.

I steered the boat directly south and was grateful for the sturdy construction as the boat bounced on the ocean calmly. Ryuudrikje was most thankful for the buffering effect the weight of the boat had upon the heaving action. Compass in hand, I maintained the steadiest course I could with the tiny paddle rudder. It was by no means a swift flight. Were it not for the shores of Cluemegnig in the distance providing some ground control points for reference, one might have been forgiven for thinking us to be just drifting with the current. Behind the boat, a slight trail of bubbles wafted listlessly in a meandering path of its own.

Ryuudrikje, completely worn, fell asleep, and night fell upon us quickly. Despite my own exhaustion, I fought against the urge to join him in slumber. I marvelled at the stars. Untrained in the constellations, I couldn't but wonder at the strange thought that people make connect-the-dot pictures out of a slight selection of stars. I kept my focus by attempting to do the same. I drew animals and people, continents and objects from the celestial bodies, and whenever I closed my eyes, I immediately forgot what I had drawn. I kept a firm hand on the tiller and shook away sleep as I repeatedly glanced at the compass.

My friend awoke with a start as the sun began to peek over the horizon. The black clouds from Cluemegnig were now all that could be seen behind us. No doubt there would be many bushed souls in that city today. Desperately tired, I showed Ryuudrikje how to steer the ship and operate the compass—which itself proved quite the novelty—and handed over control of our destiny to the young Strulbrug. I lay down and sleep overtook me with ease and Keimokaw speed.

CHAPTER 2.15

On the water, prison stories are exchanged.

I AWOKE SOMETIME later, as the day tucked itself in for its own slumber. Ryuudrikje was admirably manning the tiller and trying to figure out how to keep the wind in the luffing sails. I was worried we might be pushed off course. He kept the bow facing towards our destination to the south and our trail behind us to the north; it was a sedate progression. Far from a master shipbuilder, I had created a design that worked better in the fast-moving and hazardous torrent than here on the calm, cool ocean where it moved with the urgency of a lonely, giant tortoise.

The calm gave Ryuudrikje and me an opportunity to trade stories of the short time we had spent apart. I described to him the palace prison from which I had recently escaped and the Tegens, in particular, their leader. I told Ryuudrikje of how I had escaped, and he considered my good fortune a little insulting. As a Strulbrug, he thought it disappointing that his king would think so little of his kind as to leave the back door unlocked.

Then he told me of the island and his short stay at his prison. The island, as I had witnessed, was inhabited by several dozen prisoners, of whom about a dozen were immortals. The remainder consisted of a variety of political dissidents, amongst whom a number of Tegens could be found. This prison was the exclusive property of those who were an embarrassment to the kingdom, those whose crimes were often only the result of insulting a weak and cowardly Crown obsessed with its own stability. In this kingdom, the king was possessed of so little confidence and true power to inspire, connect, communicate, compromise, and respect others, that any who dared to possess other opinions or ideas from the official line, or speak ill of the monarch or his family, were treated as criminals. The fledgeling fourth estate was so hobbled by the powers exercised by these laws that information was not disseminated effectively.

Many of the criminals posted to the island prison could scarcely, in my mind, be considered as such. A select few might be considered intrepid and audacious journalists, others peaceful protestors, but none of them represented a true threat to the well being of others. I trust the reader will understand these prisoners' ideas and opinions were not all true and right, but in a reasonable and well-functioning society, there is always room for fact and scientifically based debate and discussion without the need to appeal to false authority.

Ryuudrikje spoke surprisingly well of the prison island. The people of Loogenage and I had been led to believe there could be no worse place on Earth, that barely enough food was sent by cable to the island to keep the residents alive, and the island was believed to be occupied by the worst offenders of the civil order. In fact, the island operated as its own miniature independent enclave within the kingdom. Inadvertently, by grouping all the dissidents together, a roundtable had been created whereby the discordants had been forced to sit and speak together to survive. The castle had become a paragon of debate and discussion. The Tegens' purist, anti-authoritarian streak had been blunted and refined by better informed and educated nonconformists. Strulbrug representatives of Ryuudrikje's network had affected the views of this group as well. Working in concert, they had designed a diminutive home out of the fortified isolated enclave.

Within the walls, what little bare earth they possessed, they converted into a garden with fruit trees, carefully hidden behind the barricades, and grew vegetables in the open to supplement the meagre foodstuffs provided by cable. This slight agricultural endeavour helped keep the prisoners well. A collection of water upstream from the Keimokaw River and the disposal of waste to the lee actually meant the prisoners enjoyed a superior sanitary standard than many in the cities. Even the Strulbrugs were encouraged to participate and experienced some of the benefits Ryuudrikje and his people had cultivated.

In truth, there was one element of humanity provided on the island that many in the kingdom of Loogenage were unaware they lacked: freedom. A man can live in pure opulence, but without freedom, having tasted it in any measure, to its pursuit alone will his time be devoted. The freedom of the island is one of the mind and spirit. The prison may encroach upon the physical freedom of its residents, but all are free to think and speak their mind without fear. Many people may believe that physical freedom is valuable, but truly the freedom of the mind and spirit are worth so much more. In spite of this, it was affirmed that many of those who had been imprisoned on the island over the years had chosen to take their chances with the river. So great were the rapids that most of the escapees reached only a few metres from shore before submerging and were never seen again. Even the strongest of swimmers would fail to make any headway, and this action was considered to be near-certain suicide.

Ryuudrikje told me of the many great plans of escape the prisoners had dreamt up during their incarceration. An abundance of time and little else affords people the opportunity to craft elaborate blueprints. One person, solo, might fall into the trap of ludicrous gimmickry, but through a group effort, they thought they had crafted a well-planned and refined operation. Ryuudrikje said that as a new initiate to the island, he had been included immediately in the regular discussion on the subject and found much had been established with clever detail. I would never see the fruits of the escape we had enabled, but it was with great hope that I looked upon this liberated group, now experts in compromise and respect, as the future of this anomalous place.

Ryuudrikje shared the same feelings. Full of hope for the future, he dreamt of being able to someday return to his free and strong homeland. I asked why he had chosen to come with me instead of staying with the Tegens. It was, he said, partly out of a desire to see more of the world than that to which he had thus far been restricted. I secretly believed it was out of a loyalty to me. Knowing I sought my own home and had yet risked all to come to his aid, he felt compelled to support and protect me as best he could. So, we floated deep into the night on a wooden tub with a single flimsy sail.

Loogenage faded behind us. In the distance, our course was laid towards a smothering fog. I hoped the fog would not prove to conceal more danger, but since it held the only way that had to me been provided, we held true to the tack.

PART THREE

GLUBDUBDRIB: NECROMANCY

CHAPTER 3.1

Sailing into the fog, the author and Ryuudrikje make landfall in a mysteriously beautiful place.

THE FOG GREW darker as we approached. Worse, a stiff wind blew straight from the concealing curtain. The wimpy sail, the possession of which had powered our slow crawl, dropped the wind. I took the oar and paddled directly into the oncoming storm. Here in the tempest, in the howling winds, blistering rain, crackling lightning, and crashing waves, the stout little boat felt more like it had in the river. It was made for this kind of punishment.

My friend was stricken by the ferocity of the storm. His recently sprouted sea legs faltered as the boat rocked to and fro. I, too, suffered from seasickness in the heart of the storm. Empowered by necessity and fuelled by adrenaline, I continued to row as an Olympian. The darkness that surrounded the ship closed in tight. Barely could I see Ryuudrikje only a few feet away from me. The air singed with electricity. My hair stood on end with cold and fright. Then my oar struck a rock. I tried to recompose myself and braced my legs against the hull. I strained to see into the thick cloud of fog and pulled on the paddle. The boat careened off a sharp, jagged rock, and the proud bow followed the weaker stern. Waves propelled us into the razor-sharp peaks. The oar in my hands, I tried to push away from the more imposing of the slag. The oar wedged in a hole. The weight of the boat jammed it and shattered the paddle into slivers about the deck.

Suddenly, the boat lurched up on an enormous wave and fell down with a clattering clash. The hull split across the bridge at the beam where both Ryuudrikje and I had taken shelter. As had the oar, the boat crumpled under the pressure, and we were flung headlong into the churning waters. The flotsam and coarse rock surrounded and bounced off the two of us. A log from the hull struck my shoulder. Needing a floatation device, I pulled it towards my body, and feeling for my semiconscious immortal companion, clasped his arms atop the float.

We were repeatedly battered and crushed upon the rocks. The log that kept us both afloat did as much harm to our bodies as it did to keep us alive. I held on to my friend as tightly as I could to keep us both draped limply over that one timber. The cold water sapped my strength, and the bruises multiplied on my arms, legs, shoulders, and back. I knew the same must be true of Ryuudrikje.

The fog then lightened slightly, and I could see clearly that he had been cut badly across his forehead and down to his eye, right through the mark of the Strulbrug. A gust of wind provided me with a quick glance of what I thought might be a small shelter nearby. I let go of the log, ducked thereunder, and pulled my friend to my chest. I leaned back into the water, and holding his back to my chest, my hands clutched over his ears in a makeshift carry, whip kicked as hard as I could towards that spot of peace.

It felt as though the winds and the waves were working against me deliberately. Each kick brought a wave over our heads. The wind blew salt into my face with every breath. I kicked and struggled against nefarious nature. I clutched my friend, certain our time on this Earth was reaching its end.

It always feels as though the last stroke is the last one you could possibly make. Perhaps it is but a trick of the mind, rewarding the individual for their efforts. It truly did seem as though I could not have kicked even one more time when my head hit a strong stone wall. I turned, and there, a foot above what I believed to be the approximate water line, was a small, protected enclave, just big enough to take shelter from the storm. I propped Ryuudrikje's arms on the lip of the cave and pulled myself out of the water. Then, carefully minding his head and neck, I plucked him from the waves as well. The water continued to lick at the ledge. Larger waves continued to roll over our legs, but we were momentarily safe. I lay my head on a cold, hard rock and wondered how long it would be until the storm would leave us. As the hours passed, the dark clouds and stormy weather persisted. Ryuudrikje, to my left, moaned as he slept. Even as he did, I was reassured in the knowledge he was all right.

Hunger eventually made itself known as remnants of our supplies began to push against our ledge as if also begging for sanctuary. I tried to pluck some of the foods out of the flotsam crashing against the wall below and succeeded in retrieving a couple apples, or at least the largest surviving parts thereof. I also pulled up a silk sheet that clung to a log. To even the least perceptive reader, it should be obvious the silk sheet was utterly drenched. I hoped to make use of it as a net with which I might retrieve a slightly better variety of food than two maimed and mutilated apples.

I wrung out the sheet while lying on my chest and tried to throw it with my forearms and wrists. I achieved no meaningful distance. A few feet away from my perch, I could see a couple jugs that, if structurally sound, should hold enough fresh water to sustain us for a short while. Unpracticed in the art of net fishing, it took many tries. I sacrificed a small degree of safety to throw from my knees instead. This innovation brought me much greater distance, but on the slippery slope of the cubby, I nearly fell back into the water. Panic raced through my veins, and I clung to the floor. After regrouping, I resolved to redouble my efforts. Many trials and frustrating failures later, I grappled a jug and carefully reeled it in. As the waves pushed and pulled, I matched their motions as best I could and moved the jug about half the distance towards me, about two feet beyond my reach. It took several more launches before I hooked it again and pulled it in towards me. Pulling it up, I took the cork out and took a small sip myself before propping up the recently awakened immortal and giving him a small amount as well.

I took the sheet, wrung it out again, as best I could, and propped it under our heads. We exchanged few words as we waited out the storm, exhausted, depleted, hurt, wet, cold, and tired.

CHAPTER 3.2

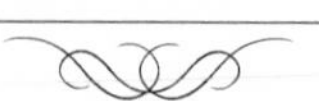

Days of unending storms and a lack of supplies force the two companions to abandon the relative safety of their roost and climb towards better prospects.

THE MINUTES TURNED quickly to hours, then to days. The storm rambled on with neither discontinuance nor diminuendo. We had fashioned of the silk a sort of funnel to catch rainwater, but our bellies rumbled, starved of food. I could not say which of us broached the idea first, but I am certain it was on both our minds. We would have to make a break for it.

We had both surveyed our options thoroughly: We could try to scale the cliff face horizontally, we could try to take to the churning waters again, or we could go vertical. The latter was the one we chose. Experienced with the waters, neither of us wished to go through that particular gauntlet again. Scaling the walls laterally might be easier, but if we fell, we would have no familiar cove of sanctuary. The upwards climb might prove the most difficult, but perhaps the rocks would be less incisive; at least if we failed, we would end up close to the relative safety of our current sanctuary. I took the silk sheet and threw one end up in an arc, hoping to blindly catch an outcrop above. After the fifth try, it stuck. By providence, it reached back down to the cave entrance. I wrapped my left hand with the silk as to form a glove. Ryuudrikje held the other end of the sheet taut and spotted for my ascent.

With learned patience, and careful movement, I tested each potential handhold. The water lashed my back, and the wind sapped the warmth from my skin. Ever so slowly, I sought out the least sharp handholds and avoided those too slippery. Upon reaching a small perch, I discovered the sheet had caught upon an outstretched root that had apparently grown close to the cliff's edge. The root was part of a dense ball of wood. I found a place to jam my arm and leg to help pull my buddy up to my level. We had only elevated a few feet, but the roots of this tree felt like true evidence that some level ground lay ahead.

The climbing was easier with the assistance of the wood. It was soaked and slippery but curved and knotted. Thanks to the root ball, we made steady progress upwards. I lost my footing on a slicked root once but caught myself. We tied the sheet around our waists to ensure that if one of us fell the other would be able to, if not catch, at least slow the descent. Unfortunately, as I reached the top of the root ball, still the cliff loomed above me. In the unnatural darkness of the perpetual deluge, I still could not make out safety ahead. The rocks had been replaced by a clay-rich soil, and I could dig out handfuls of the stuff but could not find an effective toehold.

I tried the same tossing trick with the sheet but could find no purchase above. Tying a thick knot in one end of the silk, I launched it skyward. It stuck. I held the rope, and sharing a look of powerless apprehension with my companion, I tugged hard. It stayed true. With one final look at Ryuudrikje, I tucked the rope between my legs and pulled myself towards the spouting heavens. The silk was full of water and clay, so only by manipulating its angles could I make headway, but I did. Just a few feet up, I could see the cliff's edge. I was a few feet away, so I kept climbing upwards until I reached a crotch between two sturdy branches. It was here that my knot had found a catch, and I pulled up onto the tree's limb.

Ryuudrikje followed shortly after. He proceeded more slowly than I, but he mimicked my climbing well. Soon we were both sitting on a low hanging branch of the tree. We surmised we were overhanging the combative waters at least ten metres beneath our roost.

Out of an abundance of caution, or perhaps a mixture of terror and exhaustion, we crawled along the branch towards the trunk of the tree. The bark stripped away as soggy tissue paper as we did. Hugging the branch, we reached the trunk and found a wide platform split between branches. On the side opposite the water, we scaled down a wide, strong root, exposed upwards from the ground, attached to the tree like a flying buttress. I lost my grip and slid down the root into the darkness below, crashing into a muddy puddle on the ground. Only an instant later, Ryuudrikje landed on my back.

Soaked and thoroughly muddied, our clothes tattered and drenched, we paused to laugh. It was the sort of laugh that comes from defeating impossible odds. Neither of us had said it, but we both believed our chances of survival were virtually zero. Yet here we were on solid ground. Still the storm pelted us with what seemed even greater ferocity than before, but we were safer here.

Pulling each other off the ground, we trudged through the thick, sludgy mud away from the water. Visibility was still low, but ahead, light pierced through a horizontal crack near the ground. The luminescence had a preposterous air. The slim, horizontal strip followed the natural undulation of the ground at its horizon. We approached cautiously while the storm crackled and hail pummelled us for our troubles. The fog thickened with each step until we reached out and touched…rock. It felt like perfectly polished stone.

Unmistakably, we were in front of a wall as smooth as marble but utterly lacking in colour so as to seem invisible in the dark. The stones were laid as bricks, but the mortar between them was so perfect it created a seamless finish. Above, we could see no limit, but the light had come from beneath. With Ryuudrikje in tow, I bent down to where I thought the light had come from and peered under. Beneath the wall, as clear as day, I could see to the other side of the wall. There was only a half metre or so of clearance between the wall and the ground, but it was enough to squeeze under.

Thankful to be making our way out of the hail and rain, the furious winds, and the thick electricity of the storm, we slugged our way under the thick wall at least a metre and a half wide and emerged in a sunny, warm, clear-skied field. We looked behind and saw a thick canopy of trees, densely thick in foliage, overhanging a beautiful, impenetrable, tall wall separating us from where we had come and where we now stood. Except that we had just come from there, we could not have found the gap beneath the wall from this side. On this side, light and warmth and a manicured landscape, surrounded by this great façade, were all we could see. The beauty of Loogenage, splendid as it was with its terraces and rose petals, paled in comparison to this place.

The entire land, if one assumed the entirety of this place was delimited by the great wall, which was visible but for the single expansive hill that dominated the topography, I estimated to cover about ten square kilometres. The hill seemed to have been tended to by the most flawless of gardeners. Plants of all kinds—flowers, shrubs, and trees—mixed graciously in a chaotic, yet carefully orchestrated performance of colour, shape, and size. At the peak of the hill, perched as if in a fairy tale, was a shining white palace of incomparable beauty. Every surface had been carefully selected and hewn to the highest standard. Upon the walls of the palace flowering gardens cascaded and great trees towered. Even at our great distance, we could seem them clearly. The palace, the park, and gardens that surrounded it all could only be described as the cynosure, the epitome, the apotheosis of architecture. One could stare, even at so great a distance, at the marvellous structure without remembering to wet one's eyes. An ocular siren's song, the palace stood before us proudly proclaiming itself the most impressive structure ever produced or seen.

Columns, perfectly distanced from each other, spiralled towards the sky. Onion domes and crenellations topped others. The reader might be forgiven for thinking the mixture of all these disparate styles would distract from its overall beauty, but they all played together. At the peak of the highest tower, impossible in its size, sat an orb, at least ten stories in diameter, painted as the Earth as seen from space, the bottom resting on its perch just south of Sao Paolo. Yet, I could have sworn the clouds were slowly moving, and I concluded the globe must be illuminated by a central projector at the heart of the sphere.

It would be impossible to even begin to estimate how long the two of us stood at the wall, so awed were we by its magnificence. As if cowed by a celebrity, we stood gaping at the resplendent scene before us, and to neither of us did the thought even occur to move closer.

While our minds strove to memorize every little detail of the place, our bodies suffered less distraction. It was only when the spell was broken by the fairly grumpy rumblings of my stomach that we were reminded of our position. We hiked up the hill, careful to not disturb anything. No paths nor trails were marked. Not a leaf or twig or weed, but for that which belonged to the tableau, marked any imperfection. We approached as pilgrims reaching their holy land. Even the air seemed alight with the magic of the place. At the walls of the castle, possessed of a stone both invisible and opaque at once, we approached the portcullis, itself a geometric wonder comprised of perfected Islamic and Arabesque shapes.

We could see not a guard, nor any living person beyond the castle walls. As we approached, silently as cats, the gate lifted skyward into a recess in the wall. Seeing none from whom we could seek permission, we entered.

CHAPTER 3.3

The author and Ryuudrikje make the acquaintance of the princess of Glubdubdrib.

BEHIND THE GATE, there addressing the primary corridor across a vast courtyard, measuring at least two hundred metres across and formed in a circle, stood two armies of a thousand souls if they possessed a single one. To the right, the rank and file of a Greek hoplite army stood at attention, dressed entirely from head to toe in full, unblemished, colourful garb. Counter to them stood an equally resplendent corps of Chinese soldiers as still as the Terracotta Army. Despite the numbers assembled, we heard not a whisper, shuffle, or even a breath from the soldiers.

My companion and I stood dreadfully still, fearing that at any moment a battle would be joined. Not one of the troops took notice of our intrusion, a fact we aimed to preserve. At the centre of the courtyard stood a single, solitary tower, wide enough scarcely to conceal an outhouse, but at least five stories tall and shaped as an Egyptian obelisk. In fact, down the height of the structure on the single side visible, was a darkened stretch.

Upon later examination, I would confirm the darkened stretch was possessed of carefully and intricately carved hieroglyphs in the Egyptian style.

Two doors opened from the obelisk, there in the middle of the reticent theatre of war. A woman—possessed of a long, flowing, silvery white mane that fell to her feet but was upswept by an unfiltered wind—never touched the earth. She wore a royal blue gown that reflected the light with a soft sheen. Her dress covered her entire body, from her neck downwards, and as for her hair again, it seemed to float above the path as she moved. I could not say she walked, for there was no evidence to support such a claim. She seemed to glide as though on wheels, buoyant above the ground.

Through the assembly, she drifted towards the gate, and a calming wave sprung from inside my head. I can best explain this feeling as the antithesis of a headache. It was as though my entire life had been plagued by a malady so accustomed to which I had grown, that entirely unaware of its presence I had been. The steely gaze and unflinching silence of the armies forced the tiny hairs on my skin to stand up, but I feared them not. Evidently feeling the same, without exchanging words, Ryuudrikje and I stepped fully into the courtyard in lockstep towards the enchantress.

Proximity to her incandescent beauty revealed a countenance composed of the best features from every race and a flawless complexion unmarked by even the slightest of deformity or injury. Her eyes resembled abalone, not a single colour, but seeming to reflect the light with blues, greens, browns, and all manner of shades by the refraction of the sun. Dangling over the fabric of her dress, directly upon her sternum, was a perfectly spherical opal stone. This diffracted the rainbow of light. At its centre, a patch of blue shaped as a brain with five distinct red dots near the middle of the blue. Upon this woman I looked, not with the brutish emotions of lust or longing, but as I had with the land and the castle itself, with admiration and appreciation of transcendent beauty.

I apologize to my forgiving reader. I could, and would, continue the description of my host and her castle in inexhaustible detail, but for the sake of recalling the important aspects of my travels, I must be briefer. If my povertous words would possess such greater power, the understanding reader would understand and be so much richer for it. I would sincerely wish to share the beauty with each of you, were it only possible to do so. Alas, I press on in recounting the encounter.

We stepped to a distance of about two metres from each other and paused. The soldiers to my left seemed not even to breathe so silent were they. To my right, every blink from Ryuudrikje seemed audible.

Arms outstretched as Christ the Redeemer, she spoke a single word. Off my ears this sound ricocheted and such a multifarious diversity of noise echoed within my skull. The waves collided and repeated, a symphonic orchestra of tones and syllables, and then they settled, with a clear, calm, and unmistakable, "Welcome."

The two bedraggled travellers, Ryuudrikje and I, opened our mouths at the same time. Simultaneously, in our mother tongues, he in Loogenagian and I in English, answered simply "Thank you." She smiled, and with an effortless snap of her fingers, both ranks of guards disappeared into a mist, which itself swirled and dissipated before I could even wrap my poor mind around what had happened. She bid us both to follow her into the skinny obelisk, which as disconcerted and confused as we were, we unquestioningly obliged, following her into a space I estimated from the outside to be not a decimetre wider or longer than a metre.

Our host disappeared through the door into the pitch-black space, and I followed close behind, cautiously feeling forwards to avoid running into the snow-haired maiden. I crossed the threshold and found myself to be in an impossibly enormous chamber shaped as the great ballroom in Versailles. The maiden glided across the marble floor, past elegantly carved columns, and under high vaulted ceilings with elegant paintings throughout. In this place were dozens of twittering residents who seemed far more interested in us than the ethereal guards were. We followed the woman to the far side of the room where she took a seat upon a gold and jade decorated throne. Again we stopped, and possessed of a spirit beyond my comprehension, I took a knee, and Ryuudrikje bent over and licked the floor at his feet.

She spoke again. This time she spoke in perfect English. Ryuudrikje would later remark that he was both awed and cowed at how I seemed to speak fluent Loogenagian in response. Thus, we entered into communication with Princess Beyuba of Glubdubdrib.

CHAPTER 3.4

The princess of Glubdubdrib educates the travellers about her kingdom and to them offers an unusual but an irrefusable gift.

THE PEOPLE OF this marvellous place consisted of a single tribe. The princess was the most aged of them all. Lo, her appearance belied her age. She informed us she had, in fact, bore witness to over one hundred solar years. The people of this island had once hosted visitors from a pair of kingdoms, Loogenage and Balnibarbi. At around the same time Loogenage shut its ports and scuttled her fleet, Balnibarbi, too, fell silent.

Themselves a sedentary people, those of Glubdubdrib satisfied themselves with their own superior means. As far as I was able to understand, the name "Glubdubdrib" meant the Kingdom of Magic. I hope the reader does not believe me mad, but the magiks I had witnessed sufficed to make a believer of me in their capability. In the words of Arthur C. Clarke, any sufficiently advanced technology is indistinguishable from magic. Perhaps it is so amongst the natives of this place, but there was something altogether different about their capabilities.

The single tribe of the island had once lived in towns and had a functioning harbour. Now, through devotion to their art, they had constructed the single palace where we now loitered. As near as I could understand, at least one thousand full apartments occupied this structure. Eventually, we toured a number of them, and they were all of a similar magnificence to the grand hall. We were not permitted into the private chamber of the princess, though. I could only imagine the wonders therein.

This tribe only ever married within, never with an outsider. It was thus that their unique gifts were maintained. I was told the opal, which never but hung around the princess's neck, was a sort of Babel fish. Every language it had ever been exposed to was maintained in its sphere. When used in communications, it provided the sort of instant translation to which we had become accustomed. The welcome of the sorceress had in fact been communicated to us in every language ever heard upon the Earth. The capacity to understand our own mother language amongst the thousands of others, a skill innate amongst all peoples, provided the sort of calibration necessary to ensure full translation.

The Glubdubdribians were possessed of the ability to produce more of the stones of which the wall and castle were constructed from, and they could transfer that knowledge from one to another freely. In the garden of the palace, foods of all kinds were grown within the Daedalean-interlaced vegetation. Livestock of every imaginable sort was tended to and cared for in expansive ranges.

I would have asked about how such a small numbered people, even possessed of the magic they had to me demonstrated on the first day of our visit, managed all this, but it should be known this was abundantly evident early on.

Of all the incredible abilities of the people of Glubdubdrib, the greatest by far was the ability to conjure the dead from any time in history to serve, but only within the hewn walls that surrounded the island and only for a period of a single day—not to be recalled within a period of three months. Only a single exception to this period of fallow existed: by exchanging the life of the conjurer, the deceased could be brought back within the pause.

In my mind, and no doubt that of many of my readers, an ethical dilemma came forward. It was difficult to reconcile: should one, even endowed with such powers, exorcise a resting spirit without their consent for any purpose? I voiced my concerns, but the princess held to a simple retort: The dead possess no ability to deceive or to lie, nor any impulsion to do so. They simply have no need of it in the beyond. If I wished to know whether objections existed to being drawn into the living world, I need only ask one of the many servants.

As you will understand, these people kept at their service dozens of the deceased at all times, and we were introduced to a number thereof. It was at first a surreal experience to speak to one who had been to the other side. Some of these had not breathed the air of the living these past thousands of years, and more had recently passed on. I was guaranteed, and to the concerned reader I promise, that the answers I received from each and every one, under no duress from their callers, assured me they bore no ill will at being brought to this place. They even took pleasure in the mundane or extravagant tasks asked of them, though they did not speak badly about their other existence. Being called to Glubdubdrib seemed a sort of sabbatical, as one who loves their job might take out of a desire for variety and diversion.

Our meals were served to us by the finest waiters that ever lived and were cooked by chefs such as Apicius and Mithaecus, Taillevent and Pierre de la Varenne, who had been in the employ of emperors and kings. The meals, prepared fresh from the fields of the island, were without parallel to those tasted anywhere in the world. Our rooms were prepared and cared for by the greatest hoteliers the world has ever seen. For us, the noblest and most lavish vestments were shaped by artisans of the highest order. The first visitors to the island in the life of the princess, we were treated as royalty.

Beyuba gifted Ryuudrikje and me with opals of our own, each endowed with the same brain-shaped blue and red design. It was then she offered us the most precious present I could ever have imagined. She offered each of us the chance to call any number of souls, from any point in history, for the purpose of conversation. She would grant unto each of us the services of one of her subjects endowed with the ability to recall spirits, and they would be our guides in this place. We would be permitted to speak to the evoked people candidly about their lives, but only about the time they had lived. It was forbidden to ask questions of those who cannot lie about things they do not know. We would be permitted to share details of the world, but we were not to disturb or insult the spirits.

Never before had I such a unique and cherished gift. I dare not ponder ever receiving the like again. This rare thing set my mind racing to all the people I would like to meet. The offer would begin the next morning. She offered her services for a period of not more than ten consecutive days. It is sufficient to say I was unable to sleep even for a minute that night. Possessed of a smaller breadth of history, Ryuudrikje was equally excited to call forth a number of Loogenage figures.

CHAPTER 3.5

The author lays out his plan and rationale, calls back a number of deceased, and speaks to them about a subject of paramount importance.

IN THE MORNING, though presented with the most perfect spread of foods ever collected, I am sure, my mind still raced with thoughts of the colossal figures I would call forth from their beyond. The food, surely tasting as good as any ever made, was but a cardboard façade in my mind's eye. I consumed it with such haste that the chef, were he of the living, would have certainly been disgraced and insulted. As a child who wishes only to be somewhere else, I polished off the delicacies and sought permission from my host to take her up on her offer. Behind her exotic and unfamiliar eyes, I could not but wonder at the thoughts she hid therein.

I was introduced to the man who would introduce me to such great wonders as that which my mind could not imagine on its own. Cado was, as all the people of Glubdubdrib, a relative of Princess Beyuba. Handsome in his own right, he was nearly as beautiful as the princess herself. Cado was aged more than eighty years himself, but upon looking at him, apart from his silver-white hair, one would not think him more than a fit and muscular thirty. Cado wore a tight-fitting robe of marine blue about his upper body that flowed to his ankles as a Greek toga. He wore sandals, but unlike those of Loogenage, these gave the impression of pure comfort as if he was walking upon a cloud of air that caressed his feet.

Ryuudrikje and I parted ways in the palace, each with our own guides, and were exposed to architectural marvels in the impossibly huge space that it was. The castle was home to hundreds, if not thousands, of rooms, each one unique and all endowed with examples of the most precise, ornate, elaborate, and beautiful furnishings, designs, artwork, and materials of opulent luxury with which I was completely unfamiliar. Bedrooms and common areas, bathrooms and kitchens alike were each arrayed with marvellous examples of the best art and science could possibly provide. Cado showed me such wonders as I never have seen before or since, and all the while, while I gawked at the impressive surroundings, I never felt any condescension or impatience on his part towards me. We had easy discussions about anything, and he was as open to me as a book. In spite of this, I was still focused on the even more incredible opportunity that awaited me.

As I am sure anybody would, once having decided to pursue such a thing, I prepared to call forth a prodigious number of the dead. I had sorted them out into categories in my mind: kings and emperors, queens and empresses, inventors, builders, writers, generals, athletes, military heroes, philosophers, business tycoons, scientists, artists, criminals, explorers, and other prominent leaders. I had even come up with what I thought to be a clever strategy: I would seek out common folk of various times. Perhaps the most incredible idea I had, but undoubtedly the most controversial, was to seek out the highest religious leaders.

I also sought out a few of my ancestors and recently deceased companions. With those who had actually known me, or who knew of those still alive, I made the sensible and cautious decision to keep conversation to a minimum, lest they reveal unto me something I could not bear to hear. Who would want to know that a close relative despised them, or their parents, or that they had been involved in some despicable act? To such an end, and I believe the reader to be less interested in such discussions, I shall skip over the contents under the thin veil of privacy.

To the curious amongst my readers, I will announce that my first ideas pointed towards Ancient Rome. I cannot say why I was so drawn to that place and time, but obviously an amount of time unequal has already been paid to this subject. Thinking of Rome, I considered other great empires such as Greece and Egypt, Mesopotamian civilizations like Babylon and Assyria, and then I went further afield to China, Mali, the Mughals, Incas, Aztecs, and Mayans. In my mind, it was of greater interest to explore these. For more recent context, the empires of Europe and the courts of kings and queens, all of those I could dream up I would call. I thought of a way to ensure I didn't miss somebody important out of personal ignorance. I would ask them, as I would ask my friends today, who they would have liked to speak with from the past. If my mind could store so many names, imagine what the honest minds of those incredible people could unlock? I ensured that I kept track of all the names recommended and called them forth as well, along with those who had so desired their presence.

I thought back to my ancient history classes in school. The words of one teacher rang in my head. Almost all we know of life in past times is that of the rich, powerful, and elite. We are blind to the vast majority of history because of the dearth of information about the lives of the commons. I would seek out these common people, whose names I did not know, by asking those I did for the names of the least powerful people they could name until I had an equal and representative sample from various empires and times as I have previously listed.

Apart from the powerful, I wanted to hear from the creative and brilliant and would call upon the greatest minds of whom I could think and the greatest that they could in turn. I regret that even though I spent but ten days at this oeuvre, the words, thoughts, sights, and sounds could fill a hundred volumes of the length of this story. Every word spoken is locked in my mind as a precious jewel, but I can only relate some of the more interesting.

As with every room in the castle, the chamber used to call these people was impossibly large. The space seemed to stretch farther than the entirety of the island, and above the space was a ceiling higher than the Roman Colosseum. My astonishment, shared with Ryuudrikje, was answered by my guide. Cado explained it was not the manipulation of space, but of time, that created this place. I can't begin to unravel that mystery. Perhaps if I open it to stronger minds, they might be able to explain it someday. I regret I was not able to ask him more about manipulating time to the benefit of space. He tried briefly to explain how this was accomplished, but I was either too dim to comprehend how this worked, or I simply lacked the sense that these sorcerers possessed. As a deaf child might wonder, having made a copious amount of sound sneaking into a cookie jar, how his parents knew of his deceit, so did I wonder at the abilities of the residents of this island. I digress disappointedly but shall return to my descriptions.

In this space, I was able to call not just the generals, but entire corps and field armies, even theatres. I could call not only the kings, but the entirety of their courts and servants. I could have them arranged logically. It might seem paradoxical, but calling large numbers simultaneously, entertaining as it was to see two opposing legions standing toe to toe as I had first encountered in the courtyard, provided the least depth of discovery and obviously the least intimacy.

The most famous idea I had was the one to which I must devote the least space. I sought to call forth all the greatest religious figures I could think of from history. Cado warned me about this idea and reminded me that some of the names I was asking about were indeed fictitious characters from antiquity, and thus could not be recalled, they having never actually been present in the first place. As religion is a construct of man, I understood that surely not all those figures could be real, and/or at least, the entirety of their stories and teachings could not. Certainly, they would prove in direct contrast to one another in some places. I tried to call Jesus of Nazareth, Saul of Tarsus, Muhammad, Buddha, Mirza Ghulam Ahmad, David, John the Baptist, Abraham, Moses, Joseph Smith, the Saptarshi, Lao Tzu, Zoroaster, Tiresias, Cassandra, Livius, and many others. I called them all together simultaneously. Of those who heeded the call, with no animosity shared between them, they requested but three things.

Firstly, and it was agreed upon by all of these people, was that the attendance roll for this gathering of minds should not ever be shared. It would be of no benefit to them or their followers to hold confirmation of their presence or absence. For my own sake, controverting the beliefs of their followers, or those of false and fictional prophets, would surely only lead to harm.

Secondly, they demanded that the veracity of their prophecies (true or false) equally should never be shared with the public. Again, it is in my own best interests to not appear to present myself as a prophet. And I most certainly did not want not to deny their existences, the proof of which is no less circumstantial in the absence of faith than their own fictions.

Thirdly, and unlike their other two demands, they asked that I convey a single and simple message verbatim: "That no god, deity, or supernatural being, of any pantheon, be they many or single, as espoused by the true and accurate religion(s) of the world, if indeed there be one or more, finds amusement, pleasure, or benefit in the slaying of another human either in his/her/their name or the defence thereof." They made clear that even though some of those present had apparently advocated for such actions while on Earth, the correct interpretation of all their teachings was that in no case was the killing of another justified for religious means.

Cado implored me to report their wishes truthfully and completely. The respect held for those departed on the island of Glubdubdrib was supreme. Besides, those people gathered possessed so great a power, such a tremendous conviction, and so compelling a will that I cannot but accede to their wills, and on this subject say no more, now or ever.

CHAPTER 3.6

The author calls back a number of world leaders to learn of their lives and times.

ON THE SECOND day of my commuting with those antecedents, I took to calling upon the leaders of history. At my beck were all the most and least successful monarchs, autocrats, both inherited and self-made, and those elevated to power by the will of the consensus of the people. If even had I spent a quarter of an hour individually with each person with whom I wished to speak, I could have passed the ten days many times over. Thus, I called back small groups of contemporaries, particularly those who had been fierce rivals in life.

One such group I called were European heads of state during the French Revolution and the Napoleonic wars: Francis I, Frederick VI, Muhammad Ali, Charles Louis, George III, Louis II, John VI, Frederick William III, Alexander I, Joseph I, Charles XIII, and of course Napoleon himself. I preserved the American heads of state separate, being more interested in gathering them together in a different group.

My first discovery, petty though it may appear, was that Napoleon stood at or above the line of each of the others, except George III, who towered above them all at a height slightly greater than my own, perhaps two full metres. Le petit caporal was certainly short by today's standards, standing maybe only around one hundred and sixty-five centimetres. Compared to those around him though, he was roundly similar. I cannot explain it myself, why he reported his height to be one hundred and fifty-five centimetres, but surely, by the measures with which I am familiar, this he was not.

My second discovery related principally to the respect and esteem with which he was now held by his peers. In life, they all admitted to holding nothing but spite, hatred, loathing, and contempt for the upstart, ignoble, degenerate king. In death, free of the machinations of state and culture and the necessities of life, so being complicated by the entanglements of their birthrights, several of their number broadcast freely their respect and admiration for the man who had risen from minor nobility to establish a powerful state and a great many achievements therein. I sensed, and it was confirmed, that many bore him some jealousy by the freedom he achieved for himself and his people and with which he was able to rule so freely. Such a discovery would prove a theme amongst the many good leaders with whom I shared time. Bound by their servitude and loyalty to the people and the state over which they presided, few were able to enact the sweeping reforms and programs, positive though they truly believed they could prove, for the pain that would be caused by their actions. It was those who held their convictions above the immediate needs of their servants who were able to achieve the largest changes in society. So it was for Napoleon, who, being freed of the history of his family, and the divine right of kings, could enact so many changes to the state of France, and gradually, the continent of Europe.

For his part, like so many of the tyrants I interviewed, Napoleon would heap such great praise upon those who were responsible for his eventual defeat, exile, and ultimate death. Acknowledging their praise for his achievements in so little time, he held firm that the greatest accomplishment of all belonged to them in his defeat and destruction.

Another discovery to be made was the role religion played in the lives of so many of these great leaders. The official religions of most great people, of course, are well documented, it being in the national interest and the power of the first estate, thereby providing support for such. History, a disgusting bastardization of modernity, has cemented such things into the common mind such that they cannot even be questioned. The identified religion, as believed by most today, is a product not entirely of the leader's own piety but of the literate classes of their day and the manipulation of that record over time by those with an agenda.

Two common threads unravelled in the presence of these men and women. Firstly, not all of them, while living, believed in the dominant religion of their time, or their role therein, but they recognized the value of adherence for the perpetuation of their wealth and office. Secondly, even those who demonstrated, wrote, or spoke out against the canon were subsequently fictitiously recorded in history or were simply believed by the misled and misinformed, both educated and not, to have been devoted followers, regardless of their declarations to the contrary. For those few leaders who spoke out firmly, and whose words could not be washed clean, the erasing of their memory from history's diary entirely was always attempted. Through such discoveries, I became disillusioned with the practices of modern history, especially regarding religion.

I spoke to the Egyptian Pharaoh Akhenaten. A proud and ambitious man who saw the cult of Amun in his time as too powerful and too great a check on his supposedly divine powers, he single-handedly changed the state's beliefs from Amun to Aten. He epitomized the strength and formidable will of the best kings in both life and death. As a man of antiquity, he was exquisitely gifted with words, and he possessed a regal stature, in both height and fitness.

His reward for his theistic gambit was continual slander and maldepiction. So powerful were the rival cultists that craftsmen engaged in engraving his image cowed to their pressure and repeatedly sculpted him with an androgynous body and a deformed jaw. Again and again, he rejected their works, and each time, the work was replaced by identical disfigurement. In speaking with his successors, including his son, Tutankhaten, who eventually bowed to the pressure of the powerful church and subsequently changed his name to Tutankamun, it became clear that a concerted effort had been made to strike Akhenaten's name from the record.

While a similar tale, that was a different time than when Constantine, emerging victorious from a series of civil wars against Maxentius and

Licinius, made use of a new religion, Christianity, to consolidate his power. He used his authority, backstopped by a string of military victories, to manufacture a story whereby angels and God himself had led him to his greatness. Who would dare argue, he revealed to me, with somebody who had achieved so much when he said that the cause of his success was divinity, the likes of which had been persecuted so long by his foes. Thus successful, he corralled the power of belief and mythology to cement his own permanent legacy. Unlike the Egyptian pharaoh, his reformations stuck, and the intimidated elite was gradually converted to his side.

While Akhenaten had the courage, or in his words, the arrogance, to force a change of religion on a powerful vested theocracy, others make good of the blind faith and trust of the theocratic authorities, seizing power themselves by purporting their unending faith regardless of the truth of it. So it was with Isabela and Ferdinand. In complete honesty, they shared cheerfully the great ruse that was their Catholic conviction and devotion.

When Isabella ascended the throne of Castile, she was the subject of repeated plots by the Archbishop of Toledo. Thereby, the beliefs of the two were shaken by their treatment at the hands of the Catholics under the archbishop's command. When they overcame their enemies, it became clear to the Catholic monarchs the power swaddled within the blanket of religion. The two of them silently formulated their great illusion, by which they would profess the highest faith in the Catholic god, a ruse that was rewarded by the pope, who then granted Isabella the Servant of God title nearly five hundred years later. Confronted by powerful Muslims, they used the stoked religious fanaticism to help drive the infidels from their lands. Their greatest achievement was recognizing the power of this religious fervour, and rather than allowing it to fade away, they claimed it for themselves and marshalled the theocratic authorities to focus upon an insignificant and unthreatening minority who were guilty only of not sharing the same religious beliefs, or even just having not shared them once. This masterful work of deception, they reported, allowed their retention of power. As recognized servants of the Catholic Church, their legitimacy could not be called into question. Isabella was granted the title, Catholic Monarch, by Pope Alexander VI, a man whom she detested thoroughly.

Many other kings and queens, emperors and empresses, and even elected officials, testified to the similar manipulation of religion and history for their own purposes. One more stands out in my mind, not because of the manipulation by the leaders themselves, but because of the gradual erosion of fact and the incorporation into the general consciousness of a state of falseness of belief. I saved for last the founding fathers of the United States to gather as a group, together united for the first time in hundreds of years.

Contemporaries of Napoleon, I wanted to speak with them about the convictions that led them to rebel against the British king and empire. Many stories about them are indeed true as reported, but so many have also been bastardized by time that the true facts are well obscured. The heroics of Paul Revere, who never truly announced the British were coming for the British were already there and all considered themselves to be British anyway, if not satisfied to be subjects of the English Crown, are the perfect example.

The founders balked at the idea of a Christian country. Jefferson chopped up the Bible, removing the mythology; he emphatically repeated that the writers of the New Testament were ignorant, unlettered men. Paul, the Apostle, was the first corrupter of the doctrines of Jesus. Having already called religious figures the day before, the compassionate reader will understand I was unable to recall them for a structured debate on the subject.

Most of the founding fathers instead practiced their own degree of deism, as did Napoleon in France. He chose to believe in a higher power but not in the nonsensical miracles and supernatural interventions that plague the King James Bible. He described his beliefs, in life, as a sect of his own. The majority of the writers of the American constitution retained some Christian belief but had strong influences from the renaissance deism. Washington, Franklin, Adams, Paine, and of course Jefferson, were the most willing to share their former beliefs.

I found most interesting their faith in the constitution they wrote was not firm, that the tenets they asserted were not to be the solid bedrock of a great nation as is so often believed today. It was for that reason gaps were left, allowing for amendment by an overwhelming majority in both the Senate and Congress. Thomas could be seen to blush when his compatriots emphasized a single quote to this effect: "Nothing is unchangeable but the inherent and unalienable rights of man." None of these men, despite the saint-like glow that has been applied to their names and records over the years by an appreciative and worshipful country, believed their knowledge to be absolute or their works to be unquestionable. Time changes, man grows wiser with greater knowledge and study, and rules are not meant to be broken but adapted to reflect the realities of the day.

I reflected on the day with Cado at the end of this day, interested to know what he thought of the people with whom we had spoken. I was surprised, but perhaps not so greatly, that he was largely unmoved by the people of the day. I postulated that it might be because these were not people of his world, or perhaps that he had already met with many of them and these things which were revelations unto me were but regular occurrences to him.

In fact, the reason for his blasé attitude was something a mixture of both thoughts. He was not particularly interested in the goings on of the outside world beyond Glubdubdrib because he simply needed not be. Great leaders and ill are no more important to him than any other person. What I found to be impressive and thought valuable insights were to him considerably less important, even trivial. I say this but realize it might sound like he was speaking with condescension. I swear to the reader that nothing could be further from the truth. He listened and learned intently, and with great interest, but separated from the influence of these people, it weighed little on him.

I found the experience similar with Ryuudrikje. Each of us were calling our own visitors, and we both were having an incredible time of it, but to speak of those with whom we had visited, the names and histories of whom were not relevant to each other, turned into no more than a superficial conversation more focused on the details of each person's existence in life than what we heard about them in death.

I bring up this point only to explain why I am sparing the reader details of Ryuudrikje's summons. My reader would require more contextual information about these people than I was able to learn in our busy time on Glubdubdrib, and this information in absentia, I think the description would be less than valuable.

CHAPTER 3.7

The author assembles a conference of inventors, thinkers, and scientists and discovers inspiration and history are most complicated phenomena.

I DESIRED TO speak not just to the political and religious powers of history but to some of the wisest minds and most creative souls that have graced my world. There, too, I discovered much of what is today considered important by the general public ought to be relegated to the dustbin of history.

In that vein, I collected a convention of some of the greatest inventors and scientists: Einstein, Newton, Galileo, Lovelace, Copernicus, Aristotle, Leonardo, Tesla, Curie, Faraday, Archimedes, Hypatia, Edison, Bell, and a vast sum more to discuss the commonalities that drove them to study. I asked each, having heard many times from the eager mouths of school teachers of his particular story, if they had struggled in their subjects as Einstein had in mathematics. In this question I was quickly set straight. Not only had Einstein not experienced any deficiency in math, he was, in fact, quite the prodigy. His failed test was the product of an underage application to a school that he failed not for want of mathematics but for the lack of mastery of the French language of the school, as well as botany and zoology. As seems to be so often the case, the accepted story was not the true story—that of a prodigal genius who manufactured world-changing ideas—but the fiction of a poor student turned successful could better motivate the ordinary soul to develop into the prodigy.

It was thus so when I asked about the inspiration of Sir Isaac Newton. What person today is not aware that an apple fell from a tree onto Newton's head, and he, in a moment of genius and revelation, created the theory of gravity? It was not, he reported, a sudden stroke, but it was, after considerable study and devotion to his art, that such a discovery was made. It was to his deep sadness that the thought that his life's work had been converted into a child's story intimating that anybody could solve great problems so easily as with a mild head trauma. He posited that the root of the story was that he chose to describe gravity in entertaining circles by describing the nature of an apple's fall: Why but for the effects of gravity does an apple fall downwards directly without fail?

It was so with Archimedes and Darwin. Archimedes never once ran naked through the streets exclaiming his "eureka" moment. He carefully studied objects, and his dedication led him to use a combination of buoyancy and mass to solve for the density of an irregular solid. Galileo himself confirmed similar suspicions with regards to the story. Archimedes developed his own theory of buoyancy, and scales were far easier to come by than a device which could carefully track fluid displacement. Archimedes said to me that it makes for a pretty fiction, if a bit scandalous for his preferences, but there was no truth to the story.

Darwin is reported by history to have been struck by a similar epiphany when he visited the Galapagos Islands; even the record shows that while the islands most undoubtedly provided inspiration for his theory, he spent two dozen years refining and developing the theory before he released *On the Origin of Species* in 1859, 24 years after visiting the islands in 1835. Each of these men lamented that their sincere hard work and dedication had been usurped by fairy tale and good fortune. None regretted any positive role their derived fictions could have had on encouraging work in the sciences but feared they might lead to a corner-cutting, short-term-results-driven academia.

Amongst the great minds assembled—most likely the highest cumulative intelligence gathered in one place—I felt utterly dwarfed by their mental acuity. The common threads I could find amongst the group were as simple as one could possibly imagine: a passionate devotion to the pursuit of knowledge, the careful analysis of all the facts, meticulous questioning and experimentation on all presented assumptions, a natural propensity towards deep and scrupulous thought, a liberating opportunity enabling their studies, and a rejection of presumption and constructed limitations. In the absence of any of these elements, no great advances would have been procured for humanity.

The accomplishments of these minds could scarcely be documented in a single tome. History, I concluded, is not written by the victors as we are led to believe. These thinkers must surely be remembered unfortunately by storytellers who fashion out of their own biases, whether intentionally or not, a more pleasant and easily consumable anecdote that can be stored in the collective consciousness of mankind.

These gifted individuals demonstrated to me another of their crucial skills, though I will not belittle myself and suggest I am unintelligent or slow. My more sarcastic readers might decry such a statement. In the presence of those who had studied a particular area and had advanced their understandings to such an enormously incomparable degree, it only occurred to me much later that I probably should have felt overwhelmed by their knowledge. Though they each conferred their story in their own language, despite them being translated for me by the opal, they might have presented such stories at such a level as to be unattainable to me. Yet the larger part of these great scientists were able to convey their thoughts and their ideas to me in a manner that I could digest while equally explaining the highest concepts in the manner that garnered them fame in life. Such is the greatest achievement of the best-known geniuses of history: the ability to delve deep into challenging, difficult, complicated, even labyrinthine sciences and yet to emerge with the ability to convey concisely and with clarity the most salient and pertinent essences of their discoveries.

CHAPTER 3.8

The author brings together artists and creative minds to understand the importance of art in the world.

HAVING HAD SURROUNDED myself with the most astounding men and women of science, the preeminent leaders of history, and the leading insightful theological players, I sought a respite amongst the most famous and talented artists. All those that had left their mark by tickling the ear, creating spectacles for the eyes, energizing the heart, and inspiring the mind through paint, music, literature, poetry, and performance I sought out to lighten the mood. In my mind, gathering the bards and the jesters, the scribes and the painters who had lightened the spirits of the world could do no differently for me. The weight of the gift the princess of this island had for me delivered weighed heavy upon on my shoulders.

I beseeched Cado to allow me to see these people in the beautiful openness of the island. I felt that while leaders and brilliant people could be confined to the enchanted palace complex, the risen spirits of artists could be best enjoyed in the splendour of nature.

Cado acceded to my wishes, and I asked to call these people forth expecting to have our spirits raised and our days brightened. I secretly hoped to elicit a pleasurable experience for Cado as well. I might be giving the impression he was cold and aloof. I would describe his attitude not as such but as a wise elder who enjoyed my world through my eyes second-hand. Yet I also did not think of him as other than a friend. As a friend, I hoped I would bring him some joy as I enjoyed the gift he was giving me. Alas, I did not find the gaiety and joy I thought universal amongst these ethereal beings I called.

Instead, I found the spirit that drove many to the arts was less one of frivolity and more one of a tortured soul in search of acceptance, or even one driven by competition. Born into circumstances that allowed them to practice, just as with the scientists with whom I had conversed the day before, these prodigies of art and culture were impelled to follow and perfect their craft, if not by themselves, then by their parents, guardians, teachers, or even friends.

Particularly so amongst the eldest of the spirits, their innate desire was often blunted by strict boundaries and powerful patrons who demanded the fruits of their labours. These artists became obsessed with their talent and sought out those who shared similar gifts, craving the approval they so deserved for the incredible sacrifices demanded of them. Their celebrity, combined with their introversion, provided a perfect avenue for the misinterpretation of their persons.

So it was with Vincent van Gogh, who to me appeared a humble and reticent man. Cured, but not himself cognizant of his previous madness, in the afterlife, the misrepresentation was in fact confirmed by Paul Gauguin. The two artists had originally found each other and become friends. They had worked together in search of the best of their art, but each had confessed to possessing extreme jealousy of the other's abilities in life. Their friendship had been punctuated when an argument broke out between them as Paul had set to leave one night, and Vincent had thrown a glass of absinthe at Paul's head, grazing and drawing blood from just over his ear. In a fit of anger, Gauguin had drawn his epee and swiftly carved a portion of the drunken Vincent's ear from his head. History records the incident as a moment of self-inflicted harm done by a madman, a fiction spread by

Gauguin as his friend had indeed succumbed to insanity spurred on by the same absinthe. Gauguin himself revealed that the relationship between the two giants of impressionism had been strained by their mutual infatuation with each other's art. Such a tortured but brilliant artist was van Gogh, whose most recognizable feature ought to forever be linked to the strained pursuit of perfection.

I had gathered a number of painters together and asked them to paint with supplies from around the castle. Possessed of so little time, few took up the brush to create anything. Even after their life, the pursuit of perfection and beauty still tortured them so.

An assembly of writers, from Tolstoy to Twain, Shakespeare to Hugo, and Dickenson, Dickens, Chaucer, and Wilde graced me with their presence. To hear these people speak, with the eloquence of their incalculable vocabularies and the near magic with which they combined phrases even in their ordinary speech, was a treat to my ears. Possessed of this gift, even ordinary words produce vivid pictures and scenes in the mind. I had the audacity to ask the bard the only direct question that came to mind: whether he was indeed the author of the works attributed him. He said he could not know those works that may have fallen to his name after his passing. I listed to him those of which I was familiar, and he confirmed each of those was indeed construed in his mind and constructed by his own pen. I listened intently as they each related stories of their time and the world and inspiration they used to fashion their own fantasies on paper.

No less beautiful, it should not surprise any reader, was the ensemble of great musicians and composers. Happily, they performed for me and for each other with instruments procured from the multitudes of stores held within the castle walls. The wonderful things they could do with the brass, wood, string, or virtually any run-of-the-mill object lying about made them amongst the most fantastic of all the artists.

Their talent, again, was balanced against the darkness in their hearts. Mastery of anything takes dedication and meticulous preparation, and with a talent as precise as musical ability is known to be and the subjectivity to which its evaluation is presented, the technical refinement drains so much personal enjoyment out of the art. All too familiar is the world with the likes of Mozart, who excelled as a young boy only to descend into madness with age. How could such a child embrace a natural talent so great without succumbing so? Of course, his own history has been morphed by the power of time and art to include a jealous Salieri. Between the two of them, I found not even a little animosity. These were two contemporaries who in life had pushed the best out of each other out of mutual respect, not out of jealousy or hatred.

A pair of days spent in the presence of artistic genius is hardly something that could ever be considered a waste, but pressed by time, I was eager to commune with some other minds. I think if a reader is ever presented the same opportunity as was afforded to me, it would perhaps be in their best interest to search for more variance daily, but the idea only occurred to me some time later, and as such, was not in the cards for me.

CHAPTER 3.9

The author organizes a body of builders and architects to demonstrate their craftsmanship.

OF THE INNUMERABLE qualities of the island of Glubdubdrib, the architecture of the place deserves particular mention. The façade of the building, as described previously, contained architectural elements from every corner of the world. Many of the most famous names in architecture had a hand in its design. Artists themselves, it was fascinating to hear what inspired them when I called them together. Even more so, it was a marvel to see what they could accomplish when working together as they had done here. More than just the designers of buildings, I was curious also about those who commissioned them and the people enlisted in the construction thereof. Though much time has been spent studying the colossal Egyptian pyramids, still I sought out a few of those most famous builders, impelled by personal curiosity.

Imhotep, who first built the stepped pyramid of Djoser, amongst a laundry list of other accomplishments, was perhaps the most formidable man I have ever encountered. Driven to great achievements by a towering intellect, and of great stature and confidence, he seemed to command the field with his presence alone. The creator of the largest pyramid, Hemon, was an equally commanding manifestation. More stern and dutiful, his command was derived by his strength of will as a stern taskmaster and rigid administrator. The son of a king, Khafre, who would not entrust the construction to anybody but himself, had observed under Hemon and desired to exceed in grandeur the achievements of his father. A cruel and wicked man, Khafre showed only concern for the preservation of his name and legacy. I called upon as many grand viziers as I could find and enjoyed their conversation immensely.

So it was that I asked about the reason for building such structures. A common answer was returned. The life of a pharaoh is one that establishes numerous enemies. For so long had been recorded the desecration, theft, and mutilation of the deceased corpses of kings, they began to either hide or fortify the remains. The monarchs sought to discourage this disrespect by building pyramids to protect their bodies from this insult. Over time, the people building them developed advanced techniques that made it possible to build them bigger, taller, stronger, and out of much larger stones. Of course, a huge workforce was required, but during the flood season, when all the farms were inundated with the dangerous waters of the Nile, there was an ample supply of cheap labour to be had. Servants of the king, they were well rewarded, out of their own taxation it must be noted, but they formed the backbone of construction.

As the pyramids grew larger and larger, traps and guardians were created to protect the highly visible tombs. The pyramids became objectives themselves, a sign of strength and intimidation. Even if one could manage it, who would dare try to move the perfectly fitted rocks for an unknown prize? Khafre, of course, and his father as represented by Hemon, were most concerned of all. Wicked and despised by the people who were bound to their wills, they knew with certainty their resting places would be ruined if not well protected. Relentless glory seekers, they also desired the most ostentatious symbols of their enormity. I found these two men to be most boring and loathsome in their manner and dismissed them after a short visit.

I listened to and learned from others, led by Imhotep. They did not create on the same scale, but the number and intricacies of their works exceeded those of whom I had recently departed. They also revealed that while some pharaohs sought to protect themselves with great works, others chose a quieter and more distinguished burial. Thus it was with the Valley of the Kings, a secretive place where kings and their families were interred. Seeking a quiet peace after a tumultuous life, they had carefully carved and painted caves with hidden doors and treasures most precious to them. I can understand their fears of the afterlife. Who could know what lay ahead and what role the departed body would play therein?

I found these builders to be most enterprising. Lacking sophisticated tools, they engaged simple machines that multiplied force and energy effectively. Levers, pulleys, and inclined planes were used to redirect and manoeuvre stone. Fire was used to align the stones in perfect rows. Combined with water, fire was used to cut the gigantic bricks of the pyramids. It is not the brute force these monuments were carved with that most impresses but the innovation and cunning that overcomes ignorance. The specific techniques they used have not been repeated on such a scale since, but all the elemental techniques we know of today were perfected at this time, by these people, and through their descendants, have been passed down through the ages.

Other builders of more modern structures concurred with my opinion. They each acknowledged the impact these ancients had on their works. When I asked about their inspiration, nearly all traced their ingenuity back to the work of great antiquity. It is said we stand on the shoulders of giants. We build upon them as well.

CHAPTER 3.10

The author calls for some of the most infamous criminals in the history of the world to return to learn from their mistakes and misdeeds.

YOU MIGHT REMEMBER I noted before that I asked each of my guests about the people they would like to meet. It seemed equally interesting to ask who they would have least liked to meet in life, and the resounding response always included the greatest criminals of their time. Having heard the extraordinary revelations of so many great figures, I wondered then what some of the most terrifying people would reveal about their motivation and desires. Subsequently, how would they feel about their works in the beyond?

I shall admit, contrary to my previous vows to reveal everything about my experiences, this story was nearly omitted from my final drafts for the contents could have proven too blunt and honest for a number of my readers. After much deliberation, I decided to risk censure at the hands of my critics for the people with whom I chose to associate.

I had created a list of some of the worst figures in history that I could remember, those whose irredeemable evil are not questioned by any person of right mind. I was not interested so much in the interview of individual murderers or criminals, even those with ghastly records, but more in those who had committed crimes through the apparatus of the state over which they held power. Those demons and devils, ghouls and hoodlums of the sort who ordered the killing of millions, whose passive actions resulted in the fall of their own empires and whose actions in the name of their state or people are beyond all comparison and comprehension, held my interest.

I sensed Cado was hesitant to call these people forth. I asked him why this was so, considering they were bound to his service and unable to harm us. Without his express permission, they could do no more than speak unto us. He could not say exactly why he was hesitant to do this, but he certainly didn't like the idea very much. He recounted that these were the first people that I had called that had never been called by Glubdubdribians before. There was some excitement at this achievement, but it was tempered by his concern.

There were many tyrants and despots of history who had done ill service to humanity that I could have called. It is my belief that the worst man to ever live was Adolf Hitler, the criminal who had been responsible for the slaughter of at least eleven million civilians and intended to kill far more was the first guest of my second last day.

The Austrian's form materialized before my eyes. I felt a wave of contempt crawl from my toes to my stomach and into my heart. The most sinister impulses at my disposal urged me to find a way to hurt this man, as though in some way I could give peace to the enormous masses he had wronged. My heart beat hard in my chest. A short, frail little man with a ridiculous moustache took shape. I could barely begin to speak to this thing that stood before me. I had conversed with kings and queens, great and poor. Not a single time did I experience such a depth of feeling as the hatred I bore for this one. He held no passion in his eyes. The fire of his own hatred had long since been exterminated by his own hand. The monster in my presence was a pathetic shell of the man his propagandists had promoted.

Through clenched teeth, and choking back tears at the thought of what he had done, I could only ask one word of him at first. Why? I must admit I really didn't care to hear a word of his answer. I expected him at any moment to launch into a vile diatribe against the Jewish people or spout some utter nonsense about the inferiority of one race over another or one religion over another. Instead, he uttered quietly it was about fear, hatred, and power. Confessing he was obsessed with power and was himself a fortunate coward, he shared how he had fled military service in Austria only to be pressed into service in Germany. Wounded several times, he used his cunning to fabricate stories of honour and bravery. He learned to marshal the fear that bit him to the core and realized the value of distraction and scapegoats as he himself had fallen victim. In himself, he saw the strength fear could have in mustering passions and used it to whip a defeated people into action. He admitted his actions were of a magnitude worse than anything else of which he had heard, but despite this admission, the snake had a look in his eye. He remained proud his name would live forever, if even as the worst example of the evil side of the nature of man. I could scarcely bear to look upon his face as I saw the edges of his lips curl upwards in a smirk at the thought of his enduring legacy. For this man to believe himself a success gutted me more than I had imagined. I asked Cado to expel him from this place. He did so politely, with great concern, and with urgency.

I was forced to take a break after this encounter. In the span of only a couple minutes, I had confronted the worst my imagination could conceive. I felt I had erroneously humanized this demon and I needed some time to recover. I sat on a bench in the casting area and buried my head in my hands. Cado called upon Ryuudrikje and Beyuba to come, and together they cared for me as we recessed.

My melancholy mood I forced to the side, for I was reminded of the singular opportunity in my hands and the limited window availed to me. I sought to better understand more than just the one pathetic mortal life I had just witnessed. I thanked my friends and once again we set about calling back spirits. Cado remained uncomfortable and voiced his concerns with more emphasis, but I felt confident nobody could have the singular effect on me that the first one had had. I would buffer myself against these feelings and be sure not to give power to these beasts to impact me anymore.

So, I called upon a number of other recent rulers that had caused harm to a great number of people. I called upon Josef Stalin, for his starvation of the people of the Ukraine, Emperor Hirohito for the massacre of the Chinese at Nanking, Talaat Pasha for the Armenian Genocide, Pol Pot for the Killing Fields of the Khmer Rouge, Leopold II for his destruction of the Congolese, and Kim Il Sung, for starving his own people and subjecting them to terrifying purges and laws that found guilt by association. This list of crimes is by no means complete, but I list only the principal crime that stuck out in my mind. Each of these I called forth individually, having little desire to be outnumbered by these men of ill repute. They all shared a similar story: a lust for power propelled by a fear of their own people, or of the people they desired to rule. Each of them, in turn, admitted a deep-rooted fear, and every successful grasp of the ladder and increase in power found them further vexed by the same crippling paranoia. In turn, they spread their anxieties onto those closest to them and projected disquiet upon those whom they believed to be the least trustworthy. The worse their atrocities became, the more they had to fear reprisals and the more innocent souls they found they had to dispose. A person consumed by fear—whether of a different ethnic group, religious sect, ideology, race, history, or any other manufactured difference—in possession of great power may only succeed in creating misery.

Then I delved farther into the past, calling upon leaders such as Elizabeth Bathory, Robespierre, and Vlad the Impaler from the medieval and renaissance periods. Robespierre shared much in common with those more recent tyrants possessed of a deep fear of others with power and who had turned ruthlessly even upon those who had been his comrades. Elizabeth Bathory was simply insane, and in death, admitted her deep regret at the awful actions she had taken in life. She was now doomed to remember her misdeeds for eternity. Vlad presented a more interesting case study. A man at the crossroads of two empires and civilizations, he spoke of his mistreatment at the hands both of the Ottoman and Hungarian Empires, both of which pulled at him in an international tug-of-war. The ruler of a principality that continued to be the subject of frequent wars, he sought to use fear as his weapon and even in death reported his deeds were justified given his circumstances and geopolitical position. I believe that in his words there was an honest regret at having committed his crimes that was all but masked by a perceived duty to his people.

I sought to speak to criminals of even more ancient history and sought out the Romans, Caligula and Nero. Caligula, similar to Ms. Bathory, had been driven mad and his mind had scarcely recorded his crimes. Nero, known best for having fiddled while Rome burned, professed his innocence. His claim, undeniably true given the circumstances of our meeting, was that he was not even in Rome when the great fire burned but was in Antium. Still perturbed in death, he spoke of being dismayed at the lack of love of his subjects for him. He tried to lighten spirits and make people happy with public performances, but as the emperor, his actions in theatre and the arts only lowered his standing in their eyes. In another attempt to cheer the populace, he tried to compete in games but could not find a competitor willing to risk an emperor's wrath in any arena, and so he found only emptiness. Hated by the people whose affection he sought, he worried his legacy would be tainted. When the fire burned Rome, he used his own monies and time to search for and assist the missing. His palaces he ordered opened to shelter the displaced, and still he found hatred. To help the population recover, he funded a huge construction project to build new homes out of bricks and a great palace to employ the people. Sadly, he would never find that which he sought.

Next up was Attila the Hun, who had sacked Rome and marauded about Europe. Attila, too, recognized the value of fear. A tremendous man of great courage, he gave himself the moniker, "The Scourge of God" to put fear into the hearts of his enemies. His deeds were recorded as criminal by the literate classes, which were primarily Roman in his time. Amongst his own people, of whom he asked that I call representatives, his reputation was great and their love for him and his leadership sincere.

Lastly, some recommended I talk to a figure from Greek mythology, Menestheus. Known for his role leading the Athenian army in the war at Troy, a number of his contemporaries referred to him as the greatest Grecian villain. They accused him of having caused the collapse of the Mycenaean civilization, so I asked him directly. Menestheus may have been an utter coward, but he had a sharp mind for conspiracy and tactics. He spoke meagrely and quietly, but there could be little doubt of the intelligence burning in his eyes. In the siege of Troy, he possessed but a weak fragment of an army but compensated with great tactics. Seeing his position diminished, he felt the other kingdoms of Greece were plotting against him. Carefully and strategically, he infiltrated their palaces. He proudly announced to me he had key officials murdered. Beset by an unknown enemy, for in their presence he seemed to be their friend, they undertook a defensive building spree that consumed huge amounts of resources. Little did they know their enemy was already safely inside the walls. Menestheus undermined all his allies' towns and left them economically crippled, wrecked by distrust, and eventually subject to invasion by the Dorians. His malfeasances have gone unheeded in history by virtue of his clever stealth and rightly placed trust in loyal lieutenants. This shrewd, crafty, and wholly paranoid man must truly have been one of the greatest villains to have ever walked the Earth, and yet his story is never told, a true testament to the success of his tactics.

In the absence of knowledge, tolerance, acceptance, and trust, fear blooms like a fire unchecked, and in a weak but powerful vessel, shall manifest those goals that lead only to hurt and ruin. A coward may appear firm and strong at first, but their weakness and foolishness, accompanied only with the harm they create, shall be their only lasting legacy.

Cado looked back upon me at the end of this session with care, and I demonstrated to him that I had recovered from my earlier weakness. I felt stronger, and he seemed to have benefited from a completely new perspective that the Glubdubdrubians had not thought of before. It is unusual to be the first person to ever think of something, and Cado was impressed, even pleased, to have experienced this session.

CHAPTER 3.11

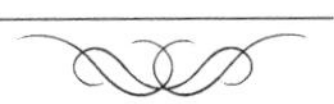

The author spends his last day on the island of the sorcerers with his family and is offered one final gift.

ON MY LAST day on this island, I sought the comfort of my friends and ancestors. The only exceptions I made were to not call the recently deceased and those closest to me. My preceding day speaking with the worst of humanity only reinforced that decision. I had saved them for last because I hoped to keep the best memory of my time with them. In that vein, I called grandparents and great aunts and uncles and the few close friends who had passed on too soon. Cado, on this day, left me alone with my family.

In these people's presence, I finally felt calmed and soothed. I thought about asking them questions, bound to honesty as they were, about their lives and thoughts but thought better of it. I feared I sought not their honest feelings and thoughts but only the validation and confirmation of what I believed. I was in no way strong enough to handle the sort of rejection that full honesty might betray. Hopefully my reader will forgive me this, but my time with my family was the most intimate, personal, and private time of my entire life. I will not share any further details but to say I appreciated it more sincerely and honestly than I could possibly relate.

True to her word, at the end of the tenth day, the princess concluded the arrangement I had enjoyed and informed Ryuudrikje—who had also called upon a number of figures unfamiliar to me from his island—and me that our time on Glubdubdrib was now at an end.

Surprisingly, she offered one last gift to each of us. She would not permit us time or resources to construct vessels with which to leave the island but would grant us a one-time opportunity to travel to one of two places instantly. The sorcerers of Glubdubdrib had long had a relationship with Loogenage and another kingdom unknown to me called Laputa. These skilled sorcerers had carefully constructed pathways in the fabric of time that allowed a person to pass from here to one of those places.

Ryuudrikje and I faced a decision: return to Loogenage or forge onward to this new, unknown place. Ryuudrikje struggled with the dilemma. The princess confirmed that once we crossed to the other place, the portal would close and could only be opened again by one of her people, and there would be none of those present at our destination. Ryuudrikje felt a sense of duty both to return to his people and towards me that I had seen before. I could read it in his hesitation and the sad longing in his eyes that I knew only too well. I knew he needed approval to go home. He must have known, too, that I could not go back to that place. We both knew there would be little chance we would either of us see or hear of each other again. With a manly nod, followed by a sincere hug, we revealed our decisions to the princess.

The next morning, at a specific time I estimated to be close to 10:00 am, for they used not the common, 24-hour, 60-minute clock with which we are familiar, we were taken to a stone circle that to me looked much like Stonehenge. A ring of magicians, including Beyuba, Cado, and Ryuudrikje's necromancer, manipulated an unseen force, and in the centre of the stones was a field, unmistakeably in Loogenage. Ryuudrikje recognized it immediately, and as sternly instructed, rushed into the field without hesitation. With a look back and a deep bow, the portal closed behind him. Almost instantly after, another gate opened, and the inner ring was replaced by a slanted floor of imperfectly cut stone, so out of place for

Glubdubdrib. I dashed into the space, and looking out from whence I had come, could see no sign of the magicians or the unaged princess. I knew I must be in Laputa.

PART FOUR

LAPUTA ON BALNIBARBI: ISLAND DOWN

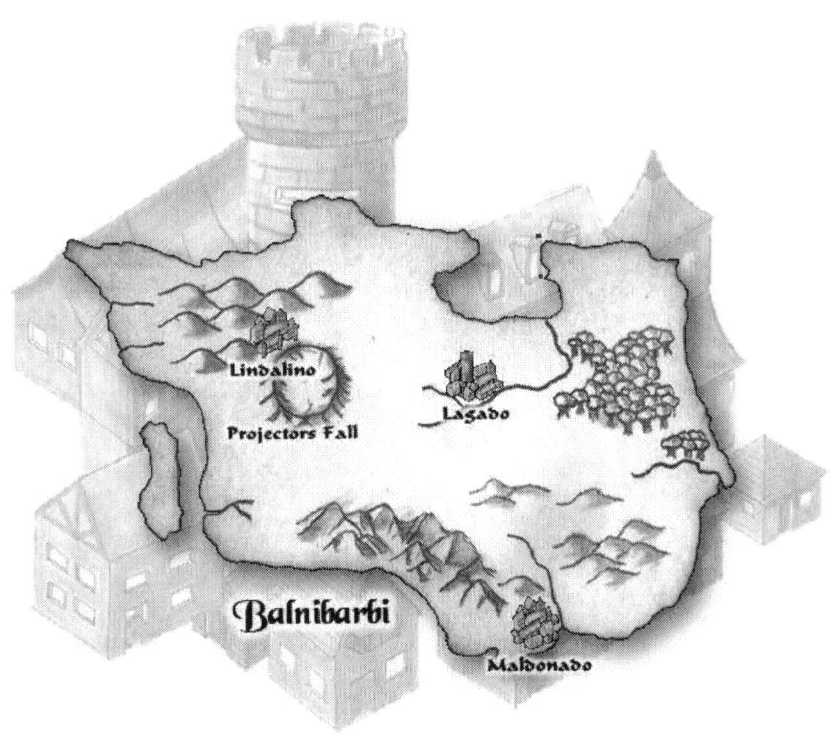

CHAPTER 4.1

Alone again in another foreign place, the author gathers his bearings and seeks to find his way homewards.

IT WAS TO my own apprehension that I arrived in this place. As a wave washes over the sands of a beach, I appeared in a large stone room. The light of my source was replaced by dimness and dreariness. The air seemed to crush near the floor with a musty, dust-covered staleness most unfamiliar to my nose and eyes.

My balance was thrown as the floor shifted immediately from level to a slope of nearly thirty degrees. The masonry beneath my feet being covered in nearly an inch of dust and cobweb, I slipped and fell to the ground. I slid off a slight platform and down into a corner of the room, leaving a clearing through the grit, utterly disheveling my clothes. As I slowly slid, I caught little nooks and crannies with my toes and fingers before flipping onto my backside and sliding down the floor as a child on the playground slide. I descended slowly, but I could see that breaking my fall was a pile of copper and glass, dusty and thoroughly ruined, so I slowed myself more, dragging my hands at my sides, and crashed gently into the garbage heap.

I tried to best position my feet such that they would land upon a large, unbroken fragment. This was challenging considering the thick covering of untended age. At the terminus of my descent, I slid off one spherical vessel and sliced my shirt on a second broken shard. Remaining still, I rested briefly to regain my senses and composure in this new place.

I looked around the room. The room was shaped as a cup, with me and the floor at the base. The entire cup was tilted at an angle of thirty degrees. At its centre was a huge, polished stone embedded deep within a sort of dais at least six metres across. Directly above that was a domed ceiling of a height of at least eighty metres and a hole as wide as forty or so metres in diameter, from which light filtered through. The walls were as though they had been hewn directly out of the earth. Rough, but refinished by amateur masons. The stone floor was poorly crafted, with circular patterns apparent along my cleared trail. The deficient craftmanship left the unfinished holes in the floor I had vainly used to try to restrain my momentum. The only light came in from the ceiling, and I sensed the cup-shaped room was more of a well or crevasse that perhaps had occurred naturally but been expanded.

I looked to my footing and dusted off several pieces of the debris upon which I terminated my descent. Every piece I could see was smashed. I couldn't know yet whether this was from a natural incident that perhaps left the floor at such a state or from violence at the hands of man. There were telescopes of great size, but each had their lenses smashed beyond all use. There were similarly devastated astrolabes, planispheres, armillary spheres, and celestial spheres scattered about. I needed little time to conclude this place was once an observatory, but the duration of its abandonment I could barely fathom. Such was the state of the forsaken observatory that I held little hope at all of finding a soul alive in this place. The room itself was plain. Apart from the polished stone at the centre and the dome at the top, it was monotonously flat and poorly finished, with a huge pile of smashed equipment at the lowest part of the tilted floor.

Not far from my position on the wall to my right side was a door, slightly elevated compared to my current position. The room, being nearly the size of a football field, with cracks and gaps in the walls, might have concealed many secrets under its dust, but the door appeared the only way out of or into the room. I began a controlled ascent.

I failed to gain a handhold easily in the thick dust, so I sought an aid in the crushed astronomical equipment and discovered bones mixed amongst the debris. Little concerned with the ominous omen that such a find might portend, I picked up the broken femur and quickly scrounged a sharp fibia. I used the skeletal remains as an ice axe, sticking them within the cracks in the floor, and pulled myself carefully up to the door.

Upon opening the door, I was faced with a single option: a poorly constructed spiral staircase that wound its way up and away. The spiral staircase, and everything else, being at the thirty-degree tilt, had sections that went down and other sections that were nearly vertical. It was only the presence of a gap down the centre of the staircase that allowed me to climb the sections that would otherwise have been vertical leaps.

After many hours of hard climbing, and more falls than I cared to count, I reached the top of the stairwell and another floor. Dusk was falling, and in this strange, diagonally oriented world, I tucked my head onto the last flat stairwell loop and rested for the night.

CHAPTER 4.2

Day breaks and the author emerges from the chasm to evaluate the island of Laputa.

I CAN ASSURE my readers that a sleep on a slanted spiral stairwell falls slightly short of a five-star review. Compared to the accommodation of Glubdubdrib, it was a step or two down. I awoke in the morning to find the sun already well overhead in the sky. From my vantage point, the island of Laputa seemed deserted and devoid of life. I poked my head from the terraced borehole cautiously as would a hunted fugitive. It was with a mix of dismay and relief when I surfaced that I found not a soul on the wide stone roof. The chasm from which light entered the observatory and from which I had climbed sat some fifteen metres to one side of the roof. Upon cautious investigation, I confirmed it was boring directly to that room. The platform upon which I stood continued right around the chasm and was protected by a small little wall a half metre tall at most, made of oddly shaped bricks that never quite fit together. The chasm itself was shaped as a circle with crenellated metre-tall walls. In the distance on all sides, towers and spires reached up from the ground at the same slant as the ground around me, but at least sixty percent lay in abject ruin, much like the instruments of the observatory.

Carefully walking the edges of the roof, I was to discover four semi-spherical basins on four diametrically opposed sides of the central platform upon which I stood. Into each, a complex series of channels and pathways connected like the centre of a spiderweb. It was no stretch to assume that by some calamity, this entire place had been thrust up at thirty degrees from its intent and that these basins would have once been collective. The entirety of the island, if reoriented towards normality, could best itself be described as a densely built-up castle-town in the shape of a bowl. Once, no doubt, this would have been a beautiful place, but the unknown catastrophe that had befallen it had caused irreparable damage.

The bowl-shaped island was enormous in size. Alternating rings of bare—but for the weeds—soil and rubbled housing sloped up to a height of at least a hundred yards. The view gave me the inspiring perspective of standing in a wide colosseum, twice as tall and a hundred times wider. In the centre of this incomparable amphitheatre, on the very focal point of the island, I could almost see the entirety of the island. I thought better of an instinct to let escape a yell for the amusement of an echo. I could see no sign of life here in this place, but I was lacking in necessary security for such an audacious effort.

To one side, the entire wall of the bowl climbed high into the sky, overhanging beyond vertical at its edge. On the other side, the shattered bowl rested just at sixty degrees above horizontal, still sloping towards the focal point. I considered the origins of this place and felt, and still feel today, that on a geological basis, this island was probably the caldera of a once-active volcano, treated and worked by human hands into a medieval-type palatial city of some forgotten fame.

Under different circumstances, I might have found adventure in trying to climb to the highest points. Instead, I took the easier path and leapt from stone to stone out of the caldera. Even at a decent pace, this took the better part of two hours, and I slowed as I reached the edge. There, as I crested over the outer stone walls of the bowl city, stretched out wide before me was the more typical sight of a more recognizable, vanilla island. Hills and valleys, rivers and forests stretched out over a great distance, and the sloped city of the caldera behind rested on a high plateau, of which ended in a thirty metre inverted descent into a forest below.

I looked down from my perch and was greeted by a pleasing sight. Across a wide gap, standing atop a tall wooden observation platform, at quite some distance from the ruined town, I could see at least a hundred people wandering about. I fancied them looking and pointing directly at me.

To my right, about a hundred metres away, had been assembled the least sturdy looking stairwell. Built of timber that looked like the undesirable leftovers from a grade-B lumberyard, it was the only visible way down from my perch. I took comfort in the evidence it had been recently used. Nevertheless, I clung with white knuckles to the railings built at uneven heights all the way down.

I reached the bottom late that afternoon and was immediately surrounded by several emaciated men wearing ridiculous-looking uniforms that appeared to be much like a child's pyjamas. Stars, moons, harps, and lutes decorated all their saggy clothes.

The strange men in pyjamas swiftly took me into custody. I imagined I might be a match for a group of underfed officers, but I acceded to their demands without a fight and was taken to a nearby station made of log in the middle of a densely forested area. There, I was escorted to a single, solid oak table suitable for seating a dozen. They forced me into a chair and then abandoned me in the cedar-scented hall.

The station was supported by thick wooden walls. So perfect were the joints that one could be forgiven for thinking the building had been fashioned from a single tree. No paintings, photos, or other art decorated the walls, which possessed a sort of natural beauty by virtue of their minimalist nature. Two doors adorned the room: the one from which I had entered and one at the opposite side. As I waited momentarily for something or someone, I noticed a distinct lack of windows in the room.

Then the door swung open and in walked a man with a purpose and confidence that mismatched his garb. His body was, in fact, more emaciated than any other I have ever, before or since, witnessed in person. He pulled out a chair, and I was quite sure the effort would cause his arms to break under the tension of the act. He sat down, took my measure, and calmly laid his gaunt arms on the table.

CHAPTER 4.3

The author is questioned by the figure of authority about his trespassing of Projectors Fall and learns of the history and fall of Laputa.

AFTER A FORTNIGHT on Glubdubdrib, I had grown accustomed to the translation of the opal gem now concealed beneath my robes. The man seemed to wait for me to break the silence, and I introduced myself and said I travelled here from Canada by way of Glubdubdrib. The man threw his hands over his ears as the sound of all known languages ricocheted in his skull—as only recently they had through my own. When his internal struggle subsided, and he seized upon the understanding thereof, he recomposed, and with great authority, presented himself.

The man introduced himself as Weimar Obers, the Executive Vice-Constable Chief President of Public Interest and Lavatorial Facilities of Projectors Fall Monument of Laputa. I am still incredulous at the translation abilities of the stone, for surely a number of words in this rather unwieldy title must have no parallel in English. Pleasantries apparently having been concluded, he pressed directly into the thrust of his examination. What was my purpose for trespassing in the monument of the Democratic People's Republic of Free Balnibarbi?

One can understand my personal quandary. To reveal the teleporteous nature of my recent travel would have seemed an insult to this man of many titles. I saw minimal technology that would lead me to suppose they possessed an even rudimentary understanding of flight. I could see that in his mind, I could only have climbed that stairwell to enter the reserve and had therefore willfully trespassed on this apparently sacred ground.

Instead, I played ignorant to his question, pretending not to understand, and in full honest truth, I really did not understand my mode of travel. So, I attempted to deflect and asked him about this place and about Projectors Fall, of which he spoke so reverentially. I must have struck a particularly passionate chord with the park ranger—for I think that best describes his actual position. His interest in the site temporarily overwhelmed his purpose, and he launched into a full lesson as an ignored teacher with much to share when tempted with an enthusiastic pupil eager to engage.

Weimar's story began with Umbali Tung, a man of apparently divine origin (which one dare not question), who had led the people against an oppressive regime. This man, born as prophesized by the crabs of the shore, had shown the way to bringing down a great, but corrupt, power.

I received at least an hour's worth of tutelage about this precious leader, Umbali Tung, who though long deceased remained a fixture of the politics of the island. Knowing that to do otherwise was foolhardy, I listened with attention and feigned interest as the ranger told me of astrological events that presaged the hero's coming, his athletic achievements in sports foreign to me, and of his incomparable genius in virtually all fields. I allowed the scrawny man to gush on about this obviously fictitious person while mentally trying to piece together more likely explanations for things.

As near as I can tell, this legendary figure was a narcissistic man of average intelligence who inherited a significant fortune, as far as the impoverished people of this country so considered. Through a series of fairly unfair dealings, he expanded his wealth through zero-sum games that made others far poorer. When an opportunity came up that enabled him to seize power, he did so ruthlessly while suppressing the voices of any who opposed him with intimidation, and where necessary, force. My interviewer presented the same information as examples of his drive, ambition, and business acumen, which in this land were repeatedly documented even after his passing around two hundred and fifty years ago. He had bravely brought a voice to a forgotten majority and created a cult of personality founded on a fear of others that persisted even to that day.

I gradually steered the conversation towards the once-floating, by means of magnetism, island of Laputa from which I had arrived to learn what it was that had befallen the place. I was informed that for many hundreds of years, the island of Balnibarbi had been ruled from the island of Laputa, which in his incredible story was once capable of levitation. A king presided over the entire country unchallenged and never left Laputa or visited his demesne in Balnibarbi. Weimar spoke dismissively of the royal island and its residents, particularly the men, who he reported were so focused on unimportant, scholarly, cerebral pursuits that they fell into introspective stupors as they conceived of theories built upon theories founded not in any sort of physical science but ever elaborate, all-encompassing interpretations and understandings of the world and cosmos.

The women of Laputa, excluded from such activities and not especially interested in their opposite gender, had taken a great interest in the men of the island below. While their mates distracted themselves with byzantine thought experiments, these women took leave of the island in ever-increasing numbers, choosing often the least desirable amongst the commoners of Balnibarbi. The women, being so transparent with their own sexuality, were easy prey for the more predatory, the more muscular, and the less intelligent Balnibarbi men, they being so unlike the men the women were acquainted with. It was one of these women, reputedly a princess, who having quietly escaped from the flying castle in the sky to the mainland by means of a descended basket, encountered the glorious leader.

I connected the two disparate thoughts together but didn't share the obvious coincidence that the man speaking had just compared their perfect saviour (Umbali Tung) to a low-brow, inferior stiff. I hope the reader might overlook my editorial comment, but my amusement was great. This woman, entranced by her common lover, had passed along news that a certain disaster was soon to eradicate all life from the planet. A particular comet, having long been traced through the skies, was certain to strike the Earth in short order and wouldst terminate all beings in due time. The men of Laputa had become obsessed with their impending doom—the tracking and the monitoring of it—that they ceased to focus on any other issue at all. More than thirty years they spent watching the comet, while below, the low-born people prepared a coup.

Umbali Tung had acquired power by slandering and ruining others in the city of Lindalino. He had leveraged his fame and fortune and had used others to establish a criminal empire built on fear and intimidation. He had used the imperfect machinery of the state to grow his asset base. While his resources and power grew in civil society, so did his desire to expand his power, and to strike out from under the literal and figurative shadow of the flying island above. Mr. Tung had developed a plan that took advantage of his business experience. In retrospect, it seems a little too clever for one of his dealings. More likely than not, some of his more intelligent sycophantic followers had concocted the scheme for which he subsequently took credit.

The Tung Organization had constructed a series of magnetic towers at the city's expense. The towers had been built by contractors of the leader, allowing him to further enrich himself in the process, I was told. I thought it interesting this conflict of interest was seen not to be insidious but rather an indication of his cunning and strength. These towers had been fashioned so they could be raised and lowered rapidly from the ground to a height of one hundred pitars, the minimum height the island was allowed to descend over Lindalino. They had then been aligned in two rows, the first row possessing three towers each of positive and negative charges and the second row possessing four negatively charged towers.

The people of Balnibarbi had built this weapon to be used if the prognostication of the Laputan king proved false, which, as the Mr. Tung predicted, it did. This was not a bad bet to take. If the world did come to an end, then it didn't matter what was done, but if not, then preparing was the best course of action. On the day the world was to end, the princess had informed the king she was leaving the island to live with the leader of Lindalino. Her father, so preoccupied was he with his observations in the royal observatory, had dismissed her assertions as irrelevant. When the offending comet eventually failed to materialize, its trajectory having been miscalculated, he, the king, had flown into a rage and directed the island to ruin the city entirely. As the empyrean island floated, Mr. Tung had ordered the people of the city to raise the first three negative towers of the first row, which tilted and sped the approach of the then-positively charged Laputa. By means of manipulating an enormous lodestone, the royals had attempted to compensate for the interference of the negative towers, which were only to be replaced by the positive towers of the first row and the negative towers of the second behind it.

The attempted corrections of the Laputian navigator, communicated from a great distance, had only exacerbated the tilt, and the island had come crashing down into Balnibarbi, close to the city of Lindalino. The leader of the rebels, Umbali Tung, had seized the opportunity to invade the downed island and had mindlessly slaughtered every soul who had survived the cataclysm. They'd sought out all instruments of oppression and had destroyed every trace of the tyrants. The Balnibarbeans had rejoiced at their triumph and had lavished title, power, and wealth upon their liberator who had founded this new glorious republic, with himself as the first and only voice of truth and reason. He had subsequently banned all others from visiting the now grounded former imperial capital and out of it had created the national monument of Projectors Fall, dedicated to his own bravery, heroism, and sacrifice. I was confident he could not have understood the meaning of that word, having at no time heard any indication he had ever sacrificed anything of his own for anybody but himself.

It was at this point that my professor and interrogator realized that he had, for the past several hours, been derelict in his duties towards me, a captured trespasser at this same place, and as night began to fall, he slapped me in chains and secured me to an iron ring on the wall. Evidently aware he had been fooled, he stormed out of the room, leaving me alone once again to process that which had with me been shared so liberally.

My attempted circumvention of the questions posed by Weimar had only delayed my full and complete interrogation. I fully anticipated that in the morning my questioning would continue anew. Not the slightest morsel of food had been offered me, no bed upon which to repose, nor any other comfort in the hall of the station. Once I may have thought it impossible, but given my experiences, I was growing accustomed to such conditions.

CHAPTER 4.4

The author is transferred to the city to continue the investigation and shares with the reader his thoughts about the countryside and the city of Lindalino.

IN THE MORNING, Weimar returned grumpy and uncommunicative. He seized my shackles and shoved me outside to a waiting cart being pushed, not pulled, by a troika of gaunt, ill-behaved horses, all wearing the same astrological pyjama-uniform as Weimar. I was positioned to the left of the driver, and with a loud yell over his shoulder to our equine engine, we slowly started forwards, leaving Weimar behind. I could see Weimar looked defeated. His shoulders slumped, his head low, there was little of the confident energy I first saw.

The cart was particularly unstable. The horses shoved courageously against a rigid wooden frame that propelled the carriage, but each rock or root on the unpaved gravel road jolted and threatened to upset the entire cart. Gradually, we made our way towards the city.

Along the way, we passed many dusty fields with scarce crops scattered in patches. I saw no sign of irrigation or any significant industry taking place in what could only be the innermost of Von Thunen's rings. In all directions, save for the *montagne* monument to our left, were vast, empty fields. Nary a one showed the capacity for meaningful production. Ahead, as we slowly rounded the fallen capital, a gritty city resembling a classic western town came into view, nestled at the feet of twin volcanic peaks. In the middle of the city sat a solitary, imposing castle, golden and taller than every other structure. It was to this edifice I was being taken. As we approached the city, Lindalino I suspected, the houses could be seen to have been constructed quite recently but in a shabbier style to that which I had expected. A huge wooden palisade, built in a similar manner to the homes surrounding most of the city, offered a weak defence against an unknown enemy, with gaping holes like a picket fence. Unless besieged by a most incompetent enemy, surely no meaningful protection would be afforded at all.

Along ramshackle streets, we wound through neighbourhoods of intense poverty. One would struggle to find a more distasteful and despicable sight. Slight children played weakly in the streets while adults wandered about with little direction or meaning. Concerned mostly with their own struggles, they approached me, begging for anything we could offer. Of course, as a prisoner, I had nothing to give. The driver tossed a few coins when the crowds became too thick. The rabble chased and squabbled over the tiny prizes.

The imposing structure of the castle loomed large, and every street seemed to lead to that hub. While grand in scale, in contrast with the impoverished masses that huddled around its great walls, it projected a ludicrous opulence, almost as if to taunt the commoners.

The castle was fortified heavily, with heavily armoured guards carrying crossbows, pikes, and daggers. We rumbled up to the gate, and the driver's uniform allowed us to pass directly into the main courtyard. All the walls, both inside and out of every building and tower, were painted or constructed, I could not tell which, in the same glowing gold, the monotony of which could scarcely be overstated. Despite the wealth apparently concentrated herein, little more plant life could be found in here as compared to the barren fields outside the city. I was forced off the wagon and transferred into a squat auric building where I was stripped down, relieved of all personal items, and provided an unpatterned smock. A man in flowing robes patterned with musical instruments of lutes and lyres entered the room from behind me and spoke to me in a strange tongue. For the first time in many weeks, I could not understand him.

He spoke, but not a word of his utterances made any sense to my ears. I tried to speak too, but it was clear that neither his nor my words were coming across. I tried to indicate a need for the opal, but as frustration mounted and still we were unable to communicate, Weimar was sent for and appeared. He too began to speak in the same language as his superior. He and the other gentleman began to argue, and Weimar gestured frequently at me, no doubt indicating I had spoken to him just fine the day previous. Frustration grew to anger, and a guard struck me in the back of the head with a heavy gauntlet. Starved of food these past couple days, I succumbed easily and slumped to the floor in a heap.

CHAPTER 4.5

The author wakes in a prison cell once again and makes strides to understand the language of Balnibarbi.

IT WOULD SEEM I have a habit of ending up in the prisons of remote and isolated island nations. Once again, when I awoke with a cracking headache and various other stiffness and soreness, I found myself in a wooden prison, in a common space with at least fifty other convicts.

In this country, forgotten and lost to the world as it had been, a prison may have well suited me as well as almost any other place. In Balnibarbi, almost the only location where one could reliably find food and drink was in the custody of the state. Hence in Balnibarbi's prisons, many of the inmates are confined by choice, having committed lesser offences that resulted in their institutionalization. In fact, as I would learn, the prison population of this country exceeded any other of which I have heard. Freedom is the only luxury of which the prisoners possess much less of than their uninhibited brethren.

My new home was a common prison cell with mud floors, thick

wooden bars, and few guards, separated from other similar enclosures by wafer-thin walls of paper. The food was delivered by air daily on magnetic flying machines called cobadopters. One meal, scarcely sufficient upon which to survive, was flown in for each prisoner. Strangely, or perhaps not, in general, the prisoners were well behaved. In one corner of the cell, a trough had been cut. This served as a sewage canal to the city river that could be heard in the distance but was unseen.

Having few activities or responsibilities, many of my fellow inmates took to the immersive instruction of Balnibarbean language and history. The inmates were not the most intelligent I have encountered and scarcely learned more English than the Yahoos achieved. I shall not suffer my readers the details of this instruction, but it was neither as swift and phenomenal as the people of Loogenage nor as foreign and strange as the Huhuneem. The mud floor made for a decent chalkboard, and free of the constraints of time, my companions proved patient and skilful tutors.

The prison was easily escapable, it being made of wood and paper and containing a team of deconstructors at the ready in the form of the prisoners. They were loathe to the prospect of liberty, though, and the starvation that attended it, and so no attempts were made.

I learned more, too, of the floating island of Laputa and the rebellious leader. In spite of their plight, though one should suppose they were quite accepting of it, they spoke of Umbali Tung with the same reverence I had experienced with Weimar. They felt certain their country, once a trading nation in contact with the world but now entirely isolated and self-focused, must undoubtedly be the greatest—if not the only—civilized state remaining in the world.

I was told of a most maligned and impotent academy of projectors. The prisoners spoke disparagingly about these men of "science" who had locked themselves away performing the most fantastical and farcical experiments in the name of progress. These projectors had outlandish ideas and spent vast fortunes chasing the impossible, most of which only resulted in abject and undeniable failure. Not a single man of the fifty in my company could name a single improvement that had been derived from the academy directly, though a great fortune had been wasted there.

Mr. Umbali Tung of Balnibarbi, having overthrown the king of Laputa, set about dismantling the Academy of Projectors. He rejected the notion of progress and science as a costly and unproductive venture that had only led to the impoverishment of the people. One of his first acts had been to normalize and standardize production techniques based on an interpretation of the golden age of the people of Balnibarbi several generations before the foundation of the academy. Farming practices had been set into law, and water management, urban planning, and codes of construction had been additionally so cemented. The study of theory of any nature had been forbidden, it having resulted in the hubris of Laputa and the erroneous calculation of the end of times. Mr. Tung had then crowned himself the Grand President and Eternal Minister of Balnibarbi.

The prisoners were happy to elaborate upon the practices that had been codified into law. A farmer must only till his soil on the day following a full moon, it being understood that the heavens' effect upon fertility is greatest on this day. Livestock must remain outdoors in their natural habitat even in the winter, an edict that had resulted in the extinction of many species, I later confirmed. Water from streams and rivers, having been exposed to pollutants such as human and animal faeces, must not be used to irrigate; only water collected from rain or hand-pumped wells was to be used in agriculture. Fertilizers were to be sterilized by fire before being applied to crops lest the contaminants be passed back into the food chain.

The tone of these explanations was primarily a pining nostalgia to a time past, or perhaps imagined, when this country was wealthier and more productive. They blamed the tyranny of Laputa and the corruption of the Academy of Projectors for their misery. So hated was the flying island that the word could not be spoken without being accompanied by some gesture of disgust by all present. For a time, I thought the name actually to be two distinct words—La Puta—followed by an oral discharge as an unusual vocalization, unused in any language to which I had been exposed.

The rejection of the old order was so encompassing and complete that little idiosyncrasies of language had resulted, such as the addition of letters to words or a completely different pronunciation of elemental properties. Bizarre to my mind was the thought of punishing something as benign as a language as if a whipping boy for the perceived crimes of its users. It was made even more bizarre because the people modifying it were themselves the largest, and perhaps only, subgroup of that linguistic family. As believed by the prisoners of this jail, perhaps the lot one might expect least predisposed to the reverence of the current order, the changes and statutes of the current order seemed reasonable and good.

The current leaders of Balnibarbi were hereditary descendants of Mr. Tung, he credited with the defeat of Laputa. The prisoners, by virtue of a never-ending propaganda cycle and pleased with what they perceived to be a new golden age come true, respected that family as the right and truthful leaders of the kingdom. Elections were unnecessary because all evidence supplied by the state showed that the leading family had widespread approval and support amongst the people.

The reader may be certain that surrounded by a half century of fervent supporters, and prisoners of a jail, I was not particularly motivated to dispute any of their evidence, especially considering my limited interaction with the country. It certainly seemed clear to me that Balnibarbi was perhaps the poorest country I had ever visited, and far from a crescending golden age, it seemed they were deep in famine and depression as evidenced by their attenuated frames. Perhaps things were worse before, and speaking relatively, this was better, but I struggled to see how that could possibly be.

Whilst engaged in conversation with the prisoners, I felt a number of their kind had begun to look ill upon me and started to suspect there was growing a distrust for a stranger who knew nothing of this place but somehow still possessed cognitive abilities. On a few occasions, I admit to having let some judgements slip in pointed questions about the success of this regulation or the rationale behind that behaviour. I started to feel as a child in a school that outperforms their peers and is publicly ostracized for their abilities. It became evident that not only did the people of Balnibarbi reject the Academy of Projectors and its unfruitful endeavours but also any learned intelligence whatsoever. I asked about education in this land and was unsurprised by the response that there was no education system, formal or otherwise. Even the basic skills of reading and writing, so widely available and learned in my home country, were shunned viciously here.

In the absence of learning and the evasion of critical thinking, I asked how leaders were selected and how accounts were managed. The responses to my questions grew shorter and terser as the days passed, but I gathered that celebrity had replaced acumen and skill here. The more popular an individual, for whatever reason, the more weight was put behind any idea they proposed. The aristocracy were self-sustained almost exclusively by their charismatic personalities and their endless self-promotion. Wealth or fame guaranteed the other in a self-perpetuating and terrifying cycle. Fame provided a platform the wealthy could purchase or borrow. Fame itself became a most valuable commodity.

Increasingly, the jailbirds distanced themselves from me insofar as possible in this confined space. Fewer and fewer came to possess the gumption to scab the growing blockade against communication with me. I was clearly not one of them.

I was most certainly lucky the prisoners with whom I shared this cell were not violent offenders of any kind. In an actual turn of fact, they were quite opposed to any cruel behaviour apart from the anti-me personality clique. I was excluded from their discussions and pointedly confined to a corner of the prison structure. They held newly frequent discussions without me.

After a few days of close-quarter, congested solitary confinement, they reached a critical decision. They would break me out of jail, not because they wished to be freed ahead of their scheduled releases, but instead to alleviate their forced suffering caused by my presence. It was no difficult task, I was told, to break out of this prison; the way out was basically unguarded. The bars, with a little work, could be simply removed with a bit of group effort. They were convinced I would starve to death outside the walls of the prison, and so weren't too concerned about my fate, but knew if a body was found on the premises, those deemed guilty would be subject to a less agreeable security-level penitentiary.

The plan was simple. Schedules were well known, and apart from the delivery of food by cobadopter, no oversight of the prisoners was performed. The prison was located in a shallow but vast quarry, and the sewage canal system ran like a dendritic tree. If I were to follow the flow, they told me, it would take me to an outflow that would eventually lead back to a river downstream of the largest city that was not the capital, Lagado. Lagado, being the once capital and seat of power on Balnibarbi for the Laputa government was not well admired in the country. While populous, it was host to unpopular facilities such as the prison. What happened to me beyond the quarry walls once I made it to the river was of little to no concern to my company.

Escape from a Balnibarbi prison was as easy as described. The prisoners shifted a prison bar to the side and released me with a small enterprise. I was able to punch small holes in the paper walls above the sewage canals and escape through a rancid but spacious outflow tunnel designed to handle stormwater runoff from the quarry. The paper walls are paired, one on each side of the runoff trough, and so I was able to cut my way through the prison without alerting any other cell. Only a few minutes after my release from the cell, I reached the wall of the quarry and followed an eroded streambed to the river. I rested about a hundred metres upstream of the effluent drainage area.

CHAPTER 4.6

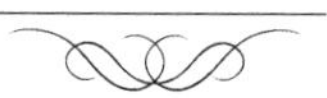

Free once again, the author seeks out safety and stability in the woodlands of Balnibarbi.

WAKING UP AT the edge of a river with no prospects, friends, resources, or any kind of support network is hardly the ideal way to travel a foreign country like Balnibarbi. Thus I woke, cold and hungry, somewhere near the once capital of this country, Lagado, wearing the uniform of an escaped convict and smelling quite ripe from the method by which I had effected the escape. My first resolution was to find fresh water and food. Too many times had I seen the consequences of drinking straight from a river or stream in the wilderness. I was eager to avoid the extra burden of giardiasis or any other nasty parasites, so I hiked the riverbank upstream hoping to find a spring, or a well, or some indication of safe potability.

A wide assortment of berries tempted me as I climbed and scrabbled, leapt and waded, ducked and crawled beside the river. None of the fruits on offer seemed familiar to me, and I would advise any traveller to avoid eating vegetation, particularly on an empty stomach, with which one is not thoroughly certain and familiar. While decisions and spirits draw worse with hunger, I was able to keep my wits about me, I think, during my long and uncomfortable march.

The river upon whose shores Lagado was founded was a small one, familiar in size and scale to the Elbow River that flows through Calgary, Alberta, in the home country to which I so desperately longed to get home. The watercourse had cut a moderate channel in the ground and was difficult to traverse due to large rocks and a meandering pattern. I thought it could not be navigated even by canoe. Frequent portage over fordable gravel sections likely would render such a venture inefficient in the extreme. It may have been possible, though, during high flow periods to float down the river on an inflated raft or inner tube, if the traveller was so inclined. Short sections of rapids might even make such a passage quite entertaining.

Across one of these sections of rapids, wedged between two cliffs, I came across a portly looking gentleman sitting on a fallen tree that bridged the river. The man held a rudimentary fishing pole as he sat with his barefoot feet dangling over the water. A couple metres below him bubbled the river as he jerked, twisted, and cast his lure. His clothes appeared far more comfortable than the uniforms the officials of the monument and court wore, and though short and loose, were more durable. He looked casual and relaxed and much like a sleepy wizard. Above everything else, particularly in comparison to the others I had seen in this land, he was even a little chubby. I felt for this reason he might be able to help me at least find an edible meal.

I thought I had been stealthy in my approach, but in his homeland he had me at a disadvantage. After a few minutes of silent observation, he called me out from my cover, having apparently seen me long before I him. Gradually I was coaxed out of my hiding spot after I carefully made certain it was I to whom he spoke. He bid me approach with gestures unfamiliar, but, with my young understanding of Balnibarbean, I at least knew I was his intended audience. He pointed to the side of the cliff upon which I stood, and I was surprised to see a sturdy looking, well-placed ladder there in plain view. Somehow, despite what I had thought to be careful surveillance, I hadn't noticed the ladder. I climbed it to the top of the rock, and he crossed over to my side, ambling comfortably on his log.

He greeted me confidently. In spite of giving up nearly a foot of height to me, his resolute determination, probably combined with my aching head and empty stomach, put him at an advantage. From my clothes, he knew exactly from where I had come but wasn't the least concerned. As soon as I spoke, my thick accent betrayed I was not from Lagado, Lindalino, or Maldonado. He asked me, with such a strange manner and accent, from which of the bailiwicks I had come. I told him I came not from Balnibarbi at all, but instead from a land over the seas by way of Glubdubdrib. Actually, he would explain to me sometime later that he and his people had been waiting the entirety of my internment. They knew about me and patiently waited for the inevitable escape.

The island of necromancers was one with which my new acquaintance was apparently familiar. Unlike the prisoners and officials I had so far encountered in this place, he was eager to hear about my experiences and knowledge. I have come to think of this as the time when I truly arrived in Balnibarbi. My time in the prison was more of an extended period of quarantine imposed by a xenophobic aristocracy determined to preserve their way of life by slamming shut their borders to any comers.

My new friend introduced himself as Ven Munodi, a member of a colony near to Lagado and a short walk from this place. He offered a drink from his water skin, which I gratefully accepted. I drank thirstily and he pulled from a pocket a bit of bread, which I devoured and for which I subsequently thanked him. At once, I was invited to return with him to the colony. He asked if I would be willing to share my experiences and knowledge with the others of his tribe. Seeing no reason to withhold information from like-minded individuals, and verily at his mercy, I happily assented, and immediately we set out towards the village.

As we walked, I noted these fields were well irrigated, with lush green fruit trees growing amidst fields of wheat, paddies of rice, and gardens of vegetables, carefully tended to and cared for. Neatly laid paths and a well-maintained aqueduct crossed the fields, and at a distance, a stone wall could be seen. Ahead lay a densely packed cluster of wood and stone houses, with barns, various types of livestock, and a functioning windmill at the centre of a courtyard. The houses were between one and three stories tall, painted white, and handsomely constructed with decks, terraces, framed windows with red shutters, and brightly coloured doors. In the yards, a dozen children played and fed the chickens. In one barn, a man was milking a cow. This town was equipped with a library, a small mill, a community hall that served as a school and gathering place, and homes for a hundred and twenty inhabitants. Each of these people appeared healthy and well fed, a welcome contrast to their neighbours.

At my sight, the children rushed to Ven and bombarded him with a stream of questions about me, and he suggested they instead ask me. Thirsty for knowledge, all at once they peppered me with questions. Who was I? Why was I here? They even asked my thoughts on everything from farming practices, to politics, to the Noboos, about whom I would learn much more soon.

Rescuing me from the chaos, Ven ushered the children aside and told them there would be more than enough time for them to ask their questions, one at a time, later. First it was time for dinner. They voiced their protests and disappointment but accepted the deal gradually and quickly became distracted by a jolly little game for four. The game involved drawing a big circle in the dirt and dividing the circle into quarters, representing the territory of each player. A soft ball was thrown into the air at the centre of the circle, and whoever was in the quarter it landed in picked it up and tried to throw it at another player. If successful in striking that player without having the ball caught, the thrower could take the predetermined short stick and carve out a portion of the territory belonging to whom they had hit. The game repeated until one player controlled all of the territories of the circle, and then they began again.

While I watched the children play, the men and women of the town assembled together in a communal kitchen and prepared a shared feast. It smelled delicious: a combination of meats, vegetables, fruits, and freshly baked bread. I was invited to dine at the head of one of the long tables in the courtyard, and we sat down to eat a most charming meal.

CHAPTER 4.7

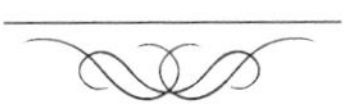

The Nauka, the Noboos, and the cult of celebrity.

AT DINNER, IT took but a moment after we had dished out the food for the people closest to interrogate me in earnest as I ate roasted chicken, baked potatoes, bread, and corn. Word of an outsider who couldn't speak Balnibarbean and had been jailed for trespassing in Projectors Fall had even reached this small commune. The commune was known as the Nauka Colony by the residents.

They impatiently asked me about everything from world geography to geopolitics, math, science, art, literature, history, technology, and every other manner of thing that could be queried. Barely could I finish a single sentence before a new question was raised. I feared the context of my responses was occasionally lost in the clamour. The adults' thirst for knowledge was exceeded by the children who had come first, so time stretched on deep into the night.

Ven and many of the others were descendants of a lord of Laputa who had established an estate of some size during the reign of that kingdom and had resisted the efforts of the state to standardize all production. Acting as a semi-autonomous town unto itself, the Naukans were frowned upon by their neighbours, thus the walls to keep disagreeable people out. The state tolerated the existence of this little community because they provided as a tax almost all the food needed for the prison. Secretly, the Naukans were many times more productive than their neighbours.

This community based its knowledge on fact and science, unlike the others. They confirmed much of what was said by the prisoners but elaborated that the current ruling regime harkened to a time of romantic delusion.

The Naukans welcomed me to join them in their farming and showed me how they made use of simple tools, technology, and careful planning to optimize the production of the land. Contrary to state policy, they had dug wells and constructed an aqueduct. Farms were tilled according to the weather, not according to the moon. They had closely studied fertilizer using controlled experiments to determine the optimal amounts, timing, and composition. Similar experimentation had improved yields by means of artificial selection. The crops that produced the best fruit or yields were not consumed but were replanted the next year, giving way to ever better and more productive fields.

Through education and literacy, these children were all able to read and write. The knowledge of one generation was passed down completely and accurately to the next, and much was rescued from the library of Lagado after the original election of the current regime. Ven granted me a tour of the schoolhouse, which was rustic and reminiscent of single-room schools one might expect of a small western town in the early 1900s. It was quaint, but the quality of the education matters more upon the qualifications of the teacher than upon the structures and supplies that attend to it, and the Naukans placed great emphasis on raising their children. In the same way the best crops were replanted, the wisest of the Naukans spent the most time raising the children to ensure the next generation were ever better and more productive. The lord of this estate at the time of Mr. Tung recognized a malevolent tone—amid suggestions the marvelled leader himself didn't read—about learning and stole a great many books. Only days later, all buildings of education and learning had been destroyed by the machinations of the state.

In a society that despises the wise and intelligent, as was the case on the island of Balnibarbi, there are costs associated with opposition and success. Thereby, the Naukans possessed virtually no rights in society and were excluded from all but their own affairs within their estate. The tax rate imposed upon their production was punitive and spitefully high. Predictably, this only had the effect of driving ever greater innovation.

The estate was regularly picketed by jealous neighbours who believed the success of the Naukans was directly responsible for their own failures. A group of protest-happy locals called the Noboos gleefully manufactured false (for all they knew) claims against the colony, so Nauka retained a night watch to keep an eye on the Noboos as they would even resort to sabotage in an effort to discredit and destroy the Nauka.

I stayed with the Nauka for three months. On four different occasions I helped chase off marauding Noboos who tried to burn the crops or destroy the aqueduct. It is probably to the good fortune of the Nauka that the people of Balnibarbi are not by their natures violent. This might have something to do with the lack of food, which in short bursts makes people angry and violent, but deprived of sufficient substance for long enough, as was typical of the people of Balnibarbi, reduces their resistance to minimal levels. The only instances of homicidal behaviour told to me had to do directly with Laputa, both from the leaders thereof who were known to use the floating island as a weapon and from the man who oversaw its downfall.

The Naukans reported that Balnibarbi was indeed once a prosperous and productive land. Several generations before the overthrow of Laputa, the country was well connected and produced more food than it needed. It was the founding of the Academy of Projectors that led to the erosion of their society. The Nauka bore little in the way of respect for the island of Laputa and painted a familiar picture of a place ruled by a people entirely obsessed with astronomy and music at the expense of all other arts and sciences. In fact, they had often replaced other scientific instruments with poorly fitting astronomical equivalents. Measures had been made by tools made of spheres and circles, but not, as I noted, ellipses. Lines, not being common in the cosmos, had not been considered proper math.

Furthermore, the Naukans described the inhabitants of Laputa as perpetually distracted by their own thoughts and completely unaware of practical science. So distracted they were reported to have been that entire corps of Balnibarbeans had been employed in whacking their eyes, ears, and mouths with little flails to remind them to look, listen, or speak at appropriate times. Despite these shortcomings, the Nauka did not blame Laputa. It was the Balnibarbeans who had gone up and learned from the Laputians and had returned obsessed with the same false science of pure theory without experimentation that set up the academy, modified all the practices over a period of eighty years, and had eventually given rise to the rebellion and ultimately the anti-intelligentsia movement.

It was to me reported, however, that the seed and foundation of the modern problems faced by Balnibarbi were the direct result of the cult of celebrity. Nurtured and evolved by the ruling family, the outright rejection of fair and rational debate supported by science and authority had been replaced by a trust in the power of celebrity. Power and trust flowed not to well-grounded ideas and measurable success, but to the loudest voices, belonging to often the least qualified persons. Artists of all types—including musicians, actors, painters, writers, and sculptors—who found success in their particular media found their every thought seized upon and followed as divine gospel. If power corrupts even the most intelligent, imagine what it does to those who possess little of that attribute.

Without evidence to support their claims and ideas, these powerful celebrities rose to ever greater heights. The more outlandish their voice, the greater their fame grew and the more sensational their following. By soapbox pronouncement, they could enact sweeping reforms across the country. If they spoke too eloquently, or with too great a poise, they, too, were cast out as the surviving fear of the tyranny of the projectors kept the people, and particularly the Noboos, vigilant.

The Naukans believed the cult of celebrity was fostered and encouraged by the ruling family. Nobody possessed greater celebrity than they. It was even rumoured in the small community that any celebrity that rose too high without close alliance to the ruling family would often disappear suddenly and without warning. These disappearances were explained away by the vices of their success. Some believed the aristocracy, in an act of self-preservation, took matters into its own hands. Those luckiest of the high risers were married into the leading family, thus ensuring the concentration of fame and fortune. So goes the tyranny of the popular and the ruin of Balnibarbi.

CHAPTER 4.8

The author plans to use his own small amount of fame to create change on the island.

A FUNNY THING OCCURRED to me during my stay with the Nauka. This small, isolated, nearly off-the-grid, unconnected colony was aware of my existence without meeting me. Word of my presence, escape from prison, and disappearance had circled back to the Naukan colony. I became aware I had achieved some small measure of fame on the island of Balnibarbi.

Because the Naukans had explained the power celebrity could wield in this land, and I recognized the extreme poverty and deplorable living conditions of the people, I felt compelled to help lift the people out of their hardship. I believed I could demonstrate the value of learning and experimentation and measured progress supported by evidence, and in so doing, bring prosperity and growth to this forgotten backwater. I knew I had originally intended to keep my profile low, but not being a machine and with no prime directive to follow, my decisions and ideas changed and modified as more information became available.

I told Ven of my plan. He counselled against the idea, warning that anybody who spoke out as I intended to do would certainly be branded a traitor to the revolution. If my words could not be twisted to support the status quo, then I would likely not be heard from again. He didn't say so, but I also felt he feared retribution against his Nauka Colony. I tried to assuage his fears by assuring him I would not speak a word of his colony directly or drop any meaningful hint that I had ever heard of or visited this place if it were to come up.

He adjured and coaxed me to, at the very least, be circumspect, to plan what I was going to say and how I would say it. Most importantly, he cautioned me to not show the poise, confidence, education, or intelligence he knew I possessed. He welcomed me to stay with them as long as I needed. It was partly the gesture of a polite host but more a guarantee that I had enough time to properly prepare, plan, and unfortunately, dumb down my words so the common Balnibarbean would thus find them accessible and tolerable. Though it is a tragedy to conceal intelligence, and to lower one's standards for fear of persecution by those jealous or fearful thereof, it was an unfortunate necessity in this self-righteous, ignorant, and nonrational place.

Thereafter, I took to crafting my coup. I worked to minimize my accent, shorten my words, and reduce the verbosity with which I spoke. Clever and witty remarks would only get me into trouble. I had to strike a balance between elucidating my key message and a sharing a foolishly simple understanding of how the world works.

I needed a convincing alibi for my time with the Nauka, so with their help, I fabricated a story of being lost in the forest near the river. Being a simple man, it had never occurred to me to leave my small encampment to explore the area. My ability to speak Balnibarbean one day and not the next was to be explained dementedly as the result of trauma from my imprisonment. A history of head injury was to explain any inconsistencies in my story, not that any was likely be probed deeply.

After several weeks of preparation and with the assistance of the Nauka, who prepared me for low-brow debates and illogical conversations and—more importantly—taught me to speak louder and target increasingly wild accusations at anybody who dared to disagree with me—a sort of idiotic doubling down on a bad argument—I felt as ready as I ever was going to be to take on this world.

The Nauka were even kind enough to help me establish a camp in the forest outside of Lagado, build a small lean-to and a fire, and plant evidence to support the contention that for the past few months I had been living off the land. We built up the site near enough that I could be certain somebody would come across me within a number of days, particularly if I kept the fire burning and pouring out a consistent billow of smoke.

All that done, I said as many goodbyes as I could, but Ven was the last to leave. He wished me good luck and returned my prison clothes, which they had tarnished to make realistic my woodsy claim. I thanked him for his hospitality, and he thanked me for sharing the news of the world with his people. We wished each other fair fortunes ahead.

Afterwards, I tended the fire and made a smoky mess of the place. True to our expectation, I was soon discovered by a child wandering out on his own into the forest. We had built the camp barely a hundred metres from the edge of the town, and the child who found me was playing in what was, in effect, his backyard. He walked up to me without any hint of fear and asked who I was. I had nearly forgotten the normal Balnibarbean form, but the skinny child quickly reminded me of my purpose. I told him I was a traveller named Cygnus from another land. His tone became suspicious, and he asked if I was the one who had been caught vandalizing the Projectors Fall monument.

In that moment, I realized my story had been modified during the time I was missing to augment the story of my capture and to elevate the standing of the men who had caught me. I would later learn I was a giant who had fought against a team of valiant public-interest constables. Hereafter, due to the never-ending title, I'll just refer to them as park rangers. They had managed to subdue me despite my many inherent advantages and bring me to justice. As I am quite tall, particularly measured against the malnourished Balnibarbean standards, the child felt no need question the fable he had been told. I affirmed I was indeed the same giant.

As children are wont to do, he was quite pleased to have made this discovery. Apparently unaware of the risk of talking to an avowed criminal, giant, and escaped convict, he asked me to come meet his parents. Again, I acceded to his wishes and followed him home to his family. It was a short walk, and when I arrived, the family was sensibly unnerved by my appearance. They sat me down at a table in the yard outside their modest shack. The child's mother, while ostensibly returning inside to fetch something, sent their eldest daughter in full flight away down the street. I made a show of not noticing the deception when the woman returned with nothing to demonstrate of her absence. With spurious and obviously false politeness, we nervously talked about my time in the woods and how I had survived so long on my own.

After several minutes, a team of police officers returned with the daughter to take me into custody, and the family breathed a sigh of relief as the officers begged me to follow them back to the station, which I *reluctantly* agreed to. The little boy that had found me tried to chase after us, yelling that he had rescued me, that he had found me, and that he should get any reward as his parents swiftly restrained him.

It was a short walk to the police station through the same sorts of streets as I had experienced in Lindalino. The houses could have been easily interchangeable between the two towns. The road was equally poorly constructed. Unlike Lindalino, Lagado only boasted a small castle that could not be said to tower over the landscape. The police station was much like the ranger station, but in lieu of logs, the police station was made of stone.

The officers sat me down at a similar table to the one I had previously encountered in the rangers' station and began to ask many of the same questions. This time, I had no need to deflect and deceive the investigators, except with my prepared statement. I told them unnecessarily detailed accounts of how I had wandered to the camp location in a bit of a stupor after escaping the prison. I had set up camp, found food from the river and forest, and managed to survive. Finishing off my sad tale, I said that as a humble man, I didn't think to explore to my north and stuck to foraging areas where I had been consistently successful. My ruse was sufficiently convincing, and I was escorted without chains to the castle at the centre of the city.

As we walked, crowds began to gather. I felt hopeful my preposterous plan might actually work. The officers took me to the district office to meet their superiors. I repeated the same fiction, and as before, they accepted it. Cooperative though I was, I still remained, in fact, an escaped convict. They insisted I remain in custody in the castle but assured me I would be well taken care of. True to their word, I was. I stayed in a cell in the castle alone for a few days, while outside my story grew and my celebrity rose. On the third day, word came I was to travel back to Lindalino to visit the ruling family. Such an offer was not one to be taken lightly. With feigned, but apparently sincere, reverence, I accepted this offer.

All the officers wished to be part of the procession bringing me to the president and his family. I was escorted out of town in a huge parade. Again, people came out to watch as the strange foreigner was celebrated and transferred to the golden palace. A carnival atmosphere preceded me. Surrounded by energy and excitement, the few hours between the cities passed quite quickly, this sojourn being quite the opposite of my previous travels in this land.

On this occasion, when I entered the golden centre of power, I was greeted quite differently. I was ushered not to the squat judge's court, but instead into the largest, tallest tower on the entire island as repeatedly advertised to me with pompous bravado. The main audience chamber, which for a supposedly democratic nation appeared more as a throne room with great golden pillars, was filled with courtiers lining the walls, while at the far end of the room, seated on a fantastically ornate, golden chair, sat Grand President Tung of Balnibarbi.

CHAPTER 4.9

The author attempts to cautiously effecta radical culture change in Balnibarbi.

GRAND PRESIDENT TUNG of Balnibarbi could trace his descent directly, patrilinealy, back to the overthrower of Laputa. Presumptuous, pretentious, and vain, he was a pompous, bombastic, narcissistic manipulator of the public will. He was dressed in the same flowing robes as most of his officials, but as with nearly everything in his immediate surroundings, they were gold in colour.

I am not partial to the tiresome monotony of golden yellow. Whilst I could recognize the beauty of the craftsmanship that went into the place, the ostentatious demonstration of abundance was grossly over the top. I had encountered vile windbags recently, but not in their own palaces, and I had not been subject to repeated lies and false truths. Should the reader possess the opportunity to visit with this inflated soul, it is my recommendation he be avoided.

The man, his hair bleached to resemble the unvarying surroundings, addressed me, speaking down to me as the inferior being he obviously believed me to be. I carefully drew upon all the strength and intestinal fortitude I could muster and smiled and nodded at many of his sometimes nonsensical, and other times insane, ramblings. So conceited a fellow was he that he never once stopped talking about his own magnificence, his wonderful triumphs, or the wealth he had accumulated. I knew from the ranger, prisoners, and Naukans he had inherited most of his wealth, the rest having been extracted from his subjects. I felt little respect for the man before me.

He boasted and bragged about the greatness of Balnibarbi, its glorious achievements, and how it was the subject of awe and astonishment the world over. Not lost on me was that this island had been long forgotten by the world, thereby rendering the hypocrisy of his purported international fame in the truest hermit kingdom laughable. His triumph and attainment spread no further than its shores. Even then, the evidence of his munificence was overshadowed by the smallest of mites. His people considered themselves the best, and the rest of the world, if they could even know of this pompous group, would also have thought differently.

He spoke at me—not to me or with me—for nearly an hour. It was the most tedious and testing display of silent theatre I have ever been forced to perform. I waited as he spoke, and his advisors and courtiers nodded and agreed with each claim, for him to stop and ask me a question, any question, but such a request never came. At the end of his soliloquy, he finished by acknowledging my presence only as a testament to his vast prodigiousness, and with a wave, indicated I was to leave the way I had come, my purpose evidently having been achieved.

I was grateful to be relieved of his presence and knew in my mind I had also accomplished that which I had set out to do. In a single day, I had gone from being a foreigner that had trespassed upon a national monument to an exotic celebrity who had met the Grand President. Thousands of people had personally bore witness to me, and now they had invested in me. Fame. I was famous as famous could be, with every man, woman, and child in the two cities of Lindalino and Lagado claiming they had seen me personally en route to meet the president. Even in the third city of Maldonado, people claimed they were present that day. They all pretended to carry a small claim to fame. I had looked their way, or blinked, or any other trivial, unprovable thing.

I was brought back to the castle in Lagado by a member of the upper class. No doubt was in my mind that the only people with direct access to the palace or the president were of such a class. This gentleman was particularly eager to be my close acquaintance. Hiaru was a lanky, gangly man, with sunken dark eyes that protruded and pierced whatever he stared at. The strange stare is what I remember most about his appearance. I can't recall ever seeing him blink. His skin was pale by the standards of Balnibarbi and glistened with a thin layer of sweat that never quite beaded or fell, just always coated his skin. His hair was thin, patchy, but where present, long and dark. He kept it combed to cover all the bald patches in a vainglorious attempt to disguise himself. He was also, to my discomfort, particularly touchy-feely. I wished I could offer him a towel, for each time he put an arm around me, or grabbed my arm, I felt the cold clammy sweat that seemed to linger on me as it did on him.

I was assigned a small room. The police had completed the transition from my arresters to my guards and public relations team. Under the direction of Hiaru, they worked to ensure that everybody knew I was here and that the president had spoken with me. Hiaru made it abundantly clear to everybody that he was the conduit necessary if anybody wished to speak with me. The castle was mobbed with people hoping to get a glance of the giant stranger who had spoken with the president himself. A gift was left in my room, evidently from the daughter of the president: my opal pendant. If I doubted my performance, this put my mind at ease. The symbolism of this gift was clear. I was to be included in the aristocratic class.

Over the next days, Hiaru and I made every effort to connect with my fans and supporters. I left the castle at every opportunity to shake hands, kiss babies, and grant audiences with the common folk like a travelling rock star. Hiaru clung to my arm as though the moistened contact kept us attached like glue. I bore the burden of his perpetual accompaniment as best as I could manage. While noisome and malodorous, he was a valuable means to an end. His own avarice and simple vocabulary I used to keep myself grounded to the level of the common people.

I kept my answers short and simple and credited luck and good fortune for my deliverance. Gradually, I started to toss out concealed knocks against the authorities. These were tiny needles none would suspect as I carefully concealed the message in the words I wasn't saying. I never once granted the president any credit for my arrival or survival. I started to hint at other ways to do things and would ask childlike questions about things I knew already while playing ignorant, innocent, and downright stupid. At first, Hiaru was pleased to answer my birdbrained queries. I knew well he was trying to bask in my reflected glow, and by extension, increase his fame and power.

Each day, I grew a little bolder in my commentary. One by one, I started to explore the benefits of basic innovations. I found a part of the audience willing to listen and learn even if they didn't realize what was happening. The Noboos were less impressed, though, and soon I found my gallery comprised of less-than-devoted fans. My mucilaginous companion kept on his smiling, happy face, but the neutral, and even negative, reactions from the crowds obviously wore heavily on his aspirations.

I tried to carefully craft my questions and comments in a way that didn't blatantly contradict any known edicts. Even those mandates with the most complicated barriers still had ways around which I could squeak. I bent rules without breaking them. The glow about me was fading rapidly. I was still highly sought after and very famous, but no longer was the bloom on the rose. I continued to travel about, and the common folk were still enthusiastic about making my acquaintance, but Hiaru slowly drifted out of my immediate orbit, and my police team, once inseparable, found more important matters with which to deal and occupy their time.

One day, I returned to the castle to find my accommodations had expired and I would need to find an alternate domicile, for no longer was the president as eager to host and bear the costs of retaining me in his inner circle.

CHAPTER 4.10

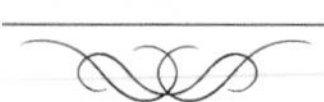

The author learns how fleeting celebrity can be and is swiftly reallocated.

IN A MATTER of weeks, I found a poor farmer keen to accept my presence. Across his property, he had recently created a crude irrigation canal connected to a rain-catching pond. I connected that pond to the stream with an underground pipe to keep the pond full at all times, regardless of the weather. Along this canal grew more than any other part of his farm, and in fact, more than the entire farm. As far as an observer could tell, the water was just rainwater collected in this basin. It wouldn't stand up to scrutiny, but it also didn't scream violation.

I took manure, created a closed-burn vessel that only *appeared* to burn anything, and quietly spread the results, compounding the positive effects of proper watering. This meant that instead of the treatment destroying most of the nutrients, he retained a much greater quantity to produce more value. His crops grew in parallel to my celebrity, but so, too, did the risks multiply.

Word spread that the foreigner had strange new ideas about farming and they seemed to be working well. I blasted anybody who suggested that what I was doing was immoral by accusing them of some misdeed, all-too-often entirely unrelated to what was being suggested. The farm at which I stayed grew in wealth and stature. So, too, did the farmer, and he became a bit of a person of fame.

Hiaru began to appear around the farm as signs of a resurgence of my celebrity began to appear. There was no place for him on the farm, and he was unaccustomed to physical labour of any sort. Unlike at the palace, Hiaru was no longer benefiting from my proximity, and his serpentine smile rarely showed on his lips anymore. I didn't exactly push him away, but I was not particularly receptive towards his advances and clumsy efforts to participate. In his mind, I'm sure he harkened back to the time only so very recently when he was basking in the limelight and enjoying all the spoils it offered him. Now he was getting jealous as the soil didn't reflect the glow as the golden palace walls had a tendency to do.

The results were speaking for themselves, but I was being asked again to speak as well. I was riding a wave of success, and I started becoming careless, usinglarger words and more complicated ideas. I carefully avoided discussing the leadership or contradicting the laws of the land, but even the dullest of citizens could see I wasn't quite the same person I had been. Doubts about me started to grow.

Naturally, a few people who found value in what I was saying were drawn into my orbit, while those who disagreed, particularly the Noboos, congregated beyond my awareness. Thereafter, I was surrounded with hangers-on who concealed from me in an echo chamber the growing questions. Surrounded by adoring fans, and divided from my critics, I grew bolder and bolder. Close to me once again was Hiaru. I was unaware of the change in his cloying behaviour. He enjoyed the company of my admirers but took extended leaves as well. I spoke more freely, and my circle lapped up every word and idea with relish.

I had overstepped my celebrity. Stories began circulating that I was questioning the president. This scandal and its significance was not lost on me, but the president himself had skin in my game. He had granted me an audience and spoken well of me afterwards. Hence, the goodwill of the president bought me some time when a neighbour of my host farm accused me of stealing and ruining his crops. He said I had uprooted his crops and transferred them at night to the other farm to claim as my own. His slanderous words caught fire and spread as fast as my own fame had done only months before. As before, when the going got rough, Hiaru made himself scarce.

The Noboos seized on the accusations as evidence of my prevarication and began twisting the words of my speeches into antigovernment, anticonstitutional rants. I found my most innocent and factual statements about improving yields were being talked about widely but in the context that I had openly challenged the laws. The first claimant against me became two and then several. They all told the same story: I had stolen from their lands to better contrast the production and falsify the benefits of my insidious agenda.

The people of Balnibarbi were whipped into a frenzy against me, and I knew that soon I would be disappeared. The farm was devastated by the accusers. The rain-catching basin was filled in, and my entourage dwindled rapidly. Those who had been my friends and supporters abandoned me for fear they might be implicated in my heinous scheme against Grand President Tung.

Finally, a particular friend approached me and told me it was time to leave. I was surprised to see him here, but I knew if he was, I must trust his words. It was not difficult to assemble my things to leave. In the middle of the night, I stole off into the darkness. As far as the public of Balnibarbi were concerned, I was never heard from again.

Of course, I went back to the Nauka Colony. Once again, I sought their asylum and assistance. I would not be able to work in the fields or assist with anything in open sight, my countenance now being immediately recognizable in this land. I stayed out of sight in one of the barns.

It seemed Ven was quite a capable friend. He let me in on a little secret: he had followed me to the castle. He had attended the presentations and noted my surroundings. Carefully, far more so than I, he had established a relationship with my escort Hiaru, who was always eager to make a connection. Ven had stayed entirely out of my spotlight but kept a close watch on me. When I began to throw caution to the wind, he had maintained his distance but kept in touch with Hiaru. Ven had even established himself in the Noboo community. He had been present as the two parties, Hiaru and the Noboos, came together. He had witnessed Hiaru pass on stories and ideas. It was Hiaru that had convinced the neighbour to slander me, and it was Hiaru that had gleefully reported to the president my transgressions, true, partly true, and complete fabrications alike. Hiaru had been playing both sides, and seeing an opportunity to capitalize on my downfall, he had ultimately been the one to sell me out. When Ven came to me at the farm and suggested I depart, I only had a matter of a few hours before the Noboos and the police were to have come and quietly dispose of me.

While I stayed hidden in the barns, the Nauka helped me to build a float boat. Well constructed but limited in size to what was communicable to a distant beach, the raft would serve as yet another escape to the sea. They supplied me with ample food, storage containers that would repel most water built into the boat, and a pair of collapsible sails. It took only a week to prepare. Again, under the cloak of darkness, we carried it on a sledge through the countryside to the sea. The Nauka farm, as mentioned, was close to Lagado, which was inland on the northern part of the island. The agreed point of departure was on the south shore, requiring a long, all-night pull. The Naukans were intimately familiar with the island and experts at avoiding detection or arousing suspicion. We crossed the country without incident, despite the object of our transportation.

Ven brought along three strong men to help launch the craft. We quickly tipped and hauled it into a quiet harbour. I thanked Ven and the Naukans again and took the opal from my neck as a token of my thanks. After a battle of who could be more polite, he graciously accepted the valuable. I boarded the ship, grabbed a pair of finely shaped oars, and rowed out of the harbour in the early dawn hours. Still today I should like to know what became of this place, but I know never am I likely to find out.

PART FIVE

BROBADINGOG: ENORMITY

CHAPTER 5.1

The author is stranded at sea and rescued by a passing vessel.

THRICE HAVE I found myself leaving an island and floating out to sea. Each time, my vessel proved a match for the waters, and with each passing experience, I grew more comfortable, and perhaps unreasonably confident, in my ability to find land or rescue. I hope I have sufficiently related the loneliness, fear, trepidation, and uncertainty of the perils of open-sea travel. Once more, without navigation aid nor power greater than the sun and the winds, did I experience this singularly unique feeling. On this journey, I was best prepared, better than at any time before, and so was I ready for a prolonged period.

The Nauka had left me with a fishing rod and net with which I could hopefully catch some meals to supplement the salted rations of bread and ham they had prepared. Further to their ingenuity, they had provided a black clay basin in the shape of a doughnut and a glass that slanted in towards the middle. In the centre of the doughnut was a receiving cup. Properly assembled, I could put salt water in the doughnut basin and allow the sun to evaporate the water, which then would condense upon the lid and collect like rain in the central glass. This invention provided me with a replaceable, if limited, amount of water. I even had a knife with which I carved a notch in the side of the boat for each day I was at sea.

It proved an altogether more civilized journey, thanks to the Nauka. I ended up at sea for forty-six days, floating freely in the South Pacific Ocean. Not a professional angler, I only managed to catch a single example of one unknown species of fish. Without a means to cook it but with the sun, I abandoned that enterprise and hoped I shouldn't come to regret it. On the forty-sixth day, I spotted a large vessel. It was unmistakably a cruise ship. If I was to be spotted by chance in the world's largest expanse of open ocean, what better way than by a ship loaded with sightseeing tourists who could spot my bright red sails in the water?

We were separated by quite some distance, but I waved the sail and raised the biggest commotion possible. For what felt an eternity, the boat appeared not to see me. I had fully abandoned hope when a horn blasted three times. I rose from the deck to wave and holler once again. This had the intended effect. The boat gradually turned around and approached. My now vast experience at sea taught me that if I wanted to be found, I should not stop waving lest they think me a regular seafarer.

The ship pulled up, and I read on the hull first the brand name of the cruise, Starboard Cruise Lines, then in smaller typeface, the name of my rescuer, the Intrepid Traveler.

A rescue boat was dropped from the deck with a small crew on board. They approached, asked in English if I was all right, and calmly raised me back up on deck. I related my story to the first mate and was visited by the ship's doctor to guarantee my health. They offered me a spare room as they travelled towards Easter Island. My situation was related back to civilization, and I enjoyed a free cruise across the Pacific, speaking of my travels with the tourists and providing to them a sort of unplanned entertainment.

I was told I was spotted not by the crew but instead by a woman on the top deck. She, having seen me, was unsure of the nature of her discovery. She sought out her binoculars, and after a while watching, decided to alert a crew member, who initiated the man-overboard protocol. By the time I heard the three horn blasts, which were Morse code for O(scar) to let the crew know there was a man overboard, they had swung around to collect me. Any further delay by the woman, and the ship would likely have not been able to confirm her news. Once having counted all souls aboard, they would have continued on their course unabated.

We arrived on Rapa Nui, and the cruise line offered me, free of charge (fortunately as I possessed no material wealth on my person), passage back to Chile, and further, on to Florida and Halifax. As far as I could tell, I had two options: I could make landfall in Chile and then fly or try an extended drive back home to Canada, which would require multiple explanations and interviews with consulates, media, and authorities, or I could remain on board a luxury cruise ship, enjoying the comforts afforded me, and arrive in Halifax, home and safe at last. I chose the latter, as I'm sure the reader would understand, given my past associations with flying over the ocean.

The cruise passed smoothly, and a few weeks later, I disembarked from the Intrepid Traveler in Halifax, Nova Scotia, where I was reunited with my family for the first time in a couple years.

I think the reader might be interested in knowing what goes on in between interviews, story requests, television appearances, etc. Once more, by all legal interpretations, I had been declared deceased and had to be brought back to life in a strictly legal sense. Doing this involves reams of paperwork, witnesses, notaries, tests, judges, lawyers, and numerous hearings to validate one's claim that they truly are who they say they are. More than a little skepticism greets someone who has twice been dead for several years. Accusations fly from those who didn't know you personally. I'm certain my keen contemporary reader might have heard I was accused of being everything from a spy to an alien masquerading as a human. The process of coming back to life is slow and tedious as compared to the subsequent glamorous appearances on late night talk shows and various news networks.

A comfortable life can be achieved simply through speaking engagements. Numerous publishers sought to buy my story, but I stuck to my convictions that only I could rightfully share the thoughts and experiences I had in recent times achieved. After only a few months back in familiar civilization, I established a personal fortune and the comfort of one with means. No longer did I have any material needs, but eager to share my story, I found once again my life took me to the skies. I did not have to toil as one of the crew, though. Instead, I enjoyed first-class amenities, and as compensation for twice-repeated issues, I was provided passage without personal outlay.

I wonder sometimes whether executives of the airline struggled with the thought of promoting my presence on the plane. Perhaps they thought to use it as a story of how, despite disaster, I was still willing to fly with them, but then perhaps they thought drawing back the curtain and inadvertently promoting their two calamities with the same man on board both times would work against them. When one writes such a statement, it forces the consideration of whether I was a bad omen, a talisman of bad luck, or perhaps even a guilty party. Knowing I had no role in either accident, and not believing in luck or divine providence, these thoughts were easy for me to cast aside. Certainly though, there must have been others who considered them with greater purpose.

In my spare time, I took courses in aviation. Having found myself twice in a situation of peril and twice having no ability to preserve myself from said danger, I thought it clever to arm myself with knowledge of flight. Between speeches to gathered dignitaries and admirous crowds, I dove deep into study. I felt it wise to be able to pilot any machine upon which I might find myself passenger. Over two years, while accumulating wealth and various honours, most I believe to have been undeserved, I earned my wings at a rapid pace. I talked to counsellors and therapists about my fears, and they generally agreed that facing the fear served better utility than avoiding it.

CHAPTER 5.2

The author is interrupted on a flight to Japan and makes landfall in a strange place.

AFTER ONLY TWENTY-FOUR months back on land and hundreds more uneventful, yet nerve-wracking flights, I was flying from Seattle to Japan to address an international conference on geography as a keynote speaker. I shan't bother the reader with the more inane details of the flight. I'm certain few care what I ate or watched on the screen, but I did sit in the first row of the first-class section. As had become customary, the pilot and copilot welcomed me aboard. It pleased them to have their picture taken with a man of celebrity to show their friends and family.

Having worked the other side, I tried to be as polite and undemanding as possible on every flight, knowing the burdens faced by the crew with a large number of tired, bored, excited, and restless passengers. I noted, or perhaps in retrospect I observed, but thought little of the behaviour of one of the crew who seemed preoccupied and demonstrated little of the trained courtesy of an experienced crew member. She, an attractive young woman with tired blue eyes, was less bubbly and friendly. She spent the lion's share of her time at the front of the cabin out of sight of the passengers. I've never found a flight enjoyable when it seems someone is under the weather of circumstance, and I tried to engage her in polite conversation. I could barely pull from her the tersest responses as though I had offended her in some way. My faltering efforts at cordial and amicable communication rebuffed, she seemed to withdraw further into herself, an unusual reaction from an occupation so extroverted in nature.

I wouldn't have to wait long to understand the source of her anxiety. Once in the air, and only an hour or so into the flight, four young, brawny men with black masks over their faces and gloves on their hands concealing every detail of their identities burst forth from behind the curtain dividing the classes. Each of them possessed a thin blade a foot long and demonstrably sharp enough to slice through the leather of an aeroplane chair. I can't say how it was the men had evaded security with such devices. By their shape, I conjectured they may have been hidden within a hollow metal tube disguised as part of a bag.

The hijackers took great care to establish their dominance, through their yelling and posturing. A man who stood up to impede their progress was swiftly dispatched. No other, including, I am ashamed to admit, me, challenged their convictions further. The attendant suddenly had more life and took a leading role in commanding the attention of the passengers with the radio, of which she seemed to possess complete control. The hijackers were, in fact, petty thieves. They demanded the occupants of the plane empty their carry-on luggage and wallets that the men may alleviate them of their burdens.

The passengers were herded to the middle of the plane and made to huddle together in close proximity along with the crew. I found myself—a celebrity and recognizable man—quite vulnerable. The woman pulled me from the group and took me to the front section. She ordered three children from the assembled passengers to be brought to the front of the plane and sat them in the first row. The gang blocked them in, holding the knives to their throats. It was made clear to me that if I failed to cooperate, they would be killed. She also stressed their intent was to seize control of the craft and land it at a friendly, unmonitored airstrip in Northern British Columbia.

My marching orders were simple: I was to stand and smile at the camera while the pilot listened to a story relayed by radio by the reprobate malefactor. The story was that I would like to come and visit the pilot in the cockpit and would return the favour by having my picture taken with them. It became clear my participation was not just fortune but planned and preordained.

The pilot resisted slightly, and the criminals grew weary and nervous, but he eventually relented. He unlocked the door of the cockpit, allowing the previously reticent attendant to open it, and two of the brutes launched forwards from their seats. One hammered the pilot's head at the same time as the other brute removed the pilot's seatbelt with the hilt of a blade, rendering him unconscious in a heap on the floor. Exhibiting his quick reflexes, the copilot radioed for help. The lowlife thug nearest to him drew his blade and ended the broadcast.

The woman cursed him, seized his knife, and prematurely completed his journey as well. She pointed it at the other while I stood well back out of the way. She decried the idiocy of the dead hijacker's actions. With both pilot and copilot unable to act, they had no way to land the plane. Furthermore, with his last action, the copilot had alerted the authorities. Certainly, they would not be able to land anywhere as planned had they even the ability to do so. Their careful plan had unwoven rapidly into a tangled mess. So, too, deteriorated their command and control.

Two of the remaining attackers jumped into the cockpit and pushed buttons, pulled on the control stick, and flipped toggles, apparently at random, in an effort to fly the plane. Outside, the woman had decided to hold her sword tightly to my throat, preventing me from speaking. It was a most uncomfortable position, considering the increasing instability of the aircraft.

One of the men threw the plane into a dive, steeply descending. The woman fell backwards hard against the opposite side of the fuselage. I grabbed the jump seat and swung into the cockpit where the two amateur pilots were both distracted and injured. I should not like to describe myself as heroic, being that I was partially, if involuntarily, to blame for our present circumstance. Once there, I overcame the two hijackers with their own weapons, they having been cast aside so the men could work to control the jet. In the cabin behind me, I heard the passengers had similarly overwhelmed their one remaining guard and were working their way forwards towards the cockpit.

I took control of the stick and did my best to pull the plane out of the dive, but I could barely make a dent in our descent. A passenger arrived, and as I was identifiably not wearing the black balaclava of the attacker, took the seat next to me in the copilot's chair. He grabbed the radio with a trained hand and sent in a mayday message. He then proceeded to inform the passengers to take a seat and assume a crash-landing position as instructed in the opening flight demonstration. I was relieved to see he had a similar comfort level as I amidst all this massive discomfort. In the cockpit of the plane, together we gradually slowed our descent. We plummeted through the clouds, and ahead, we could see we were heading directly for a landmass of enormous size. To the north was visible a string of volcanic mountains. The rest of the landmass that could be seen was a dark, verdant green.

While we were making progress, it was clear we weren't going to be able to bring the bird back up fast enough to avoid the collision. We looked for, and found, a lake in which we might attempt to ditch the plane in a somewhat softer manner. That this body of water was only a degree or two off our current path—therefore, we didn't have to add to our efforts to right the plane the effort to steer in that direction—only aided us.

The dilemma of a dive is that the faster you allow the plane to go, the easier it is to recover, yet faced with the prospect of a crash, one would rather minimize aerial velocity. We pulled hard and were able to end the dive in time. We scraped over the tops of gigantic trees, having erred in our estimate of the distance to the lake by several hundred metres.

The plane brushed through the woods as sickening screeches echoed and the exterior was treated to a new paint job. The plane slowed in starts with each tree we struck. As we descended, two great trees tore the tips off the wings, and with a last heave of control, we pulled the nose up in time to see the edge of the lake appear before us. The plane skated along the top of the water, coming to a full stop near the shore. The emergency exits opened, and the passengers who were able jumped out every emergency exit and door available to them.

Few of the survivors chose to run towards the front of the plane, they mostly having taken up seats near the back. I grabbed one of the hijackers' knives, thinking it might come in handy wherever we had landed. My copilot and I jumped from the front exit out into the lake. We swam with all we could to the edge of the lake where we watched several other passengers still jumping into the water.

Without warning, a dark shadow attached to a monstrous hand as large as two full-grown men reached from the sky and tried to pluck the plane out of the water. Failing, the behemoth decided to crush the plane as a child frustrated with a toy. A deafening wail split our ears. We ran from the shore of the lake, the copilot and I and a few of the surviving passengers who had made it this far, for fear of being found by this being.

We ran into a field of grass, which was as tall we, sometimes taller in places. As it swayed in the wind, the sound was as a small tree creaking under a heavy load. In the nook of a proper tree at least thirty metres tall, if I could estimate at all, we gathered and took stock of our position and endeavoured to reconcile our experience.

CHAPTER 5.3

The survivors set up camp and face unprecedented struggles in this strange new place.

ALL ASSEMBLED, ONLY a dozen people gathered in the nook of the tree. We stood close together, greatly traumatized by what we had just seen. The reader may think that after my experiences thus far, I might have been numbed to such an effect, but I can assure the reader nothing could have been further from the truth.

The autumn air was crisp. We needed to create a shelter to stay warm, particularly given the strong winds that continued to buffet both us and the long, thick grass. The decision was made to divide up some of the more important tasks as we would have need of food and water before long and fire and shelter to keep us warm. However, there was a little disagreement amongst our ragtag group. Instead of sticking to this one place, some felt we would be better off finding out where we were and establishing contact with the local authorities.

The rift split the group down the middle. Six people set off to find help. I counted six, including myself, who thought it wiser to stay put and try to survive while we waited for rescue. Of those who chose to remain, my copilot, two other men, and two women made up our corps. I asked for volunteers to search the nearby area for food and water and for others to construct the shelter and collect firewood. The two women and the copilot elected to search for nourishment. The remaining three of us set about the task of establishing residence in this place.

We chose a spot of land near to the tree on the side opposite the water of the lake. The trunk of the tree, three metres in diameter, provided a great deal of shelter. This was a much-appreciated cover against the waters of the lake, which were whipped into a frenzy by the heavy winds. Water sprayed and slammed into the tree like little water balloons. While the winds blew, we would stay well away from the lake and the monster we had witnessed therein.

The lake itself was about sixty metres in diameter. Judging from the still exposed vertical stabilizer of the plane, it could not be much deeper than six metres. Many logs littered the forest floor, but few were small enough to haul back to the campsite. At least an abundance of pine needles, if they could be considered such, for they measured nearly a decimetre long, covered the ground. Hence, there was not much need to go far to collect firewood as the needles themselves would prove excellent fuel.

More pressing was shelter. It seemed that, surrounded by trees of prodigious girth and height, ordinary-sized twigs never fell. Only the smallest of twigs, the length of my arm, from these monumental topiaries could be moved back to the campsite by one man. The three of us had to work together to carry larger sticks. Pine cones were also abundant, but at a metre in length, and as heavy as large stones, they were entirely unhelpful. I should also note that the smell coming off the pine cones was so strong that a number of times I was forced to recoil from the overwhelming fresh pine scent.

After several hours of laborious heavy lifting and work, we had collected a mound of large twigs and cleared a space about three metres in diameter a few metres from the tree. One of the men tried to make use of his glasses to start a fire as he'd seen done on TV back home. The other man and I worked at the shelter. Against the tree we settled the larger logs we could manoeuvre, building a long hollow, and used the pine needles to cover the walls.

The second team came back with a most humorous collection of berries and nuts. They reported that only a small distance away, perhaps fifteen minutes, they had discovered an enormous orange vegetable that tasted of carrot, just barely exposed in the soil. The group had collected a leaf at least as large as a 1,200 × 2,400 mm chunk of plywood and were hauling raspberries as large as bowls, a strawberry as big as my head, and some cracked peanuts nearly the size of the raspberries. Between the three of them, they were dragging the leaf like a tarpaulin across the ground, working in coordination to move the various foods over obstacles as an indigenous would use a travoise.

Each of the berries was more than enough food for us to go an entire day as a group and held plenty of water. We failed to strike up a fire, but the shelter alone proved a match for the elements for the night. In the morning, we left two men working to start the fire while four of us went back to where the fruit and vegetables had been found.

It was as told, a short walk to the garden. Not more than twenty minutes on, we arrived at the mammoth carrot. The dirt of the garden was dark brown and black and smelled of freshly turned earth. The one carrot top stuck out a dozen centimetres from the ground. As though a sandworm of Arrakis had been here, a chunk had been bitten out of it. We discovered as we investigated further that at equal distances of one metre, more distinctive sprouts, as tall as us, could be seen. I began to imagine, as fanciful as it was at the time, that we were in some giant's garden. Before this, I had hoped the enormous hand and foot had been figments of my imagination. I now suspected they were not. My next thought was, considering what the giant had done to the aeroplane that had done little to merit such treatment, what might he do to an interloper in his garden, eating his produce like a rabbit.

I suggested we had better move quickly and perhaps only carry as much as we could individually before running back to our burrow. Our raspberries looked as red pineapples and nearly as large; the pistils thereupon caused great injury to me as they carved my arm like little knives. We each hustled with armfuls of berries and nuts like bank robbers making off with the loot.

On our way back home, we came across a troop of cat-sized black ants gathering leaves and shipping them back in an orderly queue. We dared not get too close to the oversized insects for fear of their sharp mandibles. Under the cover of the forest, I felt safe enough from the threat of the giant gardeners that we waited patiently for a break in their line. After a few minutes, it became clear these leaf-cutter ants were not soon to offer such a reprieve. We were forced to decide between an indefinitely long detour or some other interceding action.

I harkened back to my days as a child playing with insects on vacation and thought about what was drawing the ants on this path. Even a small interruption might be enough to distract them from their course, so I and two other survivors hoisted the largest twig we could manage, carefully stood it on end as a long log, and mindful not to crush one of the ants, which we feared could result in our swarming, dropped it directly on the path.

Surely enough, the line broke as the ants behind the twig struggled to make sense of the missing pheromone trail. I goaded the others into taking advantage of the brief reprieve. Picking up a few of the razor-sharp berries, I stifled a yelp. The others joined me as we Red-Rovered our way through the gap in the line. I cast a glance over my shoulder as we made good our escape to see that the ants had, no sooner than we had crossed their line, climbed around and over the impediment in their path and were sorting out a stack of climbed-upon comrades.

We made it back to the camp with an ample supply of food and set about focusing on creating a fire with the supplies at hand. We hoped this time to secure a warm camp and shelter for the night—and equally—a shield against other indigenous life. The only weapons at our disposal, however, were sticks and twigs, pebbles, and the hijacker's sword that I had kept with me this whole time.

CHAPTER 5.4

Fire brings greater dangers, and the author encounters more wildlife and native life.

WE FAILED ONCE again to create a fire that night. Despite the chill and hardship, all souls reported again in the morning. We were hidden in the forest, and I knew our chances of rescue diminished by the day. Apart from the small lake nearby, wherein our conveyance still must sit partially emerged, a magnet for rescuers should they stumble upon this place, I could think of no safe place to establish our SOS. Any rescue, we decided, would be most drawn to smoke and fire, so that continued—our stockpiles plentiful with nuts and berries—to be our primary focus.

The six of us worked hard to generate fire. Creating that one precious spark eluded us for so long. Finally, on our third day, we were able to create a small puff of smoke. This triumph impelled us to redouble our efforts. A short while later, perhaps several minutes for the time seemed again to pass both quickly and slowly at once, sparks started to fly. As we fanned it with leaves, the fire caught and grew amongst the needles. Once lit, the fire spread quickly. If not for the clearing around the needles, it likely would have spread uncontrolled. We fenced in the fire with some rocks and with the utmost of care, rested a green leaf near the fire to create the smoke we knew we needed to draw attention to our plight.

It was overexuberance on our behalf that turned our small signal and campfire into a raging bonfire later that day. We kept the ground timber a distance away and kept throwing the largest sticks we could muster onto the inferno. We watched the tongues of flame lick the sky, our bodies warmed by the heat, and our spirits rose like the embers to the heavens. What had begun as a simple, important, necessity of survival became an ostentatious display of contempt for the power of nature. It was a foolhardy show of vanity.

The crackling of the blaze and our own expressive conversation obscured the approaching danger. I had sought refuge from the smoke and found myself opposite the others when I felt a buffeting of the wind at my back. Alarmed, I spun around to see a pair of giant pygmy moths with wingspans exceeding a metre. Attracted by the fire, or perhaps thereby confused, the moths had begun to circle.

I yelled out a warning and my companions jumped up. Vigorously, we tried to swat them from our camp. It was as though we were trying to repel a pair of determined hawks. It was a reflex to try to expel the interlopers. Great in size, the flying insects' proboscis invoked little direct threat until the wind from an unfortunately timed synchronized flap of their wings caused the fire to tip over. Still, we remained focused on the threat from the skies as the fire spread to the surrounding underbrush. Only too late did we realize our mistake. We pivoted towards the real danger. It was eminently clear we were fighting a battle already long since lost. The fire grew hot and I was forced to retreat. On the opposite side, the other five likewise were repulsed backwards.

Without any supplies to suppress the scorching conflagration, ever further from the camp was I pressed. Sparks and embers flew and created new pyres. A sea of flames split me ever further from the others. It took a little longer, but eventually the trees began to catch fire. The flames curled ever higher into the sky. The only clearing, apart from the lake—of which was on the opposite side of the blaze from me—was on the other side of the garden. Thus, it was to this direction I flew.

The inferno grew at an ever-increasing rate. My flight evolved from cautious retreat to full-fledged panic. I stumbled over needles and twigs but kept moving as fast as I could. At first, I felt I was putting distance between the fire and me. Soon, though, it seemed clear the fire was outpacing me comfortably. In the late twilight, I burst into the garden, a firebreak against the danger, and then into a dark, chest-high field of grass. I continued through the grass that struck my body like slalom poles. Propelled by adrenaline and a ceaseless instinct for self-preservation, I ignored the punishing bruises growing on my arms, chest, and legs. Scarcely daring to peer over my shoulder, I sought only to distance myself from the unfeeling, all-consuming fire.

Amidst the grass, I stumbled upon a brick plateau about half a metre off the ground. I ran to the centre of the brick pathway and looked back towards the forest behind. I had run at least a hundred metres through the grass. In the distance, the fire had not quite emerged from the copse. In the red glow, I looked upon the trees of prodigious height. Not too far distant, facing out towards the field, was a ten-story wall of mud and wattle, if wattle can be said to be formed of woven logs. Twenty metres further along the brick path, now illuminated by the spreading fire, was a rectangular door eighty feet tall.

If I could have forgotten about the immediate danger, I would have marvelled at the size of this wall; it was as if a small skyscraper had been made of such simple material. I wandered aimlessly towards it, but from a distance, a thunderous but melodic boom filled the air. The ground shook from the power of the ear-splitting tumult, which repeated itself at regular intervals until the castle-sized door swung suddenly wide, drawing a rush of wind that pulled me right off my feet and into the formidable structure. Over my head loomed a foot twice as long as my entire body was tall. The ground shook under its weight. The owner bounded into the yard from which I had come. I could see he was shaped as a man but was at least ten times my size in all dimensions. In the yard, he was joined by dozens more of his kin, and they set upon fighting the blaze as a bucket brigade.

My mind struggled to maintain the scale of the scene. At a distance of a hundred metres, they seemed as close to me as if they were but ten away. Their booming voices were so low as to be unintelligible to me. From the threshold of the door, but carefully tucked to the side, lest another giant should from the house emerge, I observed their heroic battle.

The bedlam in the yard once again distracted me from a more real threat. Over my head descended a woven cage. I was whooshed off my feet and clattered heavily against the wooden walls of my cage. I let out a yell as my leg crunched against the floor that had moments ago been the ceiling. My entire cage was lifted off the ground by another titan, placed on a shelf, a lid put over the top, and abandoned.

As the behemoths worked in the yard, daylight was failing and my surroundings turning to pitch black, so I paced my cage, testing every hole, wall, pit, or cranny. Eventually deprived of light, I found I could not escape. Despairingly, I lay down in a corner to rest and await my fate in the morning light.

CHAPTER 5.5

The morning brings new wonders but also new trials and tribulations for the author in the home of a giant.

IT WOULD NOT be accurate to report a good sleep was had that night. Apart from the fact I was being concealed inside a wicker basket of enormous size, the noise from the firefighting and the town bell—as I would later discover to be the repeated melodic thrashing—persisted for a long while. Late into the night, the combatants returned to the house. Heavy of foot and stumbling around in the dark, they raised quite the clatter themselves. In low tones, one deep voice bellowed through the small house as through a subwoofer. A second, slightly higher, voice responded. To describe the voice as anything higher than the deepest bass would be to do it a disservice. I had little doubt a conversation was being had but could no more make heads or tails of it than I could the discussion of a pod of whales.

In the morning, the bells recommenced their assault on my ears as they greeted the morning. Inside my basket cage, a small amount of light filtered in. Through the gaps, I saw a common space and kitchen, all to the same scale of everything else I had seen. Any estimates I could make relied on assumptions not well comparable to the world from which I had come. I compared the length of the master of the house's stride to my own and found it to be twelve times greater. Many readers have tried to suggest other ways I could have better formulated this estimate. I did not know his height or comparably how tall he was to his people; therefore, I could not establish a valid metric, nor was I to have a wealth of measuring devices with which to create such during my stay here.

I suppose I digress too much from my travel. Whilst I believe it understandable that I focus on the most visible distinction between my hosts and myself, I shall instead focus more on what occurred.

In the morning, as the family of the house came to the table, their low, sonorous voices filled the air. I strained against the walls of the basket to see my captors. They appeared to me to be oblivious to my presence, not altogether surprising considering my insignificant size and concealment in the basket. I could make out four titanic individuals in the room. I saw bits and pieces of them, particularly when they were furthest from the table, and concluded to my own understanding they were probably a family: a mother and father, a girl and a boy child. Based on their relative size, I deduced the boy was the youngest.

I could easily see the boy was the most excitable of the four. He bounced around the room full of the vim and vigour typical of youth and boomed in a voice as loud, but higher in pitch, than those of the night before. I recognized in his shoes the lake-stomping monster, and I shuddered to think of the damage he had recklessly caused. None of the giants seemed to be at all aware of my presence. I watched them go about their activities that morning before they all left to go about, I presume, their days.

Perhaps the reader might be interested to hear more about the daily routine of a family of giants. From my observations, there is little to report of any substance or interest. Breakfast was produced out of locally grown foods, both animal and vegetable, and served on the table, upon which my cage had been placed. The family ate together. I could perceive two doors, one of which was used almost exclusively by the parents, and one by the children. I didn't suppose this rustic abode possessed running water or electricity, nor any form of heating apart from the fireplace. The food was prepared fresh on the counter after having been harvested from the yard directly.

I would hazard to say that reduced by an order of magnitude in size, this home would not have looked out of place four hundred years ago in Europe or the North American colonies.

The smell of the food taunted me inside the cage, but none of the titans made any effort to provide me with a needed repast. The food not consumed seemed to me to be a monumental amount yet was left on the table to waste. I strained my arms, but I could not reach the food, not even a morsel of a crumb. Resigned once again, I settled back down and decided that when the family returned, I would try to gain their attention.

Several hours later, the boy returned, along with another of equal size and energy. This time, I saw a different look in his eye and felt I could be certain of who had hidden me in the basket. He looked into the parent's room and the children's room while his friend stood at the door looking out into the yard, stealing glances back. The boy came and picked up the basket suddenly, forcing me to my knees. Then he tipped me out onto the table. The pain of the action was immense as I tumbled out and slammed into the table. While I attempted to recover, the boys pushed me around the table with their hands, sliding me about the surface. They laughed and spoke to each other, and me, but I couldn't make out a word. So deep was the bass of their voices that I can best describe the sound as a tuba.

As is common of boys, they thought up a million things to do with their strange new pet. They measured me against whatever they could find and pushed food my way. I was at least able to steal a nibble of a chunk of bread they left within my grasp. This drew an awful laughter from the pair. I covered my ears and cowered from the sound. It seemed the boy of the house understood. He grew quiet and addressed me as calmly and quietly as he could. In that way, I was better able to separate the sounds into probable words, though I could still little understand their meaning. I tried to yell as loud as I could. It was clear the boy could hear what I was saying, but he could not make sense of my ramblings. His friend, on the other hand, grew bored of this activity. He knocked me over onto my back with a flick of his freckled wrist and drew out a knife almost a metre in length with a dull edge not less than a centimetre in width. He pressed a finger against my chest, crushing me to the table and knocking every last ounce of wind out of my lungs as could ever there have been stored. I felt a couple ribs break under the pressure and was unable to let a single protest fly. He lowered the knife towards my leg, no doubt intending to dismember me as a cruel child might a trapped spider or mouse.

Suddenly, the knife and the finger were removed from me. A crash like a car accident echoed around me. Winded and broken, I watched the two boys fighting and yelling, once again causing my eardrums to thunder. They smashed into the wooden furniture and the table. While they fought on the other side of the room, I felt the vibrations through the table. I suppose I could say the boy of the house was my champion. I could only hope he would vanquish his enemy quickly and thereafter acquire me some urgently needed attention.

The battle had gone on for several minutes when the mother barreled through the door herself, picked up both boys by their ears, and ended the fight. The universality of childhood fights was evident. I supposed she must have told them to be quiet and to explain themselves. This hypothesis was supported when her son pointed directly at my prone body on the table. As though she was looking at a dead rat in her food, she let out a scream I felt almost certain would rupture my eardrum. She composed herself and slowly came to the table herself and poked at my tiny feet with her gigantic hands. She jostled me a little, and I struggled as best I could if only to prove I was still alive.

Sending the other boy away, she took care of me in partnership with her boy. They rolled out a blanket on the table, a napkin I would soon realize, and peeled me off the table with a knife's flat edge, gently dropping me onto the pillowy tissue. I was unable to talk beyond a strained whisper, such was the nature of my injury, but fortunately, the boy seemed to remember and urged the mother to speak in hushed tones. They provided me with a thimble, about the size of a cup, full of water I drank and several crumbs of bread and berries from their breakfast, which I did my best, staving off the pain, to eat.

A most compassionate family I was fortunate to have found. When the daughter came home, she immediately took to caring for me and building things out of discarded supplies. The father returned last, and as I will mention for the last time, I could not understand a word of his ultra-low voice. Clearly, he was being brought up to speed on what or who had been discovered. I was the centre of conversation at the table that night, and my protector, the young boy, made sure nobody spoke much above a whisper. I endeavoured to place myself in their position. If a tiny human, not more than fifteen centimetres tall, had suddenly been found in my kitchen, how would I handle it? To their credit, and with my respect, I found they provided a diligent service to me.

I can also say keeping a one-twelfth-sized man would normally not be a great burden. Only a tiny amount of food, space, and water are required for his care. The evidence further supported my supposition that the family considered me to be their de facto pet, to which I have already alluded. That night, they placed the wicker basket over my bed, and unable to file a grievance, I allowed myself to drift into a painful, motionless sleep.

CHAPTER 5.6

As the author's bones mend, he makes strides to better understand his new masters and their home. The author also makes a friend and develops his own following.

I CAN SAY little negative about the family of giants who played host to me and kept me safe where possible. Daily, they made improvements to my little terrarium. These improvements included a better bed made of a finer thread, a cleaner thimble for my drink, and some fanciful additions like a doll larger than I to keep me company.

I never could comprehend the booming voices of the adults. Their sounds were too low, and my tiny ears were unable to break apart the syllables and words. In contrast, I was able to perceive the enunciation of the children. Of equal importance to me, it became clear that, unlike their parents who lacked the ability to hear my high pitch, the young, especially the boy, could hear me.

The boy spent most of his spare time with me. From him, I was able to learn a few words. For my voice to be caught, he would have to place his head extremely close to my mouth. I would stick my head almost fully into his ear and speak to him like an amplified bass-boosted ear bud. For his part, we established the greater his distance in the room, the better I was able to understand him with a degree of comfort.

I learned numbers and letters first. They possessed ten fingers and toes, as do we, but their numerical system was a base twelve, dozenal or duodecimal system. Understanding this system caused me a great headache, but I believe it now to be the single superior device of their people. The alphabet was more limited with only twenty letters. Three of those represented not sounds, nor characters or hieroglyphics, but logograms like the ampersand. The three words so defined included a letter for yes, or agreement, called "zite," another for no, or disagreement, "bote," and the third used in place of articles, "tel." Their restricted alphabet limited linguistic flexibility and forced words to be much longer to avoid homophones and homonyms. Furthermore, of the twenty letters, ten of them were the equivalent of our vowels. Where one here might pronounce the letter "e" in numerous ways, such as "shed," "pretty," "be," "anthem," "sergeant," or "café," the giant's language was simpler and more like Latin, where there is only one way to pronounce a given letter.

I shan't burden the reader with the entire alphabet, or a list of the words that were communicated, but for the name of the island and the people who thus hailed from it. Both shared the same noun, which is most difficult to pronounce effectively. At my best effort, it can be translated into English as "Brobadingog." Politics being generally beyond the understanding of a child of ten, as well as the history or geography of the place, I was only able to learn a small amount in my time in his care.

I was well cared for, and word of the curiosity in the farmer's house spread. I couldn't tell if it was spread by the family or perhaps the red-haired friend who had nearly bisected me. Only a few days after I was rescued, people started coming by to visit and gawk at the unique tiny man. The family set clear boundaries, and the boy jealously guarded me against harm. He was eager to show off all the magical things I could do, like talk, walk, and any number of simple tricks. The boy showed me off as a most treasured toy or pet. The rest of the family began to treat me more as a circus performer or a conversation piece for their friends and neighbours.

On a few occasions, I suffered mistreatment at the hands of a guest or when a family member forgot to lower their voice. These were few and far between. Having seen the damage the red-haired boy did just by pressing down on my chest, I was handled sparingly and with the utmost of care at all times. Food was plentiful and generously offered as the amount of food needed to keep me fit and healthy was barely more than crumbs by the standard Brobadingog fare. I should say that in my short time there, I grew quite fond of my host family.

I became aware from the boy, whose name, Blaedil, is difficult to pronounce indeed, that word of my existence and incredible abilities was spreading far amongst the people. There was barely time enough in the day to satisfy the requests to see, watch, observe, or gawk at me. I could not confirm it, but the family seemed to grow in possessions by my presence. I suspected a toll was being charged for adults to view the tiny treasure.

CHAPTER 5.7

The author recounts two narrow escapes during his stay with the Brobadingog family and the resulting change of scenery.

ONE AFTERNOON, ABOUT a week after my arrival in this house, as I rested before the family returned from their daily activities, I woke to a startling sound. Most days, the family allowed me to sleep without a cover. I benefited from the freedom this afforded, even stranded too high above the floor to chance a jump.

On this day, I woke when I heard a roar as if from a lion, and I jumped to my feet. This caused no little pain in my still fractured ribs. Startled, the sleep dashed from my eyes in a hurry, I instinctively drew the hijacker's thin sword I carried awkwardly on my hip. Snarling in front of me, hissing and growling like a big dog, was a rat the size of a small bear.

Given I hailed originally from Alberta, I'd never before seen a rat of any scale. Clearly, this was a rodent of unusual size. On all fours it came up almost to my neck. It stood only a few feet from me, sniffing and snorting at what I assume it intended to be its next meal. I could be certain there was not even a minute chance I could escape. Flight would be more dangerous than fighting, if I could even manage to outrun the beast long enough to reach the counter's edge.

I couldn't guess what posturing would bring the best result to my situation, but I didn't think much of the thought of playing dead while the scavenger took great big nibbles out of me. Instead, I chose to make myself as large as I could and bellowed loudly and firmly. Arms stretched high and wide, I waved and gestured like a crazed fan, hoping to discourage the rat's approach.

The overgrown rat made a mockery of my posture, standing on its hind legs, towering well above me, his sharp teeth and claws bearing down. I stabbed out against his belly. He let loose another roar as one paw slashed me across the face. Three deep gashes began to ooze blood. I can't recall whether I screamed or made any indication at all, but I pulled the sword defensively and cut a deep line in its paw.

The rat reared up once again. This time I ran directly into the core of the rodent and aimed for what I hoped would be its heart. I undershot by almost a full three decimetres and struck something soft I believed was its liver. The rat tried to claw at my back. I held tight to its stomach and jabbed repeatedly, getting soaked in a foul-smelling red ichor. It tried to bite down on my head. Each time I felt his chest pull away to enable the agile action necessary, I stabbed up into its chin.

I landed a dozen stabs before I finally achieved a killing shot. This time, as the rat pulled back to bite my head, I saw a moment of exposure at its neck and used a two-handed axe swing. I sliced through both the left and right jugular veins and the trachea, straight through. The rat crashed down upon me, his crushing weight completely covering me. The table stained red with a mixture of our bloods. Under his bulk and hobbled by old and new injuries, I was pinned to the table. I strained to breathe. The epinephrine slowly receded from my body, and the pain of the deep cuts all over my body began to sink in.

I could not extricate myself. I was sure that when the boy returned, it would be quite the horrifying sight to see his pet's bed and home covered in blood and a dead rat smothering him. And so it was. When he came in the door, he screamed in terror. He ran over, pulled the rat off me, and threw it across the room while sobbing uncontrollably. He thought me dead. I could not foretell his actions should that belief take deeper root, so I raised the sword into the air and dropped it on the table. It made just enough noise, like a pin dropping. The boy stopped and reevaluated the situation. I moved my arms a little to the side, lying flat on my stomach, signalling my continued survival. It was the last action for me on that day. The effort drained the last of my stamina and I faded right out.

I would wake sometime later, that day or another. I had been laid upon a fresh bed and covered with a blanket with only small amounts of blood thereupon. A glass sphere like a fishbowl, with big air holes cut out, now encased me. The mistake of leaving me exposed would not be repeated again.

The second incident occurred after about a month in the care of the giant family of Brobadingog. News of the tiny man had indeed spread widely. The boy said that a few of their tribe wished that I be spared the humiliation of captivity and released back into the wild. I told the boy I did not desire that, having a respectable fear of the enormous wildlife of this land. Being not a native species to this place, I had no home to which I could reasonably return, and though I would have preferred my freedom in my own land, I had witnessed and experienced the perils here. I hoped the others of my group had survived, but I had neither the mechanism with which to seek them out if they had nor the wherewithal to try. The boy was pleased I would choose him. Others would not believe he could hear me speak. The actions of such a small man as I mattered almost not at all in spite of their purported support for my person.

Early one evening, while my masters were out for the night, a titan I had once before seen, a neighbour, came to the door and opened it. Immediately, I could smell the thick smell of alcohol in the air. In his hand, he held the largest mug of drink I'd ever seen. He was determined to show me a little hospitality. He came straight to my enclosure, opened the lid roughly, and pushed the mug into my face as though I was to hold it myself. Instead, I pulled away in fear of the gesture of goodwill, and he changed his tack. He became more aggressive. He took the mug and poured the contents over me, still trying to have me drink. The ale struck me like a firehose directly on my head, having been dropped from twenty feet above. It was such a large quantity of liquid that I was utterly and completely soaked and waterlogged. A small swimming pool of water had fallen upon me, crushing me on my handkerchief bed.

I was flattened and sputtering, fully pained. The inebriated giant must have felt a moment of regret for he took a filthy cloth out of his pocket and clumsily reached down to dry me off. Vigorously, he tried to rub me dry. His action did more to beat me than to dry me off. Battered and broken, I surrendered. He threw the wet, filthy, alcohol-soaked cloth down on top of me and angrily stomped out of the room. Even dazed and confused, I still remember the crushing earthquake of his heavy-footed steps leaving.

I believe it was this last incident that spurred the family into action to protect me. I couldn't understand the reason for the boy's tears until a day later when a courier dressed in royal finery came to the house. I was carefully scooped into a well-cushioned box that he carried to a carriage. I was trundled down the road, on the way to a new master and a new home.

CHAPTER 5.8

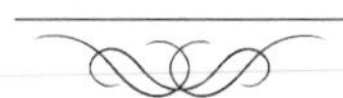

The author is resettled into a new home, and a young woman takes custody of her new prized pet.

IT BECAME CLEAR to me I had been sold, gifted, or seized by a person of greater means. The crate in which I was being transported could best be described as a gilded cage. The walls were ornately crafted with astounding attention to detail. I could perceive the rough edges of the furniture, but by the hands that crafted it, surely no imperfection could be seen. The entire floor was composed of a rich red velvet. Even my comparably tiny hands could not find fault in its make. My travelling compartment stood tall at three times my height and was circular in shape like a bird's cage.

Smooth and padded, the walls were composed of golden rods, finely detailed with flair and stylings. The lower part of the cage, rising precisely to my height of one hundred and ninety-five centimetres, was buffered with similarly smooth velvet cushioning. The carriage itself must have been designed and manufactured with the utmost of care, for as I heard it bounce and jostle, only the slightest vibration shook my cage. With the secured padding in place, I felt little disturbed.

My travelling quarters sat within the confines of the cab of the carriage. I was positioned below the level of the windows, which with the drapes being drawn closed would have provided me little view of the countryside anyway. We carried on down the road at a rapid pace. This, I hope, is understandable considering the formidable size of the horses pulling it. For what I estimated to have been an hour, I was pulled along this route. In honesty, so immense was my enjoyment of the luxury that I was able to cast aside my fears regarding my final destination.

The carriage did not stop even a single time on the journey. This fact I would reconcile when I discovered the nature of my new master, or rather, mistress. The only stop came when I reached my ultimate destination. The courier calmly, with a ceremonious flourish, pulled me and my new quarters out and carried us into an open courtyard as large as a soccer field.

It can be easy to be overwhelmed by stupendous scale, and this instance did not disappoint. The cyclopean masonry of the place was only comparable to the great pyramids of Egypt. Even so, I hazarded a guess that the height of these walls still might well have exceeded those. Swiftly but smoothly, I was carried into one of the stone-walled buildings. The stones were perfectly smooth and a brilliant white. The air smelled of lavender when the giant pushed open the door to the tower. It opened without the slightest creak, scratch, or hesitation. My courier climbed a spiral staircase up the equivalent of two giant's stories. We waited in a small—by which I should elaborate that I mean for someone the size of these people—antechamber with chairs and a table. Two more Brobadingogs stood at the door with pikes, guarding the contents of the room.

Viewing the people of this country can be difficult due to their great size and the usually significantly large angle with which it is required to discern their faces from the clouds. So it was with the guards. All features being proportionate, I found the people of this land to be quite ugly. The imperfections of their skin and teeth, which weren't well cared for in the first place, were painfully obvious to me. Even the slightest pores on the fairest of their faces looked like serious pox scars. Only from a distance could I draw a decent description of their overall features. Often, I would find myself having to extrapolate based on a meagre sample size.

One of the guards pulled a chain, the mechanism with which to call the occupant of the room. After a few moments, a girl dressed in the finest clothing I had yet encountered in this place came to the door. She squealed in delight with a sound that blasted my ears like a fog horn pressed close to me and grabbed the cage from my transporter. Without a word of appreciation, or really any acknowledgement whatsoever, she turned, ran into her room, and slammed the door behind her, a sonorous thunderclap directly behind me. As soon as the door closed, in an elevated voice, she screamed many things. No one could mistake these sounds, even at their low tone, for anything other than the eager squeals of an over-excited young lady.

She opened the cage, reached in, pulled my body from the container, then switched me to her other hand and jammed me into a palatial, if open on one side, castle on her table. Ignoring the golden cage, no more important than plastic wrapping, she granted me a tour of my new home. She pushed and prodded me through doorways and passages, all the while hollering in temporary ecstasy, exploiting her new plaything. If not for the constantly forced movement, which rapidly mutated my colouring to the purple and blue hue of bruises, this might have proven a most comfortable habitat in Brobadingog. Some of their finest craftsmen had been employed by the girl—who would awkwardly refer to herself in the third person as Princess Pitum—simply to ensure the comfort and happiness of me, her new favourite toy.

Unlike my previous masters, Princess Pitum was not interested in speaking with me or in hearing me speak. I was inclined to believe she was, in actual fact, royalty, based upon the relative wealth of she and the boy of the farm. I guessed them to be probably of similar age and size. I was, to her, a thing to amuse, entertain, and show off and about which to brag. I was one that required little of her personal care and attention. All the chores of feeding, clothing, sheltering, and all other necessities were supplied, in abundance I must admit, by the team of servants who had the displeasurable job of waiting on the princess.

Miss Pitum would carry me about the country in the same carriage that had first brought me to the palace. I was exposed to many other children of wealth and privilege. I noted the princess herself never was exposed to anyone even similar in dress or stature to the family I had first encountered. It was easy to see the pampered princess lived a most sheltered life. Without communication, I couldn't guess whether she believed herself to be better and deserving of such things, or if she thought others in her kingdom lived the same as she. I would never know the answer to this question. She barely spoke to her servants, who were only allowed in her presence the minimum time necessary to serve me. She being so high above me, in rank as well as stature, I knew there to be no chance she would deign to speak to me, except as her doll.

I had been presented to the king on an early occasion, but he didn't seem to care for the playthings of his daughter. I spent the better part of three months living in the private quarters of the princess and only on four occasions did the king, recognizable only for the crown upon his head, come to visit his daughter. It is tempting to judge, but I could speak not of the culture and expectations in this palace that would lead to such deadbeat parenting. His attitude was cold and aloof in her presence, even when he was alone with her. Never did I meet the mother of the princess. Be she queen or consort, alive or deceased, I could never discern.

The country of Brobadingog was necessarily a large kingdom to support these titans of humanity, and I was carted to awe-inspiring volcanoes in the north and wild rivers and lakes of a size of which the world must know no equal. I counted many biomes in the kingdom: badlands and deserts with cacti of prodiguous size, armed with needles as long as my arm; rainforests with trees and vines as large as skyscrapers; and savannahs, hills, and mountains of majestic rock. The kingdom itself was a true microcosm of the rest of the planet, inhabited by macrospecies in a lushly fertile landscape rich in all manner of resources.

If the giants could be compared in technology to our world, I would say they possessed a medieval style and culture. The wealth of the land and its resources and the isolation seemed to have led to a protected and uninspiringly noninnovative technological culture. I didn't often feel at risk in this place, apart from the hazards relating to being so insignificant. There never seemed to be any risk of crime or war. Nor did I perceive of any enemies of Brobadingog.

It was also clear the men ruled firmly, and the wealth was hyperconcentrated in the hands of the royal family. There was little in the way of regard for women in most instances. In this light, the country seemed dark and dreary. The contributions of women were wholly ignored, at least as far as palace life was concerned. Entirely one-half of the available workforce seemed to be allowed no place at all in the workings of the kingdom. The only women I ever saw in the palace were the lowest of servants, handmaidens of the princess, and of course, the princess herself.

As I had witnessed on previous islands, also isolated from the world, there seemed little interest in learning from a stranger in their lands. To emphasize the point, only that one young boy was ever willing to speak with me. It was a lonely time literally living in the lap of luxury, and I longed for my freedom more with each passing day. In other places to which I have travelled, there was at least some interest in what I knew or had to say. Apart from one small boy, I did not feel at all valued except as a curiosity of scale. I felt some regret I could provide no meaningful value to Brobadingog, and above all, I felt a sincere lack of direction or purpose. It is not, in spite of luxurious provision, my nature to enjoy such a rudderless existence.

CHAPTER 5.9

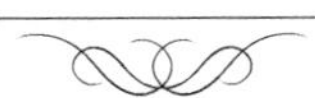

The author's short stay on Brobadingog comes to an abrupt end due to an act of carelessness, and the author is lost again to the sea.

EACH DAY PRINCESS Pitum would cart me around to whatever activities were happening: some display of horse craft, a fancy dinner, a play or concert, or—the rarest—an activity in which she actually participated. These unusual activities generally consisted of formal dinners where she would be left to her own devices while the adults entertained each other. I would be seated in a prime location immediately next to her like some prized parrot. This position afforded me many opportunities to observe the culture of the place but virtually no interaction.

At each activity, in spite of the immense size of the actors and athletes, I found it either difficult to scope the entire scene for want of distance, or equally difficult for too great an expanse. The sounds of audiences cheering, booing, applauding, or even just chatting, were despairingly deafening. When I didn't have my head buried in a pillow or my ears smothered by my shoulders, arms, or hands, the action on offer was generally slow and uninteresting. As the energy picked up around me, even amongst the not-so-fanatic, well-to-do part of the crowd in which the Crown resided, I learned quickly to duck and cover.

On one rare occasion, my mistress, the princess, took me to a beach. She had commissioned me a majestic boat, gilded with gold and jewels. It was not particularly functional as it lacked an engine or propulsion even from a sail, but it looked seaworthy and worthy of a Brobadingog fortune. Gemstones of diamond, emerald, ruby, and sapphire lined the tear-drop shaped vessel. The ballast was composed of bricks of gold and silver. It was a typically unnecessarily ostentatious craft designed to accompany the princess onto the beach and into the tide while minimizing the risk of any drop of water falling on me, her precious miniature person.

Princess Pitum took me, her living Faberge egg, out into the gentle tide and pushed and pulled me around for nearly an hour while her own attendants waited on the shore. It was the first time since I arrived in Brobadingog that I felt comfortable with the scale of anything. The waves lapped calmly and gently like one might expect of any normal beach. The tide was relaxed. Even the little princess had no trouble navigating her way around the shallows.

Something must have caught the girl's eye. Suddenly, she whipped around and started heading away from the tidal pool in which we were playing and out past the breakwater. The instant we passed that barrier the waves that crashed past the inlet grew fierce. Rollers several times larger than earlier struck against the walls of my float, and the princess started to struggle. Judging by the position of her body, a strong undertow had a grip on her legs and was tearing her out into the ocean.

The princess held onto me for a time, clutching my boat as a lifesaver and keeping me well beneath the waves. Fortuitously, this act of self-preservation buffered me from the violence of the surface. Suddenly, she let go and I burst through the surface. Sealed in the glass orb, I was thrown about viciously on deck. I pulled the sword off my hip, which had itself recently been festooned with some golden accentuation, and carved off a chunk of the velvet pillow that adorned all my conveyances on Brobadingog. I bundled myself tightly and tied myself to the middle of the boat. I held on tightly with both arms and legs, clawing desperately as the waves thrashed me to and fro.

I had at my disposal no controls to manoeuvre with and no power to effect any change. I neither dared nor cared to spare a glance away from the vessel while it bounced and danced in the waves. After a seemingly endless assault, I cleared the shallows of the beach, and the wave action dropped perceptibly. I floated on the water encased in a glass fishbowl somewhere in the North Pacific Ocean.

I knew my fishbowl only had a limited supply of air, no food, no water, and no controls. I felt no more secure than I did when I came upon the island of the Yahoos and Huhuneem in my seat-cushion raft.

My first priority was to establish an air supply. The locking mechanism was well secured from the outside. Even if I was on the outside, there was almost no chance any normal human could generate sufficient torque to tear it apart. I focused on breaking a hole in the gem-encrusted glass. I took the hilt of my sword, pommeled with a fist-sized diamond, and started hammering on a chunk of azurite embedded in the glass an arm's length above my head. This put it about ten feet above the surface of the water. The fragile gem slowly chipped and disintegrated under my sustained beating. Eventually, I managed to create a small hole in the glass. As the seal was broken, a sudden gush of air burst out of the hole as the warmer air inside depressurized into the surrounding atmosphere.

I repeated the action on several sides of my container to reduce the heat that was inevitably building in my floating greenhouse. I'm pleased to report it helped some, but only marginally was it truly effective. I considered punching more holes, but as night descended, I instead calmed myself, settled amongst the pillows, cut some of the velvet off one to act as sheets and blankets for a bed, and tried to ignore the thirst and hunger a day of hard work in the burning sun had instilled in me.

I carved out a few more pillows and made a tent out of the velvet cloth. I wiped myself off as best I could as I laid where I'd chosen to rest. I fell into a deep, dream-filled slumber as the gentle tide soothingly rocked me to sleep. It may seem counterintuitive, but I felt at peace in this place, having long ago resigned myself to my fate on Brobadingog where I truly felt no chance of rescue, escape, or return to my home and family. An end at sea seemed a reasonable conclusion to my misadventures and peregrinations, so I slept.

I didn't wake up in the morning, or at least I didn't rise. I just lay in my tent and gave myself back to sleep, hitting the snooze button until it was broken. There existed no means to signal a ship, no way to help myself, and no supplies. Night always feels the darkest just before the dawn.

CHAPTER 5.10

The author washes ashore on a new island, and he makes a remarkable discovery about the unique nature of this new island.

SOMETIME LATER, I was awakened not by the gentle currents, but by a bumping sound that came from outside my egg. The scraping and grinding, mixed with gentle bumps, startled me out of my melancholy, and I looked out to see that by some great fortune, I had landed on a rocky beach. I exhorted my tired muscles to perform one more action, and taking my sword in hand once again, bashed and battered against a large gem I thought might create a large enough opening, in absentia, for me to squeeze through. Limply at first, I began to pound on the pearl. Sensing it was not as secure as I had originally assumed, I gained confidence and struck it harder and harder until it popped directly into the water on the beach and settled amongst the rocks.

I first thought I had probably landed back on Brobadingog, it being by far the most likely place to land, considering my origins and not knowing exactly where the island was to begin with. But I couldn't have known for sure, so after slow-minded consideration, my brain being deprived of food and water and my body ill, I took the tether Princess Pitum had used to pull me around over my shoulder, wrapped it around the largest boulder I could find, and tried to tie the thick cord. I gave up after many tries and instead wedged an existing knot between two stones, which I firmed up by pulling another into position.

I probably ought not to have expended so much energy in the protection of the boat. Out of instinct I suppose, I was protecting my life raft. I wasn't satisfied with the work, but looking at the boat, I could see the tide was slightly lower than when I had drifted in. The boat was no longer bumping and grinding. It was now sitting fully exposed, beached on the rocks. I stumbled and shambled from the beach into the trees hoping to find something I could eat or drink. On a tree near the water's edge, I saw some moss, and desperate, I pulled a chunk free and jammed it into my mouth. I forced it down and swallowed it. As I worked to master my reflex to reject this food for its awful taste, I had an epiphany. The tree from which I had pulled the greenery was only about a half metre in diameter. Furthermore, the leaves on the ground about me were roughly the size of my hands. The twigs and needles on the ground were cutting my feet, not tripping me. Now I knew for certain I was not on Brobadingog, and there being few places on this Earth not inhabited by people near the ocean, I regained hope of a possible rescue.

The sun was high in the sky, near about noon. From the east, I clearly heard the sound of a small plane landing nearby. Wary of unseen dangers in the thick forest, I stayed close to the strand and crossed several small beaches before emerging at an elongated patch of contiguous sand that stretched out for a few kilometres. Most important for me, I could see several people walking and playing in the sand at some distance. I set a course towards the nearest group. They must have thought me quite the sight as I approached in a somewhat ill-fitting, but magnificently, if a little hilariously, adorned robe that had been fashioned for me in Brobadingog. This thought that I looked quite out of place only occurred to me as I got closer to the group. Those immaterial trepidations were easily washed away as I realized I may have found safety once again.

Most surprising of all was that as I neared the group, who stood with mouths agape, the children ran up and asked me in unaccented English if I was a wizard. Having not heard my mother tongue for several months, this was a shock. Conflicting emotions of joy and confusion played in my mind as I was thoroughly overwhelmed at my great luck. I stared at the children for a minute, which in hindsight must have disquieted the parents, who stepped forwards and pulled their children back. They saw my parched lips and offered me a bottle of water. I snapped out of my stunned silence and greedily drank the entirety of a large bottle before I realized my poor manners and thanked them. I asked a most pitiful question, in a quiet, unassuming, and utterly beggarly manner, "Where am I?"

One of the children offered me a most humorous answer. "Earth," they said, and a snicker turned into a laugh, which spread contagiously to everyone gathered. One of the adults offered a slightly more precise answer: Canada. I stopped laughing at once, and asked seriously, "Where?" In a series of refinements, I was informed first that I had landed in British Columbia, then Vancouver Island, close to Tofino, and then that this was Long Beach. Not only had I landed in Canada, but I had landed in a place I had once visited as a child. I broke into tears, which the children misunderstood.

The adults asked if I needed their help. I confirmed that I did, desperately. They kindly offered me some food and drove me into the town, where I once again was forced to reestablish my identity and residence. At the altruism of the small town, I was afforded food and shelter while officials came to collect me. I promised the beachcombers I wouldn't forget their goodwill. I recorded their names deep in my mind and later made certain they were well rewarded.

It took a few days to put my affairs back in order, but I was assisted by the extreme wealth aboard my boat. I enlisted the help of several young people in town, and retracing my steps, we found it floating where I had left it. We recovered the gems and the precious metal ballast, and I compensated them with one bar of gold weighing twenty kilograms. It took several trips to carry all the loot back to town. For my ten assistants, the reward amounted to more than they imagined. Altogether, I had twenty such bars of gold, ten silver, gemstones in the largest tenth percentile of their kind of a dozen types, plus the diamond on the hilt of my sword.

I was rich beyond even the wildest of imaginations. I commissioned an armoured truck to carry it to a suitable safe place and sent a diamond measured at 500 carats to the family that had found me. Some have argued the rewards I gave both to the beachgoers and to my assistants far exceeded the value of the service offered, but I was back home, safe, sound, and secure. I thought it my right to spend my serendipitous gains on whatever pleased me. I know my gesture changed the lives of these kind people for the better, so I can't be anything but happy.

PART SIX

BLAFUSECHO, SINROVIA, AND LILLIPUT: THE TINY

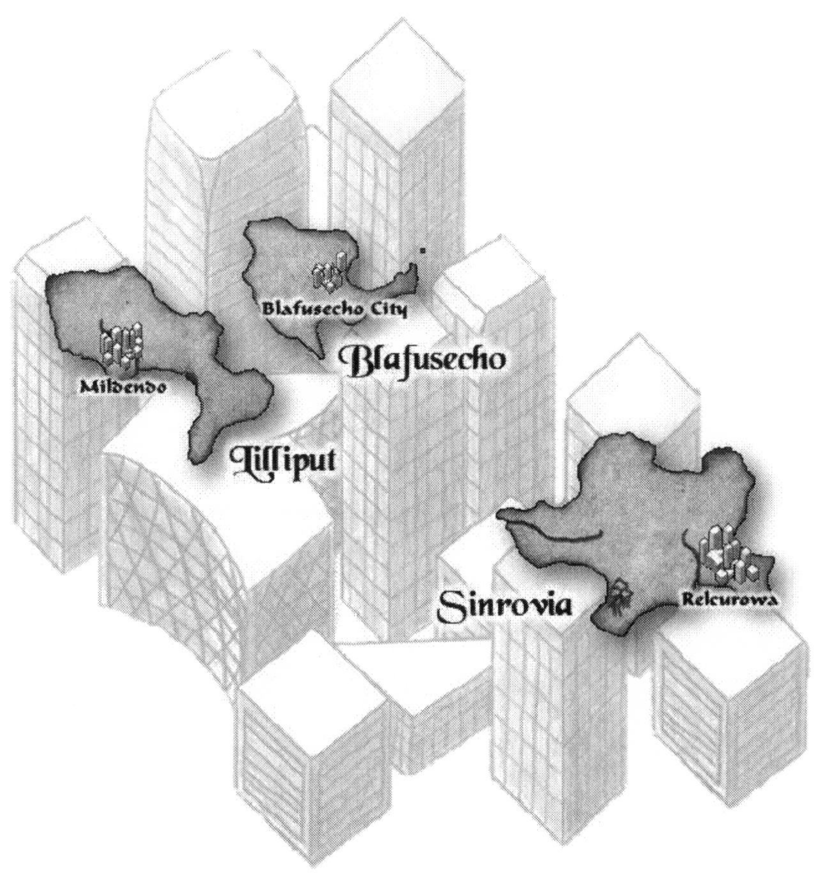

CHAPTER 6.1

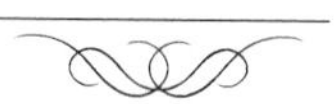

Safe at home, the author carves out a new life for himself.

THE QUESTION ASKED more frequently than any other upon my reanimation was this: How did you settle back into your old life? With all the changes that had happened in your absence and all the things that had either been retired or introduced while you were gone, how did you adjust? My answer was, and still is, patience and time. Honestly, my treasure trove from Brobadingog assisted a great deal in buffering me from culture shock.

The wealth I had accumulated before my latest misfortune was modest in comparison to what I had just acquired in precious metals and gems. It gave me options not afforded anyone else. I could have carved out a chunk of land and set it up to resemble any of the places I had encountered. I could have bought old technology and chosen to live in stasis in a time with which I was familiar and comfortable.

The technologies most difficult for me to grasp, having been away for so long with only a couple limited returns, were not those that had just recently been introduced to the world, but those that had been novel at the early part of my departure, widely adopted by the middle, and then refined and remodelled by the time I returned. Such an established level of familiarity had been gained by the majority that the simplest elements were no longer taught. Blessed with abundant resources, however, I could purchase whichever gadget I wanted, whatever was to me advised, and lessons or instructions on the usage of such technology. Leery of falling victim, I practiced patience and only explored the world in manageable chunks.

Once again, I was offered the rounds of the TV and talk show circuit. I chose to stay a little closer to home this time. Instead of sharing my story while travelling regularly, my thoughts focused on settling down and enjoying the many freedoms life has to offer.

Great fiduciary resources are certainly a most positive benefit. I would never suggest such an insult as to say otherwise, but while freeing in some aspects, it is binding in others. There comes with such resources a natural preoccupation with the protection of one's riches and monumental challenges with trust. I found it was difficult to trust anybody I hadn't known well before my travels. Even most of those I had been close with before being estranged for several years, being mindful of my money, were not as easy to believe when they presented themselves truthfully and sincerely. I felt tugged between two worlds: one of quiet hermitic solitude, trusting nobody, locked away from a world of which I had failed to be a part for some time, and one of wild gregariousness, my time and money begged for by so many and to whom I could give so much. The only choice that wasn't presented was a middle ground. It seemed to be black and white, all or nothing.

I regret my first instinct this time was towards the former option. I receded into my new home, neglected many connections, and quietly stewed over the world I had lost. Little by little, though, I began to realize that absent any direct communication and steering, the few pieces of my story, in particular relating to the island of Brobadingog, I had let slip in the ecstasy of rescue were being stitched together by storytellers and the media into a Frankenstein monster of half-truths and filler. I realized I had to tell my story, lest I be judged in absentia. The many different versions of my story had grown to paint me a coward, a thief, a criminal, or a liar. I saw my family being hurt by a fiction that barely resembled my adventures at all. I broke out of my new mansion, in which I had imprisoned myself as Princess Pitum had in Brobadingog. Knowing I couldn't repair the situation on my own, I accepted the help of a girl I had known as a child, who I had once trusted, even though she was someone with whom I had long ago lost contact.

She helped me reach back out to the world and manage my time and contacts. She let me be free, nursed me back to mental stability, and asked nothing of me in return. I think it is well known by most people familiar with my story that she and I fell in love, married, and had two wonderful children within a few years. My beautiful wife saw when my resolve was failing and propped me back up. She pushed me to be the best version of myself, for which I shall always be thankful. This part of my story has been shared before, and she herself wrote about our lives together in the years that our children were growing up. This tome, too, has been well pored over by my generous readers.

At her suggestion—or perhaps acceptance as I have always had a difficult time identifying whether an idea was hers or mine since I lived such a life of experiences—we bought a large yacht and explored the oceans in the comfort and security it provided. We sailed about the Caribbean and Mediterranean as a family, and she encouraged me to bring some friends on a trip on the Indian Ocean. I have already expressed, and continue to adhere to, a policy of nonrevealing geography. I will not elaborate further on the specifics of this leg of the journey. We hired a small crew, and with several of my closest friends, planned to visit numerous ports and sites.

The trip was to last several months, picking up and dropping off friends at various ports of call along the way, with my family learning history, geography, and all other manner of important life lessons on board. The crew and my family grew quite fond of each other, especially the captain, a Mr. Waltersson, who hailed from Fyn in Denmark. He was a tall, strong, proud man, not excessively educated, but handy and full of vigour. His wife had passed away a few years earlier, and he adopted us as his extended family, an extra grandfather to my children. We could not have asked for a better skipper.

CHAPTER 6.2

The author's luck takes a turn for the worse when a medical emergency kicks off a series of unfortunate events leading to his stranding at sea somewhere in the Indian Ocean.

AS MY LOYAL readers by now have surmised, this last adventure did not unfold the way we expected. After a few months at sea, and with several guests aboard giving us a total residency, including crew, of twenty-one souls, a tragedy befell us. We had been sailing in well-charted, open water and had been heading to port because we had a schedule that needed to be followed so three of our guests could depart and catch flights home. I had accompanied the captain on to the bridge of the ship while my family played on the main deck. Mr. Waltersson pointed out a small island in the distance with some confusion. The maps seemed to show no such land. It was a low island, probably of coral. He checked our GPS and confirmed our coordinates, but still, the island seemed otherwise undiscovered.

Suddenly, Mr. Waltersson clutched his chest. Sweat poured from his brow as this strapping man fell to the floor, breathing weakly. I caught him before he hit, slowing his fall as best I could considering his superior mass, and gently lay him down. Just as I was about to yell for help, the boat struck something firmly and lurched hard to starboard. I could hear panic below as the crew, my guests, and my family tried to assess the situation. I was certain my wife was with the children, having checked on them only minutes before, along with two of my most trusted friends, so I focused on the captain. His condition was worsening rapidly. His breathing had stopped. Even before I finished the assessment, his pulse deteriorated.

I called for help. No assistance was forthcoming. Whether my yells were not heard or were ignored for other priorities I would never know. I was alone trying to save the man, so I started CPR. For several minutes, I exerted myself in the aim of keeping some oxygenated blood in his head in case it was possible to keep him with us. In my exertions, however, I had failed to realize the boat had been sinking into the water. The bridge of the ship by this point was the only thing still above the waves. It was only when my legs, from my knees to my feet as I knelt next to the prone captain, became wet that I realized the boat was almost fully submerged.

I prayed my family was all right and they had gotten to the lifeboat. At my insistence, this was maintained and supplied with enough food, water, and fuel to easily reach the nearest island, and it contained radio equipment for emergencies. I had even gone so far as to ensure everyone, even my young children, were well trained in what to do in an emergency at sea. They were to aim for the nearest charted land mass, and once en route, to not delay for any reason. I still felt a responsibility for the captain, though, so against all better judgement, I tried to pull him through the waters that filled the only access to the bridge.

Looking down the corridor at the salty water, I knew deep in my bones there was no way I could save the man. In my delay, even my own life was likely forfeit. I exhaled deeply to purge as much carbon dioxide from my lungs as possible, took a deep breath back in, and ducked under the water. I swam first through the long hallway, but then thinking better of my circumstance, turned back to a side chamber where the scuba equipment was stored.

The equipment was all but entirely empty from a previous excursion, but I found one set still assembled. I put the regulator over my mouth and was able to breathe just a little. As the boat continued to sink, I struggled to put on some flippers, and with the tank tucked under one arm, I kicked hard towards the door, down the hallway, and onto the main deck. Free of the ship, but still deep beneath the water, I chose to abandon the already empty tank and kicked towards the surface hard. I breached the surface and swung around, hoping to find the escape craft, but the water was too choppy, so I could not find it.

As I had trained my family, I oriented myself towards the small land mass we had seen. I knew it must be at least a kilometre away based on our earlier observation, but I also knew I could not reach the original destined port without a boat. My best chance was to swim towards the island and hope for the best.

It is hardly advisable to swim as intensely as one can for long distances. The energy outlay is less efficient than a calm, gentle stroke. I kept turning around, hoping to see my family safe and coming to rescue me. I would not be that fortunate. I kept swimming, and my only thoughts were about them, the only thing that mattered a whit to me. For the first time in my awful adventures, I was concerned principally about surviving not for myself, but for my wife and children. Above all, I hoped they were well. I had no choice but to assume they were all right because it was necessary for my own sanity. In hindsight, I wasn't able to process the possibility or even the contemplation of anything else, so I swam so my children would know their father. I credit that line of thought to my survival because I did reach that island, tired and exhausted from the exertion, and I was able to swim into a shallow bay. I rolled onto my back, feeling absolutely ill, my face just above the water, and I faded to darkness.

CHAPTER 6.3

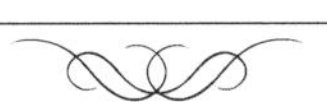

The author wakes up surrounded by boats and the inhabitants of the island he has reached, but not all is well with his new hosts.

I WOKE TO a high-pitched amelodic discord I failed to identify with my eyes closed. Something akin to the buzzing of bees, a hummingbird, or a small fan brushed past my ear, and I reflexively reached to swat it away, but my arm would not obey. I felt a dull pain in the back of my head, which was rested upon a hard piece of wood. My arms, legs, hands, feet, waist, and neck I found to be bound to the ground with strong steel-like cables, and any movement of my head was limited by wooden panels to which my head was strapped across the forehead like a neck stabilization kit. I felt the waves on my chest and against the side of my head. I was still in the water of the cove.

The buzz whizzed past my ear once again. I easily traced its sound back to its source, now that my eyes were open, as a small drone hovered in front of my eyes at a distance of only a decimetre or two. The drone was shaped as a ring. Above the hollow centre was a small conical platform raised by six rigid beams. In the cone stood a tiny man, between fifteen and sixteen centimetres in height, small enough that he could easily fit in my hand. He operated the controls of his little flying saucer, which emitted only a quiet hum at this distance, and propelled a steady current of air towards me.

As I focused on him in the bright sunlight, I became aware of several more of the single-person aircraft. At my sides in the water was the thrumming of a number of model boats. The noises were all high in pitch but low in volume. Together though, the sound they emitted was notable.

I perceived all the miniature aircraft creating a formation. My eyes wearily and warily took in the scene before me. Each of the pilots possessed a small stick that they pointed at me, their minuscule eyes cautious and concerned. I smelled electricity in the air and sensed the fear and trepidation evident on the faces of my tiny captors. Then the man in the centre of the formation approached more closely, and with an amplifier to his lips, shouted out a stream of fast-paced, high-pitched words beginning with something that sounded a bit like Latin, "*Quinbus Flestrin*."

Alas, I could not understand the words, the intent, or even the tone of the message. I would better understand this name in time. I resolved to reply to him in Latin first, then in French, and finally in Spanish, these sounding most akin to what I had heard from him. I opened my mouth to answer, and the first word I spoke aloud, as I endeavoured to speak with some authority, sent the flying machines zipping away, and to my left in the water, I heard an amplified voice shout, "*Tolgo Pulnac*!"

Suddenly, a hundred crackles of light and sound filled the air, and my left arm, leg, and cheek stung as though bitten simultaneously by several dozen bees in quick succession. The sharp and sudden pain caused me to scream and recoil into my ligatures. This reaction forced the assembled forces at my right to join the barrage from my left, and I smelled my charred skin.

The speaker from the flying machine flew back over my head, having regained control of his wayward vessel more rapidly than his companions. He directed his microscopic megaphone to each of my sides in turn and repeated urgently, "*Langro! Langro!*" The assault faded away. The courageous speaker, a Hurgo, in the words of his people, lowered his machine onto my stomach, disembarked, and confidently strode up to my chest. I felt his little feet climbing towards my face.

The man was well dressed, but by the standards of a British Navy officer from colonial times. Like a fifteen centimetre doll, he climbed into my line of sight. I marvelled at the diminutive creature who stood in front of me. I realized that in my pain and recoiling from the first volley, I had managed to loosen the bonds on my right hand just enough to pull them free. I did this as slowly as I possibly could for fear of another round from my assailants. The petite captain on my chest held his megaphone up and spoke once again. I tried to indicate to him using just facial expressions that I didn't understand his words.

He stood upon me like a hunter upon his prey. I drew my hand cautiously out of the water and took great care to not appear hostile. I raised it to my head and indicated to him that I wished for water. I was apparently successful. He signalled to one side and a fountain stream was arched over my head. Gradually, its location was recalibrated until it fell into my mouth a few seconds later. The liquid was not like any water that ever before had I tasted. Desperate, I drank greedily and excepting for a sneeze that erupted when the fountain sputtered into my nose, I put down as much of the drink as fast as I could.

The source of the beverage apparently ran dry as the bright sun continued to rise overhead. I tried to indicate a desire to eat as well, but my arm was getting very heavy, very quickly. The man on my chest spoke slower, and the sun above split into two. The flying machines multiplied, blurred, and then faded into nothingness.

CHAPTER 6.4

The author wakes up on solid ground, but still in chains, and is introduced to several dignitaries and locals.

I WOULD WAKE up slowly and groggily. It would be explained to me later that I had been drugged with a potent anaesthetic. I couldn't have realized this at the time, but the dose they had given me was sufficient to kill several hundred of their kind. So acute and accurate was their understanding of mathematics that they could precisely assess my size and dose me accordingly.

I woke up outside an aircraft hangar on a tarmac. As with the people, this was scaled down significantly in size. Around my neck was a collar of metal with fifty cables secured to hooks and tied to the ground forming about me a maypole. I could sit, stand, and lie down, but my movement was restricted to a small semisphere as defined by the length of my bindings. About my head flew a constellation of the same disc-copters, carefully outside of my reach.

At first, I tried to rise but staggered under the fading influence of the sleep agent. Instead I settled upon a knee. In addition to the flying machines, I was surrounded by several corps of miniature soldiers with minuscule guns, tanks, and all manner of vehicles to which I can't even compare. Were I to be freed from my bonds, I felt more than a match for this army. I realized then that the injuries I had sustained in the prior attack appeared to have healed. I didn't know how long I had been under the influence, but apart from the lingering effects, I felt, strangely, in pretty good shape.

To one side of me, opposite the doorway to the hangar, was erected a scaffold podium a metre and a half tall, with platforms at each floor and pads upon which the small *Telluqua*, as the flying discs I learned were known, could land.

A particularly well-appointed Telluqua moored itself just off the platform at the height of my head. Five diminutive officials, each wearing formal versions of the same sailor uniform, strode onto the deck to be joined by the original speaker. I was addressed again as Quinbus Flestrin. This was followed in quick succession by a rapid patter I could not understand. It again felt like a mixture of Latin, with perhaps some Arabic pronunciations. I have never had the privilege to learn languages from that region, so I can't say particularly confidently if the language matched a known one or not.

In a quiet voice, as I remembered the sharp pains of the tiny projectiles in my skin, I endeavoured to address the small men and women. Dear reader, I have urged the publisher to accept a modification to the story from previous versions to clarify that although all five officials wore a similar uniform, two of the three, including the one at the centre, were in fact, women, and I would soon learn she was the Hurga Degul, or leading minister in English parlance, of the Island of Blafusecho.

Though I spoke in every language in which I possessed any mastery, my words were only met with confusion. The ministers whispered to each other in disagreement, I judged, by the way they leaned into each other and spoke directly into each other's ears and frequently shook their heads. I found it difficult to clearly hear the higher tones of the females of this place in this place. They seemed scarcely more than a squeak. The deeper male voices held enough tenor as to be more easily discernable. Still, I understood not a single word spoken. I was careful to make no hostile movements, nor to demonstrate any ill intents. For this I was rewarded by the leader, who gestured for others to bring forwards a series of plates with food and drink.

The food was placed on the largest plates these tiny people could create. The food consisted of meat resembling steak but was truly whole sides of cattle and numerous poultry I ate whole, each equal in size to perhaps a plum. To speak ill of their preparation would be to do them a great disservice. The food was prepared with care and was most excellently cooked. As I devoured dozens of their chickens, I thought about the displeasure of a chef to spend so long preparing such a feast only to have it gobbled in a single bite. I was, however, more skeptical about the drink they had prepared for me in a barrel, which was close in size, for me, to a small glass. I showed my skepticism, which must have been understood. The captain who first spoke to me boarded his Telluqua and took a cupful of it himself as a guarantee.

Having apparently seen enough of me, the leader and her entourage sped away in their Telluqua. I would learn from future mini visitors the importance of this encounter. The Hurga Degul had adjudged me to be a peaceful, rational being. I was therefore deserving of their assistance, she and her people having a great compassion for those in need. Of the ministers, two had voted to provide me with their support, one had abstained, while a third, one of the men, vociferously objected to my presence on their island. On the command of the Degul, I was to be provisioned with food enough to satisfy almost two thousand of her citizens, as computed by my relative proportions. I was roughly twelve times their normal size, and so my volume must require 1,728 times the nourishment.

A dozen of the best teachers from her land were assigned to instruct me in their language, culture, history, and other important subjects. A dozen of their finest weavers were also assigned to measure and prepare for me proper dressing. They took careful note of my belongings. Many weeks later, after learning their language, I was allowed to view these notes:

> The Quinbus Flestrin wears about his wrist an engine that drums at regular intervals-approximately in time with his heartbeat-and three spinning bars rotate about its centre.

The shape and design are similar to the Gulver artifact of Lilliput but for a few extra details. The piece is produced of a shiny metal, composed of a prodigious quantity of gold and silver. In a compartment in his Ranju-lo (shorts pocket), a matching pair of semi-transparent dark glass panels are attached to a flexible and folding metal frame whose pliable extensions stretch to the length of a small woman or an elder child.

Reading this note will, I'm certain, raise a number of important and well-merited questions to the astute reader. Rest assured, I will elucidate further on the subjects of Gulver and Lilliput, the former being one, similar to me, who once visited this island, and the latter being the name of the nearest island nation to Blafusecho.

Apart from shorts, I was wearing no other clothing at this point. Thankfully, enormous efforts were undertaken to fashion for me a suit appropriate, and consistent, with the style of the island. I was larger than the standard reams of textile at their disposal, so the weavers were forced to stitch together a quilt of like fabrics. I was told this was found to be a frustratingly imperfect manufacture but there was little more they could do. In the end, after only a few days of labour, they had fashioned for me a handsome—if antique in style—shirt, coat, breeches, socks, and even a tough pair of wrap boots. They closely examined the zipper on my shorts and begged that they could study it. Having observed me operate it, to expel my various wastes, they were impressed by its clever and simple design.

I would spend several months in their tutelage under the supervision of the first who spoke to me, a captain by the name of Nockin. Provisioned with proficient professors, distracted by little during my lessons, I picked up the language relatively quickly. As soon as I was able, I asked to have the bindings cut, that I might explore Blafusecho myself.

The Hurga Degul and her ministers, both together and separately, took the liberty of visiting me officially on numerous occasions, at least once a week each, and took commensurate pleasure in my progress given the way they had earlier voted on my staying. Those compassionate two and the Degul took the most pleasure; the neutral minister seemed pleased I was not causing undue harm, while the contrary representative, a man by the name of Malièr, showed frustration, particularly with the prodigious resources required to sustain me. Malièr continued to quietly agitate against my ubiety in this place. They addressed me as Quinbus Flestrin, a title that meant the Man Mountain. I also learned I was not the first Quinbus Flestrin to land on this island, but that another, Gulver, had graced their shores many years before.

On the day I requested my liberty, the Hurga Degul and the council was summoned. She had long expected this request, so she and her people had conferred and created a covenant I would be required to accept before she could grant my request:

Article 1: *The Quinbus Flestrin, being of so great a size, shall reserve his movements to grade-level roads of sufficient width as to allow unencumbered movement.*

Article 2: *As per Article 1, the Quinbus Flestrin must not enter any metropolitan area, particularly the capital, Blafusecho City, for the risk of accidental damage to structure and people is too great.*

Article 3: *The Quinbus Flestrin must not hurt, maim, or kill any citizen of Blafusecho.*

Article 4: *As a subject of the realm, the Quinbus Flestrin must perform services as required by the government insofar as they do not violate any other article of the agreement.*

Article 5: *The Quinbus Flestrin may not depart from the island without prior approval and acknowledgement of the government of Blafusecho.*

Article 6: *The Quinbus Flestrin must not engage in diplomacy or discussions with foreign governments in the absence of Blafusechan officials.*

Article 7: *The Quinbus Flestrin is bound by the normal orders and laws of the nation of Blafusecho, insofar as they relate to his ability.*

Article 8: *In return, the Quinbus Flestrin shall be afforded the rights and privileges of all citizens of Blafusecho, as well as sufficient food and* *drink at the rate of 1,728 times the average consumption of an ordinary Blafusechan.*

I readily accepted the terms put forward. Some of the indeterminates vexed me somewhat though. Not being familiar with the laws of the realm, I was forced to accept a degree of uncertainty in agreeing to these terms. I had learned from my teachers a smidgeon of news and information about the neighbours of this place, but rather than repeat hearsay, I would have preferred to report about them from first-person accounts. It was clear I wouldn't get that opportunity, given Article 5. Article 5 was particularly vexing not only to me, but even more so to Malièr. It was still his fancy that I leave Blafusecho. Not only did this pact allow me to stay here, but it actually bound me to stay unless otherwise offered a chance to leave.

The treatise I signed was titled the "Lumos Hulga Pesso Desmar Lon Composo," which translated into the "Oath of Peace with The Leading Minister and Her Country." I was freed of my bonds by Nockin, who took great pleasure in the honour. After nine months confined to the hangar and the tarmac there surrounding, I was at liberty to explore this country of which I was now officially a citizen and equal, if not in stature, at least by law.

CHAPTER 6.5

The author explores the island and notes the many systems in place in the nation of Blafusecho.

ONCE LIBERATED OF the hangar and chains that had been my home and binding these past months, my first request was to explore the bay wherein I had washed ashore. Malière accompanied me to my landing harbour across the Blafusechan countryside. On my sojourn to my point of arrival, I took in the surroundings and was struck not only by the beauty of the country, but also by its similarity to many of the great countries and cities to which I have been fortunate to visit.

The houses were charming, and well maintained, if only a couple decimetres or so in height to match with the needs of the inhabitants therein. Each field, productive and green, was irrigated and tended carefully and arranged in a hexagonal grid. Each side of a hexagonal field amounted to twenty blustrugs, roughly equal to sixteen metres. At the centre of each field was a central pivot for irrigation that watered the fields in a perfect circle, right to the edge of the roadways. In the corners of each field, where the centre pivot did not reach, the houses and farm equipment were retained. Between each field on either side of the roadway were rows of trees, not usually more than a metre in height. The roads were a width of one metre, and the trees were low enough and close enough to afford a person of my height a long, undisturbed view of the country. Malière informed me that despite the idyllic fields and productive appearances, the island country of Blafusecho was actually near to collapse, unable to provide its own people with any sort of nutritional surplus, that the land was worked to the fullest degree and still the people were on the precipice of starvation at all times. Only by the generosity of the neighbouring state in trading with Blafusecho did Malière suggest that the people of this land continued to thrive.

I was impressed by the distance the industrious Blafusechans had transported my hulking, dormant body along this network. I would guess they had pulled me at least a kilometre from the beach to the hangar. To clarify for scale, this work would have been akin to hauling a large house several miles with little warning, preparation, or prior skill.

When I reached the bay, I saw it was surrounded by little homes I had not noticed upon my arrival, and a sandy tidal beach stretched out to a thin rocky reef. I briefly thought of the inhabitants of this place encountering a giant such as me in their backyards unexpectedly. I laughed a little at the unfathomable reality I presented them. It was little wonder in hindsight that I awoke bound on that first day; my arrival would have been quite the news story.

I searched the horizon and explored the local area almost every day. I made my near-daily pilgrimages with different ministers and the Hurga Degul herself. Of course, I was searching for and longing to see those most important to me, or at least for some confirmation of their deliverance. I had at my disposal no method to communicate with anyone or to travel anywhere beyond the island. It was a melancholy habit, to visit that harbour. It bore a hole in my stomach each time. I trust the compassionate reader will excuse my brevity, but even thinking about my lost family today wrenches my soul.

In contrast to my personal turmoil, I should like to describe the beauty and magnificence of the culture and society of the island nation of Blafusecho. I would travel to several of their cities, but as agreed, not within the limits for fear of causing damage. Each time, I would be greeted at the gates by throngs of citizens eager to view the Quinbus Flestrin. Their cities were well planned. The core areas had skyscrapers several metres in height. Public transit ran throughout each of their cities, and energy was derived from a variety of sources, including small windmills, solar plants, and miniature hydro-electric generators. Even rainfall was captured by each building, and through gravitational force, the water generated power while providing greywater to the facilities.

These innovative people possessed a number of advanced technologies such as their numerous flying machines. Such is the degree and mastery of miniaturization, at least compared to my clumsy fingers, that I had great difficulty understanding how the flying machines worked. Despite the best efforts of my teachers, it was difficult to project schematics at a scale I could read.

It was on one trip to the capital, Blafusecho City, that I first noticed a number of small signs planted all about the roads. Colourful and diverse, they dotted nearly every major intersection or thoroughfare visible from my accepted vantage beyond the city limits. I asked the Hurga about this and she told me about the political structure, as these signs were a tool of their democratic campaign, which would inevitably, due to term limits, spell the end of her governance of this nation.

Beyond technological innovations, their society had developed some of the most impressive social structures ever I have heard or witnessed. As with many of the greatest countries in the world, their government consisted of a constitutionally bound democracy. The system is full of checks and balances, but great efforts are made to ensure a transparent, functional, and equitable system of government.

The Hurga explained that all elected officials were required to demonstrate a commitment to public service. This is a measure of actual work, not financial donation. Wealthy individuals were no more likely to achieve high office than those less so. All officials must take a specified education program in the operations of government, history, and foreign relations. They must pass, depending on the level of their desired post, public service examinations to prove their competency. The entirety of their life must be made public and transparent before the electorate. This includes any records of criminal behaviour, taxes and business dealings, and personal history. All potential conflicts of interest are avoided by a system that requires public servants, beyond front-line management, to divest of all their private holdings. The proceeds from this are combined with a public pension to pay for their lives after their service is complete. I found the description most enviable, and greatly desirable, for to be a servant of the people is to dedicate oneself entirely to the cause.

Theirs was a representative democracy. Representatives were selected in public elections if they met the above requirements. These representatives were understood to stand for the people that elected them and were to such responsible. Their role was to make decisions on behalf of their constituency; thus, no referenda were required. Party politics were strictly forbidden. It had been found that political parties eroded public confidence in officials split between loyalty to their party and to the electorate. Instead, each representative was necessarily an independent body who voted on and proposed bills as they best understood the will of those who had put them in power. Decisions were made based on a pure majority. In the absence of a party system, as an astute reader will deduce, the individuals had to negotiate, compromise, and communicate eloquently to get general bills passed.

Complimentary to the checks and balances imposed on individuals, the system itself included a variety of systemic checks, such as their five branches of government. The executive was represented by a single person, the Hurgo or Hurga Degul. A judicial branch was composed of a hierarchical court structure, the qualified members thereof, being in good standing, proposed candidates for the higher courts, from which the executive and legislative branches selected their preference. The legislative branch then was trisected to handle issues of modifiable aerial unit problems. One was the Assembly, comprised of members from the smallest geographic unit, representing about one thousand of their people; the Congress, which represented about one hundred thousand people; and the Parliament, which with ten members, was the smallest branch of government, with each member of Parliament representing one million eligible voters.

Every position in all branches served a limited term. This was undoubtedly complicated on paper, but the various components functioned together to ensure no single branch possessed too much power or too great an authority over the destiny of the people.

To both share with the world the potential of this system and to currently spare the reader too long a diversion, I am in the process of writing a complete description of the politics of Blafusecho, which is close to print even now, and will refrain from expending further ink in this document, which is meant more to be a summary of my travels and of this place.

On a sojourn with Nockin to several cities, I noticed, as is often common in the outskirts of cities, public structures were less frequently found, they being more commonly clustered in the higher density parishes and precincts. That did not mean there were none available. I noted a number of exceptionally constructed and maintained buildings that stood out from the low houses even near the periphery and was told these were schools. There was quite a range of architectures and qualities present. Some of the schools were large considering their surroundings, others had extensive and carefully manicured fields. There were no consistent designs for these structures, which led to a number of questions for Nockin.

Nockin described to me, and I found great satisfaction learning of, the system of economy. The market worked freely with protective bureaucratic oversight accountable to the elected bodies. It was the motto of their system that "a million hands left to their own self-interest will achieve the greatest success, but the commons they exploit need to be stewarded and secured." The entire Blafusechan system functioned as a free market with oversight, but not interruption, from the government and bureaucratic departments.

The elected bodies worked with the bureaucracy in such a way that the government defined the standards at the advice of the bureaucracy. The government departments were tasked with determining at what cost entrepreneurs could provide each service. This was not an idle evaluation. In the absence of willing bidders, as to be explained further, the bureaucracy was then to provide those services at the assessed fee, with a fixed budget.

Once the governing body had established the standards, and the responsible department the fair fee, any licensed enterprise could elect to provide that service with the budgeted government subsidy applied. That enterprise could choose to charge more for superior service but had to meet the standards and be subjected to frequent surprise inspection to ensure quality was maintained. The businesses operating the services were thereby incentivized to find ways to provide services at lower costs to improve profit margins but also had to compete with other providers for clients, which increased quality.

I've been told an example might better illustrate their luminous system, so I will use the example of education. Before I begin, I need affirm education was compulsory in this state. All children were required to attend, between the ages of three and eighteen years, a licensed facility.

Their government set the standards and curriculum as advised by the department of education, which itself was comprised of leading educators as elected by the students of Blafusecho. The department took those standards into account and proposed a fee structure at which they could provide those services. In this example, if an average student, if such a thing exists, could be educated annually at a rate of $1,000, then the government afforded a contract to any licensed provider to educate a student. The government then granted the sum of $1,000 to the enterprise for each student under tutelage.

The business could then choose to charge nothing extra, they may levy additional fees if they believed their service was superior and the market willing to pay them, or they could pay a portion of the subsidy to the families of their children as an incentive to choose their school. This way, several schools could be found in the same area competing for students. Some catered to higher income students and some to lower, but all were required to meet or exceed the same standards and to teach the same curriculum. Failure to meet the guidelines, which I was informed is unusual in this place, resulted in a suspension of the licence. In such a case, temporarily, the department provided services in place.

Parents were free to select the school they wished their children to attend. The competition led to innovation, efficiency, and better facilities and academic performance. One need only look at the marvellous technology that abounded in this land of miniatures to understand the high quality of their education system.

The same philosophy and economic policy applied to all other services including health care, which is, of course, provided universally, the needs of the poor being no less important than those of the wealthy, which is never the case in systems of nongovernmental health care. These policies also applied to infrastructure and construction, power generation, emergency services, and even the departments of refuse and incarceration.

I can assure the reader there is scarcely a more beautiful place than a prison on Blafusecho. They were not designed purely for punishment, but for education and rehabilitation. Inmates were granted the privilege of selecting their institution, which may sound problematic, but the prisons were held to the same standard of quality as any other. The treatment of the prisoners was prescribed within certain tolerances. As a result, the most attractive correctional facilities drew more prisoners, and the less well maintained and equipped tended to suffer.

I would also speak well of the religion of Blafusecho. Constitutionally, the country was secular, but it demanded not just tolerance, but acceptance of all faiths, there being several denominations on the island.

There was, officially and demonstrably, a full separation between church and state. Careful definitions had been established to differentiate the two. Religion is based on a belief. Belief is based not on repeatable, unquestionable evidence, but rather on stories or interpretations. Science is defined as a system of measurable, repeatable, evidence-based understandings. Science can be disproven and changed, but religion can never be fully proven.

Symbols were allowed and accepted, but they could not be permanently fixed to any office of government or any licensed provider of an official, subsidized service. It must be noted that unlicensed providers were not allowed to provide any of the centrally sanctioned services. A school may not operate without the subsidy of the government as an extra-state enterprise.

The judicial system was not blind but instead looked in all directions. I found a fairness unparalleled in any modern society, for an accuser could suffer the same punishment they asked for those they accused. Again, I shall elaborate for the suspicious reader. This only happens when the accuser is found beyond reasonable doubt to have initialized their litigation under false, spurious, or specious motivation.

Legal costs are divided equally, whereby a wealthy plaintiff or defendant must provide his counterpart with equal legal costs without condition.

The counterpart may refuse the funds, but they must be made available to balance the scales of justice between wealthy and poor. I was told this discourages lawsuits by big corporations and wealthy individuals against those who would otherwise be unable to defend themselves. In the event one party was found guilty, either of spurious litigation or of the crime of which they were accused, all legal costs were then owed by that party.

Take this exemplar case. A plaintiff sues a defendant for damages amounting to one million dollars and spends ten thousand dollars on legal fees. The defendant, having not the means to spend equally on his defence, is granted a judicial loan by the plaintiff for an equal amount to prepare their defence at the same standard. At a macro scale, three outcomes are possible:

1. The defendant is found guilty, and in addition to the punitive damages of one million dollars, they must also pay the plaintiff the full cost of both parties' legal fees.

2. The plaintiff is found to have initiated the lawsuit speculatively, or for reasons not of legal but of vindictive nature; the plaintiff must pay the defendant the full cost of the proposed punitive damages, one million dollars, and forfeits the money they spent and loaned for legal costs.

3. Neither side is found to be guilty of offence, and while the case was justified, the defendant is not found to be guilty. Neither side pays punitive damages, and the judicial loan is forfeit.

It took me some time to realize the value of the proposition, but my tutors implored me to understand this had the desired result of discouraging heavy-handed legal tactics. It reduced the need for, particularly, the poor to settle cases in which they otherwise would not have had the resources with which to compete. In truth, the beautiful justice herein created a system of fairness before the law with respect to the wealth of the parties.

Additionally, courts and cases were presented anonymously. Jurists are not allowed to know either the identity of the accuser or the defendant but instead are presented thoroughly anonymous facts and figures with testimony concealing the identity of the speaker. This protected against bias in favour of or against a celebrity or any who may be known to the jurists.

Finally, punishment value and sentence were not determined by the plaintiff or prosecutor, but by the jurists and the judge based on evidence and accounting. The prosecution or litigator was required to submit a requested sum. If the amount awarded varied too greatly from the request, the plaintiff could be subjected to dual liability whereby the defendant could be guilty of one crime while the prosecution was guilty of contempt.

This concept of criminal punishment is unique in the world, and certainly can require a different cultural bent, but as I was repeatedly assured, there can be no better system than one that protects the fairness of all participants carefully and equally.

Nockin and Malière took me on a tour of one of the larger military bases, and with the entire base present, described to me the posture of Blafusechan armed forces. Nockin reported that the military of Blafusecho was well developed, though limited. Malière openly held a contrasting view of the military as well, suggesting it was not well developed, that it was weak and unable to deter threats. He freely divulged that so poor were the fighting capabilities of the Blafusechan military that any neighbouring people might consider invading.

They did agree on the structure of the forces. Military service was required of all citizens at age eighteen, functionally an extension of the education system. Skills taught included survival, service to the common good, and basic weapons and strategy training. In times of peace, which had been the case for many consecutive years, their responsibilities were entirely nonviolent. The main goals of military service were to establish well-rounded, healthy, well-trained citizens. As the reader will see, this kept military costs down, but unfortunately, limited spending in this area also resulted in some susceptibility to aggression.

In my estimation, the analyses of both Malière and Nockin were both accurate, but it was unsettling to me to hear a minister of the government speak so honestly and disparagingly of the armed forces directly in their presence. It could not be a great boost to morale to hear one's own leaders speak about them so.

I shan't go into more detail, and I hope the reader will forgive, for this is not an intended money grab to ask my kind readers to buy future volumes, but my publisher has begged that I keep my travelogue to as few pages as possible. I truly believe the content of my history and the culture of Blafusecho will contain sufficient depth as to sate the desires of my audience.

CHAPTER 6.6

Word of the author's existence and exploration of Blafusecho do not go unnoticed by the island's jealous neighbours. Demands are placed upon the country and the author that cannot go unheeded.

THE OBSERVANT READER might wonder why a tiny nation like Blafusecho would require an army at all, and from whom they needed fear invasion. An even more astute one might have noted the Gulver artifact of Lilliput. As I lived amongst the Blafusechans, so I learned this minuscule nation was actually one of three. A near neighbour, separated by a straight of only five thousand blustrugs, was named Lilliput. This nation had for a long time been a rival of Blafusecho. Farther afield lay the third, larger, island of Sinrovia. This land had only been discovered a few hundred years ago and had become embroiled in competition and frequent combat with the two other neighbours.

All three islands spoke the same language. Apart from this, and the size of the inhabitants, they shared precious little else in common. Because I certainly prefer to relate only those things I have personally witnessed, I will defer discussion about those two islands but to say that even in their observance of your humble author, they shared some extreme differences of opinion.

As one can imagine, the three countries were in constant and close communication. Hostilities and issues of trust were legion. When the presence of the Quinbus Flestrin was made known, which must obviously have not taken particularly long, Sinrovia was the first to send a delegation. The delegate sought not just to see me, but to demand my immediate relocation to the country of his people. Yet not only did I consider myself to be an amateur ambassador at best, but I had long ago sworn an oath to the people of Blafusecho. I could not leave this place without their blessing.

And, too, as one might understand from my glowing descriptions of the offices of this country, I quite liked it here. I tried each day to contribute something meaningful to the country that hosted me. I dug levees and dykes and conducted other heavy, by their standards, labour. Even so, it was clear the deleterious effect someone who consumed the resources of hundreds would have on such a nation. Just keeping me alive was the full-time occupation of an army of craftsmen, cooks, seamstresses, farmers, and so much more. Worse still was the impact my heavy and clumsy feet had on the roads and infrastructure. I credit only luck that I had not inadvertently crushed somebody since on a couple occasions, I had been alerted by my flying tutors to a pending disaster.

The Sinrovian delegations returned frequently from about the fifth month I lived in Blafusecho. They repeatedly and aggressively demanded my liberation from my oath, it being meaningless due to my divinity.

I need speak on this subject briefly. It seemed the people of Sinrovia believed in a giant by the name of Gulver who visited the islands of Lilliput and Blafusecho hundreds of years ago. He had fled Lilliput upon learning they intended to blind him and escaped into the sea. Numerous adventurers took to the sea to find their god, this giant. By accident, they landed on the shores of Sinrovia, which was assumed to be his home and promised land. I can't say whether this man was like me, a stranded traveller, or if he was actually of some other origin, for the Lilliputians believed he came from the heavens. I never advertised nor represented myself as such. When the Lilliputian believers of the Man Mountain settled Sinrovia, Blafusecho followed suit. A hundred years of war over the colonial holding broke out.

Eventually this ended when Sinrovia, split between the eastern (Lilliput) and western (Blafusecho) colonies, declared their independence of both and merged to form one imperfect union.

The delegations assured me with grand promises I would not only be well cared for but they held resources plentiful enough to not be unduly impacted by the maintenance of a titan.

Not long after the Sinrovians began visiting, so too did the envoy and ambassador of Lilliput. Lilliput demanded of the Blafusechans to transfer my person forthwith to answer for my crimes. The believed me to be the Gulver. In spite of great changes in their society, they still held to the sentences passed down from the king long ago.

The country of Blafusecho was not predisposed to the idea of surrendering me to either of their rivals. I knew Blafusecho was struggling to feed itself without having a giant to care for, so I sought permission of the Hurga Degul to allow me to go to Sinrovia, they being the ones with the more attractive offer on the table for me. In honesty, the choice between having my eyes gouged out by Lilliput seemed only marginally more offensive than living as a deity in Sinrovia.

My requests were rejected initially out of an altruistic desire to help one in need and a feeling of responsibility for my plight. Gradually, with the assistance of Malière, I convinced her of the benefits of my decision. She relented and granted me the freedom to travel to Sinrovia.

CHAPTER 6.7

Custody of the Quinbus Flestrin is transferred to the island nation of Sinrovia, where he resettles once again in a relatively luxurious home. All is not well in the three islands, and the author recounts the culture of this kingdom.

ON THE DAY I was to relocate to Sinrovia, a large number of those with whom I had interacted showed up. First amongst these were Nockin and the Hurga Degul. After the better part of a year in their company and learning of their wonderful kingdom, I shed tears with them over my departure. Of the people assigned to me and my teachers, each spoke with me one on one, despite the fact that my voice injured their ears even with my hushed tones. I thanked them for their help and promised that if they ever needed me, and I was able to come to their aid, I would not hesitate.

The Sinrovians brought with them a huge cargo vessel, like a super-tanker hollowed out, tugged by four powerful ships. Blessed with the same mathematical prowess as the Blafusechans, they, too, had accurately assessed my weight. The ship was sufficient to stay afloat as we made the long passage across the sea. I say it was a long passage in that we travelled at a sedate pace. The distance itself was only about five kilometres. I reckon the water could scarcely have been more than seven metres at its most abyssal depth.

When we arrived in the capital, Relcurowa, I was sore from the hard boat but interested in my new home. My escort parked me in the middle of the harbour and asked that I climb out. Not more than twenty metres away stood the skyline of Relcurowa. Their skyscrapers reached at least thirty metres yet were as thin as ten metres wide at the ground, truly monumental architecture when compared to the people that built it and impressive in scale even for one of my height. The buildings were of a diverse array of architectural forms, though many were built to the same specifications. I assumed this was done to save on design costs. At my ear flew a flying machine of a different sort, more like a small dirigible. From it sprouted a familiar language but a new voice.

I was being addressed by the president of Sinrovia, the largest and most powerful of the three nations, he boasted bombastically. He was an obviously proud man, if only the size of my hand. He welcomed me home excitedly and guided me towards the home that had been readied and maintained for me these past hundred years.

The home the people of Sinrovia had in mind was a squat building, roughly a metre in height at the middle. The walls bowed out and converged about three metres from end to end. The entire building had been designed as a curved isosceles triangle with the short edge being smooth, shiny, and flat. The roof was adorned with cords and cables that hung with knots and hooks, like a miniature stadium. The entire facility resembled a clam with a mohawk. The short, flat edge was the access point, at least for one of my size. The entire superstructure rested atop a stone foundation, which itself raised about half a metre from the ground. I was informed the house was a state-sponsored historical replica of a famous Gulverian artifact and was used as a house of worship by the state religion.

The entrance to my new home had been carved into the substructure another half a metre above ground level as well as an extra half metre below it. Altogether, it was clear little expense had been spared in the intricate carvings and artistry evident just from the main gateway. The doors were motorized and pulled into the adjoining foundational walls.

I ducked through the portal and found myself in an amphitheatre, further embedding my impression of a clam. The vaulted ceiling above my head reached an apex from the door to the sharpest point on its opposite side. The ground was a mirror of the ceiling, with seating laid out across either side and a pulpit at the pointed end. Positioned at the top of the stone foundation level, where the superstructure and substructure met, were five flattened ceiling joists that ran the entire span. The trees used must have been the most significant on the island, for to scale they need have been equivalent to twenty-four metres of consistently wide lumber, for they were a good three decimetres wide as well. From these crossbeams were hung a number of banners and flags, imagery and iconography depicting the actions of the great Gulver. The space was not particularly spacious but more like crawling into a cross between a casket, cathedral, and arena. It did provide shelter and warmth and an eerie familiarity with respect to the proportionate-in-scale architecture.

I was provided with a guide, though many of the kingdom felt an omniscient being such as myself must have no real need for such a thing. I was to be shown every corner of the country if I desired. No expense was to be spared to my honour.

The first question I asked of my guide, Sedekoorb, was about their religion. Actually, it wasn't so much a question I asked, but the automatic subject that she first broached. I would ask the reader to consider what else one would talk of when faced with a prospective deity of their religion. I knew nothing of their religion, for it wasn't presented to me on Blafusecho, and when I asked, it was as though a hero were asking a follower to answer an examination about their favourite subject. She jumped into a sermon that would put the most firebrand preachers to shame. She said there were two versions of the same religion that dominated the majority of Sinrovia. The Truthists believed Gulver—and she indicated she meant me—was the one true god. The Gripprians believed he was a representative of the true god. This simple distinction had apparently led to frequent dispute, debate, and even civil war. Almost every good citizen of Sinrovia believed in one or the other of these two beliefs. A bizarre and inexplicable egg-related heresy had long been represented in the fringes of society. Sedekoorb said the teachings of Gulver were simple and yet most important to the people of these islands.

This Gulver had taught that the ends always justify the means, recounting a story of how he extinguished a fire in the palace of Lilliput by means of urination and explaining it was to be understood as a parable to such effect. He had fought against oppression. He had sought his freedom from the tyranny of Lilliput. He had showed a love for the sea. Sedekoorb said she was a Gripprian who believed Gulver (me) was a representative. I insisted I was neither he, nor a god, nor had I ever previously been to this place. She knew I must be presenting myself falsely, for she believed that at the very least, I must be a like representative.

I found any argument or debate on this matter was not particularly worthy of my time or efforts, for deeply engrained were her beliefs. I sought to know more about their history, and I began to see some patterns emerge. Through their wars with their established neighbours to gain their independence, the island had become downright paranoid. They were certain that at any time one or the other island would engage in a surprise attack and take away their liberty. My guide proudly exclaimed their military was many times larger than both of their rivals combined. When I pressed the obvious disconnect between the fear of invasion and the immense superiority of their weapons, I found the point to be lost on her.

Their history of oppression at the hands of the big- and little-endian heretics and their colonization had instilled a powerful desire to tolerate other religions. The state was nominally secular, and not only my guide but any government representative with whom I spoke boasted about the moral superiority and tolerance of religion. In fact, it was clear they devoted a disproportionate amount of state resources towards religious study, such as was evident in the enormous house that for a hundred years had sat empty but for church services.

On the subject of government, in Sinrovia, there were two families that exchanged power every five years. One came from the west side of the island and the other from the east. A relic of the island's split, the two families could agree on little. In the west, the family of Barrum was a paternalistic, right-of-centre government that preferred to leave everything free of any government involvement, except for the military, which they saw as a critical, and perhaps the most important, government institution. The Enauch family from the east were far to the left of their competitors, with a desire to see a more socialist approach to government. As such, there was an arrangement in place whereby one family was in charge of the legislative branch and the other the executive at all times. Neither was willing to negotiate or even speak calmly to one another. A perpetual government gridlock had persisted as long as anybody could remember.

It seemed neither family was capable of seeing even a quantum of good in the other, either personally or politically. I tried with a number of people to ask two simple questions I still feel probe into the most important characteristics of political leadership. I think even at home today these questions would prove the most valuable that could be asked of any political candidate seeking election: Sincerely, what is the best attribute of your competitor(s), and what is the most important policy they espouse and how would you, without writing it off entirely, make it better for the people it is intended to serve?

Unfortunately, I also found the polarity of their beliefs had rendered them all unable to think of the good or even the positives of the other side. If only they could recognize and accept their opponents, surely more could be accomplished, and better.

The inability of the government to make decisions had allowed the market to roar freely, and it had done so with abandon. It was characterized by hypercompetition, wasteful production, excessive volume, and viciously underhanded practices. To be certain, the industry of Sinrovia was capable of incredible feats, but at the cost of so many people trampled in its wake.

This served only to bolster the military, the only consistently functioning arm of the government, and a well-funded one at that. The poor were ushered into military service almost by necessity, while many of the wealthy would deign to join those ranks. The poorer west was overrepresented in the armed forces of Sinrovia.

The education system and judicial system were equally unfair. The courts were reported to me to be, as is the case in most of the civilized countries of the world, blind. The evidence was ample that celebrities and the wealthy were able to manipulate the system or downright corrupt it to achieve more lenient judgements. Judges were appointed to lifetime tenure and held their cushy posts until the last moment to keep the balance of power in their favour. These lifetime appointments served to create a sort of entitlement. Therefore, the judges were accountable to nobody at all.

In this land of plenty, I found there to be little worth emulating or reporting. I was well cared for, with a rich abundance and variety of food and other necessities delivered daily. I heard the rumblings and the debates over whether I was the Quinbus Flestrin, Gulver, a god, a representative, or some false prophet. The most amusing theory I heard was that I was perhaps a Trojan horse of Blafusechan design. All the while, the country of Lilliput continued to lobby for my return to that land to face my punishment for the insult I allegedly caused them.

As diplomacy raged on, I was informed by members of the Congress of Sinrovia about the demands of Lilliput, that they were threatening war over me. It was decided that representatives of the three island nations, and I, would meet to discuss my future.

CHAPTER 6.8

The three-nations' conference is convened to determine the author's fate, but it becomes evident soon after it begins that the talks were a front to distract from other events.

I SHALL HEREAFTER describe the strangest show of international diplomacy that ever before I have witnessed. Most intriguing, at least as far as your author is concerned, was the fact that I was, in essence, being simultaneously represented as a three-hundred-year-old criminal, an immortal god or his messenger, or a simple wayward traveller. Each of the three countries represented—Blafusecho, Lilliput, and Sinrovia—held deep to their convictions that I was as they believed me to be. It seemed unlikely these three mutually exclusive alternatives were likely to be reconciled through debate by even the most convincing of orators or negotiators.

At the request of the new Hurgo Degul, and the insistence of the president of Sinrovia, I was included in the conference as an equal member, a fourth quasi-nation. I was a literal behemoth surrounded by diminutive giants of their peoples. It is with bemusement that I relate I had been elevated to the status of an entire nation unto myself, and this was the one thing that could be agreed upon by all three others involved. Apart from this one point of agreement, the three nations, due to a long history of war, religious and economic differences, and incompatible ideologies had created a conference built on a foundation that would envy sand for stability. I don't really know even today how one negotiates with somebody who disagrees on every last thing with you, and this symposium would not clarify this.

As I anticipated, each nation took a firm position. Lilliput spoke passionately about the harm I had caused them many years ago and the permanent loss of face and honour my despoiling of the royal family had caused. It apparently was of little consequence that through a revolution, the peasantry of that kingdom had overthrown that same monarchy and installed a tyrannical despot on the throne. Sinrovia demanded I be allowed to stay in their kingdom, the one place I would be appropriately worshipped and where surely I could provide the most value. It also seemed not hypocritical to these people that they reported a secular state but were thus engaged in the diplomatic effort to maintain their patron deity. Blafusecho wanted only that I be comfortable with whatever decision was made. They requested but that I be granted the opportunity to select my home and not be subject to crimes I could in no way answer for nor could those who had been directly affected attest to. I questioned Blafusecho's ability, given the limited resources of the island, to sustain me without cost to their people. The new Hurgo became confused and irritated by my words, they being slanderous of his nation. He protested that Blafusecho produced more than enough resources to support me. He demanded that I explain myself, and in a muddle, I explained to him incorrectly about that which he knew far more than I could hope to.

The conference had been scheduled to extend over a period of two weeks. It was full of the ceremony and extravagance typical of such state events. After the third day, the façade was exposed. Lilliput agents were sitting at the table talking about their rights and their national suffering when word filtered into Sinrovia that Lilliput armed forces had invaded Blafusecho suddenly and deliberately, seizing a large chunk of territory nearest to the island of Lilliput. In short order, the news was confirmed, and the tone of the conference shifted.

Their ruse having been exposed and their coup now a fait accompli, the ambassador of Lilliput announced bravely that because of the unwillingness of Blafusecho and Sinrovia to surrender the convicted criminal Gulver—and to end the oppression of Lilliputian civilians living in Blafusecho—the empire of Lilliput had liberated lands that were historically, and by means of the subjugated minority present, rightfully the territory of Lilliput.

These words terminated the conference, the true aim being made entirely transparent. Sinrovia was not going to surrender their prize. The Blafusechan ambassadors were not able to consider anything but the immediate plight of their peoples. At once, all three nations stormed out of my house, and with all haste, fled back to their capitals.

I felt my heart racing as I considered the crime reported. I set out immediately towards the western shore to head back to Blafusecho to help as best I could. The Sinrovian president beseeched me to refrain for fear I would be harmed, but I batted his complaints away, literally, as I swatted his flying machine off.

I made good time, the island being around five kilometres in diameter. Heart pounding, I charged into the Sinrovian Sea, upsetting several fishing vessels at anchor off the coast. I cared little. I felt a loyalty and responsibility towards the tiny land I had grown to care for deeply. A marathon of a swim awaited me, but I knew the way, and the water being not so deep, I felt confident I could cross the divide.

CHAPTER 6.9

The author aims to change the course of the conflict and realizes the problems inherent in intervention.

ACROSS THE SINROVIAN Sea, I swam calmly and steadily. My heart told me to sprint, but my head balanced me and ensured I swam at a moderate, controlled pace. It must have taken well over an hour to complete the distance. Close to shore, it shallowed out enough that I could touch the ground while holding my head just above the surface of the water, thus allowing me to walk the rest of the way.

I daresay, the break from my long swim was probably the most beneficial opportunity. Not only did it provide a reprieve from my effort and allow me to regain some strength, but as I approached the shore, having missed my target and ending up in Lilliput, I could see the invading navy in the strait. They were focused on the action on the Blafusechan shore and manned with but a skeleton crew. I kept my head as low as I could in the water, and as quietly and stealthily as I could, I approached.

Despite their inferior size, their fire power and armament I feared could do some damage. I remembered well the small projectiles of Blafusecho.

Those handheld weapons were surely of lesser calibre compared to what these battleships could pack. I smelled the diesel fires of the navy and the smoke of the guns. They were all pointed towards the Blafusecho shore. I seized my opportunity. The two largest warships were the furthest from the beaches. Five smaller ones, which I supposed to be landing craft, were much closer. I came as near as I dared, gulped a big lungful of air and dove beneath the surface.

When I got close enough to the battleships, I emerged from the water abruptly. Panic gripped both of the ships as I lifted the first over my head like a barbell and carried it towards Lilliput. The ship was about three metres long and exceedingly heavy. I paid little mind to the burden as I planned to lay it down on solid ground. As I neared its home, I saw a lake near enough to the water that I adjusted my plan. As gently as I could manage, I lowered it into the landlocked body of water.

I returned to retrieve the second battleship. I expected them to be ready, and indeed they were, but manned with only a small crew, only a few of the guns were loaded. As the guns spun in my direction, I breached the water like an orca and flopped hard, causing a wave that lifted the ship and washed the decks. Like a child in a pool, I splashed in the water and kept the enemy on the defensive, protecting themselves from a most hostile sea. Still close, I again dove under and hoisted the second vessel. To the lake I returned and cautiously dropped this vessel into the water as well.

I repeated these actions several more times, picking up the smaller warships and landing craft, each time adding to the armada in the pond. Eventually, I was comfortable that I had disabled the navy, but I could still see small missiles flying from Lilliput to Blafusecho. The half metre long weapons flew low over the ground. I could have tried to intercept them, but I thought it better to remove their launchers.

Tracing the missiles back to their launch points, I crushed the mobile launchers under my feet and knocked over the aircraft control towers at the two active air force bases on Lilliput.

I believed I had prevented the continuing invasion from proceeding, and I demanded to speak directly to the tyrant of Lilliput after following the longest road in Lilliput to arrive at its capital. I bellowed as loudly as I could that he should come forth and speak to me. As I marched, I was struck by the fertility of the land and the poverty of the infrastructure and buildings. I beg the forgiveness of the reader, considering the circumstances and urgency of the visit, but I really didn't appreciate my surroundings as much as I would like. As I approached the capital, Mildendo, I could see it was indeed a large place, but not like Relcurowa or Blafusecho City. It sprawled with few high-rises but numerous tenements and small, dilapidated homes.

With most of their military mobilized on the front for action with Blafusecho, there was not a large home force. Only a few distracting tanks had been posted, and they were rarely able to get a shot off—and never very close to me as I could see them long before they came into range and could move faster than they. Eventually, several armed helicopters were dispatched, but as with the tanks, they could not match my speed and agility. Armed with small munitions, they only caused a sting when their bullets bounced off my skin. My eyes I protected with my sunglasses. I received scarcely a glancing blow in the engagement. They kept their distance too, fearing my wrath. The greater their distance proportionally, so decreased the risk they presented to me.

I started pulling trees out of the ground like weeds and threw a few in the general direction of the helicopters for good measure. Seeing they were not going to defeat me, they conceded the field. A new chopper swooped up from Mildendo and flew towards me without guns mounted.

It came straight for me. It was as clear as day this was the leader's conveyance. I had proven to be superior to anything he could throw at me and was coming to surrender, or so I thought. The speakers on board the autogyro allowed me to hear the president, speaking with a confidence and arrogance that well masked any fear he must surely have been feeling. A grizzled veteran of espionage and diplomacy, he would not show me any sign of weakness. He announced that I, a convicted felon, was under arrest for my crimes against his people, and more, for having taken up cause with Lilliput's rivals. He demanded I cease and desist in my hostility and surrender myself to their authorities that I may be justly punished.

Perhaps I should have been intimidated by this man, but I certainly felt no such thing, so I yelled back I would not capitulate from my position of strength. If he did not himself stop his warmongering and open hostility, I would be forced to not just disable, but destroy, his entire armed forces.

Predictably, he rejected my proposal and demanded I stop protecting those people who were in the process of persecuting and subjugating his own. Then he ratcheted up his warning, threatening to do more than just capture his supposed rightful holdings, but to also claim the entirety of Blafusecho. I could see no progress would be made with this man of steel and lies, so I told him I would give him twenty-four hours to recall his forces from Blafusecho. No sooner had I completed my ultimatum when a dozen jet bombers roared overhead towards Mildendo from the south and east.

In their wake, on the ground, fires blossomed from the houses. Smoke raised high into the sky. I became a secondary issue. The Lilliputian leader spun back towards his city.

As Lilliput had done during the negotiations, so Sinrovia was taking advantage of the bonus I had handed to them on a silver platter. While the army of Lilliput was stranded in hostile territory on Blafusecho, Sinrovia had sent their army to capture and subjugate their enemies on Lilliput. As I could not imagine Sinrovia releasing their ambitions, I knew a weakened Lilliput, heathens as Sinrovia considered them to be, would surely present too great a prize.

I'd had no intention of so unbalancing what had been a fragile peace, but I could see that what I had done had been directly contrary to my intended aim of protecting the weak from the strong and aggressive. I had merely rendered them weak as well.

Two wrongs may not sum up to a positive, but two negatives multiplied can turn to good. I made up my mind to double down on my gamble, and for the second time that day, I headed back across the Sinrovian Sea.

Just as I had done with the Lilliput forces, I rounded up the Sinrovian ships at sea. I pulled them all back and deposited them all in a lake well inland. Unlike the Lilliputians who considered me a criminal, the soldiers of Sinrovia could no more stand against their god than their own mothers. I felt not a single weapon fired against me from the ships. I filled two large lakes with the Sinrovian Navy, commanded the mobile missile launchers to surrender their arms to me, and grounded the planes in a swamp.

The president came out to beg me to stop, to forgive him for his arrogance. I was determined to end the war once and for all. I am proud to report that I'm all but certain not a man, woman, or child was injured more than incidental bumps, bruises, or scratches, mostly caused by the panic initiated by my actions. I left the entirety of both Lilliput's and Sinrovia's armies, minus the missiles and their launchers, in perfect, inoperable condition.

I said one last thing to the Sinrovian president as I walked back towards Relcurowa. I said I would not tolerate—and it would not be right—for those machines of war to be recovered, rearmed, and used in aggression.

I headed to my abode, it being late in the day now, and I tore it out of the ground. The house, being a replica of the rowboat the Gulver had rowed away in, I hoped I would be able to make similar use of and avoid a third crossing of the sea that day. As I went, I grabbed several of the disabled missiles and piled them into the dinghy, as well as a small collection of livestock from some particularly eager farmers I passed on the way.

The boat did float, so I launched it into the water and paddled my way back to Blafusecho.

CHAPTER 6.10

The author evaluates the damage to Blafusecho and plans to leave these cursed islands once and for all.

IT WAS A slower, but more peaceful, crossing. I arrived back at Blafusecho in the middle of the night. This time, I aimed more to the north and east and landed on a peninsula close to the capital. I pulled the boat out of the water with great effort and slept therein for the night. I couldn't risk walking in the dark for fear of an accident. Having disposed of the armed forces of both aggressive belligerents and having hauled around several heavy, if tiny, warships, I felt I could risk, and had earned, this rest.

In the morning, I woke from my rest, secured the boat firmly upon the shore, and set out to evaluate the damage. What I found impacted me deeply. Blafusecho City was severely damaged by missiles and aircraft, at least forty percent was completely destroyed and in ruins, but at least my efforts to cut supply lines had indeed had an important impact. The battle lines were still a long way from the metropolis. In spite of that, a great deal of loss had occurred. Fires still burned all over the city, and the lands around were not much better off. Blafusecho City was a good distance away from the Lilliputian landing but had still been heavily struck by aerial assault.

The well-trained people of Blafusecho had done well to impede the progress of their enemy, but a beachhead had been established in the south. Absent the support of their supply lines, it was only a matter of time before the Lilliputians would be forced to surrender, but how to handle the stranded troops was a problem. No nation possessed an available navy, and Blafusecho was certainly uninterested in leaving an enemy force on their soil. The war was over and everybody knew it. All that remained was pain and suffering. I spoke with the new Hurgo Degul and offered to transport the soldiers of Lilliput back home, off this island. Seeing my proposal was wise, he agreed. I suggested the same to the commander of the Lilliputians. He too complied.

Before I allowed the Lilliputians on board my house/church/boat, I demanded they hand over all weapons. I took them and threw them deep into the ocean. I moved the belligerents back to their homes in my personal conveyance, which I pulled behind me to Lilliput. The soldiers felt they were still right and represented the best of the islands, but I cared little to hear their thoughts at this point. I was so little concerned about the state of Lilliput that after settling the last handful of sailors back on their homeland, I didn't bother to look back. I settled back onto my boat and rowed slowly back to Blafusecho.

I could see the country was devastated and could not support me even to a fraction of their previous degree. The war had laid bare that Malière was a Lilliputian spy; he had worked magic in convincing me to leave Blafusecho. The island had been a viable host, but with all certainty, they no longer would be. They felt in my debt, but I could not ask that they provide anything but some bare necessities.

Lilliput would have still happily taken me in and blinded me at the first available opportunity, and Sinrovia still eagerly sought to please and honour me as a god, but I would not parade myself falsely as such. It was tiresome to be looked upon that way, and especially by a people for whom I held so little respect. Blafusecho was, of course, my preference, but I would not, could not continue to be their burden. I considered the good I might do as a giant in their lands helping with rebuilding, but it wasn't for me.

I had been liberated of my oath towards Blafusecho. With a heavy heart, I accepted a few parachutes that I filled with water from a stream and packed them into my boat. I made sure I had a good collection of preserveable food, which I demanded as compensation from Lilliput and Sinrovia. From a place of pure interest, I also gathered a small collection of miniature cattle, goats, sheep, chickens, pigs, and vegetables, and set off into the ocean. This time felt I knew which way I needed travel to find the nearest port: due east.

CHAPTER 6.11

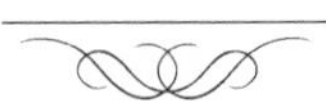

The author returns from his final adventure and receives the worst news.

I PADDLED EASTWARD, and after a day or so, I spotted an island with trees of appropriate size. I landed on the shore and explored a little, hoping for a similar fortune as when I landed on Vancouver Island. This time I was not in luck, so I set up camp, found some food and water, used a broken missile to create a fire, and settled in for the night.

Early the next morning, a plane flew overhead. I cracked a few missiles like flares and launched them to draw the attention of the passing pilot. Soon, an Indonesian vessel was dispatched and arrived on my shore, and even better, an English speaker was aboard. It took little time for the crew to understand and pick me up. I was safe again. My own safety assured, I only cared to know about one single thing.

A lump filled my throat as I asked if they knew anything about my family. I could barely get the words out. I'd hoped if a famous, wealthy family had been rescued in the last couple years, it might have made sufficient waves that people might know about it. The English speaker shrugged, and my heart sank. He asked his crewmates, but they too knew nothing about me or my family.

When the ship docked in Padang, I asked again. Each person I asked raised their shoulders, shrugged, or indicated they did not know. Finally, I found a person who was familiar with the event. He said he was certain there had been no known survivors; my family and crew had been lost at sea. My heart broke. I crumbled to the ground. My knees failed and the blood drained from my body. I had lost everything and now had nothing left. Every other time I had found salvation; I was the one lost and found. In repatriation, I recovered everything and everyone I had loved. But not this time. I begged the man that he be lying or unsure. Apologetically, he was adamant he was not.

My determination failed. I could not find words to explain where I had been. Authorities interviewed me about my whereabouts in broken English. I was transported back to Jakarta and the Canadian Embassy where, once again, efforts were once again initiated to bring me back to life.

I asked to speak to my parents at home, my only surviving family, and was given a video phone. As the phone rang, I thought about my family and the trials my repeated adventures must have caused them.

It rang for what seemed like forever, but finally, they picked up the line. The room in which they stood was dark, all the lights turned off as it was the middle of the night there. The connection was bad and broken by static. Then the light turned on, and there, in front of my eyes, like a ghost brought back to life, tears pouring freely, was not my mother or father, but my baby girl, now a couple years older, and beside her my son, grinning from ear to ear yelling, "Daddy!" My wife hugged them both from behind.

It isn't within my ability to explain the incredible feeling I felt then. I was more than excited to return to my home and my beautiful, forgiving family. I won't share any more about what we said. That is for me and my family alone. Shortly thereafter, I flew home for a final time, my peregrinations now complete. My greatest struggles and challenges were now behind me.

I settled back in at home with my wonderful family. While they filled me in on the details of their time without me, again, I don't care to share more details about them and their pains, and I trust my gracious reader will grant me the privacy I desire for my family.

It is for my children, with whom I look forward to spending time every day, and about whom I never go a moment without thinking, that I have recorded my experiences in this book. I swore from the outset to relate only that which is true and complete. My hope is my children will read this long after I'm gone and be proud of their father, and somehow, find it within them to forgive my temporary absence.

Thus, I conclude my account. I thank my patient reader for trudging through my meandering recollections and wish you all the best in your own adventures.

Cygnus

AUTHOR BRETT M. WIENS

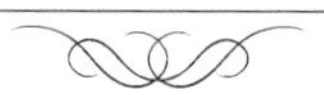

Brett M. Wiens was born, raised, and continues to reside in Calgary, Alberta with his wife and two children. He attended the University of Calgary where he received his bachelor's degree in Geography and a masters of Geographic Information Systems. He has traveled to four continents and is constantly learning new languages from French to Spanish, Latin, Italian, and a little American Sign Language.

Manufactured by Amazon.ca
Bolton, ON